Jill Mansell lives with her family in Bristol. She used to work in the field of Clinical Neurophysiology but now writes full time. She watches far too much TV and would love to be one of those super-sporty types but basically can't be bothered. Nor can she cook – having once attempted to bake a cake for the hospital's Christmas Fair, she was forced to watch while her co-workers played frisbee with it. But she's good at Twitter!

Just *Heavenly*. Just *Jill*.

Praise for YOU AND ME, ALWAYS:

'The sweetest love story of the year' *Fabulous*

'Fans of PS, I LOVE YOU will enjoy this funny and heart-warming read' *Bella*

'Achingly romantic . . . we loved it!' *Heat*

'The twists are great fun . . . and hold the happy ending tantal-isingly at bay . . . Plenty . . . to warm all our hearts' *Telegraph*

'A glorious, heartwarming romantic read' *Woman & Home*

Jill Mansell

you and me, Always

headline
review

Copyright © 2016 Jill Mansell

The right of Jill Mansell to be identified as the Author of
the Work has been asserted by her in accordance with the
Copyright, Designs and Patents Act 1988.

Map copyright © 2015 Laura Hall

First published in Great Britain in 2016 by HEADLINE REVIEW
An imprint of HEADLINE PUBLISHING GROUP

First published in paperback in 2016 by HEADLINE REVIEW
An imprint of HEADLINE PUBLISHING GROUP

1

Cataloguing in Publication Data is available from the British Library

ISBN 978 1 4722 3593 0 (A-Format)
ISBN 978 1 4722 0887 3 (B-Format)

Typeset in Bembo by Palimpsest Book Production Limited, Falkirk, Stirlingshire

Printed and bound in Great Britain by
CPI Group (UK) Ltd, Croydon, CR0 4YY

MIX
Paper from
responsible sources
FSC® C104740
www.fsc.org

Headline's policy is to use papers that are natural, renewable and recyclable products
and made from wood grown in well-managed forests and other controlled sources. The
logging and manufacturing processes are expected to conform to the environmental
regulations of the country of origin.

HEADLINE PUBLISHING GROUP
An Hachette UK Company
Carmelite House
50 Victoria Embankment
London EC4Y 0DZ

www.headline.co.uk
www.hachette.co.uk

Acknowledgements

A big thank you to Ossie Hickman, who first suggested I should feature a pilot in this book, and who then answered all my questions on matters piloty and aeronautical.

Stanton

THE STAR INN

Langley

to the Valley →

Chapter 1

There he was, sitting in the sun outside the Star Inn. Lily slowed and parked the van outside Goldstone House, next to the pub. Dan saw her and waved, and her stomach tightened at the sight of him, as it always had done. There was just something about the languid angles of his body, those long legs in black jeans stretched out in front of him, the tilt of his head as he chatted on his phone and laughed at something that had been said.

The tightening didn't mean anything, though, Lily knew that. It had evolved as a kind of Pavlovian reaction, a habit that had become ingrained over the years simply because Dan Rafferty was so physically attractive. The good thing was, the fact that he knew he was attractive, and traded on it shamelessly with all concerned, meant the idea of an actual relationship with him was the very last thing anyone in their right mind would want.

And since she was in her right mind, thankfully she was safe.

'Lily, Lily.' Dan's eyes crinkled and he pushed his dark glasses to the top of his head as she jumped down from the van. 'My most favourite girl in the world.'

See? This was what he was like. 'And you're the most annoying boy.'

'I'm not a boy. I'm a man.'

He was twenty-seven, two years older than she was. Technically he might be a man, but when you'd known each other since childhood, it just seemed wrong somehow.

'You used to put frogspawn in the hood of my anorak,' said Lily. 'You'll always be a boy to me. Where's your car, anyway?'

'Over in Chipping Norton.' Dan had texted her earlier asking if she could give him a lift to go and pick it up.

'Why?' As if she couldn't guess.

'Best not to ask. The usual, basically. Good wine and bad women. Well, one bad woman taking shameless advantage.' He gestured to the still full cup of coffee on the table in front of him. 'Are you in a tearing hurry, or can I get you a drink?'

Lily checked her watch. It was twenty past six. She'd spent the last three hours delivering a marble-topped table and a set of Victorian chimney pots to a customer in Chippenham, but work was now over for the day and the rest of her evening was free.

'Go on then, I'll have a Coke.' She joined him at the table, unsticking the back of her T-shirt from her shoulder blades and flapping the front of it to cool down her ribcage while Dan disappeared inside to order the drink.

When he returned, she took the glass and said, 'Cheers, thanks. Why couldn't Patsy give you a lift back to your car?'

'She's out. Gone on a date. With a mystery man off the internet.'

Lily perked up. 'Ooh, what's he like?'

'No idea.' Dan shrugged. 'That's the whole point of him being a mystery. She didn't want me to meet him.'

'Well, after last time with the chap from Chepstow, who could blame her?'

'Welsh William.' He shrugged. 'That wasn't my fault. He was the one who challenged me to an arm-wrestling match. He was just showing off, trying to prove how strong he was.'

'You could have let him win,' said Lily.

'Me?' Dan looked horrified. 'Why? He was an idiot. Patsy wouldn't want someone like him anyway.'

Which was true enough. Ah well, maybe this new one might be an improvement. Lily swirled the ice cubes in her glass and took a gulp of Coke, then paused as her attention was drawn to a stocky man on a bicycle heading along the main street directly towards them. He was wearing an orange cycling helmet that clashed with his red face and turquoise Lycra leggings. As his legs pumped the pedals, he appeared to be talking to himself.

By this time Dan had turned and was watching him too. It wasn't until the man had drawn closer that they realised he wasn't riding an ordinary bike; it was a tandem. Nor was he having a conversation with himself; he was loudly addressing his cycling companion behind him.

'. . . and in September of two thousand and thirteen . . . or it might have been the October come to think of it . . . anyway, that was when I cycled from Ravenglass to South Shields alongside Hadrian's Wall, and that's one hundred and seventy-four miles in total, so it's quite a trek, but the views were phenomenal . . . then the following March I did the Devon coast-to-coast, from Ilfracombe to Plymouth . . .'

'Whoops,' Lily breathed as the tandem drew nearer still and they were finally able to see who was on the back of it. Dan sprayed coffee and rocked forward on his seat. Poor Patsy, clearly mortified as her companion continued at top volume, saw them watching and pulled an *Oh God* face.

And then they were passing the pub, their legs moving in unison as the pedals turned and the tyres made a dry swishing noise on the hot, dusty tarmac. Patsy's date was still facing forwards, talking loudly for her benefit as he informed her of the importance of keeping up a nice steady rhythm.

Which made Dan, predictably, crack up with silent laughter. As the tandem moved on, Patsy glanced over at them for a moment, shook her head in despair and mouthed the words: *Help me.*

Oh dear, but it was hard not to laugh. At the junction at the end of the high street, the traffic lights turned red and the tandem dutifully slowed to a halt. They watched as Patsy put her feet down and turned back to give them a look of mortification and misery, whilst her date continued his loud monologue.

'How does she get herself into these situations?' Dan marvelled. He gestured to his sister and mimed diving sideways off the bike.

Up ahead, taking her weight on her feet and raising her bottom from the saddle, Patsy let go of the handlebars. The traffic lights changed to amber, then to green. Her companion pressed down on the front pedals and the tandem moved off, leaving Patsy standing in the road behind it. Evidently still entranced by the sound of his own voice, and oblivious to the fact that he'd lost his pedalling partner, the man who'd been her date continued on down the road.

Dan took a quick photo on his phone before the tandem completely disappeared from view. He grinned at Lily and said, 'Ha, brilliant. That's this year's Christmas card sorted.'

Patsy stood in the centre of the road and watched as Derek energetically cycled off without her. She couldn't quite believe he hadn't noticed she'd gone.

Why did this kind of situation always seem to happen to her? Derek had sounded so *nice* in his emails. He'd given her no cause whatsoever to suspect he was a secret cycling fanatic with a deep and detailed knowledge of every single cycleway in the UK and a passion for sharing *all* this information with her in a maximum-volume never-ending monotone.

If she'd known, the entire relationship could have been nipped in the bud before it even had time to become a bud. Some women might not mind the idea of sailing through life on the back of a tandem, but Patsy definitely wasn't one of them.

She sighed and brushed away the loose strands of hair that were sticking to her forehead. And now Dan and Lily were beckoning her towards them, no doubt finding her predicament hilarious. What she should have done, of course, was to tap Derek on the shoulder, politely explain that they might as well give up now, then shake hands, say goodbye and wish him better luck next time.

That would have been the normal way, the dignified way to go about it.

Oh God, poor Derek. She really shouldn't have done that to him.

Then again, poor *her*.

Chapter 2

'OK,' said Dan when Patsy reached them. 'First things first. Does he know where you live?'

'No.' She shook her head. 'We arranged to meet at the café in the garden centre. He was already waiting for me when I got there, so I didn't know about the bike thing.'

Dan raised an eyebrow. 'You mean the turquoise Lycra leggings didn't give it away?'

Patsy pulled a face at her brother, eight years younger but annoyingly so much more in control of his own life than she was of hers. 'They were hidden under the table, if you must know. We chatted for ten minutes and he said something about getting some exercise and exploring the area, but I thought we were going for a walk and that was why he'd said I should wear trousers and flat shoes.' Never happier than when she was in four-inch heels, Patsy indicated the pale pink leather ballet pumps on her feet; and to think she'd gone out and bought them specially for today's date.

'But he presumably stood up at some point, which means you saw what he was wearing. And then he took you outside and showed you his tandem. Not a euphemism,' said Dan. 'Yet you still went ahead and climbed on to it.'

'You see, this is the difference between us. You just can't understand,' said Patsy. 'If you don't want to do something, you don't do it. But when it happens to me . . .'

'You were too embarrassed to say no.' Lily leapt to her defence.

'Exactly.'

'You're a people-pleaser.'

'I am!' Was that so bad? When you were a hairdresser, it kind of went with the territory. If you didn't please people, you wouldn't last long in the job.

'She didn't want to hurt his feelings,' Lily told Dan, who was notoriously less concerned with how other people felt.

'In that case, better leave the next few minutes to me.' With a nod in the direction of the end of the road, Dan said, 'He's on his way back now.'

Bugger, so he was. Patsy said, 'I don't want to see him!' But if she tried to disappear inside the pub now, Derek would spot her running away from him.

'Come on, into the van.' Evidently having worked out the angles, Lily pressed auto-unlock. 'He won't be able to see you from here.'

Ducking down, heart thumping, Patsy kept out of view and jumped into the back of the van, pulling the door almost shut behind her with seconds to spare. She heard the squeak of the bike's brakes and the swish of tyres as Derek pulled up less than six feet away. His face wasn't visible – thankfully – but through the crack in the door she was able to see Lily and Dan.

'Hello.' Derek paused to clear his throat. 'Erm . . . I was wondering if you'd seen my cycling partner. She was with me when we came past a few minutes ago. Dark hair, pink shirt, jeans . . .'

'And you've managed to lose her somewhere?' Dan looked amused.

'Well, yes. Apparently so.'

'Actually, we did see her,' said Dan. 'She ran past us just now at quite a speed, heading in that direction.' He pointed to the right. 'She was on her mobile, calling for a cab to come and pick her up.'

'Oh. Right.'

'On the bright side,' Dan continued, 'at least it means she didn't fall off the back of your tandem. You don't have to send out a search party or wonder if she's lying dead in a ditch.'

'Hmm.' Her erstwhile date didn't sound particularly relieved.

'Oh dear. Is she your wife?'

'Good God, no. Thank goodness,' Derek snorted.

Charming. Although under the circumstances, he was allowed to be a bit cross.

'I like your leggings.' Changing the subject, Dan asked innocently, 'Where did you get them?'

'These? Ah well, they're from a specialist sportswear company, I order them online and—'

'No! Barbara, over here,' Lily blurted out. Patsy heard the sudden patter of paws, accompanied by a yelp of excitement. 'Barbara, don't do that, get *down* . . .'

Too late. Patsy made a futile grab at the van's back door, but there was no handle on the inside. A huge black paw effortlessly hooked the door open and Barbara appeared, barking in joyful recognition and wagging her tail.

Patsy wanted to die. Once, years ago, she'd been having a wee in the loo on the train when, without warning, the automatic door had slid open.

This was worse.

Derek stared into the van and she felt her skin prickle with shame. Since Barbara was now attempting to clamber up and join her, Patsy instead jumped down. 'I'm sorry,' she said.

'And so you should be.' He was still astride the front saddle of the tandem, his expression stony. 'I thought we were going for a nice twenty-mile ride.'

Which was an oxymoron if ever she'd heard one. Nevertheless, she looked penitent. 'I know. I'm not really a bicycle-y sort of person.'

His jaw jutted. 'You should have told me.'

'I didn't want to hurt your feelings.'

'Out of interest,' Dan joined in, 'why didn't you warn her you were going to turn up on a tandem?'

Derek shot him an impatient look. 'Because then she would have made some excuse and ducked out. Everyone always does. It's something you have to experience first, *then* you fall in love with it. I'm serious.' Sweat dripped from his ruddy forehead as he nodded vigorously, pale eyes alight with fervour. 'There's nothing better in the world than cycling.'

Personally, Patsy thought a nice gin and tonic beat cycling hands down. She shrugged and said, 'Anyway, I'm sorry I ran away.'

'It's no great loss.' Derek was dismissive now. 'You're not my type anyway. To be honest, anyone who wears make-up isn't my cup of tea. It's not your fault,' he amended. 'I should have stipulated that in my advert.'

Patsy nodded. 'It might have been an idea.' And she should have stipulated that she wasn't interested in anyone who wore turquoise Lycra leggings. 'Well, bye then.'

'Goodbye. And just so you know, if anyone asks how our date went, I'm afraid I'm not going to be able to give you a good review.'

'That's fine.' Patsy thought it was probably more than fine, it was a blessing. Aloud she said, 'I deserve it.'

Together they watched as Derek, for the second time, cycled off down the street.

'And another one bites the dust,' said Dan.

Barbara, the huge black Labrador who belonged to one of the most regular of the pub's regulars, placed her paw on Patsy's knee as if sympathising with her tragic still-manless state.

'I did ask him not to ride through the village, but he ignored me.' Patsy relived her horror when she'd realised he was going to go ahead and do it anyway. When you were on the back of a tandem, you didn't have much choice in the matter.

'I don't think I want to speak to you any more.' Dan was shaking his head at her. 'You shameless strumpet, plastering your face in . . . eurgh, all that disgusting *make-up*.'

Patsy picked up a cardboard beer mat and spun it at him like a weapon. Frustratingly, he employed his lightning reflexes to catch it, then flipped it into the air so that Barbara could leap up and grab it in her mouth.

'Come on then.' Lily finished her drink and stood up, gesturing to Dan and jangling her keys. 'Let's get you back to your car.'

Dan rose to his feet and gave Patsy a hug. 'Bye then. See you in a couple of weeks. And don't worry, there has to be someone decent out there. We'll find him for you eventually.'

She hugged him in turn; they might tease each other endlessly, but he was her little brother — albeit a foot taller than her — and she loved him to bits.

'Don't worry about me. I'm fine. And you look after yourself.' Drawing back, she shook her head at him. 'I still can't believe they let you fly actual planes.'

Dan grinned. 'That's nothing. I can't believe I let you cut my hair.'

He stowed his travel case in the back of the van, ruffled Barbara's ears by way of an au revoir and jumped into the passenger seat. Lily, starting the engine, leaned out of the driver's window and said, 'See you tomorrow.'

Tomorrow was Lily's birthday; she would be twenty-five. Patsy smiled, because they all knew it was set to be an especially significant day. She nodded and waved at them both. 'Oh yes, you definitely will.'

The van pulled away and disappeared up the road. Barbara, panting in the heat and now in search of shade and a bowl of cold water, wandered back inside the pub. And Patsy, finding herself with an unexpectedly free evening, set off in the direction of home.

As she was letting herself into the cottage, her phone began to ring. Surprised by the name on the screen, she answered it and said, 'Rosa, hello! How are things with you? It's been *ages*.'

Rosa had worked for her here at the salon years ago. Now married and living in London with her taxi-driver husband and three young children, she'd stayed in touch via Facebook, but they hadn't seen each other since the birth of Rosa's middle child. The good intentions were always there, but – as they had a habit of doing – life and work had simply got in the way.

'Everything's great!' Rosa sounded buoyant. 'OK, now listen, I've got something to ask you. And this might sound a bit weird, but I promise you it's not bad weird.'

'Okaaay.' Intrigued, Patsy picked up the crumb-strewn plate and empty Twix wrapper Dan had left on the coffee table; honestly, for someone without an ounce of fat on him, he didn't half eat some rubbish. 'What's it about?'

'A friend of a friend needs a favour. Nothing illegal. But it has to be someone who can definitely keep a secret.' Rosa paused, as in the background another phone began to ring. 'Which is why I thought of you.'

Chapter 3

A bird was singing loudly in the honeysuckle outside Lily's bedroom window. Coral would probably know what kind of bird, but Lily didn't have a clue. It sounded very cheerful, though. She opened her eyes and saw from the dazzle of light slicing through the gap in the curtains that it was destined to be another hot, sunny day.

It's my birthday. I'm twenty-five!

And so lucky . . .

She slid out of bed, knowing that when she opened the door, the tray would be outside. It always was; over the years it had been a tradition from which they'd never wavered.

And indeed it was there, on the wine-red landing carpet, the rectangular silver tray bearing a single rosebud in a squat silver vase, a glass of freshly squeezed orange juice, a sealed envelope and a small flat package wrapped in silver and yellow striped paper and tied with curly silver ribbons.

From her mum.

Lily bent down, picked up the tray and carefully carried it back into her room, laying it on the bedside table so nothing would topple over. Drifting up from downstairs she could hear sounds of movement, the clink of china, the murmur of voices on the radio, doors being opened and closed.

But this, now, was private, to be shared between her and her mother. Just the two of them.

For the very last time.

Lily took a sip of orange juice and opened the envelope. Whereas all the other letters had been written on thick lilac writing paper, this one was on a plain white sheet of A4. But the handwriting was the same, instantly recognisable with its extravagant loops and swirls. She ran the tips of her fingers over the paper, the first person to touch it since her mum had written the words, then lifted it to her nose and inhaled to see if it retained any recognisable scent.

No, it just smelled of paper.

OK, here goes. She took a steadying breath and began to read.

Hello, my dearest darling girl, and happy happy birthday! You're twenty-five and I wish you all the love and happiness in the world. (I'm going to trust you here, and assume you haven't opened your letters early. It's a possibility by now, and it doesn't matter a bit if you have, but I still kind of hope you managed to control your impatience and wait, so I can talk to my twenty-five-year-old daughter. Woman to woman!)

I wonder if you look like me? Is your hair still long and madly curly? It's so hard to imagine what you're like now, but I do know for sure that you are kind, thoughtful, loving and beautiful on the inside and out. I hope your life is as happy as it deserves to be. Have you found a wonderful partner yet? Are you married? Maybe you have a child . . . wow, that's an incredible thought! I could be a grandma by now! Well if I am, I bet you're a fantastic mother. (And if you don't have children, you're still fantastic anyway.)

A tear was trickling down Lily's cheek. She paused and wiped it away. She could hear her mum's voice so clearly, it was almost as if she were here in the room, saying the words to her.

She continued to read:

I didn't know how long to continue writing to you on your birthday, sweetheart. A part of me wanted to carry on until you were a hundred! But it looks as if the decision has been made for me, as the last few days haven't been great. I'm writing this in the hospital (hence the less than glamorous paper) and it's becoming harder to concentrate. They're upping my morphine so I'm going to be sleeping a lot more from now on. And I don't want to start scribbling gibberish, so this is another reason to make this the last letter.

I have a little present for you too! Is it there? Have you already opened it? If not, let me just explain that it mightn't have cost a lot, but it's my most precious and treasured possession – apart from you, obviously, my beautiful darling girl – which is why I want you to have it now. It was given to me on my nineteenth birthday by Declan Madison. He was my first love and – as it turned out – the *only* love of my life. How I wish our relationship could have lasted – although if it had, then I never would have got involved with your father and we wouldn't have had you! (Something else I wonder – will you get to know your father at some stage? Are you in touch with each other? Did he turn out to be not so bad after all? So many questions!)

Anyway, I'm passing on to you what Declan gave to me, and I really hope you like it. Has Coral told you about him? She will have done, I'm sure. He really was a lovely boy. We had the best time together – it was just the timing that was wrong. And if it's strange to think of you being twenty-five now, it's equally strange to imagine Declan being forty-eight. That's old!

I hope you're still in touch with Coral and Nick. And Patsy, too! I hope I chose the right people to look after you, my darling. I did the best I could. More than anything I wish I could have stayed with you, but sadly that hasn't been possible.

Thank you for being the light of my life, the very best thing that ever happened to me. I wish you nothing but love, health and happiness.

Happy birthday, beautiful Lily.

All all *all* my everlasting love, sweetheart.

You and me, always.

Mum xxx

There, done, and the tears were now flowing down Lily's face in earnest. Every letter ended with those same words: *You and me, always.* She and her mum had said it to each other each night at bedtime; it had been their mantra, their secret promise to each other. Whatever might happen – and it *had* happened – nothing could break the bond that existed between them.

She would reread the letter over and over in the years ahead, but never again for the first time. This was why she'd always preferred to open the envelopes in private. When it was done and she'd had the chance to compose herself once more, she would go downstairs and begin the rest of her birthday.

Rubbing her eyes and her wet face on the hem of her T-shirt, Lily picked up the wrapped present and carefully untied the silver ribbon bow. Over the past seventeen years, the Sellotape had lost its stickiness and acquired a light brown tinge; when she nudged it, it loosened beneath her touch.

She unfolded the striped wrapping paper, then the nest of tissue beneath it. The bangle was narrow and silver, randomly studded with tiny sparkling stones that were unlikely to be diamonds. But it was pretty, catching the light as she turned it this way and that. And she dimly remembered it too; vague memories from early childhood were beginning to resurface, of exploring bedroom drawers and boxes containing various bits of jewellery, seeing and trying on the bangle, which at the time had been far too big for her. Back then, at the age of five or six, she'd far preferred to hang assorted strings of beads around her neck and shuffle around in her mum's high heels, pretending to be a grown-up.

A few months after that, her mum had fallen ill and the difficult times had begun. Lily knew now how hard it must have been for everyone, attempting to shield her from the worst of it and pretend everything wasn't as bad as it actually was. Her mum had done her best to carry on doing as much as possible with her, between the repeated stays in hospital. Coral and Nick had asked her what colour she'd like her new bedroom to be, and had redecorated accordingly, for when she spent time with them. And Patsy, her babysitter, had spoiled her endlessly, taking her out on day trips, creating treasure hunts and keeping her entertained when – let's face it – most eighteen-year-old girls would far rather be chasing after boys and having fun with friends their own age.

17

When her mother had finally died, between them they had showered her with so much genuine love that she'd never once had to worry about what would happen to her. It had all been arranged; everything had been taken care of. Coral and Nick had welcomed her into their household, allowing her to grieve but always there for her, patiently helping her settle into her new life with them. Of course she'd missed her mum dreadfully, but she'd been surrounded with warmth and affection, and as time passed, the grief subsided. She might no longer have a birth mother, but Coral had definitely been the next best thing.

She slid the silver bangle on to her left wrist and gazed across at the framed photograph on her bedside table. The photo had been taken here, in the garden of Goldstone House, on her first birthday, when she'd still been a beaming bald baby with only a few teeth to her name. There she was, sitting happily on her mum's lap, with Nick and Coral to one side and Patsy laughing as she made a futile grab for a blurry toddler who was actually Dan racing past with a water pistol in each hand and a small dog in hot pursuit.

Lily had no memory, of course, of the day itself. But it was one of her favourite photographs because everyone in it looked so completely happy and relaxed.

She *had* been lucky. Tragedy might have touched her life, but she'd come through it. And Coral, in turn, had come through for her.

Which was why, twenty-four years on from that first birthday, she was still so glad to be here.

Chapter 4

Lily found Coral on the terrace, aiming her watering can at the hanging baskets outside the French windows. Turning at the sound of Lily's footsteps behind her, she managed to send a spray of water over her own bare feet.

'Darling, happy birthday!' Putting down the watering can, she came over and held out her arms. They hugged each other, then Coral pulled back so she could see Lily's face. 'How are you? All OK?'

Lily nodded. 'I'm fine. You know, bit emotional, but it was nice, too.' She indicated the envelope in her hand. 'You can read it. And this was the present.' Holding up her other arm, she showed Coral the bangle on her wrist. 'I kind of remember it used to be in her dressing-table drawer.'

'I remember it too. And I'd always wondered what happened to it.' Admiring the bangle, Coral nodded and said, 'All this time it's been wrapped up, waiting for you.'

'It was a present from her boyfriend when she was nineteen. Declan.'

'That's right.' Coral smiled, taking the letter from her. 'He was Jo's first love. She always called him the one that got away.'

Lily nodded. They'd talked about him before, of course,

although Coral had never met Declan herself. After leaving school, her mum had taken a gap year, travelling to Spain and meeting Declan when they were both working at a restaurant on Las Ramblas in Barcelona. They'd spent eleven months together, enjoying each other's company, the social life and the high-octane buzzing energy of the capital city of Catalonia. Everything had been perfect until the time had come to return to the UK and take up their places at university, Declan at St Andrews, her mother in Exeter.

This was when the perennial problem had arisen: would they be able to keep a long-distance relationship going when they were separated by a distance of over four hundred miles?

The answer had turned out to be no; it would have been just too hard, the distance that bit too great. There had been endless agonising, tears had been shed and the hopelessness of the situation had been discussed over and over again. But finally they'd conceded defeat and agreed to go their separate ways. The love affair was over.

Eventually, of course, her mum had met someone else and ended up accidentally getting pregnant. When the new boyfriend had found out about the pregnancy, he'd wanted nothing more to do with her. Whereupon her mum, devastated but far too proud to beg, had granted his wish.

What a charmer.

Anyway, who needed a man like that in their life? You'd have to be mad or desperate. Lily did what she'd always done and mentally erased the thought of her biological father from her mind. Instead she watched as Coral finished reading the letter. When she came to the end, unshed tears glimmered in her eyes and she drew Lily to her for another hug.

'Her letters sound just like her. It's as if I can hear her saying every word.'

Lily nodded. 'I know.'

'It's a beautiful letter,' said Coral. She checked her watch. 'Forty minutes before we have to open up. We'd better go inside. There *might* be more cards and presents to open in the kitchen.'

It had turned out to be a busy morning; it might be her birthday, but there was still work to do. When Coral and Nick had inherited Goldstone House from Nick's parents, they had taken over the business too. Goldstone Salvage & Treasure was a destination reclamation company that attracted visitors from miles around. Amateurs and professionals alike came to Stanton Langley in search of items for their homes, gardens and businesses. Every day was different; you never knew who would be buying or selling, or what might pass through the yard. Flagstones, wooden beams and French antique radiators jostled for position with giant chandeliers, period fireplaces, garden sculptures and eclectic items from theatre companies and old film sets. Next to a selection of ornate bed frames and church pews was a Tornado jet fighter cone. Stone gargoyles sat between mullioned windows and a cast-iron kissing gate. Wooden wall panels and original red postboxes mingled with a giant swan-shaped bed and life-sized statues of Adam and the Ants.

It was now midday. Lily had just finished helping a man load an Italian marble sink into the back of his Volvo.

'Well I'm impressed.' The man's wife shook her head in admiration. 'I can't believe you just did that.'

'I know, I'm stronger than I look. There, all done.' Lily dusted her hands on the sides of her shorts and waved the couple off as the phone in her pocket began to ring.

'Lily! Happy birthday,' said Dan.

'Hi! Thanks for the flowers. They're amazing.' The florist had delivered them an hour earlier, a typically over-the-top explosion of birds of paradise, stunning yellow roses, deep purple gerbera and fuchsia-pink peonies the size of dinner plates.

'They've arrived, then? Good. I asked for thistles, nettles and a few old dandelions.'

'That's exactly what they sent me.'

He laughed. 'Listen, that's not why I called. I've messed up and I need you to help me out.'

'Have you crashed your aeroplane? Because if you want me to take the blame and say I was driving at the time, they might be suspicious.'

'If you're going to call it *driving*, the authorities might have an inkling you're not a qualified pilot,' said Dan.

'Honestly, you people are so pernickety. Go on then,' said Lily, 'tell me what you've done.'

'OK, I bought Patsy tickets to see Beyoncé in concert for her birthday and they arrived yesterday. I checked everything was in order and thought I'd keep the envelope in my suitcase so Patsy wouldn't find them. But I searched the case this morning and the envelope isn't in there. So it has to be somewhere in my room. I must have thrown it and missed, and it's on the floor under the bed.'

'Ah,' said Lily. Patsy was a fiend with a vacuum cleaner; she even cleaned bits of the house that didn't show.

'And if I tell her there's something under the bed but she mustn't look at it, she'll just—'

'Look at it.' Lily nodded; the ability to resist temptation had never been one of Patsy's strong points.

'Exactly. And there are photos of Beyoncé all over the wallet holding the tickets. So look, can you get in and hide them? Or better still, take them out of the house?'

'No problem, I'll sort it this afternoon.'

22

'You're a star.' Dan paused. 'How was the letter from your mum?'

Touched that he'd asked, Lily said, 'It was so lovely.'

'Good. Well I'd better get a move on. Sounds like the passengers are getting restless because we haven't taken off yet.'

'Yeah, right. Bye.' She smiled, because he wouldn't really be calling her from the plane as it waited on the runway.

Except a minute after hanging up, she received a message with a photo attached, of Dan wearing his pilot's uniform and headset, grinning at her from his seat in the cockpit as he held up a piece of paper, across which was scrawled in red felt tip: HAPPY BIRTHDAY, DEAR TICKET COLLECTOR, HAPPY BIRTHDAY TO YOUUUU! x

Chapter 5

Patsy was finding it hard to concentrate, what with the gigantic secret that was currently occupying her mind. Her heart did a double skip when Erica Braithwaite suddenly said, 'So who was that fellow then, yesterday?'

OK, relax, she said *yesterday*. The secret hadn't been blown; Erica was talking about Derek. Exhaling with relief, Patsy saw that she was being beadily observed via the mirror in front of them. Around the salon she could feel the antennae of the other clients begin to twitch. That was the thing about having mirrors everywhere; there was no place to hide.

'Which fellow?' It was pointless even prevaricating, but she did it anyway. Hopefully she just looked embarrassed, rather than as if she were harbouring a secret about someone else entirely.

God, though, it was stressful. How on earth did undercover policemen do it?

'Come on, love, you know who I mean,' said Erica. 'On the bicycle made for two.'

Oh well, maybe a bit of distraction was what she needed.

Across the salon, Will was pretending not to be listening as he carried on combing out Jess Carrington's freshly dyed hair.

'It was a first date,' said Patsy. 'I think it's safe to say there won't be a second.'

'Ah, bless your heart. Dumped you already, has he?'

'No!' Honestly, sometimes the urge to let the scissors slip and just give the tip of an ear a tiny nick was almost irresistible. 'I was the one who didn't want to see him again. He wasn't my type.'

'Well by all accounts he did look a bit of a wally,' Erica retorted. 'Then again, beggars can't be choosers, can they?'

Were all old people the same, or were the elderly inhabitants of Stanton Langley truly in a league of their own? 'Thanks, Erica,' Patsy said, 'but I'm *not* a beggar and I'm *always* going to be a chooser.'

'Sure about that, love?' Over by the row of sinks, Mary Southam spluttered with chesty laughter. 'Only when it comes to men, you haven't exactly made the best choices so far.'

That set them all off, naturally. Some jokes never grew old. Patsy was only too aware that she was a source of entertainment to many of her regular clientele. And they didn't mean it maliciously, either; they just found her situation hilarious.

Which was fair enough, really; to any outsider, hers would be a comical predicament to be in.

Will wasn't getting involved, but when she glanced over at him once more, she could see he was trying hard not to smile.

'Will?' Patsy called across the salon. 'When you start cutting Mary's hair, make sure you do her fringe lopsided.'

More laughter, then general conversation resumed, leaving Patsy to wonder if anyone's life ever really went according to plan. When she thought back to her early twenties, she'd been so confident that her own life would. Some people enjoyed being single, gadding about and playing the field, the more partners the better. But she'd never yearned for those kinds of adventures, had known from very early on that all she really wanted was to meet the right man and settle down, get married and have babies, just be normal and happy and average, like a family in a children's story book . . .

Oh yes, the single life had definitely never been for her. Relationship-wise, her late teens and early twenties had been messy and unfulfilling, until at twenty-three she'd met Sean and the longed-for story-book romance had miraculously begun to come true. She'd gone along with friends to a rugby club dance, and Sean had approached her with a typically laddish chat-up line, confiding that he knew she wouldn't want anything to do with him, but *please* could she save him from the ridicule of his teammates and allow him to buy her just one drink?

It had ended up being such a great evening. Sean was lovely, with wavy fair hair and a gorgeous smile. He had a broken nose that only added character to his broad, chiselled face, and wide shoulders as befitted any self-respecting rugby player. They'd hit it off at once. She'd laughed at his terrible jokes, and in turn, he'd paid her compliments and sounded as if he meant them. They had danced together, not awfully well but with plenty of enthusiasm. And at the end of the evening he'd kissed her then said, 'God, you're amazing, I can't believe this is happening . . . I had no idea this was going to turn out to be the best night of my life.'

Patsy bit her lip at the memory; even now, all these years later, she could still recall his comments almost word for word. At the time, she'd memorised them, sensing that her life was about to change in a major way. She'd even fantasised that one day she would be able to tell her teenage daughters all about the magical night when their parents had first met. And the girls might laugh and squeal, pretending to be grossed out by the idea that their mother and father had ever been young, but secretly they'd love hearing the story of how their happy family unit had come about.

Except the happy family unit had never transpired. For the first few years together she'd thought everything was fine, but it turned out that in order for a marriage to really work, *both* partners had to be happy with it.

That had been the stumbling block. And it had come as something of a shock, too, discovering that her big, noisy, cheerful rugby-playing husband had fallen in love with someone else . . .

'The birthday girl's on her way over.' From his position by the window, Will raised his voice to be heard above the blast of the hairdryer he was now wielding. 'Not booked in for anything, is she?'

'No.' Grateful for the distraction, Patsy craned her neck to see Lily making her way across the street. Her heart lifted at the sight of her, that extravagant mane of blond curls bouncing around her shoulders, her brown eyes bright. She was wearing a dark blue Goldstone T-shirt with the Salvage & Treasure logo on the front, a pair of white shorts and light blue flip-flops. Her legs were slim and tanned from spending so much time outside. She was already waving at Will through the full-length window as she approached the salon. And everyone inside was turning to smile and greet her when she pushed open the door.

Lily was the darling of Stanton Langley; everyone loved and was protective of her following the tragic early loss of her mum. The saying 'it takes a village to raise a child' had turned out to contain more than a kernel of truth in Lily's case. Over the years they had all played their part, sharing their various fields of expertise. Kath from Derring's Farm had taught her how to feed lambs and ride horses; Will had helped her get to grips with geometry; Mary from the cake shop had taught her how to bake. Patsy smiled to herself, recalling the time she'd tried to instruct Lily in the art of applying false eyelashes. Afterwards they'd gone over to the pub, where one of the strips of lashes had ended up floating in someone's pint of cider, and that had been that; Lily hadn't attempted to wear them again since.

Having greeted Will and the customers, she came over to where Patsy was working.

'Hey, you. Happy birthday.' Patsy gave her a quick kiss on the cheek. 'All OK?' Everyone knew about the last letter from Jo.

'All OK.' Lily showed her the bangle on her wrist. 'Look, Mum gave me a present.' She nodded, met Patsy's eye and mouthed, *I'm fine*.

'Good.' Patsy duly admired the bangle. 'And to what do we owe this pleasure?'

'The thing is, I really wanted to wear my navy shoes tonight, but one of the heels is falling off. So I wondered if I could borrow yours?'

'Course you can.' They were meeting later at the Star before going out to dinner in Cheltenham. 'I'll bring them with me, shall I?'

Lily shrugged. 'Actually, it's easier if you give me your key and I'll go and pick them up now.'

Ha, like *that* was going to happen.

'It's honestly not a problem,' said Patsy. 'I'll bring them over this evening.' Now she *really* felt like an undercover agent; no way was she giving Lily her key.

Lily said, 'Oh, but I could save you the trouble. And, you know, try them on and make sure they fit me.'

OK, time to put a stop to this. 'You tried them on the other

28

week. You already know they fit you.' With an air of great firmness Patsy said, 'Don't worry, I'll bring them tonight. *Now*.' She turned back to Erica and ran a comb through the back of her hair. 'How much did you say you wanted off?'

Chapter 6

That had gone well, then. Patsy's stubbornness had been mildly puzzling, but by the time Lily had made her way back down the high street, she was pretty certain she'd worked out the likely reason. Patsy was house proud and tidy; chances were that she'd left the kitchen in a mess for once and was embarrassed at not having cleaned up.

Lily was amused by the idea; as if something like that would matter to *her*. But when people had OCD tendencies, you couldn't sway them. Patsy liked everything in her house to be pristine and perfect, and it would bother her to feel as if she'd been seen to let her high standards slip.

It was yet another reason why she was so likely to vacuum under Dan's bed and find the envelope he really didn't want her to find.

That was the thing about Dan: he could be so thoughtful sometimes. Arranging a surprise like that for Patsy was the kind of gesture so many men wouldn't bother to think of. Realising that she couldn't give up, Lily took the keys out of her shorts pocket and unlocked the passenger door of the transit van. She removed a small leather pouch from the glove compartment, jumped back down and hurried across the street. The sooner the envelope had been retrieved, the sooner she could relax and forget about it.

Banner Lane, leading off the high street, was narrow and curved round to the left. Each of the cottages was set back, with long paths separating them from their front gates, and the trees and shrubs in the gardens afforded the properties complete privacy.

Not that the neighbours were likely to call the police if any of them happened to see her breaking into Patsy's home, but it was still easier without an audience.

Also, did it technically count as breaking in when you weren't actually breaking anything?

At the front door, Lily unzipped the narrow leather pouch and selected two of the steel picks for the task in hand. Lock-picking was a skill Nick had taught her as a teenager; when you worked in a reclamation yard, it came in useful. Closed chests, drawers, boxes and desks regularly turned up minus their keys and needed opening. It was a handy trick, learned from months of practice at the kitchen table with an assortment of old locks. If you didn't have professional equipment, you could open standard locks with a thin strip of metal cut from a drinks can, and an unbent paperclip.

Leaning in close, Lily slid the first pick into the lock on the front door. She listened to the tiny clicking noises it made as it scratched at the inner walls.

OK, this wasn't the most basic lock on the market, but with a bit more work, she'd still be able to release it. She gave the door a push with the flat of her left hand, then gripped the edge of the lock face and pulled it back towards her before choosing another pick and trying again. For a moment she felt the oddest sensation, as if she were being watched, and she had to turn and check that no one was standing on the path behind her.

But it was just her overactive imagination; there wasn't anyone there.

It took another thirty seconds, then Lily heard the final click she'd been waiting for. Bingo. The lock retracted, she pushed the door open and . . .

It closed in her face.

What?

She stared at the door. It hadn't *swung* shut. Someone had pushed it.

From the inside.

She blinked. It definitely wasn't Patsy. And it couldn't be Dan. Could it? No, there was no way even Dan would have been able to jump out of his plane and race all the way back here to play a stupid trick on her.

Unnerved, Lily said, 'Who's in there?'

No reply. She hammered on the door and called out, 'What's going on?'

Nothing.

Just to be on the safe side, in case Dan had only been pretending to be flying today, she raised her voice and said, 'Dan, is that you?'

Silence.

OK, this was ridiculous; was there actually someone inside or had she just imagined it? Had a window been left open at the back of the house, causing a gust of wind to make the front door *feel* as if it were being pushed shut by an invisible hand?

Because if she called the police and they came over and the place turned out to be empty, she'd look like a complete lemon.

The more she thought about it, the more likely it seemed that it had been the wind. Still clutching the picks, she fed the second one into the keyhole in order to begin the process again.

'Get away from the door,' warned a low male voice from inside, 'or I'm calling the police.'

What? *What?* Leaping back as if she'd been electrocuted, Lily stared ahead in disbelief.

'I mean it. I'll do it if you don't get away from this house.'

'Hang on a minute,' said Lily, fuelled with sudden outrage. '*You're* calling the police? What are you even talking about? *I'm* the one who's going to call the police!'

'OK, calm down. Don't call them.' There was a pause, then the voice said, 'Who are you?'

God, he had a colossal nerve. 'Never mind me, who are *you*?'

'I'm staying here. I'm Patsy's guest.'

'Well that's a complete lie for a start, because I saw her just now and she'd have told me.' Moving further away from the door – because he didn't sound dangerous, but you never knew – Lily pulled out her phone. 'Right, I'm calling nine nine nine.'

'*Don't.*'

'Too late. Doing it.' Her hands had suddenly started shaking. She'd never actually dialled 999 before, and now she'd pressed 666 by mistake, which was probably the number you called when you needed an emergency exorcism.

At that moment the front door opened and the voice said, 'OK, please don't. I wasn't lying before. I'm allowed to be here, I promise.'

A couple of years ago, Lily had been at work shifting a stack of Victorian picture frames when someone behind her had asked how much they cost. Turning to reply, she'd found herself face to face with the deputy prime minister. It had been one of those completely surreal moments when you see someone you've only ever seen before on TV but all of a sudden they're

33

off the screen, out from behind the glass and unexpectedly inhabiting the real world.

Another time she'd been making a delivery in Oxford, sitting in the van waiting for the lights to change, and the girl with the eyebrows who did the local weather forecast on TV had crossed the road in front of her. Just like any normal person.

Neither of those experiences, however, began to compare with this one. A weather girl and a nerdy politician in socks and sandals were no match for what was happening now.

If it *was* actually happening and she wasn't having a particularly lifelike dream.

But really, what on earth was Eddie Tessler doing in Patsy's cottage?

Eyes narrowed, expression distinctly unamused, he checked there was no one else in sight, then said, 'You'd better come inside.' As if there was nothing he'd like less.

He headed back in, turned and waited for Lily to follow him, then closed the door firmly behind her.

To be honest, it was hardly surprising he didn't want to be seen. As far as many people were concerned, Eddie Tessler was currently right up there at the top of the most-wanted list.

It had only been two or three years ago that he'd sprung to the public's attention when he'd written a screenplay, sold it to one of the major studios and starred in the subsequent smash-hit film. Prior to that, he'd been an unknown, intermittently employed actor with no money, zero prospects and a run-down one-bedroomed flat in Camden. Then the film had been released and pretty much overnight Eddie Tessler found himself catapulted into the shiniest of spotlights. His life changed out of all recognition, everyone suddenly wanted to know every last thing about him and he no longer had a private life.

Before long, he began to find the endless attention wildly irritating.

Then last week it had all hit the fan. Word got out that he had allegedly been having a torrid secret affair with the co-star of his just-wrapped third film. The co-star happened to be married to a *major* A-list actor/director, who wasn't at all happy to discover that his lissom young wife appeared to have been playing away behind his back. The press had gone wild, the paparazzi had followed everyone concerned in ever-more-excitable packs, and one of them had ended up being knocked off his motorbike. Then yesterday Eddie had given them the slip. He'd disappeared and no one knew where he was. There'd even been rumours that the furious A-list actor/director might have used some of his dodgy Italian Mafia connections and arranged to have him taken care of.

Except that clearly hadn't happened, because he was here.

Of all the bizarre hideouts in the world, he'd chosen Patsy's cottage in Stanton Langley in the Cotswolds.

As you do.

Chapter 7

'OK, do me a favour,' said Eddie Tessler. 'Could you just turn your phone off and put it down somewhere I can see it?'

'Without you even saying please?' said Lily. 'I don't think so.'

Manners were manners, after all.

He was watching her intently. 'Sorry. *Please.*'

'Why should I?'

'Because I don't want you taking a photograph of me. These days it's all people ever seem to do.' He paused, raking his fingers through his over-long light brown hair, then said it again. 'Please.'

Lily switched off her phone and placed it on the table between them. 'OK, what are you doing here?'

'Keeping myself hidden, obviously. What about you?' He looked pointedly at the lock-picking case in her hand. 'Why were you breaking in?'

To be fair, it was a reasonable question. They were facing each other now, both wary, not trusting each other an inch.

'Patsy's my friend. I've just this minute been to see her. She didn't want to lend me her key and I couldn't understand why, but I needed to get in here.'

'Why were you so desperate to get in?'

If he could be blunt, so could she. 'To stop her finding something her brother accidentally left out.'

'Drugs, you mean?'

'No!' Lily shot him a look of disbelief.

'Gun?'

'Are you crazy?' This time she did a worried double-take. 'Why, have you found a gun?'

He shook his head. 'Just wondering what he left out that he doesn't want his sister to see.'

'Well stop jumping to conclusions. It's up in his room. If you give me two minutes, I'll go and get it.'

'It's my room at the moment,' said Eddie Tessler. 'I'll come with you.'

'Why? Do you think I'm going to steal your underpants?'

Another look; he clearly still didn't trust her an inch. 'I don't know anything about you. I don't know what you might try to do.'

He walked behind her up the staircase and across the landing, and Lily caught a hint of his aftershave. It really was the weirdest sensation, being this close to someone you'd only seen before on a cinema screen. He might only be three years older than her, but their lives were worlds apart.

In Dan's bedroom, there was a single holdall on the floor beneath the window. The curtains were closed, the bed had been slept in and the duvet was still rumpled. She knelt down, lifted the valance around the edge of the bed and saw the envelope at once, just out of reach.

It was another weird feeling, spread-eagling yourself on the carpet and stretching your arm under the bed all the way up to your shoulder whilst a Very Famous Person stood and watched you do it.

Her fingers touched the end of the envelope and she managed to retrieve it, wriggling backwards away from the bed like a sniper in reverse and aware that she'd tried to do it without sticking her bottom in the air.

Then she was out and back on her feet, showing the opened envelope to Eddie Tessler.

'There you go. And just so you know, I wouldn't have stolen your underpants.'

'What is it?'

'Tickets to see Beyoncé at the O2. They're a surprise for Patsy's birthday. Happy now?'

'Why would I be happy?'

'No reason at all.' God, he was tense. 'Anyway, just don't tell Patsy, or you'll spoil the surprise. Promise me.'

He gave her a look, then shook his head. 'Fine. I promise.'

'There, that wasn't so difficult, was it?'

'And you have to promise not to tell anyone I'm here.'

Lily shrugged. 'OK.'

'No one at all.'

'I heard you the first time.'

'What are you doing now?' He followed her down the staircase.

'Going back to work.'

'Not yet. Stay for a bit longer.'

'Why?'

'I want us to talk.'

She raised her eyebrows. 'Because you don't trust me.'

'Yes.'

'I just gave you my word.'

'Put it this way. People quite often say things they don't mean, make promises they're not going to keep.'

'Not me, though.'

Eddie Tessler paused, then said, 'Can you just stay anyway? For a coffee or something? I don't even know your name yet.'

He definitely wasn't saying it in a flirty way.

'Lily. Lily Harper.'

'Right.' A nod, then a brief smile to acknowledge the oddness of the situation. 'I'm Eddie.'

Which was a bit like the Queen saying, 'Hello, I'm the Queen.' Lily said, 'I still don't understand what you're doing here.' She indicated the cottage. 'How do you know Patsy?'

He made his way through to the kitchen, put two mugs under the coffee machine and switched it on. 'I don't. I went to stay with my father yesterday and the paps got there before I did. So we thought I might have more luck staying somewhere with absolutely no connection to me. That worked out well,' he added drily.

'I still don't get it. Did you just stick a pin in the phone book, call Patsy's number and ask if you could come and stay in her house?'

'Not quite. My PA was having her hair done yesterday by her sister when I called to tell her I'd arrived at my dad's and the paps were there. Her sister's name is Rose . . . no, Rosa . . .'

'Oh I know Rosa! She used to live here . . . she worked for Patsy!'

'That's right. So my PA was telling me she'd try and find somewhere I could stay and keep out of the way, and Rosa thought of this place. She knew it had complete privacy, and that Patsy could be trusted not to say anything.'

'Well that's true. She didn't even tell me.' Which was both impressive and slightly frustrating.

'Good. Let's hope you're as trustworthy as she is.'

'See, there you go again,' said Lily, irritated. 'It's actually not

39

very helpful, you know, the way you keep coming out with things like that. I'm more likely to be on your side if you tell me you *do* trust me.'

'I know. Sorry again.' He exhaled. 'But if you'd lived the kind of life I have for the last couple of years, you'd understand why I'm the way I am.'

'Poor you.' Lily half smiled and made sure she only sounded a *tad* sarcastic.

'Yeah, OK. But it's not as fantastic as people think, everyone knowing who you are and having an opinion on every damn thing you do.'

She took the coffee cup he was holding towards her, and said, 'It must be annoying. Especially if there's stuff you don't want them to find out.' *Like having an affair with your married co-star.*

'Shall we talk about you instead?' Pointedly changing the subject, Eddie Tessler sat down and said, 'So how do you know Patsy?'

'Well for a start, this is Stanton Langley. Which means everyone knows everyone. But Patsy used to babysit me when I was little. She's been like a big sister ever since.'

'Does she perm your hair to get it like that?' He made spirally gestures with his free hand.

'No. My hair does it all by itself.'

'And where do you work?'

'Goldstone Salvage and Treasure, on the high street. It's a reclamation company.'

'I haven't seen the high street. My PA drove me down here late last night. What do you do there?'

'Anything that needs doing. Order, deliver, source items for clients, buy at auction, run the website . . . we also sell online and ship worldwide.' Lily took a gulp of coffee and checked her watch. 'Coral's going to be wondering where I am. I really should get back.'

'Right.' Eddie Tessler looked as if he wanted to say something else but was thinking better of it. 'Well, you got what you came for.' He indicated the envelope in her pocket. 'I suppose I'd better not mention meeting you to Patsy.'

Oh dear, that could be tricky; now that Lily knew he was here, she wanted to be able to talk to Patsy about her secret tenant. Putting down her cup, she said, 'I pretended I needed the key so I could borrow her shoes for tonight. Why don't I take them with me, then you can tell her we met?'

He nodded in agreement. 'It'd be easier. Where are the shoes?'

'In Patsy's wardrobe. I'll get them.' As he half rose from his chair, Lily said, 'It's OK, you don't have to follow me.'

She found the shoes – midnight blue, high-heeled and fabulous – and brought them back down. Eddie Tessler's gaze flickered over her as if checking she wasn't making off with anything else.

Lily patted the pockets of her shorts, held up the shoes and did jazz hands. 'See? No underpants.'

Words she'd never expected to hear herself saying to a real-life movie star.

Eddie Tessler lifted an eyebrow. 'Unless you're wearing them.'

'Ah well. You'll never know.'

A glimmer of a smile. 'Until I go upstairs and count how many are still in my case.'

Lily couldn't help it; she burst out laughing. 'Anyway, nice to meet you. I've never spoken to a famous person before.'

'It's been nice meeting you too.' He indicated the shoes dangling by their narrow straps from her left hand. 'Where are you off to tonight? Somewhere special?'

'Very special. Out to dinner in Cheltenham with Coral and

41

Patsy. Then we'll probably come back for a few drinks at the Star.' It must sound unbelievably parochial to someone used to leading his kind of lifestyle.

He nodded, remembering. 'Patsy said she'd be out celebrating someone's birthday this evening.'

'She will be.' Lily waved a tiny imaginary flag. 'Happy birthday to me!'

Miracle of miracles, another brief smile. 'Happy birthday.'

'Thanks. Right, I'm off. Good luck with hiding from everyone. How long do you think you'll be staying here?'

'No idea. Until I get found out, I guess.' He was giving her that infuriating look again, letting her know that if he were to be rumbled, it would be her fault. 'And if that happens, I might have to tell Patsy about the Beyoncé tickets.'

It was Lily's turn to give him one of *her* looks. She opened the front door. 'You're all heart,' she said.

There hadn't been time earlier, but upstairs in her bedroom after work, Lily sat on the bed and typed Declan Madison's name into Google.

She'd mentally prepared herself in case of disappointment. He could be dead, or a serial killer, or he simply might not merit a mention on the internet. She took a deep breath and pressed 'search' . . .

And there, like magic, were the details on the screen. Lily's heart began to clatter inside her chest and her fingers tingled, because he was still alive and she'd been so afraid he might not be. There was no photograph, but she just knew instinctively that this was the right Declan Madison.

It was him.

Chapter 8

Gosh, keeping secrets was hard. Lily kept finding herself glancing across the table at Patsy, and Patsy was doing the same to her.

Because Patsy knew about Eddie Tessler, and *she* knew about Eddie Tessler, and she knew that Patsy knew she knew . . .

In the meantime, Coral was blissfully unaware and rattling on about something else entirely.

Plus, of course, they had a birthday to celebrate.

Coming to this restaurant in the Montpellier area of Cheltenham was another tradition that had begun the year her mother had died. Having been brought to Maria's months earlier and been enthralled by both the atmosphere and the fettuccine Alfredo, she'd asked to come here again for her birthday. And Maria, the owner, had made a wonderful fuss of her, bringing out the bowl of fettuccine with coloured candles stuck into it and persuading everyone in the restaurant, staff and customers alike, to sing 'Happy Birthday'. Maria, a mother of seven herself, had succeeded in making what could have been a difficult evening a triumph instead. It might not be the most upmarket and glamorous place to eat, but it was without question the most welcoming. Nine-year-old Lily had hugged Maria and declared, 'I'm always, *always* going to come here for my birthday.'

And they had done, every year since. Always the four of them when Nick had been alive, now they were down to three, but the welcome was just as warm, and Maria, like a proud and adoring grandma, still insisted on sticking candles into her food.

This evening they'd had another brilliant time, the food had been delicious and wine had been drunk.

Which wasn't helping at all.

'Who is it?' said Coral when Patsy's phone signalled the arrival of a message.

Patsy, who had glanced at the screen, gone a bit wide-eyed and hurriedly put the phone down, said, 'Sorry? No one!' Then her gaze had flickered in Lily's direction and she'd taken another glug of Soave.

'Is it Tandem Man?' Lily pulled a sympathetic face. 'Just ignore him and delete the messages. Listen, I think I might have found my mum's boyfriend.' She hadn't meant to blurt it out quite like that, but a change of subject was clearly called for. 'If it does turn out to be him, do you think he'd think it was weird if I got in touch?'

That did the trick.

'I was thinking about that too,' Coral exclaimed. 'I wondered if you'd want to do it. We never knew his surname before. I only ever heard Jo call him Declan.'

'It's an uncommon name,' said Lily. 'There's only one Declan Madison in the UK. Living in London.'

'I think you should do it!' Patsy was enthusiastic, relieved to have the attention shift away from her mystery text. 'You can tell him about the bangle. And if he's only in London, that's not far away. Would you like to meet him?'

Would she like to meet the man her mother had loved? Of course she would, more than *anything*. The idea of hearing

44

about her mum from someone who'd loved her in return was thrilling in a way Lily couldn't begin to describe.

'I would.' She nodded and scraped the last of Maria's legendary tiramisu from the plate with the back of her fork. 'But what if he says he can hardly remember her? What if Mum loved him but he was never really that bothered?' The idea had been niggling away at her all day. She held up the wrist with the bangle on it. 'What if this was Mum's most treasured possession but he's forgotten he even bought it?'

Like Dan, with his endless stream of girlfriends.

'Oh Lily, I'm sure—'

'What if he's not interested in meeting me because I'm just . . . nobody to him?'

'Then he's a complete pig,' said Patsy, 'and it's his loss. Have you got an email address for him?'

Lily shook her head. 'No, home address. He's in Notting Hill.'

'Well send him a letter and see what happens. You never know,' said Coral, 'he might be thrilled to hear from you.'

'We could go back now,' Patsy exclaimed, 'and help you write it!'

Lily frowned at her. 'I thought we were going to the Star.'

'I know, but wouldn't you rather get the letter done? We can do it at my place!'

OK, Patsy had really lost the plot now. Her voice loaded with meaning, Lily said, 'Or we could go back to *our* house.'

'What's going on?' Coral was eyeing them with suspicion. 'And don't say nothing, because something is.'

Patsy looked as if she was about to explode. 'Fine then,' she blurted out, as if Lily were being the world's biggest spoilsport. 'We'll go back to your empty house.' Pause. 'Instead of the one with the film star hiding in it.'

Lily exhaled. *Ooh dear.*

'And don't look at me like that,' Patsy wailed. 'I couldn't help it. It's been killing me all night!'

'Hang on, am I missing something here?' Coral was bemused. 'Is it a joke? Was that the punchline?'

Lily shook her head at Patsy. 'The whole reason they chose you was because they thought you could keep secrets.'

'I *can* keep secrets! Just not from Coral! I mean, it isn't fair!'

'Um, hello? You two?' Coral pointed to herself. 'I am still here, you know.'

Leaning across the table and almost knocking over the candle, Patsy whispered like a pantomime spy, 'I've got a film star in my house!'

'No!' Coral clapped a hand over her mouth. 'You stole that cardboard cut-out from the cinema? Oh Pats, what if they have CCTV? You're terrible, you really are. Honestly, you should be ashamed of yourself.'

Eddie had been in Stanton Langley for twenty-four hours now, and cabin fever was starting to set in. The cottage was very clean, but it was small. The Wi-Fi was slow, there was no satellite or cable TV and he was going out of his mind with boredom.

Which just went to show, you could dream of going away on holiday and doing absolutely nothing all day, but being on your own and doing nothing within the confines of someone else's home wasn't much fun at all.

Then again, it was still better than being endlessly followed and doorstepped by a heaving mass of paps and journalists.

Eddie tipped his head back against the sofa and heaved a sigh of irritation. It was almost eleven o'clock and there had been no reply to the text he'd regretted sending the moment it had left his phone.

A few minutes later, he heard female footsteps coming up the path, followed by the scratch of metal against the lock on the front door. Caused by a key this time, rather than a professional lock pick. He heard shuffling, muffled whispers and giggles, and smiled despite himself. Patsy was warm and likeable, and he already trusted her. As for Lily . . . well, she was likeable too. Quick-witted and quirkily attractive, with those mad blond ringlets and huge dark eyes. It wasn't just that, though. There was something about her that had struck a chord. She intrigued him.

Then the front door swung open and they burst into the living room with a clatter of high heels, Lily first, followed by Patsy waving a bottle of wine and two gigantic packets of crisps . . .

Followed by a third woman, presumably the one they'd been out to dinner with. Eddie's heart sank and his smile disappeared. Oh great, so much for thinking they were remotely trustworthy. Well done, everyone.

'OK, now listen, don't be cross.' Patsy flapped her arms to stop him in his tracks. 'I know what we promised, but it's only Coral. She doesn't count. She's one of us, and she definitely won't say anything.'

'I thought you could keep a secret.' Since she was doing him a favour, Eddie knew he couldn't actually be too cross, but he could still signal his disappointment.

'I can! I can keep loads of secrets!'

'Just not this one,' said Eddie.

'I know, but it was impossible. I knew, and Lily knew too, and there we were in the restaurant, the three of us . . . It just felt so *unfair* to leave Coral out.'

'She did do pretty well,' Lily joined in. 'She managed not to mention it for almost two hours.'

'Two whole hours? Oh well, that's all right then.'

'Please don't be like that,' said Patsy. 'It was a moment of weakness. And it's still a secret, I promise. Nobody else is going to know you're here!'

'And you did invite us back.' Lily shrugged. 'We were going to go to the pub until you sent that text. We couldn't just abandon Coral, could we? That would have been cruel.'

'You wanted company,' Patsy reminded him. 'You've got company. Just a little bit more company than you were expecting.'

She'd called it a moment of weakness. Which was basically what he'd succumbed to when he'd sent the text to Patsy saying that if she wanted to bring Lily back with her later for a nightcap, it would be fine by him.

But it was still annoying. 'Do you see where this is going, though?' he said. 'Last night only one person living in this village knew I was here. This afternoon it became two. And now it's three.'

'You know what?' said Lily suddenly. 'I think we should leave.'

'Oh darling, not you.' Coral, who had been observing the exchange from over by the door, shook her head at Lily. 'He isn't cross with you. I'll go home.' She turned to address Eddie. 'I'm so sorry about this, I really am. I'm going now.'

'I'll come with you,' said Lily.

'OK, *stop*.' Eddie shook his head in disbelief. 'This is stupid. You're here, you've seen me now, so what's the point of leaving? It's not as if it's going to erase your memory.'

'Look.' Lily was equally blunt. 'It's my birthday. You're not in the sunniest of moods. We've been out and had a fantastic evening and I really don't want the rest of it spoiled by some grumpy stranger.'

'Well if you two are going,' said Patsy, 'I'm coming with you. You're not leaving me here with him.'

'Whoa, this is getting out of hand.' Eddie marvelled at the way Patsy had broken her promise to him yet somehow he'd managed to become the bad guy. 'Can you give me a break here? I'm sorry if I was grumpy. How about if none of you leave and we open that bottle of wine?' He turned from Patsy to Lily and from Lily to Coral. 'Sorry . . . sorry . . . very very sorry. Please stay.'

And because he was Eddie Tessler, with buckets of charm and a smile capable of melting ice when he chose to use it, they did.

It was 1.30 in the morning when Lily looked across at the chiming clock and said, 'You know, we probably should be thinking of going home. It's not my birthday any more and some of us have to get up for work soon.' She pulled a face. 'Those of us who aren't film stars, I mean.'

Eddie grinned, because it wasn't every day you got to watch a girl with blond ringlets do a Michael Jackson moonwalk across a kitchen floor in a pair of stripy socks borrowed for the occasion in order to facilitate the necessary slidiness. Even more impressively, she was doing it without spilling a drop of her bright pink drink.

'I can't believe I have to cut people's hair in a few hours,' Patsy marvelled. She made extravagant scissory gestures with both hands and said, 'Imagine!'

Coral nodded in agreement. 'We should go, we really should. It's later than I thought.' She looked around, puzzled. 'What did I do with my shoes?'

'You took them off when you did the tango.' Eddie fetched them for her from the windowsill.

49

'Oh for heaven's sake, what a silly place to leave them!' Coral shook her head as she took the red stilettos and put the left one on to her right foot. 'Whoever put them there?'

As he helped her keep her balance, Eddie hid a smile, because the last couple of hours had been an experience he wouldn't forget in a hurry. Now that he'd heard the story of their joined-together lives, he understood how the three women had forged such a close bond. Coral was twelve years older than Patsy, who was in turn ten years older than Lily, but the loss of Lily's mother had pulled them together, and as the years had passed, the ties had only strengthened.

Now, after much laughter and dancing and possibly ill-advised combinations of alcohol, he was very glad he'd managed to persuade them to stay.

Then again, he was even more glad he wouldn't be having his hair cut by Patsy in the morning.

Chapter 9

Eddie Tessler wanted to kiss her, Lily could tell. She knew by the way he was gazing at her. Worse still, he seemed to know that she wanted it to happen. She heard her own breathing quicken and looked away, stretching out the tape measure in her hands and concentrating hard on the purple velvet curtains.

'What are you doing?' He moved up behind her and she felt his warm breath on the side of her neck.

'Measuring the curtains.'

'Why?'

Lily couldn't answer; she had no idea why, and now he was closer still. His mouth brushed her jawline and he murmured, 'That isn't a tape measure, by the way. It's a telephone charger. And you should probably answer that phone.'

The phone carried on ringing and Lily opened her eyes, rushing up to the surface and experiencing a mixture of disappointment and relief that it had been a dream. On the one hand, the prospect of being kissed had been thrilling; on the other, thank goodness she hadn't really been trying to measure Patsy's living-room curtains with a charger cable.

Oh God, though. Her *head*.

Wincing, she rolled over in bed and scooped her phone off the floor, which worsened the headache dramatically. She deserved some kind of medal for fortitude in the face of adversity.

'Urgh . . .' It wasn't much, but it was the best she could do.

'Morning! Is that your way of saying hello? Happy Boxing Birthday,' said Dan, who was always disgustingly cheery first thing.

'Hang on.' At least she'd had the foresight to leave a tumbler of water next to the bed, although drinking it last night might have been a wiser move. The glass clanked against her teeth as she gulped the water down in one go.

'Good night, I take it?'

'I wish you *had* taken it, then I wouldn't be feeling like this now.' Flopping back against the pillows, Lily said, 'You know Patsy's drinks cupboard? I think we may have finished the lot.'

'Oh God. Cocktails.'

'That's one way to describe them.' They'd both experienced Patsy's adventurous streak before. When the normal drinks ran out – and last night's single bottle of wine hadn't gone far between the four of them – she liked to make concoctions from whatever was in the cupboard. There had been blue curaçao, Tia Maria, lime-flavoured vodka, some weird pomegranate liqueur, Jack Daniel's . . . oh, and the raspberry Chambord.

Plenty of Chambord.

How could something so completely delicious make you feel so dreadful the next day?

'What time did you get home?' said Dan.

'Three o'clock, I think.' Lily massaged her temples. 'Your sister's a shocking influence.'

'Tell me about it. Anyway, did you manage to find those tickets?'

'I did, they're right here. They were under your bed, like you said.'

And he had no idea who had spent the last two nights *in* his bed.

'I'm always right. And you were meant to text me to let me know you'd found them. I thought you would.'

'I know, sorry. Got distracted.' By the famous person who's been sleeping in your bed. 'Hey, are you in a rush? Are you at work?'

'Not yet. I'm in Milan. Lying in bed in my hotel room. With no hangover.'

'Lucky you.'

'And no clothes on either.' He was grinning, she could tell.

'Spare me the mental picture. OK now, shush for a minute and listen.' Lily relayed to him the details of her mum's letter, then explained that she'd almost certainly tracked down Declan Madison. When she'd finished, she said, 'So I'm going to write to him!'

'You are? Why?'

'So I can let him know about Mum leaving me the bracelet he gave her. And tell him how much he meant to her . . . and then he can tell me things about her that I haven't heard before.'

'Riiiiight,' Dan said slowly.

'Why are you sounding like that?'

'I just don't want you to be hurt if he says he can't remember your mum. It was *so* long ago. They were eighteen then. I was eighteen nine years ago and I'm struggling to remember who I went out with back then.'

'You went out with Janice Frayn,' Lily reminded him patiently. 'And Tonda Whittington. And that girl with the spiky blond hair . . . she drove a yellow Fiat and had your name tattooed on her hip . . . ooh, what was she called?'

'Oh right, yes, I remember the tattoo,' said Dan. 'I didn't make her do it. She had it done as a surprise. Was her name Ellie or Ally, something like that?'

'Ania,' said Lily as it came back to her. Poor Ania, indelibly tattooed with the name of someone who couldn't even be bothered to remember hers.

'That's it. But this is what I'm saying.' Dan's tone softened. 'There's a chance this Declan chap might have forgotten your mum.'

'OK, I get the message. But they were together for nearly a year,' said Lily, 'so hopefully he hasn't forgotten her. *Hopefully*,' she added, 'he wasn't as much of a heartless bastard as you.'

Paracetamols. Long shower. Giant mug of tea. Unable to cope with the idea of actual breakfast, Lily let herself out of the house and made her way across the yard to the office, where Coral was already busy opening the post.

'Morning, darling!' Coral was as bright and cheerful as Dan had been on the phone; she was famed for her ability to knock back dubious cocktails without suffering the subsequent hangover. 'Feeling like death warmed up?'

Lily collapsed on to the chair in front of the computer. 'I'll be OK.'

'You look white. Not too ill to work?'

'Never too ill to work.' Mind over matter; if she said it with enough conviction, everything would be fine. She might even live.

Coral's eyes sparkled. 'How about a nice glass of Chambord to perk you up?'

'Don't be cruel.' The very thought.

'It was fun last night, though, wasn't it?' Lowering her voice and double-checking that no one was outside the office to overhear them, Coral added, 'With Eddie!'

The mention of his name brought the dream rushing back. Measuring curtains and getting kissed by Eddie Tessler. Lifting her still-damp hair from the back of her neck, Lily belatedly realised that that was where he'd brushed his mouth against her skin. She nodded and said faintly, 'Yes, it was . . . good.'

'So are you heading over there in your lunch break?'

'Over where?'

'To see him! You're going to write that letter, remember? He offered to help you!'

Oh God, he had. It was all coming back to her now. They'd been discussing the letter and she'd been wondering how best to word it, and Eddie had said, 'Well, why don't I give you a hand?'

Which at the time, what with him being a professional wordsmith and all, had seemed like an excellent idea.

Now, post-dream, it just felt embarrassing.

'I don't know. I should do it myself,' said Lily.

Coral looked dismayed. 'Oh go on, let him help. He'll be looking forward to a bit of company, I expect. Anyway, you can't turn him down now. It'd be rude.'

At 2.15, Lily double-knocked at the front door of Patsy's cottage, then pushed open the letter box. 'Hi, it's me.'

The door opened and she slipped inside, deliberately not thinking about the dream.

'You're late,' said Eddie Tessler.

'We've been busy. Some of us have work to do.'

'Touché. How are you feeling after last night?'

'Terrible, thanks.' It was getting easier to look at him, but still weird to think he was famous. This afternoon he was barefoot and wearing a dark blue polo shirt and board shorts, so she was even getting to see his famous legs. They were nice ones too, lean and tanned and with a pale scar across his left knee.

'And does anyone else know I'm here? Have you mentioned it to the rest of the village yet?'

'Of course I have. Didn't you hear me bellowing the announcement through my loudhailer?'

His mouth twitched. 'I'll put the kettle on. Fancy some tea and toast?'

'Perfect.'

In the kitchen, she watched from the doorway as he made the tea, sliced the loaf and took the butter out of the fridge. They really were very good legs, not off-puttingly hairy, finely muscled, with well-shaped calves and—

'I can see what you're doing, by the way.'

'What?' She jumped.

'Checking out my backside.' He pointed to the window to indicate that he'd been watching her reflection in the glass.

'Well you're wrong,' said Lily, 'because I was looking at your legs.'

'And? Are they OK?'

'Not bad.'

He laughed and began buttering the popped-up toast. 'Have you thought about how you want to write this letter?'

'Kind of. I've made a few notes. It needs to be right, though. I don't want to scare him off.'

Eddie placed everything on a tray and carried it through

to the living room. They sat down at the table facing each other and he slid over one of the plates and a mug of tea. 'Go on then, I got the gist of it last night, but tell me properly everything you know about your mum and this chap of hers. Declan.'

one

Chapter 10

Coral, of course, was the one who'd heard the story about Declan directly from Jo herself. But Lily had learned it over the years following her mum's death. She'd always loved discovering details of her mother's life, especially the happier aspects. She could pretty much recite them off by heart.

'OK, well they met in Barcelona. They were both eighteen, taking a year out after A levels before heading off to university. Mum was a waitress in a restaurant on Las Ramblas and Declan worked there behind the bar. They fancied each other from the first moment they met, apparently . . . well, Mum was stunning and she was such fun, why wouldn't he fancy her? And he was the prettiest boy she'd ever seen, like *really* good-looking. So they started seeing each other, and arranging their work schedules so they could do the same shifts and have more time off together to have fun and explore Barcelona. They'd go to the beach, swim in the sea, have adventures and just make the most of every day.'

'Because they knew it was going to come to an end,' said Eddie when she paused to take a bite of toast.

Lily chewed, swallowed and nodded. 'That's right. Mum had a place at Exeter to read English and he was due to go to St

Andrews. I mean, they couldn't have chosen two places further apart if they'd tried. I mean, hundreds and *hundreds* of miles apart. And they loved each other to bits, but what could they do? Either try and make a long-distance relationship work, or be practical and break up.' She shrugged; they both already knew the answer. 'And when it came to it, they broke up. Mum was devastated at first; it wasn't easy. But she got over it in time.'

'They were nineteen,' said Eddie. 'When you're that age, it kind of happens. Life goes on.'

'Exactly. Mum didn't forget him, though. After the first year, she wrote to him suggesting they could spend the summer break back in Barcelona, but Declan said he couldn't, he already had some other job lined up. Then a couple of days later she got a letter from someone called Theresa saying she was Declan's girlfriend now and it wasn't fair to keep pestering him; she needed to get on with her own life and let him go.'

Eddie nodded. 'Must have been hard.'

'I know. But Mum knew it was for the best. She wasn't going to beg. And the next year, she met someone else too.' Lily grimaced and took a gulp of tea. 'Keir Bourne.'

'Your father.'

'Unfortunately.'

'If it hadn't been for him, you wouldn't be here now.'

'Oh I know that. I just wish he could have turned out to be a bit less selfish, a bit more of a decent human being.' She puffed a stray curl off her forehead. 'So anyway, that was it as far as Mum and Declan were concerned. She didn't contact him after that.'

'Can I ask how you ended up here? Sorry, you don't have to tell me that.' Eddie shrugged. 'I'm just interested. I like to ask questions.'

'It's fine. Mum carried on seeing Keir, on and off. He wasn't a student; he lived with his parents in Exeter and worked for them in their car showroom. Don't laugh.' Lily pointed a finger in warning, then said, 'Actually, why not? Laugh as much as you like. I'm the biological daughter of a sleazeball used-car salesman.'

'It's OK.' Eddie wasn't laughing, but he looked as if he'd like to. 'Not your fault.'

'So anyway, it got to the end of the third year and Mum finished her finals, but she didn't do as well as she'd hoped. Then Keir's parents lost their office manager and offered her the position, and she wasn't sure what else she could do so she took the job.'

'Working for the out-laws.' Eddie shook his head. 'I'm not sure that's ever a good idea.'

'I know. She stuck it out for a few months, but it wasn't ideal. And then, at the end of October, she discovered she was pregnant.' Lily grimaced. 'Which was even less ideal. She told Keir, who told his parents. They were appalled.'

'And?'

'They accused Mum of setting out to trap their precious son, as if he was the world's greatest catch. Then they told her the problem needed taking care of. They said they'd pay for it to be dealt with and offered to take Mum to the clinic. But Mum said she'd sort it out herself.' Twisting a strand of hair around her index finger, Lily went on, 'So they gave her the exact amount in cash and prepared to wave her off. That was when she told them she'd be keeping the baby. They were horrified, of course, but there was nothing they could do about it.'

There was empathy in Eddie's silver-grey eyes. 'I hope she bought something nice with the money.'

'She bought a clapped-out blue Ford Escort – *not* from

60

them, funnily enough – and spent the rest on baby clothes and a second-hand cot. Then she left Exeter with nowhere to go.'

'No family of her own?'

Lily shook her head. 'No brothers or sisters. Just a mother who liked to drink and gamble. When Mum went off to university, her mother sold their flat to pay off the debts she'd run up at the casino. Then she married some bloke she'd met there. They refused to let Mum move in with them. So yes, she was completely on her own.'

'Yet she didn't give you up. That's pretty amazing. Sounds like your mum was quite a character.'

Lily smiled and nodded. 'Oh yes, she was amazing. She stopped the car at a service station on the M5 and bought a road map, then closed her eyes and stuck a pin in it.'

'As you do,' said Eddie.

'Well, probably not an actual pin. I expect she just pointed with her finger. And hit Nottingham, so that's where she decided to go. But as she drove on up the motorway, she realised she'd be passing quite close to the part of the Cotswolds where Coral lived. They'd been best friends through three years of uni and she'd heard all about Stanton Langley but never got to see it. She thought it'd be nice to stop on the way, pay Coral a quick visit and let her know what was happening, where she was planning to go.' Lily spread her hands and said cheerily, 'Well, you pretty much know the rest. Mum arrived here in the village, Coral persuaded her to stay the night . . . and that was it, she never left.'

'Fate,' said Eddie, finishing his last corner of toast.

'Exactly. I could have been born and lived my whole life in Nottingham.'

He pushed aside his empty plate. 'So, shall we get down to business?'

Which, like a saucy Carry-On nudge, brought memories of this morning's inappropriate dream back once more. Lily felt the little hairs on the nape of her neck prickle with embarrassment. Jumping up, she took the plates to the sink and collected a pen and notebook from her shoulder bag. Then she sat back down, uncapped the pen in businesslike fashion and said, 'Right, let's go.'

Miraculously, it didn't take long at all. Eddie told her to write from the heart, Lily jotted down what she wanted to say, and with his encouragement, the words just seemed to spill out on to the page. Twenty minutes later, it was done.

'Wow, that was easier than I thought.' She sat back, hugely impressed with herself. 'I expected it to take ages.'

Eddie smiled at her. 'I knew you could do it.'

'Do you really think it's OK?'

His gaze met hers. 'It's better than OK. It's perfect.'

'Well, thanks. You helped just by asking the right questions.' Lily tapped the open notebook, covered in the words she'd hastily scribbled down. 'I'll write it out properly and post it later. Thanks so much for helping me out.'

'My pleasure.'

'And now I'd better get back to work.' She flipped the notebook shut.

'That's a shame.' Eddie sat back. 'It's kind of nice having a bit of company.' Drily he added, 'So long as it's the right kind.'

Whoops, getting a bit hot again. 'Well, Patsy'll be home at five.'

He nodded. 'I like Patsy. She's great. We haven't talked about her ex-husband, but Rosa told my PA what happened. Must have been pretty rough for her.'

'It was.'

Eddie hesitated, then said, 'If you're not doing anything this evening, would you like to come over again?'

'God,' said Lily with a grin, 'you *are* bored.'

'Well?' Now he was smiling too.

'Can I ask you a question? Is that girlfriend of yours likely to be turning up at some stage?'

'What girlfriend?'

'Oh come on,' said Lily. 'The one that got you hiding out here in the first place. The one married to the scary movie director.'

'OK, she's not my girlfriend. I haven't slept with her. She threw herself at me to make her husband jealous because she knows *he's* been seeing someone else.' Eddie shook his head in despair. 'Seriously, the pair of them are so messed up. And as far as they're concerned, it's all extra publicity for the film, so it's fine. Never mind what it's doing to me.'

'Oh.' He certainly sounded as if he was telling the truth. 'Nice people.'

'I know. Anyway, never mind them. Will you be coming over?'

OK, how often did a good-looking famous person practically beg you to spend the evening with them? 'I'll have to consult my busy diary,' Lily said, then rose to her feet and hoisted her bag over her shoulder. 'Maybe.'

Eddie Tessler's eyes glittered. 'And if you happen to call in at the shop on your way over, white chocolate Magnums are my favourite.'

63

Chapter 11

Patsy's first client of the morning wasn't a willing one. Her name was Tamsin, and she was perfectly happy with her hair the way it was.

'Noooo,' she wailed when Patsy cautiously approached with the scissors. 'Don't! I like it like DISS.'

The child's mother shook her head. 'It can't stay like that, though, Tamsin,' she said wearily. 'Now be a good girl and sit still.'

Last night, four-year-old Tamsin had locked herself in the family bathroom with a pair of blunt scissors and spent a happy half-hour determinedly sawing away at her straight blond hair.

Just on the one side of her head.

'Sweetie, you have to be careful.' Patsy rested her hands on Tamsin's tiny shoulders. 'Because my scissors are really sharp and I don't want you to get hurt.'

Tears welled in the little girl's eyes. 'But I like my hair!'

'Tam, it can't stay like that,' her mother blurted out in despair. 'Everyone will laugh at you. Hair has to be the same on both sides otherwise it just looks *silly*.'

'NOT SILLY,' roared Tamsin, launching herself out of the chair. Like a mini superhero she ripped apart the Velcro fastening of her cape and flung it to the ground. 'NOTSILLY NOTSILLY, GETAWAYFROMME . . .'

'Oh my God, Tamsin, you are being *impossible*.' Her mother rolled her eyes. 'I'm so sorry, she's not going to let you do it,' she said to Patsy. 'We'll have to leave it for now.'

'That's OK. Not a problem.' Patsy picked up the discarded cape. 'Maybe in a day or two she'll change her mind.'

'Fingers crossed. Honestly,' said the woman, 'I think she's trying to give me a nervous breakdown. Kids, eh? Who'd have them?'

It was one of those careless, throwaway comments you heard all the time, but to Patsy the words jarred like chalk on a blackboard. A lump sprang into her throat, and when she glanced across the salon, her gaze caught Will's for a split second before he looked away.

Tamsin's mother said, 'Have you got children?'

Patsy willed the lump to reduce in size. 'No, not me.'

The woman, clearly at the end of her tether, shook her head. 'You don't know how lucky you are.'

An hour later, Patsy was putting foils into the hair of another mother, this one a not-quite-natural blond in her late twenties whose three-week-old daughter was sleeping in a new pink and grey carrying car seat. Everyone had admired little Ella, who was utterly beautiful, with downy dark hair, a rosebud mouth and delicate eyebrows that moved as she dreamed her baby dreams.

Her mother, giddy with the joy of parenthood but wiped out by the night feeds, had closed her eyes within two minutes of the first foils going in and was now also peacefully asleep.

Patsy couldn't help herself: she kept stealing glances at perfect Ella, with her tiny fingers and spiky dark lashes. If she were to pick her up, she knew exactly how that fluffy hair and silky-soft skin would feel and smell . . .

Maybe one day it would happen. Maybe one day her life would start going according to plan instead of spluttering and stalling like some clapped-out old banger. As she carried on deftly separating out the hair strands with the tail of her comb, pasting on the blue bleach and folding the foils into neat little packets, her mind wandered off in the direction it had so often wandered over the years.

Meeting and falling in love with Sean had felt so right, so perfect. It had been the happiest year of her life. Then they'd married and carried on being happy together – well, allegedly – and she had looked forward to the next stage, which was starting a family. Just as soon as they finished renovating and redecorating the cottage, it would happen. But there was no huge hurry, because they were enjoying themselves just being a couple, and there was plenty of time ahead of them for all that.

So they'd carried on having fun, socialising at the rugby club, going away on holidays abroad, meeting up with friends for parties and barbecues and enjoyable impromptu meals. She had the salon, and business was good. Sean, with his building company, always had plenty of jobs lined up. They worked hard, played hard and had fun. OK, maybe the sex had tailed off a bit over the last couple of years, but wasn't it only to be expected? Most married couples experienced that.

The marriage itself, though, had felt perfectly fine. Solid and enduring. She and Sean never really argued; they enjoyed each other's company. There had never been even the slightest hint that one day she would come home from work and hear her husband tell her he was gay.

Hardly surprisingly, it was one of those scenes that would

be seared forever into her memory: Sean, white-faced with anguish, not wanting to hurt her but knowing he must, because he simply couldn't live with the secret any more. It had been raining; the smell of dry earth soaking up water and giving out its distinctive loamy scent still reminded Patsy of that evening. Sean's voice had been strained as he'd uttered the words: 'I'm sorry, I'm gay,' and she'd said 'Shut up, you're not,' because it was about as likely as him telling her he was actually Superman and could fly.

It had felt like being trapped in an airless Perspex box, watching your own husband become a different person entirely and unable to stop it happening. He'd been wearing cargo trousers and the deep blue cotton chambray shirt she'd bought him last Christmas, and he'd said, 'I'm so, so sorry, I never wanted this to happen. I thought it would be OK, I thought I could do it, but I can't.'

That was when she'd abandoned all semblance of dignity and begged, which was shameful and embarrassing to look back on, but in her own defence, she'd been in a state of shock and disbelief. She'd told Sean he *could* do it if he just tried harder; it was a mistake, he was confused, he couldn't really be gay . . . for crying out loud, *look* at him: he drank pints of lager, he played rugby, he had *no fashion sense at all* . . .

In the five years that had passed since that world-changing evening, the fashion-sense comment had become something of a standing joke, but at the time it hadn't been remotely funny. She'd been desperate to prove to Sean that he'd made a terrible mistake.

The door to the salon swung open and Will's next client burst in with a cheery shout, causing baby Ella, startled by the sudden noise, to open her eyes and whimper. Her exhausted mother slept on. Patsy put down the bleaching brush, peeled off her thin disposable gloves and crouched in front of the baby in the car seat, gently stroking the side of her angelic face and making shushing noises to soothe her back to sleep.

Such a beautiful little thing.

Once Ella was settled once more, Patsy went back to applying the foils. Ah, the baby issue; it had seemed like the least of her worries at the time. Devastated though she'd been, she had never managed to make herself hate Sean. He'd been heart-broken too. In his own way he had still loved her. And she'd been the one who'd received the most sympathy from the inhabitants of Stanton Langley. Many of the older contingent, in particular, had been appalled with Sean for giving in to something he had no business dabbling with. A couple of vociferous women accused him of copying George Michael and Elton John and jumping on the bandwagon. He was attention-seeking, they scornfully announced, just showing off; there was no need for it.

They'd split up anyway. Sean had moved into one of the tiny houses down the road, which wasn't ideal, but the choice of available property in the vicinity was limited. Then he'd taken over as landlord of the Star and gradually his friends grew used to the idea of his sexuality and it stopped being the talk of Stanton Langley.

Until fourteen months later, when he met someone else and fell in love again. Only this time with a man.

Ironically, he had Patsy to thank for the meeting; if it hadn't been for her, the two men would never have found each other. Once she'd got used to the idea, she'd told Sean, 'Don't say I never do anything for you.'

In the years since then, Patsy had been happy for them but not so happy with herself. To begin with she'd been a wreck, a hopeless case, in no emotional state to meet anyone else.

Then she'd tentatively begun dating again, wondering each time whether this might be The One.

To which the answer was invariably no. Every single date had been a disaster, which rather indicated either that she was terribly unlucky . . . or that she might be partly to blame herself.

And now here she was at thirty-five, still utterly single and no nearer to having the family she longed for above all else. As time had passed, her lack of luck with men had become a source of entertainment for the rest of the village. Which, while not great, somehow turned out to be easier to bear than their pity and sympathy.

But it still wasn't much fun, living through the series of disappointments and knowing that as each new month passed, your eggs were becoming fewer and smaller, shrivelling up like old grapes. On the surface she might put on a good show, making fun of herself and her manless state, but inwardly it was hard sometimes not to wonder: *Why me?*

The foils were finished and her next client, Tess, had just arrived for her weekly wash and blow-dry. Leaving Ella's mother asleep, Patsy got on with shampooing Tess's hair. While they were over at the sink, Ella woke up and began to cry. Will, having just waved off his last customer, scooped her out of her car seat along with the bottle of milk that was tucked in beside her. Within seconds he had settled himself in the next chair along, scooped the baby into the crook of his arm and was feeding her like a pro.

'Look at you,' Tess marvelled. 'You're a natural.'

Will grinned. 'This is what happens when you have seven nephews and nieces. You get plenty of practice.'

Ella was noisily guzzling her feed, not bothered one iota that she was being held by a stranger. Patsy felt a clutch of envy in her stomach as she saw that tiny hand clasping Will's index finger, dark lashes batting as she gazed trustingly into his eyes.

Oh God, how many eggs *did* she have left? Was it ever going to happen to her?

'By the way, heard about your chap on the tandem,' said Tess, her head bent back over the sink. 'Bit of a no-hoper, was he?'

Still thinking about babies, Patsy said, 'Just a bit.'

'Ah, story of your life! Never mind, there's got to be someone out there for you. Tell you what, my Fred's meeting up with his steam-train mates at the weekend – he could ask around if you like, see if any of them are on the lookout for a date.'

'Oh, I don't know. I'm not sure . . .' Patsy hesitated; how could she put it delicately? She'd seen the steam-train enthusiasts at a country fair last summer and they'd sported quilted nylon waistcoats, flat caps and untrimmed beards. Plus they were all over fifty.

'What's wrong?' demanded Tess after a few seconds of uncomfortable silence.

'Well, it's just . . .' Most of them had smoked pipes too, and there'd been a fair amount of grey chest hair poking through the gaps between the straining buttons on their rather grubby checked shirts. Oh God, she just *couldn't* . . .

'Fine then,' Tess announced, evidently miffed. 'If you're going to be fussy. But it's not as if there's eligible men falling over themselves to get at you, is it? Be fair.'

Which was true, but also a bit cruel. Patsy watched as Will lifted Ella over his shoulder and expertly patted her back until she burped. She wondered what Tess would have to say if she were to suddenly announce that actually she had an eligible man hiding in her cottage *right now*.

Then again, it wasn't as if he was interested in her, so it hardly counted.

In fact, after three days and nights of him being here in Stanton Langley, she had a sneaking suspicion that the person Eddie Tessler might be romantically interested in was Lily.

Chapter 12

Sometimes, how you react to something unexpected depends entirely on the kind of day you've been having.

For Declan Madison, not for any one big reason but thanks to several small ones, it hadn't been a good day. Ridiculous traffic in central London had resulted in him being late for an important meeting. Then, returning after the meeting to his car, he'd found a deep scratch along the passenger-side panel. Two hours later, following another appointment that had run over by five minutes, he'd picked up a parking ticket.

Now, all he really wanted to do upon arriving home was sit down and relax, order a takeaway and watch a bit of mindless TV.

Except that wasn't going to happen, because Gail had organised one of her dinner parties and it was being held here in his house, which meant he was going to have to be polite to four other couples, who would spend the evening quizzing him about property prices and competing to show off about their holidays, their cars and everything else they'd achieved in their wonderful lives.

Because Gail's friends were drawn from a group Declan

privately referred to as the Perfects. The women tended to be thin and brittle, the men paunchy and rich. They attended charitable events, but mainly for the purpose of being seen to be charitable; there didn't appear to be much genuine concern for those whose lives were less wonderful than their own.

Anyway, nothing he could do about it now; downstairs was a hive of activity as the caterers prepared the meal and Gail oversaw the table arrangements.

'Darling, you're late, you need to go and get changed.' She pointed upstairs when she saw Declan in the hallway. 'Drinks at seven thirty. I need you down here by quarter past.'

'Fine.' He collected up the little pile of post waiting for him on the hall table. 'What are we having?'

'Smoked trout salad. And fillet of pork with Dijon sauce.'

Dijon sauce. Declan suppressed a sigh. He wasn't keen on mustard.

Upstairs, he kicked off his shoes and threw himself on to the bed. He was very fond of Gail, and she had some great qualities, but her enthusiasm for arranging dinner parties wasn't one of them. What would she do if he fell asleep and didn't appear?

OK, he already knew the answer to that question.

He sifted through the post, arranging the envelopes in order of interest. Bill . . . bank statement . . . yet another parking fine . . . car brochure . . . and finally something in a proper envelope with handwriting on the front.

Actual handwritten handwriting, at that.

He tore it open, mildly intrigued; who even sent letters, these days, written by hand?

Well, this person, evidently. He unfolded the good-quality sheets of pale green writing paper and took an instinctive liking to whoever's handwriting it was.

The next moment a name jumped out at him and his heart did a double beat. What? *Jo?* But how could the letter be from her, when it wasn't her writing?

And then he began to read.

Dear Declan,

Hello, you don't know me but I hope I'm sending this to the right person. My name is Lily Harper and I'm the daughter of Jo Harper. OK, I'm just going to assume you're the right Declan Madison and ask if you remember my mum. Do you? Back when you were both eighteen and working in Barcelona? Oh I do hope you do, because you meant so much to her. I'd hate to think you'd forgotten.

So anyway, the sad news is that Mum died a while ago now. Seventeen years, in fact. And I know you broke up and lost touch when you were twenty, so you must be wondering why on earth I'm writing to you now. The thing is, it was my twenty-fifth birthday a couple of days ago, and Mum left a letter for me to open. (She always has done, every year, but this is the last one.) In it, she mentioned your surname for the first time, which is how I was able to look you up. She also told me you were the love of her life. And she gave me her most treasured possession, a silver bangle that you'd given to her. I wonder if you remember that too? I'm wearing it now!

I hope you don't mind me writing to you out of the blue like this. I was brought up by Mum's fantastic best friend Coral and her late husband Nick, and have had a very happy life, living and working here in Stanton Langley, but would love to know more about my mum if you have any stories you'd be happy to share with me. You can email, or I'd be happy to come to London if you'd like to meet up. Whichever you prefer.

It would be so great to meet you, but if for any reason you don't want to be in touch, could you drop me an email just to let me know? Otherwise I'll be waiting forever, wondering if this letter ever reached you!

Best wishes and many thanks,

Lily Harper X

Declan read the letter twice more, his pulse racing each time he got to the bit telling him Jo was dead. Had been dead *for so long*. No wonder he'd never managed to trace her. He'd assumed it was because she'd married and was now using another surname. But it wasn't for that reason at all; it was because she was no longer alive.

He felt winded. It wasn't the kind of letter you ever expected to receive. It was a lot to take—

'Oh for heaven's sake, what are you *doing*?' The bedroom door had been flung open and Gail was staring at him in disbelief.

'I needed to go through the post.' Declan indicated the discarded envelopes littering the bed.

'Never mind about the post, you haven't even had your shower yet! Everyone's going to be here in ten minutes!'

He held up the sheets of writing paper. 'I've had a letter from the daughter of an old friend.'

'Declan, what am I, the invisible woman? Listen to me! You need to get ready *now*.'

Gail got a bit high-pitched when she was stressed, and at the moment she was both. Now clearly wasn't the time to be telling her about Jo. Refolding the letter, Declan swung his legs off the bed and said, 'Give me eight minutes and I'll be down.'

Chapter 13

It was seven o'clock on Saturday evening, and Patsy had just burst out laughing at something Eddie had said when the doorbell shrilled.

By now they'd developed an efficient routine. The stairs and upstairs landing were too creaky and would instantly give away the fact that someone else was there. Far simpler to just keep out of sight until Patsy had got rid of whoever it was. Eddie rose to his feet, collected up his dinner plate and wine glass, and disappeared, as silent as a ghost, into the kitchen.

Patsy pulled open her front door. 'Oh hi!' she said when she saw who was standing on the doorstep.

Her ex-husband.

And his new husband.

Sean and Will.

'Hey, how are you doing?' Sean greeted her with a brief kiss on the cheek. 'OK if we come in?'

'Um, well . . .'

'Not for long. Just a few minutes.'

'Actually, I'm a bit pushed for time.' Patsy did an ostentatious watch-check, the effect somewhat spoiled by the discovery that she'd left her watch in the kitchen.

'Me too, I have to get over to the pub. But there's something we wanted to say. Come on.' Sean guided her gently backwards into the cottage. 'Five minutes and we'll leave you in peace.'

Will and Sean, the happiest couple she knew. Patsy perched on the arm of the chair by the fireplace and they sat on the sofa opposite. Sean was wearing a charcoal-grey polo shirt and black trousers that showed off his broad, muscular physique. Will had changed out of the clothes he wore in the salon into a black T-shirt and jeans; since it was Saturday, he'd be heading off to a training session at his beloved boxing club.

'Right, so what's this about?' She definitely wasn't going to offer them a drink.

'OK, straight to the point.' Sean leaned forward, his forearms resting on his knees, fingers loosely clasped together. 'You want a baby. Time could be running out. If you decide you'd like to go ahead and have one . . . well, just so you know, I'd be happy to volunteer to be the . . . donor.'

Patsy sat back, her eyes widening in disbelief. Wow. Whatever she'd been expecting him to come out with, it hadn't been that.

Finally she said, 'What's brought this on?'

He shrugged. 'It's an offer. An idea, that's all. Something to think about.'

It was certainly *that*.

'I see you at work,' Will joined in. 'Like yesterday, when you were looking at Ella. I hear all the things people say to you, and the jokes they make about you not being able to find yourself a man. And you laugh it off, pretend it doesn't hurt.' He paused. 'But it does hurt. You know that, and we both know it too.'

'Right.' They were looking at her with genuine compassion, like parents wanting to do their very best for their child.

'And so many women get panicky and desperate,' said Sean, 'and end up having a baby with the next guy who comes along, without even stopping to wonder if he's suitable.' He gave her a serious look. 'I'm not saying you'd do that, but it happens. And the thing is, we know each other. You know I'm healthy.' After a moment's hesitation he went on, 'OK, listen, what I'm trying to say is, it could be the answer for all of us. You'd have the baby you want . . . and so would we.'

'We? You mean you and Will?'

'We've thought about it,' said Sean. 'A lot. We'd love to be involved. It's worked for other people in our situation . . .'

'Gosh.' Patsy twisted her fingers together, struggling to take in the offer.

'It's an option.' Will shrugged. 'You don't have to make any decisions now. It's just there on the table and we'd be fine with whatever you decide. Both of us,' he stressed.

'OK, well . . . thanks.' Still numb, Patsy stood up. 'I'll have a think about it.'

'You do that.' As they were leaving, Sean said, 'No hurry. And hey,' he gave her arm a squeeze, 'you never know, it could be the answer to everything.'

Will smiled and added encouragingly, 'It could be great.'

'Well,' Eddie marvelled when they'd left and she'd opened the kitchen door. 'It's all going on around here.'

Patsy exhaled, glad he wasn't pretending not to have heard everything. Of course he had; the kitchen door hadn't been completely closed and he'd been less than ten feet away from them.

'Wow.' She shook her head. 'I wasn't expecting that.'

'Is it a good surprise?' Eddie poured her a fresh glass of wine.

'No idea. I can't even begin to think about it.' They returned to the living room and she sat back down, properly this time, in the armchair. Eddie settled himself on the sofa. It was actually surprising how quickly the novelty of him being famous had worn off. She'd got used to Eddie just being himself.

'That was your ex and his other half?'

Patsy nodded; she'd already told him briefly about Sean and Will.

'They sound nice.'

'They are. And they're perfect together.'

'How did they meet?'

'All thanks to me.' Patsy smiled, though her feelings had been a little more mixed at the time. 'It was just over a year after Sean and I had split up. I'd been pretty heartbroken, but working in the salon helped. Then Rosa entered us into one of the big national hairdressing competitions in Birmingham, and the day before we were due to go up there, my gearbox exploded. So Sean offered to drive us up in his car. When we got there, he helped us carry the stuff in and set up our station.' She took a sip of wine. 'And the hairdresser at the station next to ours was Will.'

'Fate,' said Eddie.

'I know. But neither of them looked *remotely* gay. And their gaydar was rubbish. I could see them sneaking looks at each other but they genuinely didn't have a clue. The boxer and the rugby player. Bless them,' said Patsy. 'It wasn't until the end of the day that Will said something to me in passing about my husband and I told him Sean was my ex-husband. Then he said, "Oh, I'm sorry," and I said, "Actually, he's gay." And the moment I saw the look on his face, I knew for sure. I told him if he was interested he should ask for Sean's number, and he finally plucked up the courage just as we were leaving. And that was the start of it all.'

'Amazing. So then he ended up working with you.'

'They'd been seeing each other whenever they could, but Will was living up in Manchester at the time, so it wasn't ideal. Then Rosa told me she was leaving the salon, moving back to London. It was my idea that Will could take her place.' Patsy shrugged. 'And it's worked out brilliantly. He's a great hairdresser. The clients love him to bits. And so do I.'

'Hmm.' As Eddie raised a playful eyebrow, there was a double-tap at the door, signalling Lily's arrival.

Jumping up to let her in, Patsy said, 'In a non-sexy way, of course.'

It was 11.30 when a yawning Patsy said her good nights and headed up to bed.

'Night.' Lily waved and put down her coffee cup. 'I should go too.'

Eddie said, 'Why? You don't have to. Stay a bit longer.'

'You're so needy.' Lily grinned at him.

They both heard the creaking of the floorboards on the landing, then Patsy's bedroom door close behind her.

'I'm not needy. I just like talking to you.'

Which *sounded* flattering.

'Let's face it,' said Lily, 'you like talking and there aren't many of us listeners to choose from.'

'But if there were hundreds, I'd still choose you.' Eddie tilted his head to one side, grey eyes glittering.

'Don't give me your film-star smile.'

'That isn't my film-star smile. *This* is my film-star smile.' He flashed his teeth at her, arch-villain style.

'Now you look like Dick Dastardly.'

Eddie laughed. 'Not too many people say things like that to me. Maybe that's why I like you.'

'That and the mini Magnums I bring along with me.' Lily prodded the empty wrappers on the coffee table in front of them.

'They definitely help.' Amused, he said, 'Why don't you have a boyfriend?'

'You asked me that question before. I told you, it just hasn't happened.'

'You didn't say why, though. I asked Patsy earlier. She told me the real reason.'

'That I'm a horrible person and no one likes me?'

'She said she was a complete mess when her marriage broke up and you supported her through the next two years.'

Lily shrugged. 'Why wouldn't I? Patsy helped me after my mum died. Boyfriends come and go, but friends are forever.'

'Then, once Patsy was coping again, you started seeing someone and it was all going really well. And then Coral's husband died.'

She nodded. 'That's right. It was horrendous. One minute Nick was there, alive and healthy, and everything was fine. The next minute he was gone. Massive heart attack. Poor Coral, she was just bereft. So, so lost. She couldn't concentrate on anything, couldn't begin to work out how to keep the business running without Nick. He was her whole life.'

'So then you had to look after her,' said Eddie.

Lily shook her head. 'I didn't have to. I *wanted* to.'

'It must have been pretty awful for you as well. They were your surrogate parents.'

'It was awful. But worse for Coral. She needed us to help her get through it.'

'So you got rid of your boyfriend in order to do that.'

Lily smiled briefly. 'That makes me sound incredibly noble. It was more a matter of Phil showing his true colours. He was great for the first couple of weeks after the funeral, then he started complaining because I didn't want to leave Coral on her own and go out clubbing with him.'

'Nice,' said Eddie.

'I know. He told me I shouldn't fuss over her, that she needed to get used to being on her own.' Drily Lily said, 'Such a charmer. It was incredibly easy to finish with him after that.'

'His turn to get used to being on his own,' said Eddie. 'Did he take it well?'

'Not so you'd notice, but he got the message in the end. No great loss.'

'And you worked your socks off looking after Coral and keeping the business afloat. Quite a feat. You can be proud of yourself for managing that.'

'Anyone would do the same. Well, if they're half-decent human beings.'

'And not selfish gits,' said Eddie.

Lily watched as he reached over and touched the back of her hand, lightly brushing his fingertips across her knuckles. The physical contact sent a jolt of adrenalin through her. She held her breath, wondering what he meant by it. He was still stroking her hand and gazing into her eyes. The corners of his mouth curved up and he murmured, 'You're definitely half decent. At the very least.'

Her brain was all over the place. Her mouth was dry. The underlying attraction between them appeared to be swimming to the surface. All the nerve endings on the back of her hand were now so sensitive his touch was all she could think about.

When Eddie said, 'What's that?' she thought he'd found some kind of lump or a sticking-out vein.

The next moment she heard footsteps outside the front door, followed by the sound of a key being fitted into the lock.

Chapter 14

'Who the hell . . .?' Eddie was sitting up, dropping her hand.

'Only me,' said Dan as he pushed the door open. 'I thought you'd be asleep by now, that's why I didn't phone to— *Oh.*'

The pregnant pause lasted a good couple of seconds until Lily smiled and said brightly, 'Hi!'

'Hi.' Dan looked steadily at her, then at Eddie Tessler. 'Does Patsy not live here any more?'

'She went up to bed. We were just chatting.' Gesturing to Eddie and fairly sure her cheeks were red, Lily said, 'This is, um, Eddie.'

'I know. Hello.'

'Hi,' said Eddie.

'We weren't expecting you,' Lily gabbled. 'You didn't say you were coming back. We didn't even hear the car outside.'

'I parked further down, under the street lamp. We've been invited to a black-tie do on Monday so I needed to pick up my dinner suit. I'll just go and get it; Anna's waiting in the car.' As he spoke, Dan was simultaneously giving her a narrow stare and heading for the staircase.

'I'll come up with you.' Leaping to her feet, Lily followed him, catching up as he reached his bedroom doorway.

'What's going on?' Dan halted abruptly, as she'd known he would. The bed was unmade, Eddie's clothes were flung over the chair and other belongings had been scattered about.

'He's been staying for a few days, that's all.'

'In my bedroom? And no one thought to ask if that was OK with me?'

'It was a secret. We couldn't let anyone else know he was here.'

'Not even the person whose room he's been using?' Dan, whose default setting was jokey and flippant, wasn't being jokey now. Distinctly unamused, he said, 'You don't think it might have been polite to mention it?'

'Maybe,' said Lily, 'but you weren't supposed to find out.'

He shook his head in disbelief. 'A complete stranger.'

'He's not a complete stranger, though, is he? He's Eddie Tessler, you *know* who he is.'

'And I also know he's been sleeping in my bed. With you, presumably. My God—'

'What? I'm not *sleeping* with him!' Whoops, was Eddie able to overhear this, downstairs? Lowering her voice, Lily hissed, 'I'm *not*.'

'So what *are* you doing with him then? And what's he doing here?'

'OK, I'm just keeping him company. He needed somewhere to stay. His PA is Rosa's sister and Rosa suggested here. Patsy said yes, so that's how it happened. And no one else knows he's here. It's a *secret*.'

'Yes, yes, I get the message.' Dan sounded irritated. 'You don't have to keep saying it.' He pulled open the wardrobe doors, removed his dinner suit and a white dress shirt, and slid a black bow tie out of the tie rack. Lily had only seen him dressed up like that once before; hardly surprisingly, he had looked amazing in it.

'Sorry. Don't be cross,' she said as he closed the wardrobe door.

Dan turned to look directly at her. 'Sure you're not having sex with him?'

Lily shook her head, glad he couldn't tell how prickly her palms were at the thought of it. 'Absolutely sure.'

'Well make sure you don't. Because he'll try it on, guaranteed.'

'I'm not going to do anything,' she retorted. 'Don't be so suspicious.'

'And you, don't be gullible.' Dan held up a warning finger. 'Think about why he's having to hide out here in the first place. Men like that just do whatever they want.'

'I think you mean men like *you*.' Lily softened the comment with a half-smile, and this time he acknowledged the dig.

'Fine, but all the more reason to listen to me. Because I know what I'm talking about.' His phone buzzed and he glanced at it; his latest girlfriend was notoriously impatient. 'Anna's waiting. I need to go. But just remember what I said.'

'I will.' She mimed zipping her mouth shut. 'And you remember what I said too.'

They made their way downstairs, Lily marvelling at Patsy's ability to sleep through anything; once she'd gone, you could hold a rave outside her bedroom door and she wouldn't wake up.

'Bye.' Dan briefly raised a hand to Eddie.

'Bye,' said Eddie. 'Sorry about not letting you know. And thanks for—'

'Yep, have to go.'

When Dan had left, Eddie shook his head. 'He's not going to keep this to himself.'

Unsettled by Dan's earlier comments, Lily decided she should leave too. She reached for her bag and turned to Eddie; the least she could do was reassure him. 'Don't worry, he will.'

'Hey, you didn't have to sound quite so appalled, by the way. Sleeping with me wouldn't be *that* terrible.'

So he *had* overheard. And now he was making fun of her. Lily gave him a look, then quickly left before he could see that he'd made her blush.

The first paparazzi arrived the following morning, just before midday. An hour later, a couple of journalists turned up. Lily couldn't believe it; she'd been so certain she could trust Dan to keep the secret. But she knew it hadn't been Patsy or Coral, so who else could have given the game away? There simply wasn't anyone else who knew. Mortified, she sent Dan a sarcastic text message and received no reply.

At two o'clock, Patsy arrived at Goldstone and found Lily out in the yard, stacking up a range of ceramic planting pots.

'Well, he's gone.'

'Eddie?' Lily had guessed he would leave; once his cover had been blown, there'd be no reason to stay.

'Rosa's husband came down to collect him, take him back to London. It's going to be weird not having him around.'

'I know.' They'd enjoyed sharing the secret, keeping Eddie Tessler to themselves. 'Was he cross with Dan?'

'Not really. More resigned. He said he'd had five days of peace, which was better than nothing. Oh, and he asked me to say goodbye to you too, and thanks for everything.'

'Right.' Was it silly to wish he could have called into the yard, even for just half a minute, to say goodbye? Probably, but Lily still found herself thinking it. Then again, why would he? Eddie Tessler was on his way back to London, to his film-starry life peppered with paparazzi, glitz and gorgeous girls from the world of celebrity. He'd been bored and she'd provided him with a bit of undemanding company, but now he was gone. Whilst she was stuck here, lugging heavy, dusty Victorian pots around the yard. Oh, the glamour.

'And he said good luck with finding Declan,' Patsy added. 'He hopes you get to hear from him.'

She'd posted the letter on Thursday with a first-class stamp on it. Despite obsessively checking her emails since Friday, there'd been no reply so far.

'Yeah.' As Lily bent to lift the biggest, heaviest pot and shift it into a better position against the dry-stone wall, a huge spider made a bid for freedom and scuttled across her arm. 'Me too.'

Chapter 15

The letter had disappeared.

Before Friday's dinner party it had been there on his bed. Afterwards, it had gone. Declan had looked everywhere for it without success, and the more time he spent searching, the more impatient Gail had become with him.

The more impatient she'd become with him, the more he suspected that she'd quietly disposed of the letter herself.

'So she's the daughter of some girl you once went out with, and the mother's been dead for years but you still want to meet her. Even though she isn't your daughter.'

'That's right,' said Declan.

'She absolutely *definitely* isn't your daughter.'

'Absolutely definitely.'

'In that case, I don't get it. Why would you want to meet her? What's the point?'

'I just do,' Declan reiterated. How could he even begin to explain when he barely understood it himself?

'Well it just seems like a waste of time to me. Anyway, I'm going to be late for work. I'll see you tonight, yes? We'll have dinner at my place.'

He nodded, distracted. 'Um . . . yes, fine.'

'Let's have a nice Monday detox, shall we? Steamed fish and summer greens!'

Gail planted a mouthwashy kiss on his lips and left the house. *Had* she taken the letter in the hope that he would lose interest in the idea of meeting Jo's daughter?

As he watched through the window, Declan saw her pause beside the recycling boxes out on the pavement and drop something into the paper-recycling box, due to be emptied in a couple of hours' time. Then she headed off down the road to catch the bus in to work.

Feeling like a spy, Declan waited until she'd turned the corner, then left the front door on the latch and went out to check the black box. The discarded Sunday papers were in there, together with a few magazines and an assortment of junk mail. If he found Lily's letter, that was it: the relationship with Gail would be over.

Ten minutes later, he still hadn't found it. Carefully leafing through the pages of the copy of *Red* that she'd put out yesterday, he was beginning to suspect that the item he'd seen her drop into the box had been the flyer for a pizza delivery company that had come through the letter box last night. Then again, if she'd really wanted to hide the letter from him, surely she'd choose to leave it in a bin somewhere further away from the house, so that was still a possib—

A car horn tooted and Declan looked up as a silver 4x4 squealed to a halt beside him.

'Hiya!' Jumping out of the driver's seat, Carly tottered on to the pavement and threw her arms around him. 'Mwah, *mwah*. Now listen, thanks so much for Friday, we had such a great evening!'

'Our pleasure. It was good fun, wasn't it?' Carly and her husband had been the last to head off after the dinner party.

Wondering why she was here now, Declan said, 'Did you leave something behind?'

'For once, no. Quite the opposite, in fact. Honestly, what am I like?' Carly's conversations tended to be rattled out like machine-gun fire. 'Well, I *know* what I'm like, I get a few drinks down my neck and my brain goes AWOL. Anyway, I've worked out how it happened, because when I went to touch up my make-up there was someone else in the loo, so I sneaked into your bedroom instead, to use a mirror, then I couldn't find my stupid lipstick so I tipped everything out of my bag on to your bed!'

It was like finally, after days of puzzling over a fiendish crossword clue, all of a sudden realising you'd figured out the answer.

'And then I chucked it all back in, but it wasn't until this morning that I found I'd scooped up something else too. Completely by accident, of course. But I'm so sorry and I do hope you haven't been searching for it.' As she spoke, Carly was opening her bag, taking out the pale green envelope and wincing apologetically.

'Thanks.' Declan broke into a broad smile; he wouldn't tell her how long he'd spent trying to find it. 'I had wondered where it had got to. But it's not a problem; I'm just glad to have it back.'

'Well I feel terrible, but I really didn't mean it to happen. Anyway, you've got it now. And I haven't read it, I promise.'

'OK.' Declan nodded.

'Oh who am I trying to kid? Of course I read it!' The confession came tumbling out. 'Anyone who says they wouldn't do the same is a liar. A proper letter written in real handwriting? Are you kidding? Who could resist that!'

'It's fine, don't worry.' Declan didn't blame her; the chances were that he'd have done exactly the same. Interested, he said, 'And what do you think I should do?'

'OK, is there even the teeniest chance that this girl's your daughter?'

Was this the conclusion everyone was going to jump to? He shook his head. 'No chance at all.'

'Well that's a big shame. But I still think you have to meet her,' said Carly. 'She sounds so lovely! Why?' Her eyebrows rose as far as the Botox would allow. 'Don't you want to?'

'No, I really do. It's just that Gail can't understand why I would.'

'Can't she? Well, maybe she's just not that curious. Some people are, some aren't. And it's not actually anything to do with Gail anyway, is it?'

'I suppose not.' Declan smiled. 'You're right, it doesn't affect her. Fair enough.'

'Ah, she's a nice girl. You make a good couple. And now I'd better go.' Carly gave him another quick kiss on the cheek and jangled her car keys. 'Pilates – I'll be in trouble if I'm late!'

Back inside the house, Declan opened his laptop and dealt with the morning emails, but his attention kept sliding back to the letter on the table next to him. Poor Gail: to think he'd suspected her of underhand practices, when all this time she'd been completely innocent. Of course she was innocent; Gail was blunt and outspoken but never underhand.

Plus, destroying it wouldn't have stopped him from making contact with Jo's daughter anyway. He might not have been able to recall Lily's email address, but knowing she lived in Goldstone House in Stanton Langley meant he would certainly have been able to find her. He'd already looked up the village and liked what he'd seen of it online.

But now that he had the letter back, he could even more

easily send off an email and – as Lily herself had suggested – arrange for the two of them to meet up, right here in London.

Declan sat back and gazed out of the window. And yet . . . and yet, since exploring Stanton Langley via Google Earth, the idea of an email no longer seemed quite enough.

He checked his watch: it was still only 8.30 on a bright, sunny morning. Getting out of the city and heading west wasn't out of the question. He could be there by eleven. And he had no business appointments today, no other commitments, nowhere else he categorically had to be.

Which was an unusual enough situation to feel a bit like fate.

Plus, Lily might not have specified exactly whereabouts, but she'd told him she worked in Stanton Langley . . .

Once he'd escaped the clogged streets of London, the journey had been smooth. By 10.30, Declan found himself on the outskirts of the village. And then he was driving along the broad main street, lined with trees and flowers and quint-essentially quirky custard-yellow stone buildings. The sky was cloudless and cobalt blue, sunlight bounced off windows, and there were plenty of people around – as one of the jewels of the Cotswolds, Stanton Langley was something of a tourist trap, and several of the shops catered to their needs. But the place seemed to have a good feel to it, an inherent charm and warmth signalling that the residents enjoyed living here as much as outsiders loved to visit it. People were greeting each other, stopping to chat, emerging from shops and waving to those they knew. There was a bakery, a hairdresser's called Rafferty's, a mini-supermarket, a couple of restaurants, a tea room, the souvenir-type businesses and a couple of antiques shops. A large pub, the Star Inn, had plenty of tables outside it and a black Labrador lying in a patch of shade close to the entrance.

Declan knew he'd slowed down, but it wasn't until he heard an impatient bicycle bell ding-dinging behind him that he realised quite how much. Raising a hand in apology, he allowed the elderly woman to overtake him and smiled as she threw him a disparaging glance whilst pedalling regally by.

But he couldn't help himself: being here felt like stepping into his computer and experiencing Google Earth brought to life. There, next to the Star Inn, was Goldstone House. And on the other side of the property, above the entrance to what he presumed was a driveway leading round to the house, was a dark blue sign announcing in simple gold lettering: Goldstone Salvage & Treasure.

Since there was nowhere to stop, Declan carried on down the road, turned right at the end and found a small car park. Accustomed to London prices, he was amused to see from the Pay and Display sign that leaving his car here for two hours would cost a whole pound.

He bought his ticket and headed back on foot to the main street. As he approached Goldstone House, he saw two people carrying a white wrought-iron garden table out through the gates and loading it into the back of a grey van. The man was in his sixties, the woman twenty years younger. He was over-weight and grey-haired; she was slender and blond, wearing jeans and a navy T-shirt. She was talking and laughing with the man as they secured the table, tying it with blue nylon rope to the bars on the inside of the van.

When the task was completed and the blond woman turned and jumped down, Declan saw the Goldstone logo on the front of her shirt and realised that she wasn't the man's younger, prettier wife after all; she worked here.

She had blue eyes, swingy hair and the kind of narrow-hipped figure so many other women could only dream of. And if she was in her late forties, there was a good chance her name was Coral.

Chapter 16

'Hi.' Realising she was being watched, the woman dusted her hands on the sides of her jeans and said cheerily, 'Anything I can do for you?'

'Hope so.' All of a sudden, Declan no longer knew what to do with his own hands. His pulse began to speed up. Taking his car keys out of his trouser pocket for something to jangle, he promptly dropped them. Which meant having to bend down and pick them up and pray his back didn't go into spasm and make him look eighty. Finally, vertical once more, he said, 'I'm looking for Lily.'

'Oh, she's not here, I'm afraid. Did she speak to you on the phone? What's it about . . . is it something on the website? Maybe I can help you instead.'

'Er, well, what time's she likely to be back?' Not usually at a loss for words, Declan now found himself prevaricating. What if Lily hadn't told anyone else she was contacting him? Maybe she didn't want it to become public knowledge.

But as he dithered, the expression on the woman's face began to change. Her eyes widened and she raised a tentative index finger like a child in a classroom thinking she *might* know the answer.

'Wait.' She searched his face for clues, then said in wonder and disbelief, 'Are you . . . Declan?'

Her voice was beautiful, clear and gentle, with no discernible accent. He liked the way she said his name.

'Possibly.' He eyed her with amusement. 'Are you Coral?'

At that moment, a burly builder type ambled past and clapped her on the shoulder. 'She's Coral, I'm Ted, and I'm starving.'

Coral shook her head at him. 'Ted, you're always starving. The country would be knee-deep in sausage rolls if it wasn't for you. Off you go.'

Ted strolled off down the street, pausing to rub the ears of the Labrador outside the pub. Coral, her hands clasped to her chest, turned to Declan. 'You're here to see Lily! I can't believe it! She's been checking her emails every five minutes for the last four days. She was starting to think you were never going to reply.'

'The letter arrived, then it got lost, then this morning it turned up again. I know I should have emailed,' said Declan, 'but I wanted to see her in person. I couldn't wait.' He paused, disappointed. 'Except it looks like I'm going to have to.'

'Oh, not for too long; she'll be back by three. If you can stay until then.'

As if he'd leave now. Declan nodded; he'd just have to call Gail and let her know he wouldn't be back for the detox steamed fish and summer greens. 'It's OK, I can stay.'

'Hooray, that's fantastic! She's going to be *so* thrilled to see you. In fact, come here.' Coral spread her arms and gave him a hug. 'We're *all* thrilled. You have no idea how much this means to Lily.'

Declan was aware of the feel of her hands on his shoulders, the front of her T-shirt against his chest, the fresh, woody scent of the perfume she was wearing. 'Thanks. It means a lot to me too.' He paused, then said with a crooked smile, 'I don't even know why it feels so important. It just does.'

And now she was stepping back, holding him at arm's length, studying his face. 'I've seen the letter Lily wrote to you. You really were the love of Jo's life, you know.'

Hearing her repeat what Lily had said in the letter caused a surge of emotion to well up. Declan hesitated, then nodded. 'And it turns out Jo was the love of my life too.'

Did that sound melodramatic? It was true, though. He'd expected to meet someone else; he *had* met plenty of someone-elses over the years, but none of them had ever made him feel quite the way he'd felt about Jo.

'Oh, and you probably didn't know she'd died. That must have come as an awful shock.' Coral touched his arm.

'It did. I mean, it wasn't something that had ever occurred to me. I know we hadn't seen each other for all those years, but I'd assumed she was out there somewhere.' Declan shrugged. 'I always hoped she was happy.'

'Come along inside.' Guiding him through the gates of Goldstone Salvage & Treasure, Coral led him across the flag-stones, past an eclectic assortment of items for sale and into a low building that turned out to be an office.

'Marty, could you keep an eye on things out there? This is someone I need to chat to in private for ten minutes.'

Middle-aged Marty, also wearing a blue Goldstone T-shirt and jeans, nodded and left them alone. Coral offered Declan a swivel chair and perched herself on the edge of the desk next to the computer.

'Like I said, Lily should be back by three o'clock. I'm not going to call her and say you're here, because I don't want her racing back down the motorway like a maniac. And I'm not going to talk to you about her either, because that wouldn't be fair. Lily deserves to be the one who does that.'

'Absolutely.' Declan nodded in agreement.

'But you won't be disappointed.' Coral smiled at him. 'I can promise you that much. She's a gorgeous girl. I won't show you any photos. You'll see for yourself when she gets back.'

'Fair enough.' Now he knew it was definitely going to happen, he was fine to wait.

'And we're pretty busy here today, but we can chat about Jo, if you'd like to.'

'You were her best friend,' said Declan. 'I'd really like to.'

'Jo was so great. The first time we met was the day we both moved into the halls of residence at Exeter. There was this weird whacking sound coming from the room next door to mine and a voice kept saying, "Oh you *bugger*." In the end I went to see what was going on, and there was Jo trying to hit a bluebottle with a rolled-up magazine, but every time she took a swipe at it, it flew off. The first words she said to me were "Oh, hi, have you come to watch me murder my new roommate?" And at that exact moment, the bluebottle flew around her in a circle and landed on her head.'

'Ha.' Declan smiled, already glad he'd made the journey down; hearing stories about Jo wasn't only going to benefit Lily, it seemed. 'I can just picture that happening.' He could almost hear Jo saying the words, mischievous yet deadpan. Comic timing had always been her forte.

'We were friends from that moment on,' said Coral. 'It's scary to think we might not have met. If some bored office admin person had allocated us different rooms or put us in different halls . . . well, everything could have been so different.'

'The first time I saw Jo,' said Declan, 'I was just turning up for my shift at the restaurant in Barcelona. An old Scottish woman on holiday had had her purse snatched and the thief was running off down Las Ramblas. Jo had seen it happen and she raced off after him. She was still carrying her tray,' he remembered. 'The thief had an accomplice waiting for him on a moped at the end of the street. Just as he was about to jump on the back of the moped and escape, Jo threw the metal tray at him like a Frisbee and it hit him smack in the back of the legs. I saw it with my own eyes. The thief dropped the purse and went flying, the guy on the moped rode off without him and Jo picked up the purse and the tray and came back up the street to the restaurant. The old lady was sobbing with gratitude and tried to give her some money to say thank you. Jo said, "No *way*, that's the best fun I've had in weeks."'

'That's exactly what she was like.' Coral was laughing now. 'All she told me was that she once threw a tray at a thief in Barcelona. I never got to hear the whole story.' She shook her head. 'This is amazing. It's like filling in all the gaps. We could carry on doing this for hours.'

'I've brought a photograph album down with me.' Declan waved his hand in the rough direction of the car park. 'I'll wait until Lily's back. I mean, I know Jo had photos too . . .'

'Of you and her together? Oh, but she didn't. Well, she did once,' Coral hastily amended. 'I saw them when we were first at uni. But they disappeared during our second year, just vanished. Jo was distraught when she realised they'd gone missing. I'm sure it was her boyfriend. He always denied it, but I'd bet any money it was him. Anyway, Lily never got to see them, obviously, so she'll be thrilled to see your photo album.'

'Which boyfriend was this?' By the curl of her lip, Declan suspected she wasn't a fan.

'Keir. Lily's biological father.' Coral pulled an even more

disparaging face. 'Honestly, I can't tell you how much I despise that man. He left Jo high and dry, refused to have anything to do with her once he found out she was pregnant, and got his parents to do his dirty work for him. *Eurgh.*'

Declan closed his eyes briefly. Whatever had Jo been thinking, getting involved with someone who so clearly didn't deserve her?

Aloud he said, 'Why was she with him in the first place?'

'Well the trouble with some people is you don't find out what they're really like until it's too late. To begin with, he seemed fine.' Coral shrugged. 'On the surface he was good-looking and he had plenty of charm. He could be good company too, if I'm being honest. Jo would never have got together with him if he'd been awful. He was fun to have around. And they seemed happy together, until Jo got pregnant and Keir decided he wanted nothing to do with the situation. That was it, relationship over.'

'God. And how about now? Does Lily see much of him these days?'

'Who, Keir? She's never seen him.'

Declan did a double-take. 'What? Never ever?'

'His parents paid Jo to have the "inconvenience" taken care of. She told them she wasn't going to do that. So she bought a car, left Exeter and ended up here instead.'

It didn't bear thinking about. 'Poor Jo. What a thing to have to go through. She must have been—'

'Devastated?' Coral was already shaking her head. 'Maybe at first, but not for long. By the time she arrived here, she'd made up her mind. If Keir didn't want to know, he wasn't worth crying over. It was his loss and she wasn't going to waste a minute of her time wishing things could have been different. Well,' another amendment, 'between her and Keir.'

102

'So did Keir never even know he had a daughter?'

'Oh he did, after she was born. Jo wrote to tell him the news, just because she thought he should know. If he'd wanted a relationship with his daughter, she would have allowed it to happen, for Lily's sake rather than his. But it never did happen. Keir wrote back and said it was her decision to have the baby and nothing to do with him.'

'Nice.'

Coral shrugged. 'As I said. He revealed his true colours. There was never any more contact after that.'

'What, not even child support?'

She shook her head. 'You know what Jo was like. Once she made up her mind to do something, that was it. If Keir wasn't interested, he'd be the one missing out.'

Declan watched a wasp bashing itself against one of the smaller windows in the office. He did know what Jo was like. Her ability to make a decision and stick to it was something he'd been only too familiar with.

'Um, Coral?' The door opened and Marty stuck his head round. 'Sorry, but it's getting busy out here. There's a new delivery just arrived, someone's asking about the Venetian chandelier, and Mrs Ingalls wants a hand getting those church pews into the back of her truck.'

'No problem, on my way.' Coral slid down from the desk and looked at Declan. 'I'm sorry, I need to get out there. Look, do you want to go off and explore the village, then come back just before three?'

Through the open door, they heard a female voice saying, 'I've tried, I really have, but I just can't lift them by myself.'

'I can go off and explore if you want me out of the way,' said Declan. 'Or if you could do with an extra pair of hands here, I'm happy to stay and help out.'

Coral said, 'Would you? Are you sure?'

'Of course.' He rose to his feet. 'Just tell me what to do.'

For the next three and a half hours, Declan worked with Marty, lifting and carrying oversized objects, helping to load heavy items into cars and vans, and offering honest opinions when potential customers were torn between various options.

Across the yard, Coral was doing the same. Every so often Declan would pause to watch her, listening to her interactions with other people and observing the way her blond hair glistened when she moved her head. Occasionally, catching his eye, she would mouth: *Everything OK?* And he would nod, because everything was more than OK. As far as days went, this one was turning out to be pretty much perfect.

And he hadn't even met Lily yet.

Chapter 17

At twenty to three, he was outside the gates, hauling the last of a stack of Cotswold roof tiles into the back of an ancient Volvo, when a van drew up and parked half on, half off the pavement next to a sporty silver Toyota. The Toyota's owner, her arms full of flowers and shopping, was standing beside her car, rooting around in her bag for her keys.

The van was dark blue, with the Goldstone logo on the side. Declan straightened up, held his breath and waited for the driver's door to swing open.

The next moment it did, and his heart stepped up a pace as the girl who had to be Lily jumped out. Simultaneously, the silver Toyota sped away from the kerb and something fell into the road with a *thunk*. The girl who had to be Lily bent down to retrieve the pink leather purse that the driver of the Toyota had managed to leave on the roof of her car.

The next moment she was off, racing up the street after the departing Toyota, waving madly and clutching the purse in her other hand. Up ahead, the traffic lights turned from green to red and the car slowed. Declan watched as the girl carried on running, finally catching up and tapping on the Toyota's window on the passenger's side. The window slid down, the purse was handed back to its rightful owner and the girl laughed at something the driver said. Then the traffic lights changed back to green, the Toyota pulled away once more and the girl who had to be Lily began to make her way back down the main street to Goldstone House.

Had there ever been any question that this was Jo's daughter? She had her mother's mass of streaky blond ringlets, her dancing dark eyes and her infectious smile. God, it was incredible.

Coral had appeared at his side. Reading his mind, she murmured, 'Looks like Jo, doesn't she?'

Declan nodded. 'Just a bit.'

When she was only a few metres away, Lily said cheerily to Coral, 'Did you see what happened? She left her purse on the roof of her car and drove off. She'd be on her way up to Sheffield without it by now if the traffic lights hadn't turned red.'

'And if you hadn't gone chasing after her like Usain Bolt.' As she said it, Coral gave Declan a gentle nudge.

Declan looked at Lily. 'The first time I met your mum, she was doing much the same.'

Lily stopped dead in her tracks, a slew of expressions flickering across her face as she took in the unexpected words of a complete stranger. The silence probably lasted only a second, but it seemed far longer as she stared at him in disbelief. Then she saw that Coral was grinning broadly.

'Oh my God.' Her dark brown eyes fixed on him once more. 'Are you . . . Declan?'

'I am.' He nodded, breaking into a smile himself. 'And you're Lily. Hi.'

'Oh, this is *amazing*.' Lily covered her mouth. 'I was just checking my email to see if you'd been in touch yet, and now you're here, you're really *here*. Hello!'

And then she was hugging him, and it felt like hugging the daughter he'd never had. When they broke apart, Declan reached for her left wrist and studied the bangle she was wearing.

'There it is, that's the one. I bought it for Jo from a jeweller who had a tiny studio in one of the back streets of Barcelona.' He nodded in recognition. 'I can't believe I'm seeing it again all these years later. It didn't cost a lot,' he added. 'We didn't have much money to spare back then. It might turn your skin green.'

'I don't care if it does. It's beautiful.' Lily twisted her arm so the tiny embedded stones caught the light. 'Thank you for choosing it for her.'

'You two go on into the house,' said Coral. 'Me and Marty can take care of things out here.'

'You're busy,' said Declan. 'We can wait until you close, if that makes it easier.'

'Er, hello? I don't think so.' Lily was already shaking her head in mock horror at this hideous suggestion. 'You might be happy to wait another three hours,' she told him. 'But I'm not!'

Lily was feeling dizzy with discovery. 'I honestly don't know which is best,' she said when Coral joined them at 5.30 in the back garden. 'Hearing the stories or seeing the photographs.'

'Except you don't have to choose.' Declan smiled at her as he said it. 'I've got both.'

'You do have both. It's so brilliant, I can't tell you.' Lily wondered if either of them could fully understand how much this meant to her. 'This has been one of the best days of my life.'

'Shall I leave you two in peace?' said Coral. 'I'll go into the kitchen and put some food together.'

'No, don't. Stay out here with us. You have to see these photos.' Lily patted the sun-warmed cushions beside her on the garden seat. 'I could look at them forever.'

Joining her on the seat, Coral said, 'Go on then, show me.'

'I love this one.' Swivelling the open album on the table so Coral could see, Lily looked at Declan. 'You tell her. They're your stories.'

And she loved to listen to them. Maybe only someone in her position could appreciate how it felt to learn more about the person you'd loved and lost so many years ago. It felt like being presented with glorious long-buried treasure.

'That was the first one taken of the two of us together,' said Declan. 'I'd been pretty smitten by Jo from day one, when she brought down that thief with her serving tray. And I thought there was a chance she might like me too, but she was playing it cool, getting her bearings and finding her way around the new job. She'd only just arrived in Spain.'

'She fancied you rotten,' Coral supplied with a grin, 'but she needed to be certain before anything happened. She said it was like starting at a brand-new school and making friends with the first person who spoke to you, then realising a month later that you'd gone and got yourself stuck with a complete weirdo and there was no escape.' She paused. 'Not that you *were* a weirdo, of course. But you have to make sure.'

'Plus I kind of had a girlfriend,' Declan admitted, 'although I finished with her two days after first setting eyes on Jo. A week later, I told Jo she was the reason. And the day after *that*, a group of us left work at midnight and went out to join a party down on Barceloneta beach.'

'And ended up staying there all night. This was taken at seven o'clock the next morning, by one of Declan's friends.' Lily gazed lovingly at the glossy snap, with the remains of a barbecue in the foreground and a hazy sunrise behind them turning the sky palest pink and the sea liquid silver. Her mum and Declan were half sitting, half lying back on their elbows with their heads tilted together and her mum's left foot touching Declan's right ankle. It was all there in the eyes, in the secret smiles on their tanned faces, and in the glow of happiness surrounding them. They were young, they were healthy and they were free to do whatever they liked. Her mum was wearing a short ruffled skirt and an oversized white T-shirt that had slipped off one shoulder, with a pink halter-neck bikini top visible beneath it. Declan's own shorts and shirt were both wet from the sea.

'I remember Jo telling me about that night on the beach.' Coral's eyes lit up. 'Someone had a boombox and you were all dancing to Fairground Attraction. Remember that song? *It's got to be-ee-eeee-eee . . .*'

'*Perfect*,' said Declan. 'Ha, yes, we were. And we danced to that song by Bros, too. "I Owe You Nothing".'

'Bros?' Lily couldn't keep a straight face. 'That's a bit embarrassing.'

He shrugged good-naturedly. 'Tell me about it.'

To tease him, Lily sang, '*I owe you nothinnggg . . .*' and did a couple of pointy-fingered gestures into the air before suddenly wondering what she was doing and tucking her hands back down at her sides.

'That's how Jo used to dance to it,' said Declan. 'Exactly the same.'

'She had that song on a cassette tape,' Coral joined in. 'It was one of your favourites when you were little. You used to beg her to play it over and over again.'

Lily turned to her. 'I did? Really?'

'The two of you used to dance around to it together.' Coral

109

did the pointy-fingered hand movements. 'Just like that. When you were three. It was hilarious to watch – you used to take it all so seriously and get so *cross* if you ever made a mistake.'

'OK, thanks a lot, you can stop now. And to think I called *you* embarrassing,' she said ruefully to Declan.

'Hey, you were three years old. I was nineteen.'

Lily could just picture her mum and the young Declan together; she could imagine them dancing wildly on the beach as the stars faded from the sky, the sun rose above the horizon and the dawn chorus filled the air. Vying, of course, with the equally chirpy sounds of Matt and Luke Goss.

There were other photos too, of Declan and her mum either singly or together, depending on whether there had been anyone else around to take the pictures. Sometimes they were part of a group of friends, all making the most of their year in Barcelona, cavorting in the sea, climbing mountains or socialising with drinks at pavement cafés.

'You can see the connection between you.' Lily looked at Declan. 'You can *feel* it. I mean, I'm not just imagining it, am I? It's really and truly there.'

'I think so.' He nodded. 'It definitely felt like it at the time.'

'It's such a shame you broke up. Apart from me not being here if you hadn't.' It was kind of a weird thing to think about. She was inclined to believe that if her mum and Declan had stayed together and had a baby, that baby would still somehow have been her, only this time with two parents who loved each other. Wouldn't that have been nice?

'I know. If our universities hadn't been so far apart, I think we might have managed it. As it was,' said Declan, 'we ended up having—'

His phone was ringing. As he took it out of his pocket and saw the name flashing up, he winced. 'Oh God.'

'It's fine.' Coral was already on her feet. 'We'll go into the kitchen, leave you in peace.'

'No need. My fault.' Declan pressed answer. 'Gail, sorry, I'm not going to be able to get over for dinner.' Pause. 'I know, I know, I meant to and completely forgot.' Pause. 'No, I'm not in London.' Long pause. 'I'm in the Cotswolds. Stanton Langley.' Even longer pause, during which Lily and Coral were both able to hear Gail's exclamation of disbelief, followed by a rattle of words they couldn't make out.

Which was probably a good thing.

'I know, but I did,' Declan replied patiently. 'And it's been a fantastic day. Look, everything's fine. I'll speak to you tomorrow, tell you all about it then.'

'Oh dear,' said Coral when the call had ended. 'I feel terrible now. Like a mistress!' Then her cheeks turned pink at the realisation of what she'd just blurted out.

'Is your girlfriend incredibly jealous?' Lily was curious.

Declan shook his head. 'No, she's really not. Just organised and efficient. She's cooked dinner for me and I'm not there. That's why she's a bit put out.'

'Understandable,' said Coral. 'Well, if you're not rushing back, will you stay and have something to eat with us?'

Stay, stay, Lily mentally willed him. *Staaaaaaay.*

And without even being aware of the message she was sending out, Declan smiled and said easily, 'Sounds great.'

Hooray for secret messages!

'Well it might be.' Coral's eyes were sparkling. 'Keep your fingers crossed.'

Chapter 18

They moved inside. A bottle of wine was opened and Coral began putting a meal together in her characteristic slapdash-but-hopefully-successful way. An hour later they sat down at the scrubbed oak table in the kitchen and ate king prawns in chilli and garlic, followed by fried chicken with green beans, new potatoes and hollandaise. And maybe the chicken was a bit burnt and the green beans too crunchy, but who cared? The company was wonderful. For pudding they had Jaffa Cakes.

'So how exactly did you and Mum break up?' Lily was busy separating the orange jelly from the sponge part of her Jaffa Cake.

'Well basically, the distance was too great and I think we were both too proud.' Declan shrugged and stirred his coffee. 'We discussed it over and over again, with each other and with our friends. Could we cope, being that far apart? It was a ten-hour drive from Fife to Exeter, if either of us even owned a car capable of getting that far, which of course we didn't. There were no cheap airfares back then. Even trains and coaches cost more than we could afford. Which meant we wouldn't be seeing each other for months on end.'

Coral nodded sympathetically. 'Jo told me about that. It must have been so horrible for you both.'

'It was.' Declan sighed. 'Everyone else told us we'd be crazy to even try to keep things going when what we were *meant* to be doing was having fun and enjoying university life. In the end, Jo said maybe we should accept the situation and make a clean break. I was horrified, but she made it sound as if it was what she wanted, and I wasn't going to beg. So I pretended to agree.'

'She only said it in the first place because she thought it was what you secretly wanted,' said Coral.

'At the time, it didn't occur to me. Jo was upset with me, I was upset with her, and we ended up doing the thing neither of us wanted to do.' Declan raised his hands in defeat. 'And that was it, no going back. The decision had been made.'

'Oh God.' Lily was only too easily able to envisage it.

'It was pretty awful,' Declan said. 'We'd agreed not to contact each other, once we'd made the break. So I went up to St Andrews and Jo went off to Exeter, and we stuck it out. The first six months were awful, but I got through it and gradually things became easier. The following May, I started seeing someone else. Then in June, I *did* hear from Jo. She sent me a letter asking if I fancied taking off to Barcelona for the summer. But I'd already arranged a job with my flatmate's dad and I couldn't let him down. Plus, my girlfriend saw the letter and wasn't amused.'

'Was her name Theresa?' said Lily.

Startled, Declan said, 'Yes! How did you know *that*?'

'She wrote to Mum. Warned her off.'

'God, really? I had no idea.' He shrugged. 'She was way too pushy. We broke up a couple of weeks later.'

Missed opportunities, sliding doors.

'So you and Mum never saw each other again,' said Lily.

Declan hesitated for a moment, then said, 'Well, I did see Jo. Just once. But she didn't see me.'

'You saw her?' Coral straightened. 'When?'

'Halfway through second year. I'd just been missing her so much. *So* much.' He shook his head. 'It was one of those spur-of-the-moment decisions.'

'Like coming here today,' said Lily.

'But with less of a happy outcome.' Declan was rueful. 'I skipped a couple of lectures, borrowed some money and spent the whole of Friday travelling down on a coach from Fife to Exeter. Then I walked three miles to a pub called The Parrot, because the sister of a friend of mine had told me that Jo always went there on Friday nights.'

Coral nodded. 'We did.'

'Anyway, it rained. A lot. By the time I arrived, it was ten thirty and I looked as if I'd just climbed out of a pond.'

Lily drank some wine; as a story, it clearly wasn't set to end well. Across the table, Coral had the flat of her hand pressed against her sternum.

'The place was packed,' Declan continued. 'There were banners and balloons everywhere, celebrating someone's birthday, and at first I thought Jo wasn't there. Everyone was dancing, but I couldn't see her anywhere. Then suddenly the music stopped and the DJ said, "Come on then, where are they? Where are the lovebirds?" And that was when they appeared on the stage. It was Jo and the guy whose birthday it was. And they were kissing.'

'Neil . . .' Coral said faintly.

'That's right.' Declan nodded. 'He was tall, with reddish-fair hair, wearing a red rugby shirt and jeans.' The mental picture in his head was evidently as vivid now as the day he'd seen them together up on the stage. 'They had their arms wrapped around each other and they *kept* kissing, and the DJ made some jokey comment about . . . well, never mind.' He shook his head apologetically at Lily. 'I'm sure you can guess.'

'I was at that party,' said Coral.

'Well, I realised I'd chosen the wrong time to make my surprise appearance. In fact I couldn't have picked a worse night if I tried. Neil and Jo were dancing together on the stage, gazing into each other's eyes like it was their honeymoon. Jo looked amazing, just so happy.' Declan sat back on his chair, his fingers gripping his coffee cup. 'And I felt as if my heart was being ripped out.' A muscle twitched in his jaw. 'So I left. Spent the night on a plastic bench in the bus station and the next morning headed back up to Scotland. Not what you'd call the best weekend of my life.'

There was silence around the table for a few seconds. Then Lily said, 'So who was Neil? Mum didn't have that many boyfriends, and I've never heard of a Neil.'

'Oh dear,' said Coral. 'That's because he was never her boyfriend.'

Lily frowned. 'But why . . .?'

'Neil was a friend of ours. He'd been dumped by his last girlfriend, and his much better-looking older brother was down from Bristol Uni that weekend. You know what big brothers are like . . . he was always teasing Neil for not getting girls as pretty as the ones *he* got. So Jo and Neil pretended to be an item, to shut his brother up. And it worked like a charm,' said Coral. 'But it was all for show; there was never anything going on between them. Neil was just a mate.'

Declan shook his head. 'Well they fooled me too. Of all the Friday nights I could have chosen to turn up, I had to choose that one.'

'If they hadn't done that, everything could have been different,' Lily marvelled. There were so many what-ifs; life was like a ball of string with three hundred ends.

'And it was only a couple of weeks after that party,' said Coral, 'that Jo met Keir.'

Just for a moment, unshed tears pricked at the backs of Lily's eyes; talk about bad timing all round. Except she really had to stop thinking like that. *If Mum hadn't got together with Keir, I would never have been born.*

Declan left soon after midnight. At the front door, he hugged them both. 'Thanks for making me so welcome. It's been an amazing day.'

'Thank *you*,' said Lily, 'for driving all this way and coming to see us.' She smiled, inwardly desperate to know if they'd ever see him again, or if this was it. He'd met her now, assuaged his curiosity; maybe as far as he was concerned, that was enough. But she mustn't appear needy, mustn't ask if another visit could be on the cards . . .

'It's been lovely to meet you,' Coral said. 'Really, you don't know how much it's meant to Lily.'

'And to me too.' Declan glanced at the bangle on Lily's wrist. 'It's almost as if Jo meant it to happen.'

'If you come down again, you have to meet Patsy,' said Coral. 'Such a shame she's in Oxford tonight . . . she's going to be so sorry she missed you.'

Good try, thought Lily, but in all honesty, was meeting another complete stranger really that much of a draw?

'You're looking worried,' said Declan. 'What's wrong?'

Oh bugger, so much for not being needy. Lily spoke in a rush. 'We might not see you again . . . and I haven't even shown you my birthday letters yet!'

116

He smiled, first at Coral, then at her. 'Don't worry. I'll be back.'

It was three o'clock in the morning. Coral heard the grandfather clock chime downstairs in the hall and gave up on the idea of sleep. Sitting up in bed, she reached for her phone and clicked on the camera roll.

Just over two years now since Nick had died, and scrolling through the photo gallery had become her night-time comfort blanket. It was weird to think that she'd always been six months younger than him, and now she was eighteen months older than he would ever be. There were fine lines fanning out from the corners of her eyes that hadn't been there when he was alive. As the years passed, she would continue to grow old without him.

'Oh Nick.' She lightly touched the screen where his dear familiar face smiled out at her. 'I still miss you. So much.'

The last two and a bit years had been a trial, without doubt the very worst of her life. At first, the shock of losing him so suddenly had left her barely able to function. But gradually she'd begun to work through the stages of grief and rejoin the human race, even if she had often felt like an imposter, smiling and talking and generally behaving like a normal person on the surface, whilst inside all was joyless and frozen. The things she'd especially loved to do before – like sketching and painting – no longer interested her in the slightest. Arranging spur-of-the-moment weekends away had become a thing of the past, because the person she most wanted to go away with was no longer here. Weeks and months passed with glacial slowness and all she wanted was to begin to feel normal again, but it was turning out to be easier said than done.

Because Nick had been her first and only love. There'd never been anyone else. They'd met when she was sixteen and he was seventeen and it had been like finding each other's missing halves. People had laughed and told them they were crazy, how could they know they were right for each other if they didn't have other experiences to make comparisons with? But the idea of breaking up for no reason at all and spending time being unhappy apart, purely in order to satisfy their critics, seemed even crazier. So they'd metaphorically stuck two fingers up at their detractors and stayed together.

Till death us do part.

Bloody *death*. So uncompromising. So final.

Because it never gave you a second chance, did it? You couldn't apologise to God or whoever was in charge of deciding when these things should happen. You weren't allowed to strike a bargain and say, 'Look, we knew we were happy, we just didn't always realise quite *how* happy. But we do now, so *please* could you bring him back, even if it's just for a few more years?'

It didn't work that way, sadly. Once they were gone, they were gone.

So anyway, the freeze had set in and she'd imagined it would be there for good. Over the course of the last year, people had begun making the occasional half-jokey remark about how in time she would meet someone else, but the idea was ridiculous; it was on a par with being told, 'If you flap your arms really fast, you'll be able to fly.'

It just wasn't going to happen.

Coral scrolled on through the more recent photos that didn't feature Nick, then came to the ones from tonight. She'd taken some of Lily and Declan standing together smiling into the camera, as well as several more informal unposed ones.

So there it was; against all odds it had happened at last. This afternoon she had looked at Declan Madison out in the yard and seen a nice-looking man who did nothing for her. Then this evening she'd looked at him across the dinner table and experienced a jolt of attraction so out of the blue and completely unexpected that at first she hadn't known what it was.

Recognition had belatedly set in. That squiggly sensation inside her ribcage was the same squiggly sensation she'd experienced when she'd first met Nick. After the first few months it had worn off, of course, because you simply couldn't go through life feeling that way all the time. But it had always come back to ambush her at unexpected moments: when she caught sight of Nick from a distance, or saw him again after they'd been apart for a day or two. She remembered arriving back at Heathrow after visiting her cousin in Switzerland years ago, and experiencing a huge rush of adrenalin when she saw Nick waiting for her at the arrivals gate, because she loved him and still fancied him like mad and he loved her too. And when a few seconds later their eyes had met across a crowded airport and that wonderful smile had lit up his face, she vividly remembered thinking how lucky she was to have him in her life.

Until two years ago, when the luck had so cruelly run out.

So was this nature's way of letting her know she was on the road to recovery? And was it also nature's way of playing a bit of a mean trick on her?

Because it did seem slightly unfair that the first person other than Nick to make her feel this way should be the love of her best friend's life.

Not to mention already *in* a relationship.

OK, enough. Coral switched off her phone and wriggled back down in an attempt to get some sleep. Then again, maybe it was better – *safer* – to have her first post-Nick crush on someone unattainable. That way, she could get used to all the feelings without the possibility of anything actually happening.

Like learning to ride your first bike with stabilisers attached, with no risk of falling off.

Call it a practice run.

Plus, who was to say they'd ever see each other again anyway? Declan had said they would, but he might just have been saying it to be polite.

Maybe today had been her practice run and now it was over; that had been *it*.

Chapter 19

It was one of those split-second decisions you don't stop to think about. One minute Dan was enjoying himself at the barbecue on Friday evening, chatting to friends and drinking a cold beer. The next minute he was throwing the bottle aside, leaving a foamy beer fountain in his wake as he raced across the lawn to stop a three-year-old being crushed by a twenty-stone weight falling from a great height.

Well, twelve feet. High enough.

Big Al had hired the Velcro wall for his birthday barbecue. Having squeezed himself into the largest of the all-in-one Velcro suits and taken a running jump off the trampoline launch pad, he had catapulted into the air and landed – *splat* – against the wall an impressive distance off the ground and, thanks to a mid-air somersault, upside down. Letting out a yell of triumph, he was unaware that his daughter Maisie had scrambled up on to the inflatable mattress directly beneath him. Meanwhile, Big Al's Velcro suit had begun to unpeel from the wall, and once that happened, there was no way of preventing the inevitable fall . . .

'Oh my *God*!' Big Al's wife, distracted for a few seconds by their terrier making off like Groucho Marx with a barbecued chicken leg in his mouth, saw what was about to happen just as Dan flung himself across the launch pad, scooped Maisie up like a rugby ball and sent her sliding to safety. There was the escalating sound of Velcro being ripped apart directly above his head, and the twenty-stone weight that was Big Al landed on top of him instead.

Searing pain radiated from his right shoulder like a smashed mirror. Somehow still aware that small children were about, Dan managed to amend his howl of '*Fu*—' to '*Fuh . . . gahhh!*' Then, as Big Al scrambled to get off him, another jolt of pain crushed his left foot. '*Sh . . . eesh!*' yelled Dan as the two separate pain points battled for supremacy. To add insult to injury, Al elbowed him in the eye whilst clambering off the inflatable mattress. '*Owwwww.*'

'God, mate, sorry. Are you all right?'

For a supposedly intelligent maths teacher, Big Al could ask some spectacularly stupid questions. Through gritted teeth – he should probably be grateful he still *had* teeth – Dan said, 'Do I look all right?'

Maisie, clutched in her mother's arms and less than sympathetic, clapped her hands and cried happily, 'Again, Daddy! Do it again!'

'Is it your shoulder?' Maisie's mother gazed worriedly down at Dan.

'I think I heard my collarbone crack.' He was beginning to feel light-headed now. 'And something went in my foot too.'

'Oh fuck,' said Big Al.

Maisie's eyes widened with delight. 'Daddy! That's *rude*.'

Lily was working in the yard the next day when she saw a yellow VW Beetle pull up outside the entrance. About to go out and tell the driver he couldn't park there, she experienced a jolt when she spotted Dan in the passenger seat.

Their history of swapping jokey texts had ground to a halt following the decidedly non-jokey exchange that had taken place after Eddie Tessler's abrupt departure from Stanton Langley.

Hers had said: *You told someone Eddie was here. Well done.*

And Dan had texted back: *It wasn't me. But thanks for jumping to conclusions.*

Except she knew he must have done, which was why there'd been no further contact between them since.

She turned away, aware that Dan was watching her. The phone buzzed in her jeans pocket and she pulled it out.

The text from Dan said: *Sorry x*

Did he really think she was that much of a pushover? She put the phone away and made a start on carrying a recent delivery of stained glass into the barn behind the office.

Two minutes later, she heard what sounded like an old-age pensioner making their way slowly across the gravel behind her. Turning to see how she could help, Lily did a double-take when she came face to face with Dan. Oh God, what had *happened* to him?

'Again,' said Dan, 'I'm really sorry.' He paused, then added, 'Turns out it was me after all.'

The sight of him was shocking. He had a spectacularly bruised eye; a sling strapped his right arm firmly to his chest, his left foot was held off the ground and he was supporting himself with a metal crutch in his left hand.

Then again, he clearly wanted to get the apology out of the way first. Lily said, 'I knew it was you. How could *you* not know?'

He exhaled. 'Anna was with me that night, remember? As soon as I got back into the car, she knew something was up. She kept asking me what it was, wouldn't stop, so in the end I had to tell her. But I made her *promise* not to breathe a word

123

to anyone else.' He shifted his weight on his uninjured foot. 'She promised. And when word got out the next day, she swore blind she hadn't told a living soul.'

'But she had,' said Lily.

'I only found out last night. Anna told her flatmate, who told her brother. Anna's flatmate's brother, it turns out, just recently started working for a news agency in London.'

'Right.'

Dan tilted his head. 'I know. It was all my fault, but I didn't mean it to happen. And I'm very sorry.'

OK, not asking him about his injuries was actually killing her now. Furthermore, he wasn't going to be able to manage all the stairs leading to his fourth-floor flat overlooking the Clifton Suspension Bridge in Bristol. Lily said, 'Whose car did you come up in?' Because the VW Beetle hadn't been Anna's.

'Big Al's. He's a mate of mine.'

'Where's he gone?'

'Taking my cases over to the cottage. Looks like I'm back for a while. Unless Patsy's rented out my room to anyone else in the last week.'

Lily ignored the dig. 'How long will you be here for?'

'Until I can fly again. Could be two months.'

Despite everything, it would be lovely to have Dan back here. Not that she would dream of telling *him* that, of course.

'Go on then.' She gave in at last. 'What happened?'

There it was, a flicker of the old triumphant smile. 'I thought you'd never ask.'

'Well now I have.'

'Maybe I won't tell you,' said Dan.

'And maybe I'll steal that crutch and push you over,' said Lily. 'Tell me how you got yourself into this mess. Ooh, were you beaten up by some girl's jealous boyfriend?'

'Close. I saved a little kid from being crushed to death by a falling boulder.'

'Oh my God, *really*?'

'Well, not an actual boulder. It was Big Al.' Dan broke into a grin. 'But I'm still a hero. Everyone says so.'

Maybe he was, but no way was he getting off that lightly. 'A hero who can't keep a secret,' said Lily.

'Unless I'm having an affair with someone I shouldn't.' His dark eyes glittered with intent. 'Then I'm absolutely discreet.'

'Oh well, when it's in your own interests, you would be.'

Dan smiled. 'Am I forgiven? Can we be friends again now?'

He already knew he'd won her over. And he wasn't the only one who'd had difficulty keeping that particular secret. Lily heaved a dramatic sigh. 'You mean now that you're disabled and can't drive and are going to be needing lifts everywhere.'

'Is that what you're thinking? I swear that won't happen.' He clutched his heart with his unstrapped hand, the one with the crutch dangling from it. 'No favours, I promise. If you're ever driving down the road and you see me limping along slower than a snail, my face white with pain, I wouldn't even want you to stop and offer me a lift. In fact, you have to promise you'll never do that.'

'Don't worry, I won't. And if it's raining hard, I'll speed up and drive past really close, so you get splashed all over with mud.'

'I wouldn't expect anything less,' said Dan. 'It's absolutely what I deserve.'

A customer was lugging a marble statue across the gravel towards them. Lily said, 'I have to get back to work.'

'I know. So are we OK? Friends again?'

'Possibly.' She held her finger and thumb a few millimetres apart. 'About this much.'

125

'Fancy a few drinks at the Star this evening?'

'Go on then. What time?'

'Seven?'

Lily nodded. 'Seven it is.'

He gave her a playful look. 'That means you'll turn up at seven thirty, just to keep me waiting and make the point that I'm lucky to have you there at all.'

They'd known each other for so long, it was impossible to play games and not be called out on it.

'I'll get there at seven forty-five,' said Lily.

'Great. Gives me more time to chat up whoever's working behind the bar.'

'It's Sean tonight.'

'Hey, no problem, I'm an equal-opportunities chatter-upper.' Dan winked at her. 'Practice makes perfect.'

Chapter 20

At 7.30, having showered and changed into a stripy red and white jersey dress, Lily was upstairs in her bedroom patting serum on to her still-damp ringlets when she saw Dan making his way down the main street towards the Star.

Honestly, how did he manage it? He was wearing a dark purple polo shirt, narrow faded jeans and a deck shoe on his right foot. The left foot, held off the ground, was in a lime-green cast. He was indeed progressing at a painfully slow pace, pausing every few steps to wipe the palm of his left hand on the side of his jeans. As for his eye – well, what a mess. The skin around it was purple and charcoal grey, yet he still somehow managed to look good, high-cheekboned and piratical rather than like some loser who'd come off worst in a fight.

There was that familiar tightening in the pit of her stomach. As ever, Lily ignored it, because to do otherwise would be madness.

Nevertheless, she'd be lying if she didn't admit, even if just to herself, that having Dan back here for the summer would be fun. He might be exasperating sometimes – OK, often – but he was never dull.

At that moment, he glanced up at her window and saw her

looking down at him. Breaking into a grin, he raised his left arm, waved the metal crutch in the air and pretended to wobble crazily like a clown on a high wire.

Lily leaned out of the window and called down, 'If you fall over and break your other foot, it'll serve you right.'

True to form, when she joined him in the pub ten minutes later, he was perched on a stool doing his fortune-telling act on Tanya, who was working behind the bar with Sean tonight.

'. . . You have an adventurous spirit and a need for love in your life. There's a tall dark man . . . you've had a secret crush on him for years, but this could be the time you get together for a wild romantic affair.'

'This tall dark man,' said Tanya. 'Would he happen to have his arm in a sling and a bit of a limp?'

Dan frowned and peered more closely at her palm, then raised his eyebrows in surprise. 'You're right, he has!'

Down-to-earth Tanya, who was in her forties and had a husband, five children and two grandchildren, snorted with laughter. 'Ah, but a bit of a limp what?'

'Oh Tanya, you're a cruel woman.' Dan dropped her hand and sat back, shaking his head in defeat. 'You break hearts without even realising it. I'm choking up. Just give me a moment . . .'

'Yes, that's what I've heard.' Still chuckling, Tanya moved off to serve another customer.

Lily said, 'Thirty love to Tanya.'

He heaved a mournful sigh. 'She beats me every time.'

It only happened, though, because Dan allowed it to. Casting himself in the role of hapless underdog was another of his ploys to charm the opposite sex. Luckily both he and Tanya were aware he wasn't serious.

'I know all your tricks,' Lily reminded him.

'Then I'm just going to have to come up with some new ones. Anyway, never mind that now. Patsy tells me you met Declan last weekend. I want to hear all about him.'

One of Dan's good qualities was his interest and enthusiasm; when he paid attention to you, it was his full attention. He was genuinely interested in what you had to say and asked all the right questions. For the next hour, Lily told him all about Declan, showed him the photos on her phone and relayed the stories Declan had shared about her mum.

'That reminds me, I left my phone charger in Bristol.' Dan took out his own phone and grimaced at the battery sign glowing red on the screen. 'Two per cent. Nightmare. You don't have a spare, do you?'

'No, and I need mine tonight, but you can borrow it tomorrow morning.'

'I'll do that. Can I use your phone now to order another charger online?'

'Help yourself.' Sliding down from her stool, Lily pushed her phone across the bar. 'Back in two minutes. The skin around your eye's getting blacker, by the way. Does it really hurt?'

'Of course it hurts. The reason I'm not making a fuss is because I'm so incredibly brave.' He touched the skin around his eye. 'Go on, have a feel. It's hot.'

Gently Lily pressed the tips of her fingers against the dark-blue outer corner of the eyelid, where the skin was puffy and stretched.

'Ow,' Dan murmured, his gaze fixed on her face. '*Ow.*'

'You're the one who asked me to do it.'

'I wanted you to know how heroic I'm being.'

'And now I do,' said Lily. 'I suppose I'd better write to the Queen. You'll probably be awarded the Victoria Cross.'

When she returned from the loo three minutes later, Dan

was ordering the new charger. Lily bought a fresh round of drinks while he finished tapping in his details.

'Thanks.' He handed back her phone. 'It'll be here by Tuesday.'

'No problem. Won't Anna be coming over to visit you? She could bring your old one with her.'

'I think we can safely say she won't be coming over to visit me,' said Dan.

'Oh. Have you dumped her?' This inspired mixed emotions; Anna was a triumph of looks over personality, but she was the manager of a fantastic clothes shop in Bristol and had let Lily use her 60 per cent discount code when she'd ordered a couple of dresses online.

Although now that she *knew* the code, would it be very wrong to carry on using it if Anna and Dan were no longer an item?

'We don't call it dumped,' said Dan. 'But yes, it's over. Seemed like time to call it a day. Anyhow, what else has been happening while I've been away?'

Poor Anna, dismissed from his life. Another one bites the dust.

'Not much. We've been busy at the yard. Oh, we sold that giant octopus chandelier to a hotel in Miami. Got three grand for it – they didn't even haggle!'

'Excellent. And how about Eddie Tessler? Has he been in touch?'

Mini adrenalin rush. Lily casually shook her head. 'Eddie? No.'

'What, you haven't heard from him at all?' Dan sounded surprised.

She gave him a wide-eyed look. 'Why would I? He stayed with Patsy for a few days, now he's gone back to London. End of story.'

'Yes, but you spent a lot of time with him. Patsy told me all about it. She said the two of you got on well together.' He raised an eyebrow. 'Like, *really* well.'

Perspiration was prickling at the back of Lily's neck. Patsy was right, they *had* got on well. In particular, there'd been that moment when she'd thought he might be about to kiss her – oh God, that had been *such* a thrilling moment – until they'd been interrupted by the sound of a key in the front door and Dan's unexpected late-night appearance.

Yes, thanks for that, Dan, thanks a lot.

'Look, we got on fine, but that's all it was.' Lily was effortlessly dismissive.

'But didn't you wish there could have been more?'

'No!'

'Don't sound so outraged.' Dan held up his hands. 'He's a good-looking guy. Girls love him. You must have fancied him.'

'I didn't, I swear.' If she said so herself, Lily was doing a fantastic job of playing it cool. For once in her life she wasn't blushing scarlet, looking guilty or sounding like the world's most unconvincing fibber.

'Not even a tiny bit?'

Her confidence grew. 'Not even a smidgeon. I mean, nice enough guy, but not my type.'

'Well I'm impressed,' said Dan. 'I honestly thought you'd get one of your crushes on him, and fantasise about him falling under your spell.'

'Wait, what are you even talking about? For a start, I wouldn't fantasise about him,' said Lily. 'And second, what do you mean, one of my crushes? When did I last have a crush on someone?'

'That film you couldn't stop watching. *The Proposal*. Ryan Reynolds,' Dan reminded her. 'You had a massive crush on him.'

'Oh come on, it wasn't a real-life crush! He's a film star!'

'So's Eddie Tessler.'

'Fine,' said Lily. 'All the more reason not to have a crush on him.'

'Not even a secret one?'

'Not even a secret one. Why are you keeping on about it?'

'Oh, sorry, I didn't realise I was.' Dan shrugged and gave her one of his glittery apologetic smiles. 'I'll stop now.' Minuscule pause. 'I just wondered why you'd googled him twenty-seven times in the last four days, that's all.'

Too late, Lily remembered that when you found yourself on the receiving end of one of those smiles, it meant the one-upmanship wasn't about to go in your favour.

Bugger.

Actually no, never mind bugger. *Fuck.*

Aloud she said coolly, 'You mean you've been snooping? Scrolling through my phone and my private messages? That's a bit low, isn't it? Even for you.'

Now she could feel the heat emanating from her face, and her palms were so slick with perspiration that if she tried to pick up her drink, it would probably slip right through her fingers and crash back on to the table.

Which would amuse Dan no end, the bastard.

'I wasn't snooping. I'd never snoop. And I wouldn't dream of reading your private messages,' he protested. 'That would be reprehensible.'

'Plus you don't know my email password.'

'I wouldn't *want* to know it.' He looked wounded at the very thought. 'All I did was click on Safari so I could order a new charger, and there were all the pages already open. You really shouldn't leave them open like that, you know. It drains the battery.'

Lily wished she could drain *his* battery. She said, 'I didn't have twenty-seven pages open.'

'I know, there were about five. But then I checked your search history to see if there was maybe some kind of *fault* with your phone. That was when the list came up and I saw how many times you'd typed in his name.' Dan shrugged his good shoulder. 'I mean, twenty-seven. That's quite a number of times to check up on someone you're not remotely interested in.'

He wasn't even bothering to keep a straight face. Lily said, 'God, you're smug.'

'I'm not. I just happen to think honesty's the best policy. You liked him and you thought maybe he liked you. You hoped he'd be in touch, but it hasn't happened. There's no need to be embarrassed about that.'

'I'm not embarrassed.'

'You're still bright red, though,' Dan pointed out. 'Hey, it's fine, a bit of harmless cyber-stalking never hurt anyone.'

'I haven't been cyber-stalking! I looked him up on Google, that's all!'

'Twenty-seven times,' Dan murmured.

Lily took a deep breath; the temptation to throw a drink at him had never been greater. The really annoying thing was that she hadn't even realised she'd done it that often. She stared deliberately past Dan and stayed silent.

'Did he seduce you? Is that why?'

'Oh for crying out loud, *no*.'

'But you wish he had.'

'Will you *stop* trying to wind me up? I could always break your other foot.' She didn't completely mean it, but almost. Since childhood Dan had delighted in teasing her, making fun of her weaknesses, catching her out. And she'd done the same to him in return. But this time felt different, possibly because he was bang on the money: she *had* wanted more to happen and, gullibly, had thought Eddie might have been in touch. Even a brief text, a friendly couple of lines would have been enough.

Except it hadn't happened, and yes, secretly she was a bit miffed.

Plus, there was nothing more annoying than being disappointed by one man and caught out by another who you knew was never going to let you forget it.

Just to make herself feel better, Lily dipped her fingers in her drink and flicked droplets of iced spritzer at Dan. Not too much; that would be a waste.

'Cruel.' Dan bent down to greet Barbara, who had waddled over to say hello. 'See that, Barb? Now she's trying to drown me.'

Barbara wagged her tail.

'I hate you,' said Lily.

'Only some of the time.'

'Don't flatter yourself.'

'Ah, but you are secretly glad I'm back.'

'Why would I be glad? Look at you.' Lily indicated his strapped-up arm and plastered foot. 'It's not as if you're going to be any use to anyone.'

'Don't be so dismissive. I could be capable of more than you think,' Dan said playfully. 'You don't know what I can or can't do until you let me try.'

Chapter 21

At 11.30 the next morning, Lily was standing in a crowded auction room in Bristol. As she waited to bid on life-sized resin sculptures of a pair of Friesian cows, her phone – switched to silent – began to buzz in her pocket, signalling an incoming call.

'Now we come to Lot 88,' said the auctioneer. 'And if you're thinking of starting up your own farm but you're too lazy to do the milking, we've got some cattle here that could be right up your street. Or should I say farmyard, hahahaHA!'

The auctioneer fancied himself as a comedian and liked to brighten proceedings with his own brand of humour. He beamed around the room. 'Who'll start the bidding then, at three hundred pounds?'

Lily had no intention of answering her phone, obviously. Until she saw the name flashing up on the screen and let out an involuntary squeak of surprise.

Eddie.

Eddie Tessler.

OhmyGodohmyGod.

'Come on, you lot, don't you go *milking* the situation.' The auctioneer chuckled at his own wit.

'Three hundred!' a voice called out at the back.

Eddie was phoning her right here, right now. Paralysed with indecision, Lily felt her mobile buzz for the third time. Bidding at auction always prompted an adrenalin rush, and now her heart had gone into double overdrive thanks to this two-pronged assault. If it were anyone else calling she'd leave it, but this wasn't anyone else, it was Eddie. What if she returned the call later and he didn't answer it? What if this was her one and only chance to speak to him again?

'Come on, ladies and gentlemen, don't be *moo-dy*, who'll give me three fifty?'

What if he took offence and blocked her number? He was a film star; people in his position didn't take kindly to being ignored.

'Three fifty,' called out a voice to Lily's left.

'Three seventy,' said another.

'That's more like it,' the auctioneer announced. 'Now we're *moo*-ving! Who'll give me—'

'Four hundred,' shrieked Lily, a bit more high-pitched than she'd intended. In her hand, the phone buzzed for the fifth time.

Mimicking her in a squeaky falsetto, the auctioneer said, 'What was that? Four hundred from the mouse in the room?'

Above the sound of laughter someone else shouted, 'Four twenty.'

Lily already had a buyer lined up for the life-sized black and white cows; they had a regular customer with a weakness for such quirky items and a huge garden to put them in. Already backing out of the room, she yelled, 'Four fifty,' then pressed answer and said, 'Hello?'

This time, thank goodness, *not* in a helium voice.

'Hi, it's me. Eddie.'

'I know it is.' Despite the fact that she was trying to squeeze between a pair of enormous men in scratchy tweed jackets, she found herself grinning like an idiot. 'Hi.'

'Four seventy,' cried a new voice right behind her.

Oh bugger. Twisting round, Lily raised her free arm and yelled, 'Five hundred.'

'Sorry?' said Eddie.

'Five hundred from the little mouse with the curly hair,' the auctioneer announced. 'Ladies and gentlemen, any *udder* bids?'

'Five twenty,' shouted Lily, flustered.

'Whoa, little mouse, not your turn! Hold your horses,' said the auctioneer. 'Or should I say Friesians!'

'What on earth's going on?' said Eddie.

At least he couldn't see how much of a flap she was in. Pressing the phone tighter against her ear so she could hear him above the sound of everyone else laughing at her mistake, Lily said, 'I'm at an auction.'

'Sounds like a rowdy pub. What are you buying?'

'Two cows.'

'Seriously?'

'Not real ones. Life-sized models. Hang on a sec.' Someone else was bidding five hundred and twenty pounds now. Covering the phone, she countered with 'Five fifty.'

'How dare they bid against you?' Eddie sounded amused. 'So rude.'

'I know, it's a shocking breach of etiquette.'

'Want me to call back later?'

'I'll be done in just a minute if you're OK to hang on. SIX HUNDRED!'

'Ow, my ear.'

'Whoops, sorry.' This time she'd forgotten to cover the receiver.

137

'Six hundred and twenty,' said the auctioneer.

'Seven hundred pounds,' said Eddie.

'Don't do that, you'll get me muddled again.'

'Seventeen hundred.'

'Stop it.'

He was laughing now. 'Seventeen thousand.'

'Seven hundred pounds,' Lily called out, to counteract the woman across the room who had just bid six fifty.

'Any advance on seven hundred?' The auctioneer gazed around, gavel raised. 'Is that it? Are we all done at seven hundred?'

'Yes we are,' shouted Eddie, causing Lily to snort with laughter.

There were no more bids. The gavel came down and the auctioneer said, 'Well done, little mouse, the cows are yours. And I reckon you deserve a pat on the back. Get it? A *pat* on the back!'

In her ear Eddie said, 'He's amazing. Someone should give that man a headline spot at Caesar's Palace.'

Lily squeezed past the people at the back of the auction room and made her way outside.

'There, I'm in the car park. I can hear you properly now.'

'Sit down, make yourself comfortable.'

'It's a car park, not the Savoy Hotel.' But there was a stone step to one side of the building; Lily took up occupancy and stretched her legs out in front of her. It was both surreal and lovely hearing Eddie's voice again. 'Where are you, anyway?'

'In LA.'

'Wow, really?' She already knew where he was, thanks to all the diligent cyber-stalking. He'd flown over there three days ago and was in talks with James Cameron about appearing in his next movie alongside Sandra Bullock. *Oh my life, just imagine.*

'You mean you haven't been googling to see what I'm up to? My ego just crashed and burned.'

'I may have checked once or twice. Definitely no more than twenty-seven times.' Why, why did she blurt things out without thinking them through? It really wasn't doing her any favours. She kicked off her flip-flops and gazed sadly at her dusty feet. He'd think she was a stalker now for sure.

But Eddie was laughing. 'Thank you for resurrecting my ego. Even if you're only saying it to make me feel better. Can I tell you something?'

'If you must.' She felt herself begin to relax.

'I've missed talking to you. Missed our chats. I thought maybe you'd text or call. But you haven't.'

'I thought you might call me, but you didn't.' In for a penny.

'I was waiting for you.'

'I'm a girl.'

'Don't give me that. You're not shy.'

'I'm not shy,' Lily agreed. 'But you're the famous one. I'm the civilian.'

'Oh right, fair enough.' He sounded surprised.

'Do you always wait for girls to phone you first?'

'Yes.' Of course he did.

'Well then,' said Lily. 'There you go.'

'That's me told.' He was smiling, she could feel it. 'Maybe this is what I've missed. Anyway, did you hear back from that guy?'

'Johnny Depp? Yeah, he kept phoning and calling round but I've taken out a restraining order now.' The initial shock of hearing from Eddie had subsided, and they were falling back into their easy, jokey way of carrying on.

'Glad to hear it. How about your mum's boyfriend?'

'Which one?' For some reason it felt like a test. If he could remember the name, it meant he was properly interested.

139

'Are you checking to see if I was paying attention? Declan,' said Eddie. 'Declan Madison. And I want extra points for the surname.'

Pleased, Lily said, 'Ten extra points and a silver star.'

'Silver? Why not gold?'

'You only get gold if you can tell me his birthday.'

Eddie laughed. 'Has he been in touch?'

'Better than that. He turned up, spent the whole day with us. Honestly, it was fantastic. He brought photos of him and Mum together. And he had stories, so many stories. It was just brilliant, we really hit it off. Even when we weren't talking about Mum, he was still great company.' Lily did her best to make Eddie understand. 'Telling me about his sisters and his nephews, and everything he's done in the past. You know how sometimes you meet someone and it's so comfortable it feels like you've known them forever? It's weird, but it was exactly like that. And the way he talked about my mum . . . oh God, I don't know how to explain. It just kind of *got* me. It meant so much.'

'I can tell.' Eddie sounded amused. 'That's great. I'm so glad. So will you see him again?'

'I hope so. He said we will.' Suddenly struck by a thought, Lily said, 'Hang on, what time is it where you are?'

'Three forty-five. In the morning.'

'Oh my God, why are you even awake?'

'Jet lag. It's hideous.'

'Are you in *bed*?' For some reason she'd been picturing him sitting in an office in a smart suit.

He laughed. 'I am. You sound shocked.'

'I *am* shocked. I thought you had clothes on.'

'Sorry. Tell yourself I'm wearing striped pyjamas.'

'And a long woollen dressing gown. And old men's slippers.' It wasn't working at all; her brain knew better.

140

'How's Patsy?'

'Good. She's got another date lined up for tomorrow night, and this one definitely doesn't ride a tandem. She's checked.'

'Wise move.'

'Oh, and Dan's back for the next few weeks. He had an accident and broke his collarbone. And his foot. It was his girlfriend who gave the game away about you staying at Patsy's, by the way. Dan's only just found out. He's really sorry.'

'That's OK. It was bound to happen sooner or later.'

Lily could hear the lot numbers rising inside the hall; she had more items waiting to be bid on. 'Look, I'm going to have to get back to the auction . . . Coral will shoot me if I miss out on the lots she's after.'

'I'll let you go.' Eddie's voice softened. 'It's been nice to chat. Maybe you'll call me next time.'

'Maybe. What are you doing today?'

'Nothing much. Having lunch with Sandra Bullock.'

Of course he was. It was a hard life being a film star. 'Poor you,' Lily said cheerfully. 'And here's me wondering how to squeeze two model cows, a dining table and sixteen Victorian chimney pots into the back of a van. If I'm lucky, my lunch will be a doughnut and a mug of tea.'

Chapter 22

Patsy checked her face in the rear-view mirror and redid her lipstick before climbing out of the car. It never stopped being scary, but at this moment the possibilities were limitless. Secretly, she had high hopes for this evening's blind date. You never knew, this could be it.

And it wasn't a blind date either. His name was James, she'd seen enough photos of him to know exactly what he looked like, and they'd exchanged enough emails for her to be reassured that he was charming, intelligent, witty and able to spell. Basically he seemed great. Better still, when she'd asked him if he owned a bike, he'd said not since he was thirteen. Which, let's face it, was a major plus.

OK, here we go. She crossed the road and made her way into the restaurant. He was sitting at the table waiting for her. Which was always a good start. He was wearing a nice burgundy and white striped shirt and – phew – *not* a pair of turquoise Lycra leggings. Dark trousers, that was fine. Well-polished shoes, too. And a smile.

'Patsy. At last. Lovely to meet you.'

He greeted her with a genial kiss on the cheek and Patsy wondered if, years from now, they would reminisce about this first meeting. Was this the man she was destined to spend the rest of her life with? Would they have children together? Was it weird to be thinking these things within ten seconds of meeting someone?

Does he know I'm thinking them?

An hour later, she had all the answers she needed, and one more course still to go.

'. . . so then my ex-wife called me up and told me she was moving back to Oxford. And she asked me for *more* money, so I said she couldn't keep doing this. I mean, she'd already got me to pay for her to go to Santorini, and that used to be where we went on holiday when we were still together.'

'Oh, Santorini's great,' said Patsy. 'I went there with—'

'So I said to her, God, how can you be so thoughtless? And she just said I shouldn't be so sensitive, but I mean, how does she *expect* me to react?'

'Oh dear,' said Patsy. 'I'm lucky with my ex-husband, we still get on well and—'

'She does it on purpose to wind me up,' said James. 'She's always been an attention-seeker. We went to New York for our honeymoon and she spent the whole flight chatting up the guy sitting across the aisle from us.'

Maybe a change of subject would help. Patsy said, 'So where did you go on holiday when you were a child? Where did your parents—'

'And then when we got *back* from our honeymoon, I found this new number on her phone with just a P next to it, and when I rang it, I recognised his voice. It was the guy from the plane. Whose name was Paolo. You see, that's what she's like, that's what I had to put up with for five years.' James shook his head, besieged with memories of his ex-wife.

'We used to go camping in South Wales.' Patsy gave it one

143

last try. 'At a site just outside Tenby. When my little brother was four years old, he had a Superman suit and one day he jumped off the harbour wall—'

'She told me she loved me,' said James, tears springing into his eyes. 'And I was stupid enough to believe her.'

'Yes, but—'

'I can't get over the way she's still playing her games. I can't believe people still fall for them.' He opened his phone and said, 'Do you want to see a photo of us on our wedding day?'

The couple at the next table had been eavesdropping; they'd stopped talking to each other and were now sitting with their cutlery poised above their dinner plates. Patsy glanced at her watch – *almost* nine o'clock – and said, 'No thanks.'

It was the first time James hadn't interrupted her. Mainly because he was scrolling through the photos on his phone, fully intending to show her the pictures of his wedding day anyway.

'Here we are. There she is. Look at her, just look!'

The couple next to them were struggling not to laugh. Patsy didn't have any on her own phone, but purely to entertain herself she said to James, 'Would you like to see some of my wedding photos? I have them right here—'

'Three thousand pounds, that wedding dress cost. She said she wanted to look like a fairy-tale princess and I told her she'd always be *my* fairy-tale princess.'

Right on cue, Patsy's phone began to ring. She said apologetically, 'I'd better get this,' and pressed answer.

'Hi,' said Lily. 'This is your nine o'clock call. How's it going – is he as nice as you thought?'

How could she have got it so wrong, yet again? But Patsy knew why: it was because emails couldn't be interrupted in mid-sentence. James had written to her, she had replied to him and the exchanges had continued in an orderly fashion. Not until they'd met up and had a proper verbal conversation had his chronic inability to let anyone else finish a sentence become apparent.

'Oh no, he *hasn't*.' Patsy sat back in her chair and looked dismayed. 'Really? That's terrible. And the other leg's definitely broken? That's awful, poor Dan! Is he conscious?'

'That bad?' Lily sounded sympathetic. 'Come on, get yourself out of there and come home.'

'Yes, I will. I'll meet you in A&E. See you soon. Bye.' Hanging up, Patsy said, 'I'm so sorry, I'm going to have to go. My brother's in hospital . . . I need to get there straight away.'

'You haven't seen the wedding dress yet. Look at her, there she is. Isn't she beautiful?'

'Very beautiful. But I'm afraid I have to leave.'

'Funny, isn't it, how often that happens?' James was barely paying attention, his gaze still fixed on his phone. 'Seems like every time I meet up with someone new, they get a call in the middle of the first date. And it's always something urgent that means they need to rush off.'

Oh.

The awkward silence was broken only by the smothered snorts of amusement at the next table.

'Well.' Patsy took a couple of twenties out of her purse and put them down beside her plate. 'It could have something to do with the way you never listen to a word anyone else says because all you want to talk about is your ex-wife.'

She said it gently, not meanly. But James was too busy gazing at his phone once more to notice. With a sigh, he stroked the screen. 'Is it any wonder, though? She'll come back to me one day, I know she will. She's my princess.'

★ ★ ★

145

'Honestly,' Lily let herself into the cottage, 'it's like babysitting without getting paid.'

'Except I'm toilet-trained,' said Dan.

'I do hope so.' He'd called her ten minutes ago, a plaintive message asking her to come over and help him. 'What's the problem, anyway?'

'I want a cup of tea. In the living room. I mean, I can struggle to the kitchen and make a cup of tea. It's not easy, but I can just about manage it.' Dan gestured helplessly at his leg, his crutch, his strapped-up arm, and, for good measure, his spectacularly black eye. 'But I can't carry it back to the sofa.'

'You poor lamb. Have you tried balancing the cup on your head?'

He gave her a mournful look. 'Is that what you want me to do?'

'How about if we get you one of those kids' plastic lorries you pull along the floor with a piece of string? You could hold the string in your teeth,' said Lily.

'Or I could do that Snow White thing and train small wild animals to carry the cup through to the living room in a basket. Or,' Dan said pointedly, 'you could just be kind and do it yourself, to help out your poor disabled friend.'

'Hero friend. You forgot the hero bit.'

'I'm just being modest,' said Dan.

Lily made two mugs of tea, brought them through to the living room and silently willed him to make some disparaging jokey comment about Eddie Tessler still not having been in touch. She was longing for him to say it, *bursting* to be able to casually reply that in fact he had.

But Dan was now talking about the thriller she'd lent him, which was no good at all. Taking her phone out, she began glancing at the screen and turning it over and over in her

146

hands while Dan rattled on about murders and double-crossing tricksters and his own views as to who the killer was.

'. . . OK, the guy was carrying a loaf of bread.' When Dan got involved in a thriller, he *really* got involved. 'So what I'm thinking is, he could have hollowed out the loaf and hidden the gun inside . . .'

'It's no good telling me what you think,' said Lily. 'You haven't finished the book yet, so I'm not going to tell you if you're right.'

'And then when he jumps off the train, I bet he left the gun in the bag of the woman who went to the loo . . .'

'Oh, by the way, did I mention I got a call from Eddie?' She'd tried her level best to contain herself, but the words came blurting out anyway. She'd been holding them in for over thirty-three *hours*.

'And then the woman came back from the loo and slipped the gun into the pocket of the red-headed guy who'd just got on the train. Which would explain why there were crumbs in his pocket when they found his body on the tracks.'

There was a framed painting on the wall above his head, a pretty garden scene in acrylics that Coral had painted a few years back, before Nick had died and she'd abruptly abandoned her hobby. For a moment Lily fantasised about seizing it in both hands and bringing it crashing down, cartoon-style, on Dan's head.

'Oh! Unless the crumbs are something to do with the *parrot* . . .' said Dan.

'Are you listening to me?' Lily demanded. 'Did you even hear what I just said?'

Dan looked at her. Finally he nodded. 'He called you.'

'Yes!'

'And this is interesting because?'

'It's interesting because you told me he wouldn't. But he did. I mean, no big deal.' She shrugged casually, to demonstrate just how *small* a deal it was, because it wasn't as if she'd been desperate for Eddie Tessler to get back in touch. 'I'm just letting you know, seeing as you were so sure it wouldn't happen.'

'So you were right and I was wrong.' Dan smiled briefly. 'And this makes you happy, I can tell.'

'It always makes me happy when you're wrong.'

'Go on then, tell me. Am I right about the handgun being hidden inside the bread?'

No *way* was she letting him get away with changing the subject. 'Yes, that's exactly how it happened. Clever you. So anyway, Eddie called me yesterday from LA, while I was bidding at the auction. He was pretty funny. And then we had a long chat. Like, for *aaaages*. He was really interested to hear about Declan, too.'

'What time was this? Late morning? Midday?'

'Yes. Why?'

'Pretty standard,' said Dan. 'He's in LA, suffering from jet lag, lying in bed and wide awake at four in the morning with no one over there he can call.'

Lily narrowed her eyes. 'He called me because he'd missed talking to me.'

'Correction, he *told* you he called because he'd missed talking to you.'

'And he's texted me since then.' This was true; she'd sent him the photo of her mum and Declan as teenagers on the beach and Eddie had texted back: *Amazing!*

Which wasn't much, but technically it counted as a reply. And it wasn't as if Eddie didn't have other things on his mind.

'Texted,' said Dan. 'Great.'

'He had lunch with Sandra Bullock yesterday.' The logical

part of her knew he was being like this on purpose, refusing to seem impressed. But deep down he had to be. And she needed to tell him. It was like when you met someone at a party and they said super-casually, 'Oh yeah, I met Shakin' Stevens at a petrol station once, we were queuing up at the checkout together . . . I said hi to him and he said hi back, seemed like a really nice chap.'

Only much better, of course.

Shakin' Stevens or Eddie Tessler?

Be honest, which one would you rather boast about knowing?

'At the Chateau Marmont,' Lily continued in the face of Dan's apparent lack of interest. Eddie hadn't told her where they were eating, but it had been easy enough to find out. Easy, too, to delete her Google search history afterwards, which was something she would always do from now on. 'They're probably going to do a film together. Directed by James Cameron. *What?*' she said impatiently, because he was giving her one of his looks.

'You. Have you joined the Eddie Tessler fan club yet? When he flies back here, will you be waiting at the airport with a giant placard, jumping up and down and screaming his name?'

'Yes, that's exactly what I'll be doing.' Lily could feel herself getting irritated all over again. If Dan could have heard Eddie's voice yesterday when he'd said how much he'd missed talking to her, he wouldn't be making fun of her like this.

'Hey, don't be cross with me.' Reaching out with his un-injured leg, Dan gave her foot a gentle nudge. 'I'm just saying, that's all. Don't get carried away.'

'I didn't know I was.'

'Well, maybe it's easier for me to see. Maybe you just don't want to admit it. But deep down, I think you do know. The way you talked about him on Sunday night. The way you're reacting now. It's fine to have a crush on someone out of reach. I just worry that you're expecting it to . . . you know, lead to something real.'

'What with me being so physically repulsive, is that what you're trying to tell me?' OK, now she was really losing patience. 'Because I'm so ugly, no half-decent man could possibly be interested?'

'Oh come on, you know I don't mean that. I'm talking about him, not you.'

'You met him for all of thirty seconds,' said Lily.

'He's a man. A man who's used to getting a lot of attention from the opposite sex.'

'You mean he's exactly like you,' Lily pointed out. 'God help him.'

'Maybe so. But I'm just trying to help.'

'And what you're basically saying is that someone like Eddie would never be attracted to me.' Dan's habit of plain speaking, Lily discovered, was altogether less endearing when the person on the receiving end of his blunt opinions was you.

'I'm not saying that. I'm just pointing out that it wouldn't be a relationship that necessarily meant a lot to him. And I wouldn't want to see you getting hurt.'

'Hello?' Lily spread her hands in disbelief. 'Why are you even talking about it like this? There *is* no relationship!'

'Right, fine.' Dan sat back, visibly relieved. 'Well that's a good thing. Long may it last.' Catching the dangerous glint in her eye, he smiled and said, 'For your benefit, not his. You deserve better.'

It was annoying, and she wouldn't dream of ever admitting it, but maybe he was right. Time to change the subject. 'Speaking of deserving better, Patsy's date wasn't a success. She'll be home soon.'

'Did she say what was wrong with him?'

'She couldn't. He was there when I rang.'

'Shall we take bets, then?' Dan's mischievous smile was back, his attention successfully diverted from the subject of just how far out of her league Eddie Tessler was. 'A pound a go, winner takes all?' Counting off on the fingers of his functioning hand, he said, 'OK, I'll start. He made out he was forty but he's actually sixty.'

'A stranger to deodorant,' said Lily.

'Wearing a toupee that doesn't match the rest of his hair.'

'Still married.'

'Eats with his mouth open.'

'Describes his dreams in detail.'

'Wears make-up,' said Dan. 'Nothing over the top, just a bit of eyeliner, some mascara and a nice lipstick.'

See? Having driven her nuts, he was now making her smile again. How annoying was it not even being able to stay cross with him for five minutes?

'And an electronic tag,' said Lily.

Dan thought for a moment, then said, 'Or a nappy.'

Weaver's Cottage was dilapidated but not disastrously so. It had three bedrooms, one the size of a hamster cage. The kitchen was small, the Formica units ugly and cheap. The wallpaper probably dated from the 1970s, and every room was decorated a different shade of purple, apart from the bathroom, whose fittings were avocado green and matt with dust.

It was the kind of place that caused many people to grimace in distaste and hastily move on to look instead at a nice clean semi on a just-built estate. But Declan, who had been dealing in property for twenty years, wasn't put off. The Cotswold stone roof didn't have actual holes in it, the overgrown garden

151

was small but south-facing and the views from the cottage's elevated position overlooking the valley were indeed spectacular.

None of this would ever have occurred to him if Lily hadn't happened to mention it. But she had, and now it almost felt like fate. They'd been texting and emailing, and yesterday he'd told her about having just been gazumped at the last minute on a property in Kensington. The deal had fallen through and now he needed to find somewhere else to invest in. Lily had said that if he fancied buying something outside of London, there was a cottage coming up for auction on the edge of their village. She'd added that it was in a complete state but had fantastic views, and planning permission, and could look amazing once it was done up.

When he'd found the property online, Declan couldn't disagree. He'd bought country-based properties before, but not for the last few years. Maybe it would make a nice change to leave behind the hassle of snarled-up traffic and endless parking problems. It would be a sound enough investment, he knew that; there was nothing wealthy Londoners liked more than escaping to a high-spec, beautifully renovated Cotswold cottage at the weekend as a break from their frantic urban lives.

Coral's breath caught in her throat at the sight of Declan Madison making his way in through the just-opened blue and gold iron gates. 'Hello! Wow, when you said you were coming down today, I didn't realise you meant this early!'

Oh, but it was so nice to see him again. She knew he and Lily had been in regular contact, but when he'd called Lily yesterday to let them know he was coming, Coral's heart had done that skippety-excited thing and it had felt both thrilling and scary. But common sense had prevailed; as she'd decided after that sleepless night following his first visit, since nothing

152

could come of it, she was simply going to regard him as a practice run and enjoy the fact that her body was showing signs of coming back to life.

Nick wouldn't mind, she was sure. He would approve.

She greeted Declan with a kiss on the cheek and breathed him in. Hopefully with enough discretion to ensure he didn't notice.

'I'm early for a reason. Where's Lily?'

'Driving a vanload of parcels over to the depot. She'll be back by ten. We weren't expecting you before eleven.'

'OK, it'll be done by then.' Declan checked his wristwatch, then glanced over at Marty, who was making himself a coffee in the office. 'Do you have to be right here, or could Marty hold the fort for forty minutes?'

Coral found herself transfixed by his gaze, by the something unspoken he seemed to be signalling to her with his dark-ringed steel-grey eyes. For a micro-second she wondered if Declan was suggesting that Marty might like to hold the fort while he whisked her upstairs to her bedroom for forty minutes of wild, glorious, spectacular—

No, no, of *course* that wasn't what he was suggesting. Honestly, what was happening to her? It was like all her hormones had woken up after a hundred years and started going completely haywire.

All of a fluster she said, 'Of course he can. Marty can hold anything.' *Good God, my hormones have turned into innuendo-laden teenagers.* 'I mean, it's fine, we're not busy, most people don't start coming in until mid-morning. What is it you want?'

Oh phew, and there was that smile again; he really did have a way with him. Not to mention a girlfriend.

'Come with me and I'll show you.' As he spoke, Declan lightly touched her arm. 'I'm in need of your expertise.'

The Valentine Hotel was just outside Stanton Langley. When you reached the traffic lights at the end of the high street and turned left on to Norton Road, the hotel was five hundred metres further along on the right. As Declan pulled into the car park, the possibility that he'd booked a room for them bounced into Coral's head like an exuberant puppy. *OK, stop this, stop it right now, you're being ridiculous.* The next second, she saw the sign next to the entrance announcing that the local estate agent was holding a property auction here today.

There, see? Calm down, woman. Get a grip.

The auction was taking place in the Wedding Room, complete with glittering chandeliers, full-length ivory silk curtains and light sprinklings of confetti on the polished oak parquet floor, left over from last night's party. Most of the assembled bidders, by way of contrast, were a lot less glamorous.

'This one,' Declan murmured, pointing to the number in the catalogue. 'Lily told me about it yesterday. What do you think?'

They'd taken up positions at the back of the room. His warm breath in her ear was doing nothing whatsoever to calm Coral's heart rate. He was considering buying a house on the edge of the village? Right here in Stanton Langley?

Oh, come on, idiot, he's a property developer.

'To do up and sell? Good idea!' She bent her head over the catalogue so he couldn't see her face and realise she'd been thinking rogue thoughts. 'It's a bit of a mess, but easy enough to renovate. Old Malcolm lived there, but he died at Easter. Sad, but he was ninety-three.'

'And do you know any of these people?' Declan discreetly indicated the rest of the room. 'I'm the outsider here. Any information gratefully received.'

He was wearing the same aftershave as before; it smelled

delicious on his skin. Gathering herself, Coral glanced around. 'The three men standing by the door are builders,' she whispered. 'The tall woman in the red shirt runs a holiday lettings business. Those two over there are a husband and wife team who do buy-to-let. And the skinny guy at the front works for his dad; they're in property development too.'

'Thanks.'

'I don't know any of the others.'

'That's fine. If I'm bidding with them, can't go too far wrong. It's the one-off buyers who fall in love with somewhere and get carried away that you don't want to go up against.'

Coral nodded, impressed by his professional attitude. 'Do you get butterflies when you're bidding?'

Declan shook his head. 'I've been doing it for too long. That doesn't happen any more. I'm used to it.'

Of course he would be by now. Gosh, he was so cool.

Lily saw Declan and Coral making their way into the yard. 'There you are! Where have you two been?'

'Hello.' Declan greeted her with a hug. 'Sorry, there was just a little something I needed to do.'

'What kind of something?' said Lily, because he was looking incredibly pleased with himself.

He held up a bunch of keys on a cheap plastic key ring. 'Just bought a house.'

She stared at him. 'What?'

'Weaver's Cottage.' Coral was grinning.

'Oh my God, that's amazing!' Lily let out a shriek of delight. 'You actually did it!'

'You were right about it,' said Declan. 'It has real potential.' He jangled the keys. 'I'm heading back over there now.'

Oh, this was exciting. 'Can I come and have a look at it

155

with you? We're not busy here.' She looked at Coral. 'Is that OK?'

'Go on,' said Coral. 'It's fine.'

Declan said, 'Brace yourself, though. The rooms are very purple.'

But when they reached the cottage, all the work that needed doing seemed straightforward enough. Having been assured by Coral that Dempsey's was the best local building contractor by far, Declan had approached Bill Dempsey at the auction and arranged to meet him at the property. Within twenty minutes, as they made their way through the brightly painted rooms discussing ideas and taking pages of notes and measurements, he'd hired Bill to do the work that needed to be done. Ten minutes after that, he'd put calls through to the best local landscape gardener, the best painter and decorator and the best kitchen fitters in the area.

'Blimey,' said Lily, impressed. 'You don't hang about, do you?'

'Ah well, time is money.' Declan looked amused.

Lily pointed to the narrow window at the side of the cottage, which had no view to speak of but would get the sun in the morning. 'You could use stained glass in that frame.'

'Can you find some for me?' said Declan.

'Definitely. Or there's a guy in Chipping Norton who makes it. You could commission your own design . . . and this could be Coral wanting me to get back.'

It wasn't Coral. When Lily saw who was calling, she said, 'Oh, let me just take this,' and slipped outside, leaving Declan and Bill to discuss lintels and stripped-out door frames.

'Hi,' said Eddie Tessler.

'Calling me again in the middle of the night? More jet lag?'

'Maybe, but I'm about to solve that problem.'

Her ear was still tingling from the sound of his voice. 'And how are you planning on doing that?'

'By flying back to the place whose time zone I'm compatible with. What are you up to tomorrow night?'

Caught off guard, Lily said, 'You're coming back to Stanton Langley?' Oh God, what a stupid thing to say. Of course he wasn't doing that.

Eddie laughed and she felt even more ridiculous.

'Not quite, but I'm flying into Heathrow. Now listen, would you be free?'

She proceeded with caution. 'To do what?'

'You told me the other week you'd always fancied the idea of going to a movie premiere, remember?'

'I remember. And you said they were boring.'

'And *you* said maybe I thought they were boring because I was a miserable old sod.'

Oh yes, she did remember coming out with something along those lines. Lily batted away a hovering wasp and said, 'Bit rude of me. Sorry about that.'

'No problem. So how about it?'

'How about what?' She held her breath; no way was she about to jump to conclusions and make a twit of herself twice in two minutes.

'I'm going to the premiere of *Catcher* in Leicester Square tomorrow night.' Patiently he spelled it out for her. 'You told me you'd always wanted to go to a premiere. So would you like to come along with me to this one?'

Ask a silly question.

'Seriously? I'd love to. You mean I'd actually get to walk along the red carpet?' Oh wow, this was thrilling . . .

'No, I'd just sneak you in through the back door.'

What? Disappointed, Lily said, 'Oh, right.'

'Kidding,' said Eddie. 'Of course you'd be on the red carpet. But I'm warning you now, people will want to know who you are.'

'That's OK. It's not as if they'll be interested once they find out I'm a nobody. God, thanks so much for inviting me, though. What time does it start and finish, so I can book my train tickets?'

'Hey, no need, I'll send a car to pick you up around three, if that's OK, and book you into a hotel for the night. Do you have to be at work the next day?'

Lily pictured the works diary, pinned up in the office. 'Yes, I do. I'd need to be back by ten, ten thirty.'

'Fine, we'll arrange that, then. And I'll see you tomorrow afternoon. What are you going to do with your hair?'

What *was* she going to do with her hair? Her hand, moving instinctively to her head, encountered a sticky clump of old spider's web from where they'd explored the dusty attic of Weaver's Cottage. 'I'll probably wash it,' she said.

He laughed. 'Are you going to enjoy yourself at the premiere?'

'Are you serious? Of course I am!'

'In that case,' Eddie's tone was genial, 'I promise I will too.'

Chapter 23

Casually dropping the news into conversation in front of Dan was, needless to say, the best bit of all.

They'd already booked a table at the Star that evening, so that Declan could meet Patsy, Sean and Will. Then Dan had ended up tagging along too – well, limping along – what with him being incapable of preparing his own food, and the weather had been warm enough for them all to eat outside in the pub garden beneath the trees strung with silver fairy lights and hanging jars of citronella candles.

Watching them, Lily glowed with happiness at the way the group had so effortlessly expanded to include Declan. Everyone liked him and he in turn was getting on with each of them. As darkness fell and the stars came out, stories and memories continued to be swapped. Dan, refilling their glasses with wine, said, 'When I was five or six, I remember Lily's mum explaining to me how a pulley system worked. She threw a rope over one of the low branches of the ash tree in our garden to show me, then she went into the house and I tied the rope around Lily's waist and tried to haul her up into the tree.'

'Except you let go and dropped me and I landed splat on the ground,' Lily protested amidst collective laughter at the memory. 'All my growing-up years, you kept coming up with brilliant new ways to torture me and I never had the chance to get my own back because I was always two years younger than you.'

Dan clapped his good hand to his chest in disbelief. 'Are you kidding me, are you actually serious? You were *always* getting your own back on me! What about the time I fell asleep on the sofa before my first date with Cara Mason and you drew giant eyelashes on my face with felt pen?'

Oh yes, that had been brilliant. 'You couldn't have been that excited about the date if you could fall asleep two hours beforehand. Plus,' Lily reminded him, 'it's not my fault you woke up and went out to meet her without even bothering to look in a mirror first.'

'Why would I look in a mirror?' He mimed confusion. 'I'm not a girl.'

Patsy joined in, giving him a nudge. 'And there was the time I was too busy to cut your hair so Lily offered to do it instead. Remember that?'

Dan shuddered. 'How could I forget? She actually made me believe she could do it.'

Lily grinned. 'That was to pay you back for telling everyone on the school bus that I was wearing my first ever bra.'

'What?' Dan did a double-take. 'Hang on, that was when you were twelve. The hair-cutting thing happened a whole year later.'

'And do you remember how long all the boys made fun of me by twanging the back strap of my bra? They carried on doing it for *months*,' said Lily. 'Anyway, I got my revenge in the end, and it was worth the wait.'

'What about the time we went on that school trip to the water park?' Dan's dark eyes glinted in the reflected candlelight

160

as he shook his head sorrowfully at her. 'I still don't know how you managed it but I *know* it was you who swapped my swimming trunks for a bikini.'

'I have no idea why you'd think that was me.' A decade on from that triumphant occasion, Lily gave him an innocent smile. It had actually involved creeping into his house the night before and replacing the trunks in his sports bag with the old-fashioned pink bikini she'd bought for fifty pence from a charity shop.

Coral said, 'Unless it was to pay Dan back for that rumour he spread about you having a big crush on Moggy Blake.'

'Oh, Moggy.' Lily groaned at the memory of the boy who'd smelled of cat wee and followed girls around miaowing at them. The idea that she could secretly be lusting after him had been mortifying at the time.

'You know you loved him really,' said Dan.

Lily threw a French fry across the table at him. 'You were a nightmare. You still are.'

Dan picked the French fry off the front of his shirt and ate it. 'So you're the one who hid my bicycle up a tree, yet I'm the nightmare.'

'You two are like a double act,' said Declan. 'Seriously, you're Tom and Jerry.'

Everyone burst out laughing. 'That's what Mum used to call us,' Lily explained. 'All the time.'

'I was Tom,' said Dan. 'She was Jerry. Mainly on account of her enormous ears.'

'I was Jerry because I was smaller,' Lily retorted, 'and because I didn't have fleas.'

'Don't worry,' said Patsy. 'They're always like this. They love each other really.'

'In the non-physical sense,' said Lily. 'I'm not *that* stupid.'

'Lily prefers film stars these days.' Dan's tone was playful. 'If they're thousands of miles away and give her a quick call, that pretty much makes her day.'

Lily suppressed a yelp of triumph, because she'd *known* he wouldn't be able to resist mentioning Eddie and making fun of her silly crush on him. It had almost killed her not mentioning it earlier, but now that Dan had done the honours, she could go ahead. And again, totally worth the wait.

Savouring the moment and taking a sip of ice-cold wine, she gave Dan the benefit of the insouciant smile she'd practised earlier in front of the mirror. 'Actually, he's been in touch again.'

Ha, and this time she hadn't blurted it out like a small child incapable of keeping a secret for more than two minutes.

Oh yes, being insouciant was definitely the way to go.

'He has? Did he send you another text?' Dan's eyes were bright with mischief. 'Was it definitely from him, or did he get his assistant to do it?'

So smug. So, *so* smug. Lily idly tipped her wine glass this way and that, then said casually, 'Oh no, it was definitely his voice on the phone. He's flying back to the UK this evening. The reason he called was to invite me to London tomorrow night.'

Ha. Ha! Fifteen love to *me*.

Dan had been lounging back on his chair. Now his shoulders stiffened. 'Oh? To do what?'

'He asked me to go along with him to the premiere of *Catcher*. In Leicester Square.' Thirty love.

'So exciting,' Coral exclaimed. 'Have you decided yet what you're going to wear?'

'Either the yellow dress with the beading, or the red one.' It wasn't as if she had many to choose from.

'Oh, the red is *lovely*,' said Patsy. 'That's my favourite.'

'Mine too, but we'll be on the red carpet. It might make me . . . you know,' Lily gestured down at herself, 'a bit invisible.'

'*Catcher*'s set in the future,' said Dan. 'You don't like films set in the future.'

'That doesn't matter,' Coral told him. 'It's a premiere! There'll be all sorts going on!'

'How will you get home afterwards?' Dan put his drink down on the table.

'He's booked a hotel.' Forty love. 'And a car to get me there and back.' Unable to resist it, Lily added, 'Well, a limo.'

'Of course he has.' Gone was Dan's air of mischief; in the dim light and with his narrowed dark eyes and shadowed cheekbones, he now resembled Mr Darcy being all disapproving and taut-jawed.

Fantastic. Game, set and match.

'I can't wait,' said Lily. 'It's going to be amazing.'

'Just don't—' Dan stopped himself in his tracks and exhaled.

'Just don't forget to have fun?' Lily beamed triumphantly at him. 'Don't worry, I won't!'

Dan and Patsy had departed, as had Sean and Will. With just the three of them left, they'd headed next door to Goldstone House. Declan had been finishing his coffee when Lily brought downstairs the box containing all the birthday letters from her mother.

When he'd finished reading them, Declan had to gather himself for a moment before he was able to speak. Finally he said, 'Thank you for showing them to me.'

'I wanted you to see them.' Lily was winding a length of curly ribbon from the box around her index finger. 'Aren't they good?'

Declan nodded slowly, because they were better than good.

Jo had taken care to make each letter appropriate to the age Lily would have been when she read it for the first time. As she'd grown up, so the words and sentences had grown longer. 'Her voice is so clear in them,' he marvelled. 'I can hear her saying every word.'

'I know.' Coral smiled. 'We all can.'

In one of the earlier letters Jo had said, *Darling Lily, I know you'll always be happy with Coral and Nick. They love you so much – to the moon and back! And maybe one day they'll have a baby of their own, then you can all be happy together! Oh wouldn't that be fantastic?*

'Am I allowed to ask, or is it too personal?' Declan lightly tapped the relevant letter and looked at Coral. 'You didn't have any other children . . .?' It *was* a highly personal question, but somehow it seemed safe to ask it tonight.

Coral smiled briefly. 'We tried, but it just never happened. Maybe we could have tried harder, investigated other avenues . . . but we had Lily, so somehow it didn't seem as important. Thanks to this one,' she affectionately touched Lily's shoulder, 'we weren't desperate. She was Jo's gift to us. She was ours and she was enough.'

Their eyes met across the table and Declan said gently, 'That's good.'

'How about you?' said Coral. 'Did you ever want children?'

They were already aware that he didn't have any of his own. Declan said, 'I lived with a lovely woman fifteen years ago. We were together for four years. We tried for a family, Meg got pregnant, then she miscarried.' He hesitated, then said, 'Twice. Both times at ten weeks.'

'Oh I'm sorry, that must have been awful,' said Lily. 'For both of you.'

'It was a rough time,' Declan admitted. 'Meg was devastated.

We broke up a year after the second miscarriage. The good news is, I heard through friends that she married an Italian guy and went on to have healthy twin boys.' He shrugged. 'I'm happy for her.'

'Not so easy, though, is it?' There were sympathetic tears in Coral's eyes.

'It was a long time ago. I'm used to it now.' Finishing the last mouthful of coffee, Declan said, 'Life goes on.'

It was 1.30 in the morning by the time Declan arrived back in Notting Hill. When he saw the lights on in the house, he knew Gail had come over and let herself in, and was waiting for him. Well, either that or the burglar had forgotten his torch.

When he climbed the stairs and pushed open the bedroom door, she was sitting up in his bed.

'Hi,' said Declan.

'Darling, I'm sorry.' She closed her laptop and placed it on the bedside table. Her long hair gleamed in the flattering lamplight and she was wearing an elegant pistachio silk nightdress. 'What can I tell you? I was having a tough day at work, everyone else was being an idiot and I wanted to yell at them but I couldn't. Then I got your text and took it out on you.'

'Right. I guessed it might have been something like that.' Declan kept his tone neutral. When she'd messaged him earlier to ask where he was, he'd told her Stanton Langley without elaborating further. The reply had come flying back:

Sounds to me like you'd far rather be there than here. It's been nice knowing you. Goodbye.

This message had come through at three o'clock, while he'd been at Weaver's Cottage meeting with the kitchen fitter recommended to him by Coral. He'd switched off his mobile without replying.

'Come here.' Gail held out her toned arms, beckoning him closer. 'I didn't mean it. You do know I didn't mean it, don't you?'

Declan hesitated, then nodded. There were unshed tears shimmering in her eyes and she was silently pleading with him for forgiveness, which wasn't something that came naturally to her.

'I do. Listen, there's nothing to worry about. I met Lily and her friends and family. I like them all. But I like Stanton Langley too. It's a fantastic place. If you saw it, you'd understand what I'm talking about.'

Gail was nodding along enthusiastically as he said it, eager to make amends. 'I will, I'd like to. So you went there today to see Lily *and* the village. It'd be great to meet her. We could go down next weekend.'

'Fine, we'll do that. I bought a property there this morning.'

That took her aback. 'You did?'

'It's my job. I went along to the auction and snapped it up.' He shrugged. 'It's a great investment.'

'To *live* in?'

'Not to live in.' He shook his head; she knew he'd often talked about one day leaving London and moving out to Kent or maybe Berkshire. As a committed city-dweller herself, the idea was anathema to her.

'So it's just something to do up and sell on.' She looked relieved.

'I haven't decided yet. Either sell it on, or add it to the portfolio and let it out. If you did want to come and see it for yourself, you could tell me what you think.'

'I will. And I'm sorry about earlier.' Gail reached for him

and pulled his face down to hers for a kiss, then patted the mattress beside her. 'It's late, come to bed.'

'I'm pretty tired,' said Declan before she could get any ideas. 'Here, I took some photos of the cottage.' He handed her his phone and began to unbutton his shirt.

'Looks pretty run-down.' Gail scrolled through the pictures. She'd never been particularly interested in his career. 'If it weren't,' Declan explained, 'I wouldn't be buying it. See those views over the valley? That's the money shot, right there. You'll never lose on a place with views like that.'

'And this is Lily and her friends.' Already bored with photos of peeling purple wallpaper and unevenly plastered ceilings, Gail was scrolling further on through the gallery. 'Seems like a nice place, wherever it is.'

'We had dinner in the garden of the local pub, the Star Inn.'

'They all look great too.' Keen to make up for her earlier strop, she was now being extra-magnanimous. 'So that's the woman who adopted her, yes? Carol?'

'Coral.'

'Right. And the brunette?'

'That's Patsy, she's a hairdresser. She used to babysit when Lily was small and they've been close ever since.'

'And this one?' Gail pointed to Dan. 'Is he Lily's boyfriend?'

'No, they're just friends. He's Patsy's younger brother.'

'He's very good-looking.'

'And knows it.' Declan climbed into bed. 'He's an airline pilot.'

'Oh damn, *hairdresser*.' Raising her palms in despair, Gail said, 'I completely forgot, I've got an appointment at Fenn Lomax next Saturday afternoon.'

'Well you can always call them and cancel,' said Declan.

'Patsy has her own salon in Stanton Langley. I'm sure she could fit you in while we're down there.'

Gail threw back her head and barked with laughter. 'You mean I should cancel my appointment with Fenn Lomax and let some village hairdresser loose on my hair instead? Oh darling . . . ha ha ha, this is why I love you so much!'

Chapter 24

Lily couldn't stop gazing out through the tinted window of the limousine. Leicester Square was packed, ablaze with lights and buzzing with anticipation. The red carpet stretched ahead of them like a river, cordoned off from the fans squashed up against the metal barriers. There were TV cameras and reporters and security staff with earpieces and walkie-talkies milling about.

'Well?' said Eddie, next to her on the back seat. 'What d'you think?'

'It looks just like it does on the telly. Look at all the *people*.'

He smiled. 'That's kind of the point. If there's a film premiere but nobody turns up to see the stars arrive, did it ever really happen?'

'I knew it'd be busy,' said Lily, 'but I didn't think it'd be this busy.'

'Ah well, it helps that it isn't raining. Are you ready?' he added as the car moved up a few feet towards the head of the queue. 'We're next.'

Oh wow, surreal or what? The gleaming black chauffeur-driven car had collected them from the hotel just a few streets away, then crawled through the rush-hour traffic to bring them here, despite the fact that it would have been five times quicker to walk.

And now it was drawing to a halt at the head of the queue and the door was being opened. Lily took a deep breath to quell the butterflies and smoothed down the skirt of her favourite red dress to ensure she wasn't about to flash her knickers to the world.

A dazzle of flashbulbs went off and she blinked, then blinked again as Eddie intertwined his fingers with hers. The photographers were calling out his name, even as a female organiser with a clipboard was shepherding them towards the press pen.

'You wait here with me for a minute,' the organiser murmured, resting her hand on Lily's forearm. 'Let them get their shots of Eddie.'

Eddie had to stand in front of a giant backdrop featuring logos of the film and various companies advertising the event. He was wearing a gorgeously cut dark blue suit and cream shirt, and his hair was slicked back from his tanned face. Lily had never seen him looking so smart and so much like a film star; watching him now was making her stomach go a bit squiggly, if she was honest.

After a minute or two, he beckoned for her to join him, and the female organiser moved across to lead her over.

'What's your name, love?' one of the photographers called out.

Lily shook her head. 'It's OK, I'm no one.'

'Come on, tell us who you are,' said another man.

The organiser gave her a distracted nod. 'It's OK, you can tell them.'

Giving her permission. Imagine that.

'My name's Patsy,' said Lily, just for fun. And it *was* fun, because the photographers instantly began calling out: 'This way, Patsy!'

'Over here, Patsy!'

'Patsy, give us a smile!'

Out of the corner of her mouth Lily said to Eddie, 'This is the craziest thing.'

His arm was around her waist, his hip brushing against hers. 'Enjoying having your photo taken?'

'Oh yes. Although I do know I'm going to end up getting cropped out of ninety-nine per cent of them.'

He tilted his head closer to hers and murmured, 'I'm not sure I'm going to be able to remember to keep calling you Patsy.'

Lily grinned at him. 'Don't worry, I'll change it in a minute. Can you hear all those girls over there screaming your name?'

'I can now you've said it. We'll have to go along the carpet in a minute.'

'Right.' The officious organiser checked her stopwatch and signalled that it was indeed time for them to move on. 'All done here.'

The next arrivals were emerging from their limos, ready to take their place in front of the backdrop.

As the slow journey along the red carpet began, the flashes from the professional photographers' elaborate cameras became interspersed with those from the overexcited fans' mobile phones. Lily hung back while Eddie chatted to those behind the barriers and allowed himself to be photographed with them.

'Will you sign me here?' A big girl in a plunging T-shirt handed him a black felt-tip pen and patted the area above the low-cut top. She gazed at Eddie adoringly as he scrawled an autograph across her chest. When he'd finished, she said, 'I'm going to get that done as a tattoo tomorrow. Oh my God, I just love you so much!'

'I don't think you should have it tattooed there.' Lily couldn't help herself; she had to say it. As a signature, it wasn't even legible, for heaven's sake.

'Who asked you?' The overweight girl shot her an insolent stare. 'I don't give a toss what you think.'

Eddie had moved on to have a selfie taken with a squealing group. Lily noticed that the overweight girl's jacket pocket was moving. She pointed. 'What have you got in there?'

The girl stiffened. 'My mouse. What's it to you? I can bring my mouse with me if I want.'

Honestly, so defensive. 'I didn't say you couldn't. What's his name?'

'Snowball.'

Lily smiled. 'I used to have a mouse when I was younger.'

'What was yours called?'

'William.'

'That's a stupid name for a mouse.'

'I know. I don't know what I was thinking. Can I have a look at Snowball?'

'No.' The girl shook her head, then leaned across the barrier and lowered her voice. 'I don't want people to see him and start screaming. I might get kicked out.'

'Good point.' Lily nodded sympathetically. 'I once took William along to our school nativity play and got sent off the stage.'

The girl managed a faint smile. 'Are you Eddie's girlfriend?'

'No, I'm not.'

'Are you an actress?'

'No.' Lily hesitated; Eddie was waiting for her, ready to move on to the next group. 'Listen, don't get his name tattooed on your chest. It'll be there for the rest of your life.'

The girl's expression changed. 'Oh don't start that again. I *want* it to be there for the rest of my life.'

'But when you have a boyfriend, he might not like seeing someone else's name on his girlfriend's chest.'

The girl shrugged. 'I'm never going to get a boyfriend anyway. Boys don't fancy me.'

'Come along, you need to catch up with Eddie.' Steering Lily firmly on, the organiser whispered, 'We need to keep going. Thought I'd come and rescue you.'

'She wants to have Eddie's signature tattooed on her chest. I was trying to persuade her not to.'

'Ah well, not our problem.' The organiser was more concerned with keeping everyone moving to make way for Mira Knowles, the star of the show.

It was hard not to keep turning round and stealing glances at Mira Knowles, although being on the red carpet presumably meant being too cool to do so. In her mid-thirties, Mira had been acting in films since childhood and was proper Hollywood royalty. Tonight, with her hair in an intricate dark chignon and wearing a stunning full-length dress covered in tiny iridescent pearls, she radiated ice-queen glamour. Having waved to the fans but not stopped to speak to them, she was now being interviewed by a TV crew.

'And what's your name?'

'Sorry?' Lily belatedly realised someone was addressing her. 'Oh, I'm no one, I'm just here with Eddie.'

The male journalist was holding a microphone. 'You must have a name, though!'

'I'm Coral. But I'm not his girlfriend,' said Lily.

'And who are you wearing?'

'This? It's vintage. Dior, I think.' Could she be sued for telling such an outrageous lie? Whoops, and now the girl with him was photographing her. Hurriedly Lily said, 'Actually it's not Dior. It's New Look.'

'Oh dear.' The young journalist sniggered. 'You really are no one.'

Lily shrugged and said, 'I told you.'

'Don't be so rude.' The photographer rolled her eyes at the journalist. 'Nothing wrong with a bit of New Look.'

'So, Coral, do you wish you were Eddie's girlfriend? Bet you do,' said the journalist.

'I don't,' said Lily. 'He snores.'

OK, shouldn't have said that either. Embarrassed, Lily looked away and found herself glancing over again at Mira Knowles. The next moment she noticed something tiny and determined making its way at top speed across the red carpet in the direction of—

'AAAAARRRGH!' If the shriek was ear-splitting, the leap into the air that accompanied it was frankly impressive. Mira Knowles screamed again as she began hopping around in terror. With every hop, the likelihood of her spearing the mouse with a stiletto increased.

And somehow, no one else had spotted the cause of the kerfuffle.

Lily, only three or four metres away, launched herself in some kind of rugby-tackle dive and with her arms stretched out in front of her managed to grab the petrified mouse in the nick of time. She snatched it from beneath Mira's lethal high heels and rolled sideways, clutching Snowball to her chest.

'Urgh! Has it gone? Has it really gone? Oh my God, that was *so* disgusting!' Mira shuddered with revulsion, then let out another high-pitched scream as one of the security guards hauled Lily to her feet a bit too vigorously and for a moment she lost her balance, stumbling towards the actress with the mouse clasped in her hands.

OK, that wouldn't be clever, tipping Snowball headlong into Mira Knowles's fabulous cleavage. Balance regained, Lily said, 'It's fine, I'll get him away from you.' She turned, searched the crowds behind the barrier and saw the girl with Eddie's autograph scrawled across her chest.

The girl was pale with anguish as Lily handed Snowball over to her, though not before the mouse had done a little wee in her hand. Well, it had been a stressful experience for him, almost getting skewered by a Jimmy Choo.

'He didn't get hurt. Luckily.' Lily gave Snowball's tiny head a stroke and shot the girl a meaningful look.

The girl flushed, caught out. 'I thought Mira would be fine with him. When she plays characters in films, she's always really brave, never scared of anything.'

'You thought she'd pick Snowball up and bring him back to you, and then she'd talk to you about him, was that the plan?'

'Maybe. Kind of.'

'Another idea that wasn't so great.' Lily felt sorry for her. 'Listen, how about getting the tattooist to trace the signature and put it somewhere else on your body? Would you at least have a think about it?'

The girl hung her head for a second then said, 'Yeah, OK. I'll do that.'

'And make sure Snowball doesn't escape again.'

'He won't.'

It wasn't until Lily turned to make her way back to Eddie that she realised quite how many people were now taking photos of her. Flash-flash-flash went the lights, dazzling her for a moment until Eddie, grinning, reached for her hand.

'You were like the SAS, throwing yourself at Mira's feet like that. Talk about impressive.'

'I thought she was going to stamp on it and kill it.'

'She nearly did.' His grin broadened. 'You're a real mice-saver.'

'Everyone's looking at me.' Lily was finding it an unsettling experience, being the object of so many people's attention. 'Now I know what it's like for you,' she said ruefully.

'D'you want the good news or the bad news?'

'Both.'

'You're probably going to be on the front pages of the tabloids tomorrow.'

Was that the good or the bad? Lily searched his face for clues. 'And?'

'When you did your SAS thing and launched yourself across the carpet, your dress flew right up at the back.'

Oh. *Oh.* Lily sighed. 'Just my luck. Did everyone see my knickers?'

'Not quite. You had about an inch to spare.' He grinned. 'But it's a relief to know you were wearing some.'

Waaaahhh, just imagine . . .

'Come on,' said Eddie, 'don't worry about it. Mira wants to see you, and I'm sure all the journalists are going to be desperate for a word too.' He led her over to Mira. 'Here she is, then.'

And indeed, here she was.

'Hey, it's the scene-stealer,' exclaimed Mira Knowles.

'Sorry.' Lily inwardly cursed her own Britishness.

Mira smiled her dazzling film-star smile – up close, her teeth were nothing short of astonishing – and said, 'I'm kidding! You rescued me and I'm so grateful! My whole life I've been petrified of little scuttly things, and mice are, like, the scuttliest.

You were so brave doing that, catching it in your hands.' She shuddered at the mere thought. 'Urgh, so gross. Anyhow, thank you for saving me.'

'No problem. I like mice.' Lily was still hyper-aware of the cameras upon her, the journalists attempting to attract her attention, people murmuring to each other, 'Who is she?'

And other people replying, 'Her name's Patsy Somebody-or-other.'

Whereupon other voices said, 'No it's not, she's called Coral.'

'Could we have some pictures of the three of you together?' In response to the photographers, the organiser was making squeeze-up gestures with her splayed hands. The next moment Lily found herself with Eddie on one side of her and Mira Knowles on the other. It was like being in a film-star sandwich. And Mira had her arm around her waist.

Somewhere over to the left, she heard a voice say, 'Did we get the shot with her skirt flying up?'

And the reply: 'Yup.'

Then a camera crew approached them and a reporter was saying, 'Mira, how are you feeling after that close encounter?'

'Grateful towards my rescuer! She's my new best friend!' As she said it, Mira clasped Lily's hand and gave it a best-friend squeeze. This probably wasn't the moment to tell her it was also the hand Snowball had done a panicky wee on.

'Hey, Coral, turn this way!'

'Patsy! Over here!'

The organiser gave her an odd look and said, 'Which one are you?'

'Neither,' said Eddie. 'She's Lily.'

'Oh, *you're* Lily,' Mira exclaimed, turning her headlight gaze on her. 'I didn't realise! Eddie's told me all about you!'

★　★　★

Once the film was over, Mira said, 'So, what are you two up to now?'

'I was planning to take Lily out to dinner,' said Eddie. 'I've booked a table at—'

'Oh don't do that. No no no,' Mira protested, clutching Lily's hand again.

'I'm hungry, though.' Lily was torn. 'Aren't you hungry?'

'Are you serious? Look at me.' Mira indicated her whippet-thin waist and hips. 'I spend my whole life hungry. But we don't have to go *out*, do we? We're all at the same hotel, so why don't we have dinner in my suite?'

'Well . . .' Eddie wasn't sounding enthusiastic.

'Oh please,' Mira begged. 'My driver's waiting out back; he can take us there now. I'll die of boredom if you two don't keep me company. Come on,' she reiterated, intertwining Lily's fingers with her own. 'Say yes! It'll be fun!'

Chapter 25

It was one o'clock in the morning, and Eddie Tessler was marvelling at the way the seduction he'd organised with such care had spectacularly failed to go according to plan.

The more time he'd spent with Lily the other week, the more he'd liked her. Everything about her, in fact. Her quirky character appealed to him; she was funny and bright; and with those huge brown eyes and that riot of curly golden hair she almost resembled a cartoon. She was also pretty but remarkably unvain, which was a draw. For the last couple of years he felt as if all he'd encountered was girls obsessed with how they looked, from their acrylic nails to their fake tans.

So when he'd called to invite her along to this evening's premiere, he'd have been lying if he'd said he wasn't interested in getting to know her better and moving their relationship to the next level. When a twenty-five-year-old girl still lived at home with the person who was effectively her mother, it created a certain dilemma. Bringing her up to London had been intended to overcome that problem. He'd envisaged a romantic dinner *à deux*, a deepening of the attraction between them, an even more romantic moonlight walk along the glittering banks of the Thames as they made their way back to the hotel, followed by maybe one last glass of champagne in the bar before they headed, hand in hand, up to either his room or hers . . .

What he *hadn't* counted on was having this carefully planned sequence of events banjaxed by an A-list actress with a low boredom threshold and a profound love of word games.

Worse, it was pretty much his own fault. When he and Mira had been over in LA last week promoting the US release of *Catcher*, he'd found himself telling her all about Lily. He'd also stressed how natural and unaffected she was and how utterly trustworthy she'd been, keeping the secret of his stay at Stanton Langley when so many others wouldn't have been able to resist giving it away.

This had been the particular draw for Mira, who'd been famous for so much longer than he had. To be reassured that you could allow yourself to relax completely in the company of someone and not worry that they might be indiscreet was a wonderful feeling, and once Lily had said to her, 'Don't worry, I don't blab,' Mira's relief had been palpable.

Then Mira had mentioned her passion for Scrabble and that had been it, because it transpired that Lily loved Scrabble too. For the next two hours they'd all drunk whisky and gossiped and played a demon match narrowly won by Lily, who'd then gone on to introduce them to another game called Word Squares that had had Mira entranced. More whisky and laughter and boisterous debates ensued . . .

Undeniably it had been a great evening, but to say it hadn't been the kind Eddie had been looking forward to was something of an understatement.

'Oh God, we've finished the whisky!' Lily was now pointing with disbelief at the empty bottle on the table.

'It's fine, doesn't matter,' Mira assured her. 'We can call room service and get some more.'

Lily shook her head a bit wildly, her ringlets bouncing around her shoulders like springs. 'No no, we don't want more. I mean we've finished all that whisky. And I have to be up in five hours to go to work and I'm not even a whisky-drinking person . . .'

'Well you should be.' Mira had long ago kicked off her shoes and changed out of her pearl-encrusted evening dress into a camisole top and shorts. 'You drink it very well.'

Lily grinned. 'Thank you. I didn't know until tonight that I liked it.'

'Call it my gift to you. I taught you to enjoy whisky, you taught us to play Word Squares.'

'I should go to bed.'

Yes, we should, thought Eddie.

'Oh no! Just one more game, pleeeease,' Mira begged. 'I want to beat your best score.'

'You won't beat it.' Lily shook her head pityingly. 'Forty-three is a magnificent score.'

Mira bounced up and down on the sofa. 'Let me try, let me try! I love this game so much!'

'Go on then. One last game. Draw your squares,' said Lily, stifling a yawn. 'But after this I really need to go to sleep.'

'Hang on, quick bathroom break.' Leaping to her feet, Mira held up a skinny index finger. 'I'll be back in *one* minute.'

It took Eddie less than forty seconds to fetch a bottle of iced water from the minibar in the next room, but by the time he returned, Lily had already reached her limit. The notepad and pen were still resting in her lap, her bare legs were curled up beneath her and her head had fallen to one side. Her eyes were closed, her mouth was very slightly open, her breathing slow and regular.

She was fast asleep.

Back from the bathroom, Mira stared in dismay. 'Oh man, what did you let her do *that* for?'

Eddie shook his head. 'I didn't. I just went to get a drink. The next second, she was out for the count.'

'Well that's no good. Wake her up, I want another game!'

Mira was accustomed to having her every whim instantly catered for. Eddie said, 'She's wiped out. I'll get her to her room.'

'Then will *you* come back and play Word Squares with me?'

Their body clocks were both messed up after having just flown over from LA. Eddie wasn't tired either. Just disappointed.

He said, 'I'm pretty shattered too. Going to call it a night.'

A night devoid of sex, thanks to you.

'You're no fun,' Mira complained. 'That means I'm going to have to call Monty, get him over here to play Word Squares.'

Monty was the long-suffering personal assistant who travelled everywhere with Mira and would be fast asleep right now.

'You do that,' said Eddie. 'I'm sure he won't mind at all.'

He bent down, put the pen and paper on the silver-embossed coffee table and gently hauled Lily to her feet. 'Come on, I'm taking you to your room.'

Lily's eyes half opened and she nodded. 'OK.'

'Bye, sweetie! I totally forgive you for crashing out on me!' Mira had already called Monty's number and was waiting impatiently for him to pick up.

'Bye.' Lily's dark lashes flickered as she leaned against Eddie's side and allowed him to help her out of the suite. In his left hand he carried her shoes and evening bag. She smelled of whisky and shampoo and the chocolate they'd devoured between them from the minibar.

Finally they reached their rooms, adjacent to each other.

Eddie found Lily's key card in her bag and pushed open the door for her.

'I'm so tired,' Lily whispered, placing her arms around his neck. Her eyes still three-quarters closed, she gave him a clumsy kiss on the cheek. '*So* tired. Thanks for everything. I can't believe I played Scrabble with Mira Knowles.'

'And with me,' Eddie reminded her. He was clearly second best.

She nodded in agreement. 'Sorry, and with you.' Resting her face against his chest, she yawned. 'This has been the most amazing night of my life.'

'Good.' Now wasn't the time to tell her it could have been better still. With a rueful smile Eddie said, 'Don't forget. If you need anything, anything at all, I'm just next door.'

Lily nodded again, her hair brushing against the skin exposed by the V of his open-necked shirt. Eddie realised it was the most physical contact he was going to experience. Then she stepped back, took her shoes and bag and said sleepily, 'Thanks so much. G'night.'

'Night,' said Eddie as she shuffled inside and closed the door.

Lily woke with a start at 6.30. OK, time to get up, bit of a headache but nothing a grown twenty-five-year-old couldn't handle. She blinked at the elaborate ceiling cornice overhead, then scanned the room and wondered why there were no clothes strewn over the chairs. Had she actually hung them up in the wardrobe last night? Because that was uncharacteristically efficient.

Then she threw back the bedcovers and realised she was still wearing her premiere dress. Well that solved that mystery. Too much excitement, not enough sleep beforehand and a crash course in whisky had caused her to zonk out. Which was good in one way but somewhat disappointing in another, seeing as she'd wondered if last night might have ended up with altogether less sleeping going on.

Then again, if the idea had only been in her head and not Eddie's, maybe it was just as well. Imagine making a pass at him and being told, gently but firmly, that as far as he was concerned he'd only invited her along because they were friends. And with a bit of whisky inside her, she might well have been tempted to give it a go.

Oh the potential for humiliation. Thank goodness she hadn't done it.

In the shower, to distract herself from thoughts of Eddie, Lily marvelled at everything else that had happened yesterday evening: the premiere . . . the mouse . . . her dress flying up . . . eating pizza from room service with Eddie and Mira whilst teaching them how to play Word Squares . . .

Mad, just mad.

By seven o'clock, she was dressed in jeans and a T-shirt, almost ready to leave. The car would be waiting at the front entrance of the hotel at 7.15 to take her home. Should she knock on Eddie's door and say goodbye, or would he be fast asleep and unamused at being woken up?

But as she gathered together her belongings and collected up all the free things in the luxurious marble bathroom – shampoo, little sewing kit, emery boards, disposable slippers! – Lily heard the sounds of movement next door. Two minutes later, having let herself out of her own room, she hesitated, then tapped on Eddie's door.

It opened almost immediately, and there he was, evidently just out of the shower himself and wearing nothing but a white bath towel slung around his hips.

Which was slightly less than she'd ever seen him in before, and a rather impressive sight.

184

'Hey, how are you feeling?'

Lily hesitated, because the honest answer would have been: a bit dry-mouthed actually, what with you being naked under that towel.

Instead she said brightly, 'I'm great. Can't believe how shattered I was last night! Anyway, just dropped by to say thank you for inviting me. I had the best time ever.'

'Good.' His smile held a hint of wryness. 'I'm glad.'

One tiny thing had been niggling her. 'I won't really be on the front pages of the papers, will I? You weren't serious about that?'

'Who knows?' Eddie shrugged. 'To be honest, it's more likely to be a photo of Mira leaping into the air to get away from the mouse. Alongside another of the mouse itself.'

Lily nodded, reassured. 'It'll be that.'

'Did you want to come in?' He moved to one side, gesturing for her to do so.

'Better not. It's ten past seven. By the time I get downstairs, my car will be waiting.' *Get me, saying 'my car' as if I've been chauffeured around all my life.*

'OK. Well, bye.' He placed his hand at the back of her neck and drew her towards him. 'And thanks for keeping me company. I enjoyed last night far more than I usually do.'

His mouth was an inch from the side of her face, his breath toothpastey and warm. As Lily inhaled the scent of him, he gave her a brief kiss on the cheek . . . then another . . . and one more . . .

Each time his mouth had edged closer to hers, until their lips met. Then several brief kisses transformed into one long one and a rush of heat spread through Lily's stomach, because she'd wondered so often how it would feel to be kissed by Eddie Tessler.

She'd seen him kissing other girls in films, and now at last it was happening to her.

Except this time, hopefully, he wasn't acting.

On the last occasion, when it had seemed as if a kiss was imminent, they'd been interrupted by Dan's unexpected arrival at the cottage.

Dan wasn't here now.

OK, thinking about Dan had to be about *the* most irrelevant thing she could be doing. As she took a step back and gazed up into Eddie's eyes, he said, 'Coming in after all?'

It was definitely a tempting offer.

But Lily shook her head. 'I can't. The car's downstairs.'

'The car would wait. That's what they get paid to do.'

'I know, but I need to get back. For work.' It was set to be busy at the yard: Marty had the day off and they were due a visit from one of their biggest overseas buyers.

'Could you not even be a little bit late?' said Eddie.

'I really can't.'

'You're breaking my heart.'

Lily smiled. 'No I'm not.' Of course it would be possible to keep the car waiting downstairs then drive that bit faster back to Stanton Langley in order to make up the time. But if she was going to sleep with Eddie, she wanted it to be more than a ten-minute quickie.

'If I wasn't stuck doing interviews,' he murmured, 'I'd come with you.'

'I'd still have to work.'

'Not *all* the time.' He stroked the side of her face, his smile regretful. 'OK, I don't want to, but I'm going to let you go. For now.'

The way he was looking at her caused Lily's stomach to do

a mini-flip, which was doubtless what he intended. She nodded. 'OK.'

'But this is definitely unfinished business. You do know that, don't you? I like you,' said Eddie. 'And I'll call you later, OK?'

Lily emerged from the mirrored lift on the ground floor and stepped into the foyer of the hotel. Her phone rang and Eddie's name flashed up.

She pressed answer. 'Hi, did I forget something?'

'No. Just wait there. I'm on my way down.'

'Um, is that wise, considering you're not wearing any clothes?' A Carry-On scenario flashed through her brain, of Eddie emerging from the lift just as the doors closed, snatching away the towel around his hips . . .

Then she saw him descending the staircase; in twenty seconds flat he'd pulled on jeans and a T-shirt, though his feet were still bare.

'Missing you already.' He was smiling. 'Plus, how bloody rude of me not to walk you to your car.'

He picked up her overnight case, slid his hand around her waist and together they made their way out through the doors and down the steps.

When the case had been stowed in the boot of the waiting car, Eddie kissed her once more.

'What are you doing?' Lily pulled back. 'People are watching!'

'Let them watch. I don't care.'

Excited on the inside but determined not to show it, Lily said, 'Well you might not have a reputation to keep up, but some of us do.'

Chapter 26

'You made it back then,' Dan remarked when Lily came into the office at five to ten.

Was she glowing? Lily *felt* as if she might be glowing. Oh, but it was so hard to play it cool when you had this much adrenalin sloshing around your system.

'Of course I made it back.' Reaching for the charger on the desk, she plugged in her phone. 'I said I would, didn't I? What are you doing here anyway?'

'Coral called me an hour ago. She couldn't get through to you and was worried in case you'd been held up. I offered to come over and help out. I know I can't do much,' he added as Lily opened her mouth to protest, 'but I can man the phone, deal with emails and print out receipts.'

'Why would I not turn up? Have I ever let anyone down before? I forgot my charger and my phone's dead, that's all. I could have stayed longer in London if I'd wanted to,' Lily added, 'but I didn't, because I'm reliable. And when I make a promise, I keep it. You know I do.'

They stared at each other in silence. Whoops, was it the look in Dan's eyes or her own surfeit of adrenalin making her defensive? Why was she suddenly feeling *guilty*, for heaven's sake?

Finally he said, 'Did you have a nice time?'

Lily exhaled. 'Yes I did, I had an amazing time.'

'What was the film like?'

'Great!' OK, it hadn't been that great for her, what with it being sci-fi, but that was beside the point. 'And afterwards we went back to the hotel with Mira Knowles, had pizza in her suite and played word games.'

'Rock and roll,' said Dan. 'And what happened after that?'

'Why are you looking at me like that?'

'Did you sleep with him?'

'Well *that's* none of your business,' said Lily.

'I'll take that as a yes, then.'

'And so what if I did?'

'Nothing. I just thought you'd have had more sense. Because all he was doing was using you.'

'Oh, we're back to this again, are we?' Why couldn't he be happy for her? Why was he being like this, trying to spoil everything? 'Except maybe you've got it the wrong way round and I'm the one using him.'

Before Dan could reply, the door swung open and Coral exclaimed, 'You're back! Oh my God, can you believe you're on the front page of the paper? I screamed when I saw it!'

'Am I really?' Lily was startled. 'I haven't seen it. I mean, Eddie said it might happen, but I thought he was joking.'

'Show her!' Coral nodded excitedly at the newspaper lying face down beside the computer, and Dan pushed it across the desk towards Lily. Her eyes widened further still when she saw the photos and read the accompanying piece.

'You definitely chose the right dress. You looked fantastic.' Coral was bubbling with enthusiasm. 'And there's more on the next page! Everyone was wondering who on earth you were! It says you kept giving them different names and it just made

189

them all the more interested and now they want to know if you're Eddie's new girlfriend!'

The next moment, Lily's plugged-in phone began to ring and she saw that the caller was Eddie.

'Hi.' Her eyes felt as if they were actually sparkling as she listened to him. 'I know, my phone died. I've only just seen it now.'

After a bit longer she said, 'Me too. Definitely.'

Then a short time after that: 'Sounds great. Yes, I know. Of *course* I do . . . that'd be perfect . . . Yes, we will . . . brilliant . . . can't wait. Bye . . . yes, OK. Bye.' She finally hung up, aware that she was smiling like a lunatic.

'Wrong number?' said Dan.

She said, 'I'd call it the right number. Eddie's coming down here tomorrow evening to see me.'

'Oh my goodness.' Coral clasped her hands together. 'You really like him, I can tell!'

Lily nodded. 'I do,' she said simply.

Dan had turned his attention to the computer and was apparently engrossed in the words he was reading on the screen.

'Anyway, I'm back now,' Lily went on cheerfully. 'You don't need to be here any more, looking all superior and disapproving.' With a flourish she handed Dan the crutch he'd left propped up against the desk. 'You can go.'

OK, so it had been a *slightly* odd experience, having a first date under the discreet but watchful gaze of your ex-husband. On the other hand, it had meant she hadn't needed to drive anywhere, and at least the food had been guaranteed to be good.

It was just a shame that the date himself had chatted to so many women online that he'd got Patsy's details muddled up with those of another divorcee who definitely *didn't* want children at some stage in the future. After that, he couldn't get away fast enough, evidently terrified that she might force him to impregnate her before the night was out.

He'd also meticulously divided their dinner bill according to what each of them had eaten, and announced with pride that he wouldn't be tipping because he didn't believe in tips.

'Oh well, at least you didn't find out a year from now.' Sean had beckoned for her to join him up at the bar after the dreamboat had left. 'You haven't wasted any time on him.'

Patsy pulled a face. Apart from this evening. Her friend Finola had invited her to an impromptu barbecue in Chipping Norton and she'd had to say she couldn't make it because she already had a date. She wondered what the evening might have been like if she'd gone along to Finola's instead. What if the perfect man for her was there, wishing he could meet the perfect woman for him?

Not that there was any way of ever knowing the answer to that question. It was too late to go over there now.

'Cheer up. Have a drink,' said Sean, opening the wine fridge. 'Chablis?'

Chablis was her favourite. Patsy shook her head. 'Thanks, but it's OK.'

No one else was currently in earshot. Sean said, 'Don't let it get you down. Have you given any more thought to . . . you know, what we talked about before?'

'Of course I've thought about it.' She smiled faintly. 'It's not the kind of offer you forget about.'

'And?'

'I just don't know. I mean, it's nice to know it's there . . .'

'OK, I don't think we mentioned it before, but in case you were wondering, if you *did* decide you liked the idea, we'd prefer to go the turkey baster route.' Sean lowered his voice and added, 'You know, rather than . . . *au naturel*.'

'Oh! Yes, of course. I hadn't even thought of doing it that way,' said Patsy. 'I'd assumed it'd be turkey baster from the word go.'

'Right. Well that's good. So long as we both know how it would happen. But like we said before, no pressure.' Sean gave her hand a reassuring squeeze. 'Plenty of time to decide.'

Patsy nodded. Of course she'd prefer to have a baby with a partner of her own, someone who loved her for herself. But look at tonight's date – what if she ended up with someone who refused to tip because he was such a cheapskate?

Sean, meanwhile, was still holding the bottle of Chablis. 'Sure you don't want one? On the house?'

'I'm sure.' She smiled at her ex-husband, touched by his kindness. 'I'm just not in the mood for a drink.'

Chapter 27

Dan *was* in the mood for a drink. He was in the mood for several. On his way down to the shop this afternoon he'd stopped to talk to Maggie Bennett, who was taking her hyperactive three-year-old grandson out on his new tricycle. The boy, desperate to get to the playground and losing patience with his grandmother, had taken aim and cycled furiously into the back of her legs, causing Maggie to lurch forward in shock and hang on to Dan for support.

Which wouldn't normally have been a problem, except she'd grabbed him by the shoulder and, in an effort to stay upright, simultaneously stepped on his foot. Needless to say, it was his bad foot and his strapped-up shoulder. If she'd also managed to punch him in his black eye, she'd have achieved the hat-trick.

Plus poor Maggie was so mortified and apologetic that Dan had then been forced to pretend everything was fine and it hadn't hurt a bit.

At least her grandson had found it funny. That boy was definitely a Hannibal Lecter in the making.

The pain had been intense; it had carried on making itself felt all afternoon and on into the evening. Banned from the pub because Patsy was meeting another of her internet dates there, Dan dosed himself up with painkillers and stretched out on the sofa to watch *Star Wars*.

But for once, even his all-time favourite film didn't have the desired effect; it wasn't managing to distract him from thoughts of Lily with Eddie Tessler. And the more Dan thought about it, the more it bothered him. Lily had had boyfriends before – not many, but a few – and he'd been able to accept the situation, maybe because he'd looked at each of them and known instinctively that there was no need to worry; they wouldn't be around for long.

He'd always been right, too. Within a few weeks Lily would invariably lose interest and end the relationship; as soon as it became apparent to her that they weren't The One, she saw no reason to carry on seeing them simply in order to have a boyfriend in her life.

The only one who'd lasted any length of time had been Phil, but even then Dan hadn't been concerned. Phil had seemed on the surface like a nice enough guy, but Dan had known he would reveal his true colours sooner or later. It had happened following Nick's sudden death, when, sure enough, Phil had completely failed to understand why Lily would want to support Coral in her grief rather than carry on socialising with him. His lack of empathy had killed the six-month relationship stone dead and Dan had been glad, because Lily deserved so much better than someone like Phil.

That another relationship hadn't materialised in the last couple of years was purely down to the fact that she'd been so completely uninterested in meeting anyone, and somehow Dan had got used to this being the situation, had been lulled into a false sense of security. Although the logical part of his brain was aware that at some stage in the future it was bound to happen, the illogical part had been hoping it never would.

Except now the false sense of security had been ruthlessly ripped away and it felt as if a bottomless sinkhole had opened up beneath his feet. At the moment he was still hovering at ground level, like a character in a cartoon stepping off a cliff into thin air, but any moment now gravity would set in and he'd go plunging down, down, down . . .

Because while none of the other boyfriends in Lily's life had felt like a threat, Eddie Tessler did. He was in a different league altogether, and Lily was clearly both flattered and smitten.

Dan's mouth was dry, his mind in unaccustomed turmoil. While all he could do was endure it and pray for the relationship to crash and burn, he had the awful feeling it wouldn't.

Basically, why *would* Eddie Tessler lose interest in someone as funny and original and quirky and lovable as Lily? Let's face it, the attraction between them was already there; he'd heard about it from Lily and Patsy, and now he'd seen it with his own eyes.

And why wouldn't it exist? She was perfect. Hadn't he himself spent years, after all, trying to find someone who could successfully take his mind off her? He had tried, over and over again, and had failed miserably.

The film was still playing on the TV screen but Dan was paying it no attention. Instead he reached once more for his laptop and fired it up, like some kind of masochist. Because it wasn't as if all the photos of Eddie and Lily together weren't already seared indelibly into his brain.

Yet still he was compelled to look at them again, scrolling awkwardly with his left hand, clicking on link after link and experiencing a fresh stab of jealousy with each photo in turn. It was just so clear, so visible, the connection between them. The cameras had caught it perfectly, damn their miracle lenses . . . the way Eddie was looking at Lily as if he couldn't believe his luck, and the way Lily was glowing with the kind of happiness that only—

A key turned in the lock, the front door opened and Dan hurriedly closed the lid of the laptop, as guilty as if he'd been caught watching porn.

One look at Patsy's face told him the evening hadn't been a success.

'Oh dear,' said Dan. 'Marks out of ten?'

'Minus four hundred and seventy-six.'

He felt for her. 'That's a disappointing date.'

'Just your average disaster. Story of my life.' Patsy turned to look at the TV screen. 'Are you watching that?'

Which was shorthand for: please tell me you're not watching that awful film again because I'd quite like to put on *The Holiday* to cheer me up.

'No, you go ahead.' Switching off the laptop and hauling himself awkwardly to his feet, Dan winced at the pain. 'If I'm allowed back in now, I think I'll head down to the pub.'

It was eleven o'clock and Sean was calling last orders. Dan held up his empty glass. 'Yes please.'

Because eleven o'clock was far too early; he hadn't come out until 9.30 and was nowhere near finished yet.

'Are you sure?' Sean was raising an eyebrow at him in that knowing, landlordy way landlords had.

'Sure I'm sure. Absolutely. And have one for yourself.' Easing his wallet out of his jeans pocket with his left hand, Dan dropped it on the floor. 'Bugger.'

'Here, let me.' Sean came out from behind the bar and retrieved the wallet. 'Were you drinking before you came out tonight?'

'No, nope, not me. Well, yes, I was *drinking*,' said Dan. 'But only orange juice. Nothing in it, I swear.'

'You've only had four drinks here.' Sean started to wash glasses. 'You shouldn't be this far gone. What else have you taken?'

'Just painkillers. *Oh*,' said Dan. 'That could be it. We ran out of paracetamol so I had some, you know, other stuff instead. Not that kind of other stuff.' He shook his head and wavered for a moment on his bar stool. 'It was a prescription Patsy had for painkillers that time she did her back in.'

'Well that was intelligent,' Sean said drily.

'No other choice. I was in agony.' Dan grinned. 'Maggie Bennett threw herself at me this afternoon.'

'I know. You already told me.'

Had he? Ha. Dan looked at the clusters of lights behind the bar, noticed that there appeared to be more of them than usual and belatedly realised he was seeing double. It was pretty. Christmassy. He said, 'The lights look nice.'

Amused, Sean said, 'Do they?'

'Yes. And you have lovely eyes.'

'Thanks.'

'Just one more drink.'

'You can flirt with me all you like, but I'm still not serving you.'

'I feel woozy,' said Dan. He paused to consider the word: Whoozy? Whoozie? 'How do you spell woozy?'

'I spell it p-i-s-s-e-d.' Sean said sympathetically, 'You're not yourself tonight. What's going on?'

'I don't know. I think I'm having an out-of-body experience. Am I floating? I feel as if I'm floating. Don't look at me like that,' said Dan. 'I'm going through a horrible, horrible time.'

'You mean not being able to work?' Sean indicated the sling

around his neck and the aluminium crutch hooked over the side of the bar.

'Not that. Worse than that.' He really did feel as if he were floating now.

'Girl problems?'

'Kind of.' Dan paused, suddenly overcome with the need to confide the truth. 'Honestly? It's killing me, and there's nothing in the world I can do about it.'

'Something to do with Patsy?' Sean suddenly looked really concerned.

Dan shook his head – whoa, more fuzziness – and said, 'Not Patsy. Someone else. I want to tell you but I can't. Because that's the thing,' he went on helplessly. 'I can't tell anyone. It's the biggest secret of my life.'

'We have a guest,' Sean announced thirty minutes later.

Dan nodded and pointed to his own chest. 'It's me.'

'So I see.' Amused, Will cleared the slew of boxing magazines out of the way, then jumped up and helped him on to the sofa. 'Hello, guest, how are you doing? What's going on?'

'Hi, Will. Sorry about this. Sean thinks I need looking after.'

'He took some of Patsy's prescription painkillers, then came down to the pub and had a few drinks. Because he's a complete idiot.' Sean shook his head good-naturedly. 'Patsy'll be asleep by now, so I think it's best if we just keep an eye on him here.'

'Like a homeless dog.' Dan pulled an appropriately mournful face.

'Like an overmedicated homeless dog with a broken foot and a smashed-up shoulder.' Will grinned. 'So, are you ready to crash out or can I get you a coffee?'

'I don't want to sleep. I can't sleep.' Dan considered the limited options; they were unlikely to offer him a glass of red wine. 'Coffee, please. Coffee would be good. We can just chat, can't we?' He was oh so in the mood to talk.

'We'll all have coffee.' Sean nodded soothingly and looked at Will. 'Dan's been going through a hard time recently.'

'I have.' Dan nodded too and felt his head do that swimmy thing again. 'I am.'

'Oh no. Girlfriend trouble?' said Will.

'He can't tell us what it's about,' said Sean.

'I'd really like to.' Dan shrugged, forgetting how much it would hurt. 'Ow, *dammit.*' He gazed helplessly at the pair of them; they'd been through difficult times themselves, hadn't they? Yet his dilemma was different.

'That's fine,' Will reassured him. 'I'll make the coffee.'

'I want to talk about it, more than anything. But I mustn't,' said Dan. 'I just mustn't.' He held the index finger of his left hand up to his mouth to show how discreet he was. 'It's a great big *secret.*'

Chapter 28

'. . . I don't know what to do, I wish I didn't feel like this but there isn't any way to make it stop.' Dan rubbed his good hand over his stubbly jawline. 'I love her, I just really and truly love her. And the thing is, I love her too much to risk ever doing anything about it.'

There, he could hardly believe he'd said them, but the words were out. It had been like jamming a nail into a car tyre and hearing the hiss of air escaping under pressure, except instead of air it had been his deepest, darkest and most personal confession spilling out.

Oh God, though, the anguish it had caused him over the years.

Sean and Will were looking pretty startled too. As well they might.

'Seriously?' said Sean.

'I wouldn't say it if it wasn't true.'

'And you just suddenly realised this . . . what, last week?'

Ha, if only. Dan shook his head. 'Longer ago than that. Much longer.'

'How much longer?' said Will.

'Ooh, give or take a few days, it'll be nine years now.'

'*What?*'

Dan even knew the day; he could pin it down to the exact moment. He'd replayed it in his mind a thousand times. 'Remember the week in St Ives? That holiday we all went on together after I'd finished my A levels and Lily had just taken her GCSEs?'

Dan watched Sean nod in agreement. Of course Sean remembered; he'd still been married to Patsy at the time. The three of them had gone down to Cornwall with Coral, Nick and Lily, staying in a fantastic hotel overlooking the main surfing beach. The weather had been kind to them, hot sunny days melting into balmy nights. He'd met a girl whose name he'd long forgotten, and Lily had teased him because the girl had this way of gazing at him as if he were some kind of superstar. And he'd laughed about it because Lily was forever teasing him. They'd grown up together making merciless fun of each other. It was just what they did.

The change had happened on the last but one night of the holiday, surging out of nowhere with no warning at all. The adults – he might have been eighteen, but he wasn't one of the grown-ups – were starting a barbecue on the beach. He and Lily had been exploring the rocks over to the left of the bay . . .

'Um, hello, are you actually going to tell us?' said Sean. 'Or were you just going to sit there picturing the scene in your head?'

'Sorry.' It was exactly what he'd been doing. 'The evening of the barbecue. Lily was wearing a loose pink cotton sweater and jeans. I was wearing a denim shirt and orange board shorts. Lily found a baby crab in one of the rock pools. Then she spotted a bigger crab in the sea below us and said it must be the baby's mum. So I scooped up the baby crab, climbed down and slipped it back into the water. Except then *another* big crab crawled out from under one of the rocks in the pool and Lily said we hadn't reunited mother and baby at all, we'd actually separated them.' Was this too much detail? Dan found he couldn't bear to miss any of it out. 'So I called her a dipstick and she called me a murderer because the baby crab would probably die without its mum. And that was when I dived off the rocks into the sea.'

'I remember now.' Sean was nodding.

'Well I couldn't find the baby crab. But I managed to slice my knee open on the edge of a rock underwater and came up swearing. Lily thought it was hilarious and said, "Is there blood? Oh look, and there's a shark heading straight for you!" Then the next moment she saw the blood spreading in the water like a cloud and jumped in with me.'

Will's eyes were wide. '*Was* there a shark?'

'No.' Reliving the moment, Dan smiled and shook his head. 'She just jumped in for the hell of it. With all her clothes on. We swam all the way around the rocks and made our way back to the shore. My knee was still pouring with blood and Lily called me a liability and a hopeless case. Then I sat on the beach and she rinsed all the sand out of the cut. And I looked down at the back of her head with her wet hair rippling over her shoulders and suddenly out of nowhere I realised I loved her. With all my heart. And that was when she turned to look at me and said, "You know what you are, don't you? A crab-murderer with an attention-seeking knee."'

For a couple of seconds the cottage was silent.

'What happened next?' prompted Will.

'Nothing. I couldn't do anything. Or say anything. I couldn't *tell* her.' Dan marvelled at the very idea. 'She'd have laughed her head off. I'd never have lived it down. I needed time to get used to the idea, work out what I was going to do.'

'I took you back to the hotel to get your knee bandaged up,' Sean remembered. 'And you were meant to be spending the next day – the last day of the holiday – with that pretty girl you'd been seeing. What was her name?'

'Can't remember.'

'Maeve, that was it. She was from Coventry. But you called and told her you couldn't meet up after all. None of us understood why.'

'Well now you know,' said Dan.

The light-headedness was still there, along with a sense of freedom. At long last he'd bared his soul.

Sean said, 'And you've been recklessly damaging yourself ever since, desperate for Lily to show you some more sympathy.'

'Believe it or not, I didn't do all this on purpose.' Dan glanced down at his injuries.

'All this time,' Will marvelled, 'and you've never once made a move.'

'Never once.' Dan was already picturing the unfolding next scene.

'Why not?' said Will.

'I thought I'd hang fire for a bit, make sure the feelings were real. I mean, *really* real. I couldn't take the risk of rushing into anything. Plus I was about to head off to uni. I'd never waited before; it had never even occurred to me. But this was Lily we were talking about. I knew it was important. Everything had to be right.' Dan raked his fingers through his hair. 'It had to be completely right. Because if it went wrong, our whole relationship would be ruined. So I waited until the thirtieth of August.'

'Nick's birthday,' said Sean, as Dan had known he would.

Dan nodded. 'He was having one of his big parties to celebrate. Everyone was invited. It was scary to think I was going to do it at last, but exciting too. Until I was standing at the back of the marquee that evening and I overheard Lily and her friend Amber talking outside the tent. We were less than two feet away from each other, separated by a sheet of canvas, but they had no idea I was there. Amber was saying how much she fancied me – which I'd known for ages – and how she couldn't understand why Lily didn't.' He paused, his mouth dry. 'And Lily said she never had and never would fancy me, I just wasn't the kind of guy she'd ever go for, not in a million years.'

'She might not have meant it,' said Will.

'Oh she did, believe me. Why would she say it otherwise? She told Amber I wasn't her type, I was the *opposite* of her type. And she certainly sounded as if she meant it.'

'We've all said things we didn't mean, though.' Will pulled a face. 'When I was eighteen, I told everyone who'd listen that I fancied the pants off Yasmin Le Bon. Of course it was really Simon Le Bon.' He shook his head at Dan. 'I can't believe you gave up, just like that. And it never occurred to you to try again, in case she might have changed her mind?' To make his point, he indicated Sean next to him. 'Because . . . you know, sometimes people do.'

'OK, OK.' Dan raised a hand to stop him. 'You haven't heard the rest of it yet. The double whammy.' They couldn't begin to understand the lasting impact that evening had had on him; he was still able to vividly recall every second of it, every emotion, every word, every last detail. 'So there I was, I'd overheard Lily and Amber talking about me and it had come as a shock. Then they moved off, and the next moment someone was putting their hand on my shoulder. It was Nick,' said Dan. 'I hadn't even realised he'd been standing behind me. He'd heard Lily too. And I thought he was just going to make a joke about it, because he didn't know how I felt about Lily, but it turned out he *did* know. He sat me down and told me he'd seen what was happening ever since the holiday in Cornwall, had realised the way things could be going. And he said he needed to make me understand why it might not be a good idea.'

Sean was looking shocked. 'He warned you off? Like Don Corleone in *The Godfather*?'

'No, no, it wasn't a threat. Actually, it was worse than that.' If Nick had flatly refused to permit any kind of relationship, Dan knew his eighteen-year-old self would have been inclined to just go ahead and do it anyway. Instead, Nick had reasoned with him and appealed to his better nature. 'He was incredibly nice about it . . . sympathetic . . . He said it might have seemed like a good idea, but imagine what it would be like if me and Lily got together and it didn't work out? And really, we were so young, the chances were that it wouldn't last, and then how awkward would things be? Everyone in Stanton Langley doted on Lily. If I ended up breaking her heart, I wouldn't hear the end of it.' He paused, then shrugged. 'Well, he was right about that. Basically, I didn't have the best reputation, and if I hurt Lily, I'd never be forgiven. As Nick said, we could either stay as we were and be friends for life, or I could try and take things further and risk losing everything. And not just Lily. Our friends, families . . . everyone.'

'Wow,' said Will. 'Heavy.'

'But he had a point,' said Sean.

'He did.' Dan nodded in weary agreement.

'You slept with Amber that night, for a start.'

Dan shrugged and nodded again; he wasn't proud of himself for having done that. In his admittedly inadequate defence, he'd been eighteen years old and his heart had just been broken into a million pieces. It had also made Amber's night. At the time it had seemed like the only thing to do.

'Then you went off to university and slept with most of the girls there too.'

'Not *most* of them,' said Dan, although it had been a fair few. 'So anyway, you see now why I never did say anything. It would have been me versus the whole of Stanton Langley.'

Not once had it occurred to any of them that he might be the way he was purely because he wasn't allowed to make his feelings known to the one girl he truly did want and felt he could be faithful to.

But the years had rolled by and he'd grown into his role as an indefatigable ladies' man. He'd tried so hard to fall in love with another girl but it just hadn't happened. And over time he'd realised he could no longer be sure he *did* trust himself one hundred per cent. The fear was too great to take the risk, because what if he couldn't?

All the more reason not to try.

Sean had been watching him disappear into his memories. Now he said, 'So this is why you have your jokey relationship with Lily. You fake-flirt with her because it would be weird not to, but it's a double bluff because deep down you actually mean it. And you've got used to things being the way they are because it's safe and you're not risking the whole thing blowing up and hitting the fan.'

Spookily spot-on. Was it being gay that made Sean so adept at digging beneath the carefully constructed devil-may-care surface and understanding what was actually going on in his confused and despairing mind?

'Sounds about right,' said Dan.

'So what happens now?' asked Will. 'Are you going to tell her how you feel?'

206

There it was again, the serrated knife in the stomach. Dan shook his head. 'No, I'm not. I can't. All the old arguments still stand. I know what I'm like . . . I've been this way for so long now. I can't afford to take the risk of fucking up.'

More silence. Finally Sean said, 'So all this business with her and Eddie Tessler must be pretty hard for you to handle.'

'Let's just say it hasn't been the best few days of my life.'

'Maybe he'll lose interest,' said Sean.

'He might not,' said Will, unhelpfully.

Dan was suddenly overwhelmed with exhaustion; the light-headedness had dissipated, his eyelids were now heavy and his brain appeared to have been replaced by cotton wool. Under the accidental influence of drink and drugs, he'd shared his secret, which had been a relief at the time, though it wasn't as if there was anything they could do about it.

There was no magic answer.

'You mustn't tell anyone.' Through half-closed eyes he looked from Sean to Will. 'I mean it, you have to swear on your lives. Lily must never know.'

They were both nodding sympathetically. 'Don't worry, we promise,' said Sean. 'Your secret's safe with us.'

Will was smiling. 'Same. And let's face it, if you can't trust a couple of gay men who both hid their sexuality for years . . . well, who can you trust?'

Dan woke up at 6.30 the next morning. Sean and Will were both upstairs asleep. He left a note on the coffee table: *Don't worry, I'm still alive. Many thanks for last night. D. P.S. Remember, just between us.*

As he let himself out of the house, it occurred to him that anyone else catching sight of the note might think they'd had a threesome.

Limping along like Long John Silver, he paused outside the cottage and decided to head on down to the high street. The newsagent would be open; he wanted to pick up a couple of papers, and they sold painkillers too.

In the newsagent's he flicked casually – one-handedly – through some of the papers, not even admitting to himself what he was looking for.

Until he turned a page and saw the huge photo captioned: *This could be The One, says Eddie.*

Then he really wished he hadn't bothered.

'Oh my goodness,' said a blond girl, grinning across at him as she picked a copy of *Heat* magazine off the rack. 'You've been in the wars!'

She was young, pretty, clearly interested. There was a fuchsia-pink streak in her hair. Out of sheer habit, Dan flashed a brief smile in return. 'You should see the other guy.'

'I can imagine. Wow, that's what I call a black eye. Is it really painful?'

Not nearly as painful as looking at pictures of Lily with Eddie Tessler.

'I'm managing.' He wondered idly who she was.

'I'm Shaz. Hi. Saw you looking at that photo just then. If you're from around here, you must know Lily.'

Dan no longer needed to wonder. She was a journalist. 'Sorry, I can't help you.'

'Oh that's a shame. It's such a great story, real Cinderella stuff.' Shaz's eyes were bright as she said playfully, 'Now you're making me wonder if she's an ex-girlfriend of yours!'

Dan shook his head. 'No.' Limping over to the counter with the newspaper tucked under his arm, he asked Ted Wilson for a packet of paracetamol, paid for both items and made to leave.

As he reached the door, he heard Ted say to Shaz, 'If you want to know about Lily, I can tell you everything you need.'

'You can?' Shaz perked right up. 'Well that's fantastic.'

'I mean, you'll pay, will you?'

'Depending on the information, we can certainly negotiate a price.' Shaz nodded so vigorously her earrings jangled.

Dan turned in the doorway and raised his eyebrows at Ted, who had only moved into the village a couple of years ago.

'What?' said Ted defensively. 'If I don't do it, someone else will.'

'Exactly,' said Shaz.

Chapter 29

Who knew so much could happen in the space of a week?

Lily was brushing her teeth in the en-suite bathroom of her hotel room. Not up in London this time, but in the Valentine's best room, occupied for the past seven days by herself and Eddie Tessler. And if it seemed weird to others that she was staying in a hotel in her own village . . . well, it felt a bit weird to her too.

Most annoyingly, one of her all-time favourite things about hotels had been going downstairs to the dining room in the morning and enjoying a proper cooked full English breakfast.

Except when you knew the chef and the waitresses and could see them looking at you as if you were a whole different person, it all became hugely awkward and impossible.

Lunch or dinner at the Star, being served by friends, fine.

Breakfast at the Valentine, too embarrassing for words.

And as for having it delivered to your room, actually carried in on a silver tray while you stood beside the huge velvet-canopied four-poster you'd spent the night in with the hotel's current VIP . . . eurgh, no way, forget it.

Lily grimaced at her reflection in the mirror and spat tooth-paste froth into the sink. The term VIP was something else she wasn't fond of.

'What are you pulling that face for?' Emerging from the shower behind her, Eddie slicked his wet hair back with his hands.

Lily smiled, because sharing the king-sized hotel bed with Eddie was something she *was* enjoying about her stay here. She rinsed her mouth with water, spat again and said, 'It should be VFP.'

'Of course it should.' He wrapped his arms around her. 'What are you on about?'

'People say VIP but they don't mean VIP. Some people are important but most aren't,' she told him. 'It should be very famous person. That's what they really mean, isn't it? Or just FP, because most people aren't even very famous.'

'So true.' Eddie was looking amused. 'And what about me? What would I be?'

'You'd qualify as a QFP,' said Lily.

'Quintessentially famous person?'

'Quite famous.'

He pretended to bite her bare shoulder. 'Thank you for putting me in my place.'

'That's quintessentially all right. And now I need to go to work.' Well, tea and toast at home, then work.

'Do you have to?'

'You know I do. We're busier than ever.' She shook her head. 'And that's all your fault too.'

'I'm sorry.'

'Are you writing your script today?'

'I'll be trying to write my script.' It was Eddie's turn to pull a face; never having had trouble getting the words down before, he was struggling with the current storyline.

'You'll get back into it,' Lily assured him.

'It's your fault. I can't concentrate when you're around to distract me.'

She twisted round and planted a kiss on his mouth. 'Which is why I'm leaving now.'

Downstairs, as she was making her way out through the main doors and along the driveway, Lily heard a clatter of china and someone loudly hissing her name.

She turned and saw one of the waitresses hurrying after her clutching a fully laden breakfast tray. It was Jessica Raven, a sweet girl in her late teens who lived in the village with her parents and numerous brothers and sisters.

'Hi, Jess, how are you?'

'OK thanks.' Jessica glanced furtively from left to right like a cartoon burglar. 'Right, so here's the thing. None of us are allowed to ask Eddie Tessler for his autograph, but I really want one, so I was wondering . . .'

'You want me to ask Eddie for his autograph?'

'Well you're having sex with him, so it's not like he's going to say no, is it?'

Lily blinked. 'I suppose not.'

'So will you do it?'

Since she couldn't think of a reason not to, Lily said, 'OK.'

'Brilliant! Can I have ten, please?'

'Ten autographs?'

'I know, but we're a big family. They'll be dead upset if they don't get one each.'

Lily gave in. 'All right, I'll text Eddie and ask him to do it. You can pick them up from his room later.'

'Except I don't want to get sacked, so could you take them up to the yard and one of my brothers will be along to collect them later this afternoon? That way if anyone from the hotel asks, you can tell them it was nothing to do with me.'

'OK,' said Lily.

'Thanks. You're so lucky.' Jessica sighed. 'Eddie Tessler's well fit.'

212

'Um, yes.'

The younger girl broke into a complicit grin. 'I bet he's great in bed.'

Arriving at the yard at four o'clock, Eddie handed over an envelope containing the autographed cards. 'Here you go.'

'Thanks. Sorry about that,' said Lily, 'but she's a sweet girl. I didn't have the heart to say no.'

He shrugged, amused. 'What's the betting they'll be up on eBay by this evening?'

'Oh no, she wouldn't do that.' Lily shook her head vigorously. 'Don't worry, Jess isn't like that at all.'

Eddie dropped a kiss on her forehead. 'If you say so.'

Lifting her chin, Lily found his mouth and kissed him back, briefly but with great affection. Oh she did enjoy being allowed to do this. After years of concealing her true feelings for Dan, it was just so lovely to be able to act on impulse and openly demonstrate how she felt. Eddie might not be Dan, but he was now her boyfriend and she was enjoying every minute of their relationship.

She gave him one last kiss for luck. 'How's the script going?'

'Badly. Which is why I walked up here to give you these.'

'And now you can walk back to the hotel and give it another go. I'll see you at seven thirty,' said Lily. 'You have another three hours to get some words down.'

'Slave-driver,' said Eddie.

'It's my middle name.'

He smiled. 'Attractive.'

As he strolled off, Lily noticed a couple of customers surreptitiously taking photos of him on their phones. She also saw one of Jessica's younger brothers riding his bike around in tight circles on the section of pavement beyond the gates. As soon as Eddie had disappeared from view, the teenager rode into the yard, skidded to a halt in front of her and nodded at the envelope in her hand.

'Is that them?'

'Yes. Here you go.' She handed the autographs over.

'Cheers.' The boy – it was either Tim or Tom, Lily couldn't remember which – slid the envelope inside the front of his jacket.

'Not at school today?'

He looked shocked. 'Nah, I left school two weeks ago, after my GCSEs.'

'Oh, right. Any luck finding a job yet?'

'Yeah.' The boy had a cheeky lopsided grin. 'Buying and selling stuff, you know? Wheeling and dealing. I'm like a freelance entrepreneur.'

Watching him ride off in a scatter of gravel, Lily had to admire his chutzpah. He was definitely going to sell those autographs on eBay.

Chapter 30

Talk about mixed emotions. From the safety of the kitchen, Coral could hear the buzz of voices outside, the chink of glasses, the bursts of laughter. Hosting informal get-togethers at Goldstone House had always been one of her and Nick's favourite things. Following Nick's death, she'd no longer had the heart for it.

But time moved on, she was getting back into the swing of things socially, and this evening's mini-party had evolved so naturally that she'd been happy to do it. Lily and Eddie, herself and Patsy, Dan, Declan and Gail. And Gail seemed perfectly pleasant; she worked as a buyer for an upmarket London department store and had already given Coral invaluable advice about replacing the taps in the downstairs cloakroom, and the best place to order specialist light bulbs online.

All in all, what could be nicer and more relaxed?

If you didn't happen to have a stonking crush on Declan and the terrible fear that his girlfriend was able to read you like a book.

Anyway, never mind, she was just being paranoid. Of course Gail couldn't tell. And this was Lily's evening. She was lit up with happiness, even managing to upstage Eddie himself.

Everyone was getting on together just fine, Dan was back to his laid-back, wisecracking best and it hadn't even been embarrassing when one of the barmaids from next door had popped in and asked Eddie if she could have a selfie taken with him.

Despite the fact that it had ended up being seven selfies, because the girl's adrenalin-induced blinking had rendered the first six attempts not good enough.

It hadn't mattered at all, though. Eddie had submitted with good grace, and the girl, having proudly uploaded the end result to social media, was now the envy of all her female friends on Facebook.

'Come on, let's get the rest of this food through.' Lily came into the kitchen, flushed and sparkly-eyed. 'It all looks fantastic.'

'Is Eddie all right?'

'He's great.'

She was twenty-five now, old enough to settle down. In case Lily was wondering, Coral said, 'I do like him, you know. Very much.'

Lily gave her a quick hug. 'I know. Me too.'

Together they carried out the bowls of salad and dishes of salmon, curried eggs, baked tomatoes and Caribbean rice. On the terrace, Dan had taken charge of the barbecue and was deftly, one-handedly turning the steaks, sausages and marinated chicken legs. Smoky, spicy cooking smells filled the air as more food was laid out on the long table between plates, wine buckets and glasses.

'You have a beautiful garden,' Gail told Coral as music was turned on in the living room and Alicia Keys' silky voice drifted out through the propped-open French doors. 'Just lovely.'

The happy feeling in Coral's stomach mingled uneasily with the sensation that Gail was about to interrogate her in an exam for which she'd forgotten to revise.

'Thanks. We like it.' Coral gave the potato salad a stir it didn't need. 'Are you a gardener?'

'God, no, not me. All those insects and worms.' Gail shuddered. 'But I don't mind sitting in a deckchair admiring everyone else's hard work.'

She was forty years old, with her hair cut in a geometrically precise bob that emphasised her slender neck. She was beautiful, somewhat intense and clearly had wonderful dress sense.

'Oh well,' Coral said with a smile, 'we all like doing that.'

'My flat has no garden, thank goodness.' Gail began separating the pile of plates as, behind the barbecue, Dan waved his tongs like a conductor and started singing along to the music playing on the sound system.

'So you won't be helping Declan out with the one at Weaver's Cottage?'

'Ha, not a chance.' Declan had brought Gail down this afternoon and shown her the work that was being carried out on the property. She grimaced slightly. 'It still needs an awful lot doing to it.'

'Ah, but it'll be worth it in the end. And he won't have any trouble selling it on or renting it out,' said Coral. Aware of Gail's cool gaze upon her, she felt the tension ramping up. 'There's always a market for nicely done-up cottages in a picturesque setting. And people in Stanton Langley are friendly. It's a great village.'

'So Declan keeps telling me.' Gail paused, her tone measured. 'To be honest, I wondered what was going on at first. When he received that letter out of the blue from Lily. I thought maybe he was her father and wasn't admitting it.'

Halfway down the garden, with the rays from the setting sun streaming through the high branches, Lily was showing Declan how she used to climb trees as a child. As they watched her, fifteen feet off the ground, she hooked her legs over a swaying horizontal branch and hung upside down like a monkey.

A monkey wearing jeans, silver hoop earrings and flip-flops.

'Oh Jesus,' cried Declan, shielding his eyes from the sun's glare as he gazed up in horror. 'Don't do that. Come down!'

'I spent years telling her that,' Coral said fondly. 'Never made a blind bit of difference. Nick used to call her half child, half orang-utan. And no,' she went on, 'Declan isn't her father. But don't they get on well? There's a real connection between them. And it's been fantastic for Lily, meeting someone who meant so much to her mum.'

'I suppose it must be.' Gail softened slightly.

'It's so lovely seeing them together. I think it means a lot to Declan too, what with him not having any children of his own.'

'So far,' said Gail.

'Oh!' Coral's heart broke into a gallop. Her gaze slid to the glass of iced sparkling water in Gail's manicured hand. The swell of her breasts beneath the crisply cut lilac linen dress. Were they usually smaller than that? And did the fact that Declan hadn't so much as mentioned it mean he didn't yet know?

Then she became aware that Gail's head was tilted like a bird's and she was being observed with a mixture of triumph and amusement.

'I'm not pregnant, if that's what you're thinking.' The glossy, expertly lowlighted bob swung from side to side and her mouth opened to reveal dazzlingly white teeth. 'The reason I'm drinking water is because I'm driving us back to London tonight.' Picking up one of the plates, Gail began helping herself to food from the various bowls arranged along the table. 'Is the dressing on this salad oil-free?'

'Um . . . no, I'm afraid not.'

'Oh. OK.'

'I could do you some,' Coral offered helplessly, because Gail was clearly disappointed.

'Thank you, that would be great. Sorry if it's boring, but I like to take care of myself.' Gail followed her into the kitchen.

'I can see that. You have a fantastic figure.'

'I know. Well, so do you. Was your husband overweight?'

Coral was already tearing up fresh lettuce, throwing it into a bowl. She turned, surprised. 'Nick? No.'

'Oh, I just wondered. What with him dying so young of a heart attack.' Gail shrugged. 'It generally happens to people who eat too much.'

'Well not in Nick's case.'

'Sorry, am I being a bit blunt? I don't mean to be.' Picking up a bottle of balsamic vinegar, Gail coated the torn lettuce leaves.

If Gail could do it, so could she. Feeling terribly brave, Coral said, 'So are you and Declan trying for a baby?'

Gail added cherry tomatoes, cooked asparagus and discs of cucumber to the salad. 'I'm considering it. I suspect Declan regrets not having had children before. He'd be a fantastic father, don't you think?'

What was she meant to say to that? Coral nodded. 'I'm sure he would,' she murmured. 'And if it's what you want, too . . .'

'Ah well, I love Declan.' Gail shrugged elegantly. 'That's the main reason I'd be doing it. Babies aren't really my cup of tea, but if it's what he wants, I'm happy to give it a go. You never know, it might not be as bad as people make out.'

Coral was taken aback. 'What if it is?'

Gail shrugged. 'Lots of women think they don't want children, then when it all starts happening they change their mind.

My cousin was the same as me and she's got three now! So it all worked out OK in the end.'

Coral blinked. 'Right.'

'Do you find Declan attractive?' said Gail.

OK, hang on, what did she just say? Coral frowned, assuming she'd somehow misheard. 'Sorry?'

Gail repeated it. 'Declan. Do you find him attractive?'

Mortified, Coral shook her head. 'No! Why?'

'No particular reason. Just interested.' Gail was watching her with a perfectly pleasant smile on her face. 'The thing is, and I think most people would agree with me, Declan is a very attractive man. So I suppose I'm wondering why you don't think so.'

Which on the surface sounded completely plausible, but Coral was almost sure she wasn't imagining the unspoken subtext. As if Gail were perfectly well aware of Coral's experimental crush on him.

And was subtly letting her know that she knew.

Which in turn made Coral wonder – with a shudder of embarrassment – if Declan knew too.

Outside in the garden, they could hear Lily and Dan bellowing discordantly along together with Alicia Keys: 'No ONE, no one, no one . . .'

Coincidentally, it had been one of Nick's favourite songs too. He used to sing it at the top of his voice in the shower. Except it wasn't a coincidence, Coral corrected herself; the CD was being played because she'd bought it for Nick years ago and it had since become a treasured part of their collection. *Oh Nick . . .*

'I loved my husband very much,' she told Gail. 'I still do. I suppose that's the reason I don't find other men attractive.'

Are you listening, Nick? Can you hear me telling a bare-faced lie and using you as my excuse for doing it? Sweetheart, I'm so sorry, I hope you don't mind too much.

The good thing was, if he were somehow watching and listening, she thought he would understand and be fine with it.

The bad thing was, Gail was giving her the kind of look that signalled she wasn't convinced.

What was it they used to do with a woman in the olden days if she was suspected of being a witch? Throw her into water and if she drowned she was innocent. And if she floated she was found guilty, which meant they'd then burn her at the stake.

Suppressing a shiver and hoping Gail wouldn't try this method to test her out, Coral held up the bowl of salad. 'Is there anything else you'd like?'

Yes, for you to stop fancying Declan.

Gail didn't actually say this, thank goodness, but the mere idea that she could be thinking it was enough to send prickles of alarm down Coral's neck and spine.

'No, that's perfect. Thank you.' She took the bowl. 'Sorry to be a nuisance.'

'You aren't a nuisance at all.'

'Aren't I?' With a small, enigmatic smile that prompted yet more tremors of unease, Gail said, 'Well, I do hope not.'

Chapter 31

They headed back out to rejoin the others in the garden. Everyone was loading up their plates now. Dan was piling medium-rare fillet steaks into a dish, Patsy was picking the bigger slices of chilli out of her rice and giving them to Lily, and Gail was chatting to Eddie about her elderly male next-door neighbour, who had once acted on the stage with Joanna Lumley and had been helplessly besotted with her ever since.

'Ooh, crème fraiche.' Reaching past Gail, Patsy helped herself to a generous spoonful and dolloped it on her spicy rice. 'Declan?' She offered to do the same for him.

Gail said, 'People always think crème fraiche is healthier than normal double cream, but it isn't, you know. Just as many calories.'

'And every bit as delicious,' Patsy said happily as she tucked in.

Coral glanced over at Declan, and for a split second their eyes locked. He winked at her, but in a way that indicated good-natured acceptance of other people's passions and foibles rather than as a signal of anything more salacious.

Oh, but the wink and that smile . . . just seeing him here . . . how could it all have such an effect on her? Declan made her happy, Coral realised. Really happy. Her stomach lurched with longing and she wished more desperately than ever that this situation could have been different.

Because it was all very well telling yourself it was just a practice crush and you'd keep it under control, but it was turning out not to be that easy after all.

Her mouth bone dry, Coral realised how idiotic she'd been, like someone deciding they'd try taking crack cocaine just the once and everything would be fine because all they had to do was make sure they didn't become addicted.

Her gaze veered helplessly back towards Declan, who was now chatting to Patsy. It was too late, it had happened.

She was hopelessly hooked on Declan Madison, with no way of getting herself unhooked. And it was scary, as scary as—

'Chicken!'

Coral jumped, her left knee jerking against the edge of the table so that one of the almost-empty wine bottles toppled sideways, splashing drops of red wine across the white tablecloth.

As if she weren't already agonisingly aware of the mess she'd gone and got herself into.

'Whoops.' Lily stood the bottle upright and offered Coral the plate in her other hand. 'Having some chicken? Lemon on the left, bourbon on the right.'

Could she even eat anything? Coral said, 'Just a small piece, thanks. I'm waiting for Dan to grill the tiger prawns.'

'Your wish is my command,' Dan called across. 'They're ready. Bring your plate over here.'

And now he was plying her with enormous marinated prawns while gusts of smoke stung her eyes and she was forced to rub them, forgetting she was wearing mascara.

'Your make-up's run.' Dan passed her one of the soft paper napkins from the pile at his side.

So of course, as Coral was blinking and dabbing beneath her eyes, Gail spotted her and came hurrying over. 'Oh no, are you all right? I hope asking you about your husband didn't upset you!' She sounded genuinely concerned. 'I'm so sorry. Here, you've missed a bit, let me help.'

Finally all the food was served and everyone was seated around the table. Citronella candles flickering in silver holders were keeping the mosquitoes at bay, the music had been changed to Bastille, and Declan was popping the cork on a bottle of Perrier Jouët.

'A toast,' he said when the foaming contents had been divided between them. Everyone raised their glasses. 'To new friends and old.' Declan clinked his glass against Dan's and everyone else followed suit.

'Four weeks ago you'd never even heard of Stanton Langley,' Lily reminded him. 'Can you believe it?'

'Four weeks ago I'd never heard of you.' He grinned at her.

'I walked past the cottage yesterday,' said Eddie. 'Saw all the work going on. Pretty amazing how much they've managed to get done in a week.'

'They're moving fast. I'm going to be spending more time here myself, project-managing.' Declan dunked a tiger prawn in saffron mayonnaise. 'I'm planning to come down again next weekend and stay for the week, make sure everything keeps on course.'

'Where will you stay?' said Patsy.

'At the cottage. It's fine.' Declan shrugged. 'We'll have the new floor down by then. Not a problem.'

'But it wouldn't be comfortable,' Lily protested. 'Why suffer if you don't need to? That's just crazy. You can stay here!'

Oh no, no, please don't. Coral pressed her knees together beneath the table to stop them juddering uncontrollably.

224

Convinced she was being watched by Gail, and unable to meet anyone's gaze, she pretended to be absorbed in the task of batting away an insect above her head.

'Can't he?' Lily was addressing her, clearly on a mission. 'Wouldn't that make perfect sense? Declan doesn't need to stay in a half-finished cottage and sleep on the floor. He can stay in our spare room!'

'Oh look, I don't want to put you out . . .' Out of the corner of her eye, Coral could see Declan shaking his head, not wanting to be a nuisance. Next to him, Gail had put down her forkful of chicken. Oh help, if she didn't say something in the next quarter of a second, things were going to get awkward.

But she couldn't say yes . . .

And she definitely couldn't say no . . .

'You wouldn't be putting us out,' Lily declared. 'Of course you must stay with us!'

'Oh, this *mosquito* – these citronella candles aren't working at all!' Flapping her napkin at the troublesome non-existent insect, Coral said, 'Of course he can stay. Absolutely! I won't be here, which is a shame, but that doesn't matter, does it?' She flashed a bright smile across the table at Declan. 'You'll have Lily to look after you.'

Lily was looking baffled. 'Why won't you be here? Where are you going?'

Deep breath. 'To the South of France. Grimaud.'

'What?' Lily's eyes widened. 'You mean . . . that magazine piece I showed you? *Really?*'

'Really.' Coral nodded, light-headed with relief at having successfully removed herself from the situation that had prompted her snap decision. 'Well, I need to double-check first that Marty and his brother can cover for me here, which is why I hadn't mentioned anything yet. But I'm sure they'll be able to do it. When you showed me the article, I remembered how much I used to enjoy it . . . and I suddenly realised I would like to go. So I phoned them up this afternoon to check they still had spaces. And they have.' She gave a little shrug. 'I decided I'd book a place on the course.'

In actual fact, all she'd done was sign up for the company's newsletter, but they'd promptly emailed her with enticing prices for next week's holiday, so with a bit of luck there were still places available. Oh well, looked like she'd better book herself in now, pronto.

'Yay, that is brilliant!' Lily clapped her hands with delight. 'I'm *so* pleased.'

'Well now I'm intrigued,' said Gail. 'What kind of a course is this?'

Coral's shoulders had relaxed; speaking to Gail was suddenly a million times easier now the immediate danger had passed. 'It's an art course for people who want to draw and paint. I used to go when Nick was alive. They have a couple of tutors there and it's always really friendly and relaxed. You spend your days painting outside, then in the evenings everyone eats and socialises together. I haven't been on one since Nick died, but when Lily showed me the magazine, I decided that the time has come.' And who knows, she thought, now that she'd been pushed into going, she might enjoy it and be glad it had happened.

'So you're an artist.' Eddie was sounding interested. 'Hidden talents.'

'Oh no, nothing like that.' Embarrassed, Coral shook her head. 'I'm not very good.'

'Yes she is,' Lily chimed in, ever loyal.

'Do you sell your work?' said Gail.

'God, no!'

Gail was looking baffled. 'So why do you do it, then?'

Next to her, Declan said, 'Because she enjoys painting, I imagine.'

'She gives them to friends,' said Lily defensively. 'They're brilliant.' She turned to Eddie. 'The garden scene up on the wall in Patsy's living room – that's one of Coral's. She used to paint all the time.'

Eddie was suitably impressed. 'You're really good.'

Coral smiled at him. 'It's been almost three years since I last picked up a paintbrush, so we'll have to see if I can still do it.'

'Oh Lord, did I sound rude? Ignore me,' said Gail. 'I've just never been able to understand why people choose to spend hours and hours on a hobby that doesn't bring them any financial or physical reward.' She helped herself to more rice salad. 'Still, each to their own. We're all different, aren't we? If I'm no good at something, I don't do it. I'd far rather play to my strengths.' She shrugged. 'But that's just me.'

Eddie's phone began to ring and he glanced at the screen. 'Damn, it's my manager. He wouldn't be calling if it wasn't important. I'd better see what he wants.' Pushing back his chair and moving away from the table, he answered the call. He listened in silence for a couple of minutes, then murmured a few words and hung up. 'Lily?'

Lily twisted round on her seat to look at him. 'Yes?'

Coral had already sensed from Eddie's expression that the news wasn't good. Her stomach contracted with apprehension as she watched him rest his hand on Lily's bare shoulder.

'Your biological father's name is Keir Bourne, is that right?'

Lily stared. Finally she nodded. 'That's right.'

'Sorry. He's sold his story to one of the Sunday papers.'

Coral's hand covered her mouth.

Lily's eyes were huge, her face suddenly pale and tight. 'You mean the one about how he behaved like an absolute bastard, dumped my mum and never once bothered to come and see me? Wow, that's a great story.' Her voice dripped with derision. 'He's the scum of the earth and he actually wants everyone to know it.'

Eddie exhaled. 'Apparently he wants to meet you, and he needed you to hear his side of the story. He says it's time you knew the truth.'

'We already know the truth,' said Lily.

Across the table, a glass slid out of Patsy's hand and landed on the edge of her plate with a *crackkk*.

Chapter 32

Twelve years ago

Stanton Langley had never looked more Christmassy, and Patsy had never felt less festive.

Why, why did stuff like this always seem to happen to her? Had she actually been a complete monster in a previous life?

Because it sometimes felt like it.

As ever, she hadn't seen it coming. Two weeks ago, she and Alex had been a normal, happy couple, getting on as well together as any couple and looking forward to their holiday in Tenerife.

Well, Alex was still looking forward to his holiday in Tenerife, because he was on his way to the airport right now, at this very minute, with bloody Alice Sawyer, who was his brand-new girlfriend.

Instead of with her, Patsy, whom he'd so unceremoniously dumped two days ago because – get this – she was just too good for him.

Yes, he'd actually had the brass neck to utter those words. Right before admitting that he was now seeing Alice, who had a far smaller brain than she did, but much bigger boobs.

So now here she was, in the middle of December, single once more. Not to mention despairing, disillusioned and a tiny bit bitter. Because everyone else had an other half, and there was nothing guaranteed to make you feel more lonely at Christmas than being the only unattached person you knew.

I'm twenty-three years old, I've been on a diet and lost a whole stone, and I've bought myself the most gorgeous turquoise bikini.

Which no one is now going to get to see.

Not to mention the additional frustration that she'd taken a week's precious annual leave from the salon and no longer had anything to do during it.

It was two o'clock in the afternoon when Patsy first noticed the man. He was sitting at a table in the window of the café, drinking coffee and gazing out at the passers-by. He was in his mid-thirties at a guess, wearing a charcoal-grey shirt and a smart mulberry-red sweater. His hair was dark, he had nice eyes, and when he caught Patsy's eye, he smiled slightly. Not in a creepy way, though. Just a normal friendly acknowledgement that she'd seen him and he'd seen her. When you lived in a village, it was perfectly usual to smile at strangers.

In the newsagent's, Patsy bought a packet of chewing gum and a copy of *Cosmopolitan*. The shout-line on the cover was: *New Year, New You!*, which seemed like an enticing idea. On her way back down the high street, she saw that the man in the mulberry jumper was still sitting there. By chance, Patsy's stomach was rumbling, and the café happened to sell her favourite pains aux raisins.

As she pushed through the door – bugger the diet – the old-fashioned bell above it went *ting-a-ting-a-ting* and the man was smiling again, only this time to himself. Oh God, was she being too obvious? Was he laughing at her? Flushing, Patsy marched up to the counter and said, 'Just a pain aux raisins please, to take away.'

When she'd paid, she turned to leave, embarrassed now and deliberately avoiding looking at the occupant of the table over by the window. Until he said, 'Before you go, can I just tell you why I was smiling?'

'Fire away.' Patsy shrugged as if she wasn't remotely interested.

'I watched one of my favourite films on TV the other night. *It's a Wonderful Life*, with James Stewart. Do you know it?'

'Yes.' Didn't everyone on the planet know that film?

'When you opened the door just now, the bell made the exact sound it does in the film. Remember? Every time a bell rings, an angel gets its wings.'

'Right.' Patsy relaxed. 'Yes, it does sound a bit like that.'

'Exactly like that. And then you came in here in your red coat and shiny boots, looking all happy and Christmassy, and it was as if you were . . . no, never mind, I can't say it.' He shook his head, but his eyes were twinkling.

'Well you're wrong anyway,' said Patsy, 'if you think I'm happy. Because I can promise you I'm not.'

He sat back on his chair. 'You were smiling. You looked happy.'

'Crying on the inside, though.'

'What happened?'

'The same thing that always happens. When you're me, anyway.' She said it wryly. 'It's the case of the vanishing boyfriend. Well, ex-boyfriend now.'

'Seriously? His loss. Can I ask you a question?'

'Of course.' Patsy held her breath; what was it going to be?

'That bus stop across the road. Is that the only one in the village, or is there another I've missed?'

OK, not the question she'd expected, but easy enough to answer. 'No, just that one. Why?'

He shrugged. 'I'm waiting for someone. Don't want to miss them. Can I ask you another question?'

'About the timetable? It's not exactly Piccadilly Circus around here. We only have one bus an hour coming through.'

He inclined his head. 'Actually, I was going to ask if you'd like to sit down and let me buy you a coffee.'

His name was Kevin Lester, Patsy learned. He was thirty-six years old, lived in Slough and owned a small engineering company. He was divorced, keen on mountaineering and partial to eating out in nice restaurants. In his spare time he helped to raise funds for animal charities. If he didn't work such long hours, he'd definitely have a dog. And the reason for his presence in Stanton Langley was because his eccentric Aunt Ethel had announced that she wanted to meet him here today.

'She's as mad as a box of frogs,' he explained. 'Keeps changing her surname, so we don't even know where she's living now. But every year or two she gets in touch and tells me where to come so we can catch up and I can make sure she's OK. She phoned me the other evening and said I should be here this afternoon, that she'd arrive on the bus. Except she didn't specify which bus. Par for the course with Ethel.'

'But she'll definitely turn up?' said Patsy.

Kevin shrugged. 'Might, might not. You never can tell. One time, after she didn't arrive, she wrote to let me know she'd decided on a whim to visit Longleat instead to see if Lord Bath wanted another wifelet.'

'Oh God. And did he?'

'Apparently not. Anyway, tell me all about you.'

232

And so she did. He was a good listener, genuinely interested and asking lots of questions. Patsy told him about her unfortunate past history with boyfriends, but was careful to make it fun and amusing so she didn't sound like too much of a tragic loser. She talked about her hairdressing job in Cheltenham, the people she worked with in the salon and her friends here in the village. And as the minutes slid by, she found herself warming to Kevin Lester more and more.

At four o'clock, they went outside at Patsy's insistence and waited for the next bus to arrive, because if he wasn't standing out there on the pavement, she explained, Aunt Ethel might just decide to stay on the bus.

'My brother'll be on this one,' she added, 'coming home from school. Just warning you now, if he sees us together and makes a smart comment, don't take any notice.'

Five minutes later, the bus trundled into view. It pulled up with a discordant shriek of brakes and the doors concertinaed open.

'Fingers crossed,' said Patsy as Kevin put on a pair of dark-rimmed spectacles. 'I know, crazy,' he said, catching her look of surprise. 'But if I'm not wearing them, Ethel won't recognise me.'

Except there was no Aunt Ethel on the bus. Patsy was disappointed – she'd been looking forward to seeing what a seventy-something rejected wifelet looked like. Several of the older villagers, back from a day of Christmas shopping, climbed carefully down the steps with their collections of carrier bags. Then the schoolchildren bounced off the bus, in high spirits because it was almost the end of term and normal lessons had given way to having fun.

'Hiya!' Lily greeted Patsy with enthusiasm. 'Not catching the bus, are you? What's up, has your car broken down?'

Patsy shook her head. 'This is Kevin, I was just keeping him company while he waited for his aunt, but she isn't on this bus. Look at the two of you,' she added, tutting at Lily and Dan. 'Not even wearing coats.'

'It isn't cold,' Lily protested, arms spread wide to prove just how uncold it was.

Patsy smiled, because as a teenager she'd been exactly the same, and as if to prove that it was cold, snowflakes had begun to spiral lazily down from the darkening grey sky. 'You two are a lost cause.' Turning to Kevin, she explained, 'That's my little brother Dan.' Little brother was a joke – at fifteen he was already taller than her. 'And this is Lily, who I used to babysit.'

Kevin nodded briefly and said, 'Hi,' in a vague kind of way. Pausing to adjust his glasses, he added, 'Been to school, then?'

Which was possibly one of the most redundant questions of all time, but some men simply didn't know how to speak to teenagers.

'No.' Dan glanced down at his white school shirt, loosened school tie and grey school trousers. 'I've been scuba diving.' He jerked a thumb at Lily. 'And she's been to a fancy dress party.'

'Don't worry, just ignore him.' Lily shook her head sympathetically at Kevin. 'He thinks he's hilarious.'

'Er, excuse me, I am hilarious.' Dan deftly snatched the open packet of fruit pastilles from her left hand and removed the top one, holding it between his finger and thumb as if it were a priceless diamond. 'Ooh, my favourite . . .'

'Not that one! Give it back. You can take a green one, but you're not having the red!'

And that was it, they were off, Lily chasing Dan across the road and along the pavement on the other side as he darted around her, staying just out of reach. Lily's blond curls bounced around her shoulders as she took an almighty swing at him with her heavy school rucksack and finally managed to grab the fruit pastilles back.

'Help, dial nine nine nine, call the police.' Dan was doubled up with laughter. 'I'm being attacked by a lunatic . . .'

'They're like that all the time.' Patsy rolled her eyes fondly. 'It never stops.'

When Lily and Dan had disappeared through the gates of Goldstone House, she said, 'What are you going to do now? Wait for the next bus?'

'I have to. Just one more. Honestly, Aunt Ethel does my head in.' Kevin paused, his smile rueful. 'Although on the bright side, I've met you.'

They gazed at each other for several seconds as the snow gathered pace and began to fall harder around them. The street lamps were coming on now, the sky was growing darker by the minute and someone inside the Star Inn had just switched on the strings of coloured fairy lights that decorated the front of the pub.

'I think I've had enough coffee for one day,' said Kevin. 'I might try that place, just for a change of scenery. It looks nice.'

Patsy nodded, her cold hands shoved deep inside the pockets of her red wool coat. 'It is nice.'

'And do you have to be anywhere? I mean, things to do, people to see?'

She had nothing to do, nowhere else she needed to be. Other than Tenerife, obviously. She shook her head. 'No.'

Snowflakes were landing on the lenses of Kevin's spectacles and sliding down the glass. She added, 'You can take those off again now.'

He smiled, did as he was told, then said, 'Come on, let's go.'

As they crossed the rapidly whitening road, a blue Fiesta drove by with festive music booming out of it. Stealing a glance at Kevin's profile, Patsy wondered how prophetic it was that the song playing was Mariah Carey's jaunty classic 'All I Want for Christmas Is You'.

By nine o'clock in the evening, Patsy's edges were pleasantly blurred. She wasn't drunk, just happily relaxed. Tucked into a cosy corner of the pub, she and Kevin had shared a bottle of red wine, eaten chicken casserole and talked non-stop for hours. And although neither of them had referred to it, the mutual attraction between them was growing at a rate of knots. The body language was there, the not-very-accidental physical contact inescapable. Patsy's cheeks ached from smiling, her foot beneath the old oak table was resting against Kevin's, and she'd long since decided that the age gap between them wasn't too great after all.

Because when you scrolled through her past experiences with boys her own age . . . well, look how they'd turned out. Maybe an older man was just what she needed. And it wasn't as if Kevin was ancient. He was thirty-six, she was twenty-three . . . and the words of the Mariah Carey song were still playing on a loop in her brain.

All she wanted for Christmas could be sitting in front of her right now.

Needless to say, Aunt Ethel hadn't been on the five o'clock bus.

Thank goodness.

Because if she had been, Kevin would have spent the last few hours with his mad aunt instead of with her.

They ordered another bottle of delicious Barolo and Patsy said, 'You're not going to be able to drive home tonight.'

Kevin shrugged. 'I'll just have to sleep in my car.'

He was probably joking, but Patsy said, 'You can't do that, you'll freeze to death.'

'This is true.' He peered out through the window at the snow still falling steadily outside. 'Would you happen to have a sofa I could spend the night on?'

Patsy hesitated. She did, but she also had a nosy mother. Not to mention a smart-alec fifteen-year-old brother. Furthermore, she suspected Kevin was hoping for more than a sofa.

'That could be awkward. What with family . . .'

'Oh I see. Right.'

'There's a hotel down the road. The Valentine.'

'Hmm, is that the four-star one I drove past on my way here? It might cost a bit more than I can afford. Is there a cheap B&B anywhere nearby?'

There *was* a cheap B&B, at the other end of the high street. It was run by the scariest person in the Cotswolds, a bossy, judgemental woman in her sixties called Beatrice who disapproved enormously of sex before marriage.

And Kevin's index finger was now idly stroking the inside of Patsy's wrist, sending mini electricity zings shooting all the way up her arm.

'What are you thinking?' His voice was low, his gaze fixed on hers.

'There's a B&B, but it's not very nice,' Patsy fibbed. God, Beatrice would go ballistic if she knew she'd said that. 'And the landlady is quite . . .' she pulled a face, 'strict.'

'You mean she wouldn't approve of visitors?'

'She definitely wouldn't approve of visitors.'

They were in a quiet corner of the pub. No one was watching them. Kevin leaned across the table, gently pulled her forward to meet him halfway, and kissed her on the mouth.

Oh wow, more zings, mega-zings. *All I want for Christmas is yoooou.*

Sitting back but keeping hold of her hand, Kevin said, 'That isn't ideal, then. Maybe I should splash out on the hotel.' He smiled slowly and rubbed his fingers across the back of her knuckles. 'You could stay with me, if you'd like to. What do you think, hmm?'

Patsy's mouth was dry. Who knew, maybe meeting Kevin today had been fate, designed to alter the course of her life. What if, twenty years from now, telling people the story of how they'd first got together became their well-honed party-piece?

She could almost hear the older version of Kevin saying the words: 'And to think, if she hadn't said yes, we might never have seen each other again after that night. Imagine that!'

Seize the moment. Go on, do it. You can't let this chance slip by.

Patsy took a deep breath. 'OK. I'd like that.'

Kevin broke into a smile. 'That's good news. Because I don't much like staying in strange hotel rooms on my own.'

Using the payphone out in the corridor, they looked up the number of the Valentine in the Yellow Pages. Kevin called the hotel and booked a double room.

Next, Patsy phoned home and told her mother she'd be staying with a friend that night. Well, it wasn't a lie, was it?

Then they recorked the still almost-full bottle of red wine, slid it into Patsy's oversized shoulder bag and left the pub.

The walk along the high street was cold but completely magical. Snow tumbled out of the ink-black sky and multi-coloured lights and decorated Christmas trees glittered in the windows of the shops and houses they passed. Their breath formed opaque clouds of condensation, and crisp, dry snow squeaked beneath their feet. Kevin was keeping his arm around

238

her to make sure she didn't slip and fall. He was such a gentleman and he had such a nice smile. It felt like being in a film.

'Just so you know.' Patsy felt the need to say it as they passed the newsagent's where she'd bought her copy of *Cosmo*. 'I've never done this before. I mean, not on the first night. I'm not that kind of girl.'

'I know.' Kevin paused to kiss her briefly, his nose cold against her cheek. 'I can tell. But this is different. This is special.'

He could feel it too; it wasn't just her. Patsy's heart soared as she whispered, 'I think you're right.'

At two o'clock in the morning, the sound of a toilet being flushed in the next room woke Patsy from sleep. For a split second she wondered where she was. Then, remembering, she smiled and snuggled closer to Kevin, who was lying on his side facing away from her.

They'd had such a wonderful evening. Any worries that she'd been making a mistake had been swept away. They'd had another glass of wine each, made love, then talked some more, sharing the rest of the bottle of Barolo, before making love again. He was such a genuinely nice person. He no longer seemed several years older than her; he was just . . . Kevin.

Kevin Lester.

Patsy Lester.

It sounded so right. Far better than Alex's surname. Much as she'd liked Alex, if they had ended up getting married she'd have been Patsy Bacon. Which, let's face it, wasn't ideal. So many puns, so little time . . .

Ah, but Patsy Lester was fine, it was a good name. And OK, maybe this was jumping the gun, but it wasn't as if anyone would ever know she'd been thinking it.

She ran her hand lightly over his back, not enough to wake him, just to feel the warmth of his skin. Here they were, naked together on the first night of their relationship. She was never going to forget—

A door slammed on the next floor, and Kevin's arm twitched. He lifted his head for a moment, then let it fall back on to the pillow. 'Go back to bed,' he mumbled.

Patsy grinned in the darkness. People who talked in their sleep were always entertaining. When a few seconds had passed, she reached up behind her and knocked the wooden headboard with her knuckles.

Kevin let out a groan. 'Tan, she's trying to get in . . . you sort it out . . . put her back to bed.'

Patsy stopped grinning. What?

Kevin shifted in his sleep and began to snore.

Seriously, *what*?

Because people sometimes talked rubbish when they were asleep, muttering about catching potatoes and flying with dragons, but Kevin's words were rather more prosaic than that.

Who was Tan?

And who did she need to put back to bed?

Oblivious to the snoring, Patsy lay on her back and stared up at the ceiling. OK, Tan could be his ex-girlfriend, someone with a small daughter. That was completely feasible.

Of course it was.

Wasn't it?

Her toes were so tense, they were in danger of seizing up with cramp. No way could she get back to sleep now she'd heard him say those things. At least not until she'd found out the meaning behind them.

Patsy eased herself away from Kevin's sleeping form and slid silently out of bed. She wrapped herself in one of the white towelling dressing gowns hanging up behind the door, then, finding Kevin's trousers thrown over the armchair by the window, stealthily removed his wallet from the back pocket.

Everything's going to be OK, everything's going to be OK. Just breathe . . .

Locking herself in the bathroom, Patsy glanced at her reflection in the mirror above the sink. Tousled bed-hair, slightly smudged make-up and anxious eyebrows.

Don't be anxious. There has to be a perfectly simple explanation for what you heard him say.

She perched on the edge of the bath, gazed at the brown leather wallet in her lap, then took a deep breath and opened it.

'Wake up.'

'Hhurrgh . . .'

'Wake up.' Patsy was trembling with fury. She gave the double bed a kick and almost broke her toe.

'Eh?' Opening his eyes and rolling over on to his back, Kevin blinked in sleepy confusion.

Except his name wasn't Kevin.

'Wake up and answer the phone,' said Patsy. 'Your wife wants to know why you haven't come home tonight.'

'What?' That did the trick. He sat up, searched the room for the phone and saw it sitting silently on the bedside table with the receiver in place.

'You seem to have stolen someone else's wallet.' Patsy held it up, still shaking. 'Someone by the name of Keir.' She took out the Visa debit card and spun it across the bed at him. 'Keir Bourne.' The MasterCard followed it, bouncing off his chest. 'And guess what? He even looks like you.' She aimed a driving licence at his head, followed by a small colour photograph of him with a pretty red-haired woman and a girl with pigtails who looked to be about three or four years old. 'And he has a wife and a child, imagine that! You bastard . . .'

'OK, stop it. You had no right to go through my wallet.'

'You had no right to tell me your name was Kevin Lester.' It was warm in the room, but Patsy's teeth were chattering violently. 'You lied to me. You've been lying to me from the word go.'

'Look, I'm married but it's a disaster. We're only staying together until Sasha's a bit older. As soon as she's settled at school we'll make the break . . .'

'You don't live in Slough,' Patsy pointed out. 'You live in Milton Keynes. It says so on your driver's licence.'

'Look, I'm sorry.'

'Who's Kevin Lester?'

He sighed. 'Just someone I was friends with at school.'

'Does mad Aunt Ethel even exist?' Patsy paused. 'No, of course she doesn't. You made her up.'

Silence. Keir Bourne looked away.

'And in case you're wondering, I do know who you are,' said Patsy. 'Which means I know why you came here to Stanton Langley.'

More silence, broken only by the sound of her own uneven breathing.

'And now I hate myself. I feel so stupid.' Tears filled her eyes, then slid down her cheeks and dripped on to her bare feet. 'I feel grubby and gullible and used.'

'Well you shouldn't,' said Keir, 'because I didn't mean for any of this to happen. Not this between you and me. I came here for one reason . . . a completely different reason . . . and I didn't expect to meet you, but I did. All of this, the way I

242

feel about you and the way you felt about me . . . it was real.'
He swallowed, as if on the brink of tears himself. 'It *is* real.'

Patsy's voice broke. 'You're Lily's father.'

'Yes.'

'You dumped Jo. She was all alone and pregnant, and you abandoned her.'

Keir shook his head sorrowfully. 'No, no, you've got it all wrong. It wasn't my fault.'

'You're lying again.' Sobbing now, she wiped her eyes with the sleeve of the white dressing gown.

'I'm not, I swear. Please listen to me,' Keir said with anguish in his eyes. 'Just let me explain.'

Chapter 33

Twelve years on from that night, the very, very worst of her life, Patsy wondered if this one was about to eclipse it.

All around her, at the table in the garden of Goldstone House, the rest of them were discussing the situation with varying degrees of outrage and disgust. The Sunday edition of the newspaper was yet to appear online; they were waiting for it to be uploaded within the next hour or so. And who could say what might be revealed when it did?

Patsy felt sick. For all this time she'd guarded her deepest, darkest and most shameful secret. At first she'd lived in perpetual fear that one way or another the truth would come out. Then, as the years had rolled by, the terror had lessened to a low-level rumbling anxiety. Lily had continued to be completely un-interested in meeting her biological father, and that had been the best news of all.

But now . . . oh, but now Keir was wanting to make contact with his daughter, and instead of simply writing to her, he'd chosen to do it via the medium of a national newspaper. God alone knew what he might be about to say.

'Are you OK?' Coral was looking at her with concern.

'I'm afraid . . . well, not really. I'm feeling a bit . . . ill.' Patsy's hand shook as she took a sip of water, and the rim of the tumbler clattered against her teeth.

'You do look pale,' said Eddie.

'Don't try and blame my barbecuing skills,' Dan announced. 'It's too soon for food poisoning.'

Coral said, 'It might be one of those bugs.'

'I think it could be that.' Hating herself even more, Patsy nodded weakly. 'I've been feeling a bit yuck for a few hours, but it's getting worse.'

'Poor you,' Lily exclaimed. 'And you've been trying so hard to pretend nothing's wrong. If you feel sick, I bet you're dying to go home.'

'I am feeling sick.' Patsy put the tumbler down. 'I think I probably should go. Sorry.'

'Don't be silly, it's not your fault! Would you like me to walk you home?'

Patsy said, 'It's fine. Don't worry, you stay here.' Lily's compassion was only making her feel worse. 'I'd rather be on my own.' She made stay-sitting gestures, but it was too late; Lily was already out of her chair.

'You mustn't . . .' Patsy protested as Lily hugged her. 'You don't want to catch whatever I've got.'

'I won't, I never do. Poor you,' Lily said again. 'I hope you feel better soon.'

Patsy had never felt more like Judas. Her throat tight with shame and self-loathing, she murmured, 'Me too. I'm sorry.'

Lily smiled. 'Will you stop saying that? You didn't do it on purpose!'

The shameful words echoed through Patsy's brain: *Oh, but I kind of did.*

* * *

The piece appeared on the newspaper's website at just gone midnight. As soon as Dan looked up from his phone and said, 'It's there,' Lily nodded and pushed back her chair.

'I'll read it inside. Won't be long.'

'Oh darling, are you sure you don't want anyone with you?' Coral was looking concerned.

Lily gave her hand a reassuring squeeze. 'Don't worry. I'll be fine.'

In the kitchen, Lily sat down at the scrubbed oak table and opened the page on her iPad. It wasn't a case of being worried she might cry; she simply wanted to be able to concentrate and take it all in without being aware that everyone was watching her.

All these years, the fact that she'd never once googled Keir Bourne had been a source of great pride to Lily, proof that he was a nobody who meant nothing at all. The man had never shown any interest in her, so he was absolutely irrelevant to her life. What he'd done to her mum was disgusting and reprehensible and he didn't deserve to be looked up or searched out in any way whatsoever. Lily had always refused to give him the satisfaction of finding out that she'd so much as typed his name into a search engine. A man like him was beyond contempt, and that was that.

But had she been curious? OK, yes. Of course she had. And now that he'd made his move, she needed to know what he'd said.

Forewarned is forearmed, and all that.

Willing herself to stay calm and detached, she twisted the crystal-studded bangle on her left wrist and looked at the photo that had just come up on the screen, of the man who was her biological father.

Keir Bourne had been photographed looking appropriately

sincere and concerned, sitting in a chair whilst holding one of the photos of her that had appeared in last week's newspaper.

He had short brown hair that was greying very slightly at the temples. Defined eyebrows, dark eyes and the beginnings of a double chin. He wasn't ugly; you could tell he'd been good-looking when he was younger. And if she were being honest, although there wasn't any strikingly noticeable similarity, there was something about his forehead and jawline that was reminiscent of her own.

No intense thud of recognition, though, thank goodness. And no sense of longing to meet him. Also good.

Lily exhaled and realised she was still compulsively twirling her mother's bangle around her wrist. She knew from Coral that Keir Bourne had never liked having his photo taken. When her mum had been seeing him, he'd always turned away from the camera, shielding his face with his hand or simply ducking out of sight. She'd only ever seen two or three photographs of him, and they'd been poor-quality snaps taken with a cheap throwaway camera – you'd never subsequently recognise him in real life.

Plus, those snaps had been taken before she'd been born, when he was still in his early twenties. A quarter of a century had passed since then.

Once a bastard, always a bastard.

OK, that was the first hurdle over. Bracing herself, Lily turned her attention from the photo to the text and began to read.

A week ago, Lily Harper sprang to the public's attention when she rescued a runaway mouse from superstar Mira Knowles . . . or maybe rescued Mira Knowles from a runaway mouse. Today we speak to Keir Bourne, who recognised Lily from the coverage as the daughter he's been deprived of knowing all these years, thanks to the impulsive actions of Lily's runaway mother, Jo.

'You mustn't blame her mum,' Keir anxiously tells me when we meet in a café close to his home in Milton Keynes. 'She didn't mean to cause me all these years of heartache. I'm sure in her own mind Jo's intentions were good. We loved each other so much, though; I don't think she realised how deep my feelings for her were. It was the worst pain I've ever known when I found out she no longer wanted me in her – and our daughter's – life.'

He pauses to gaze at the photograph of Lily in his hand, then gathers himself to continue. 'But as the years passed, I did my best to build a new life of my own. I married and had another daughter, but was never able to forget Lily. How could I? She was my firstborn.' Keir's voice breaks as he proceeds. 'Every single day I wondered how she was and if she was missing me. Then when Lily was seven years old, I received a letter from Jo telling me she was dying of cancer and had made arrangements for our daughter to be cared for and brought up by friends of hers. I was devastated, naturally, but she insisted she didn't want me to contact her or Lily. And although it was like a knife in my chest, I felt I had no other choice than to go along with what Jo had decided. Once again I was heartbroken.

'Seeing Lily on the front page of the papers and discovering she's now dating a mega-celebrity makes me more proud than I can say, but it also tears me apart, knowing how many years of her life I've missed out on. More than anything, I wish we could meet and get to know each other properly.'

At this point, overcome with emotion, Keir wipes his eyes and asks for a drink of water. It's achingly clear how much his long-lost daughter means to him. Heaven knows, I'm a hard-nosed journalist, but even my heart goes out to this likeable man. When I suggest gently that Lily may wonder why he's left it until now to do this, Keir shakes his head and explains to me that this isn't the first time he's tried to make contact. In fact, he has met and spoken with Lily before.

What? WHAT?

'Although she didn't find out I was her father,' he explains to me. 'My intention was to be discreet. I took the day off work and travelled to Stanton Langley in search of my daughter and met up with someone who knew her very well indeed. This person told me all about her, but stressed that Lily was happy with the people she now knew as her parents and had been brainwashed over time into thinking the worst of me. I also met Lily herself and was struck by how comfortable and settled she seemed. She was beautiful, chatty and friendly, everything you could want a daughter to be. But thirteen is a tricky age and, not wanting to cause upset and emotional trauma, I took the agonising decision not to reveal my identity.

'It was the hardest decision of my life.

'Now, though, twelve years on, I feel she deserves to know that I've always loved and missed her, and that what I did was only ever for the best. If she can find it in her heart to meet me, I'd be the happiest man in the world.'

Lily sat at the table and skimmed over the words again. When the kitchen door was pushed open behind her, she knew from the rhythmic metallic clunk who it was.

She quivered at the touch of Dan's hand on her bare shoulder. And now he was standing beside her, his good arm resting against her back.

'However you're feeling right now, it's OK to feel it.' He gave her a reassuring squeeze.

'I have no idea how I feel, that's the weird thing.' Lily shrugged and unthinkingly reached up to curl her fingers around his. 'It's like my mind's gone blank.' It was also weird for there to be this amount of physical contact between them; due to the nature of their friendship, they tended not to go in for touchy-feely gestures of concern or affection. A playful thump on the arm was more their kind of thing.

'Any memory of meeting him?' said Dan.

Lily shook her head. 'None. But it's impossible – it could have happened at any time. If I was thirteen, I was helping out in the yard whenever I wasn't at school. I suppose he spoke to me there.'

'And who did he talk to? Who gave him all that personal information?'

'No idea. I can't believe someone told him so much about me and kept it a secret all these years.' She tilted her head to gaze up at him. 'Do you think Coral knew?'

'No way. She's as shocked as you.' Dan shook his head. 'She definitely didn't have any idea.'

'Everyone's going to be wondering how I am.' Lily rose to her feet. 'We should get back out there. Thanks for coming in.'

'Hey, why wouldn't I? Any time.'

They were facing each other, Dan's jean-clad thigh resting against the side of the table, the characteristic spark of amusement

250

missing for once from his dark eyes. The connection between them stretched all the way back through both their lives; he was as concerned about tonight's developments as she was. Overcome with gratitude, and suddenly experiencing a rush of confused emotion, Lily wrapped her arms around him and buried her face in his good shoulder. In turn, Dan's arm tightened around her and she felt the warmth of his breath against her ear.

'Don't worry,' he murmured into her hair. 'Whatever happens, we'll get through this.'

And although Dan had a broken foot and a strapped-up arm, Lily knew that he was on her side and would defend her to the death.

Although hopefully it wouldn't come to *that*.

Before anyone else could burst in and misconstrue the situation, she took a step back. 'I know. Thank you. Come on, we'd better go.'

Chapter 34

The alarm was set for eight the next morning. Dan, who had barely slept, lay in bed and watched the hands of the clock approach the moment the ear-splitting bell was due to go off.

He'd broken his own strict rule last night, and now he knew how right he'd been to impose it all those years ago. The rule had been: no matter what the circumstances, never, ever give in to temptation and get physically closer to Lily than you would to your bank manager.

It had been simultaneously the best and worst experience of his life, and it must never be allowed to happen again. He'd been so desperately close to losing the last vestige of control and kissing Lily in the way he'd kissed her in his imagination more times than he'd ever dream of admitting to a living soul.

One minute to eight. Mentally bracing himself for the blast of the alarm, he forced himself to stop thinking about nearly kissing Lily. They had far more important concerns today. There was every chance that her biological father might turn up.

Patsy too had had precious little sleep. Alone in her bedroom, she had read the online piece in the paper, her stomach churning

252

with fear at both Keir Bourne's words and the photograph of him twelve years on.

He hadn't mentioned her by name, which was obviously a relief, but she was chillingly aware that she wasn't out of the woods yet.

Poor Lily.

Poor me.

Except I don't deserve any sympathy, do I?

No, you don't. None at all.

All she wanted to do was stay in bed with the covers pulled over her head.

Over at the Valentine, Eddie was packing up his belongings, ready to be collected and driven to Heathrow.

'I wish I didn't have to leave you like this.' He paused and reached down to kiss Lily, who was dressed and sitting cross-legged on the king-sized bed with her iPad, studying the online comments left by the newspaper's readers.

'It's OK, I'm a grown-up. I can cope.' She returned the kiss. He had to fly over to New York for meetings, and they weren't the kind where you could call in sick with a croaky voice and cancel. 'You have your job, I have mine.'

'Do you really need to work today? What if this guy turns up?'

This guy. It was how they'd been referring to Keir Bourne.

Lily shrugged. 'If it's going to happen, it'll happen. I'm not going to hide from him. You should see the messages some people are leaving on here.' Fascinated, she scrolled through a few more.

Eddie said, 'Rule number one, never, ever read the online comments. They'll melt your brain.'

'"Does this girl think she's a celebritty now, just because she caught a mouse? How pathetick that she is so desparate for attenttion she's making up storys like this!' 'Wow,' said Lily. 'And they managed to spell almost every word wrong.'

She was doing her best to laugh it off, but just knowing that someone actually thought she'd arranged the whole thing was a kick in the gut.

Another one said, 'Why do the dad's always get the blame? Maybe the girl was just an ugly baby. Get overrrrr it!'

Next came: 'It's the woman's fault for getting herself up the duff in the first place.'

Below which someone had replied: 'Sexist pig!'

The next one said, 'Probly her mother smoked fags and was a cheating bitch and that's why he left. Like my ex missus.'

Followed by: 'How on earth is this news? Who are these people? DON'T CARE.'

Well, quite. For a split second, Lily was tempted to reply: *Hear hear!*

But no, she mustn't. That way madness lay.

She put down the iPad and sat back against the pillows, perfectly well aware that reading the comments was her way of trying to distract herself from what might happen later on today. A knot kept tightening in her stomach at the thought of finally coming face to face with Keir Bourne.

At that moment her phone rang and Dan's name flashed up. She pressed answer. 'Hey, you're awake.'

'I am. I know, it's like a miracle.' His tone softened. 'How are you?'

The way he said it, the sound of his voice, made her feel the tiniest bit better. 'Bearing up.'

'Oh God, isn't that what women do when they're having a baby? Don't tell me you've gone into labour.'

He might drive her nuts, but he'd always been able to make

her smile. 'That's bearing down. Shows how much you know about giving birth.'

Which caused Eddie, across the room, to pause a moment in the middle of folding his blue shirt.

'Thank goodness,' said Dan. 'Are you still going into work?'

'Of course.'

'Want me to keep you company?'

Touched, Lily said, 'Would you? That'd be great.'

'No problem. I'll see you in a bit.'

'How's Patsy this morning?'

'Still not herself. She's staying in bed.'

Oh dear, was there anything worse than feeling ill? 'Poor thing,' Lily said sympathetically. 'Tell her I hope she feels better soon.'

By midday, Lily was discovering that the waiting for something to happen was the worst bit. Like the day your GCSE results were due to arrive, or that sick sense of dread as you sat in the dentist's waiting room about to have your wisdom teeth wrenched out.

But that kind of physical pain was far easier to deal with; it hurt like hell for a bit, then gradually faded away and you knew the worst was over. Whereas this felt different and could have the potential to leave wounds that wouldn't heal. Because despite putting on a brave face and pretending she was fine, the nerves were really starting to kick in now. Beneath the surface she was dreading hearing something she might not want to know.

'OK?' murmured Dan when she went into the office to fetch the bubble wrap.

He knew, of course. Other people might be fooled by her couldn't-care-less manner, but not Dan. His good hand brushed against hers as he passed her the roll, and that familiar tingle zipped up her arm. In a moment of weakness Lily found herself pretending to lose her grip on the slippery plastic so that their fingers could briefly make contact again. *Zinnggg*. Stupid, but it was just something she needed this morning. Every little helped.

'Don't worry.' Dan's voice was reassuring. 'I'm here. You'll be fine.'

'I know.' She met his gaze, saw the concern and compassion in those black-lashed dark eyes. 'I just wish it would hurry up and happen.'

Forty minutes later, it did. Lily was hefting a stack of duck-egg-blue glazed stone garden troughs into the back of a customer's battered old Jaguar when she realised she was being watched by a pretty blonde girl.

When the girl turned her head to one side and Lily saw the pink streak in her hair, she knew. Dan had told her about his encounter with the journalist in Ted Wilson's shop. She finished loading the troughs into the Jaguar's boot and waved the driver off, then turned back to look at the girl. It was almost a relief to have the waiting over at last.

'Hi. I'm Shaz. Looks like you know why I'm here.' And now the girl was in front of her, beaming and enthusiastically shaking her hand. 'It's so good to finally meet you!'

'Is he here now?'

'Your dad?'

'Keir Bourne,' said Lily.

'He is.' Shaz nodded. 'Oh Lily, he's so looking forward to meeting you again. Properly this time. You have no idea how much it means to him.'

Lily swallowed; she didn't need to do this. She could walk

away now, lock herself inside the house and refuse to come out. Nobody could force her to meet him.

But that would give him more importance than he deserved. Allowing him to meet her and remaining detached would show him just how much of an irrelevance he was in her life.

Plus it would get it out of the way. Done and dusted. Then she could have her mild curiosity assuaged and go back to ignoring him once more.

Even as these thoughts were spinning – for the millionth time – through her brain, Lily was aware of the sound of car doors slamming a short distance away, followed by footsteps crossing the road towards her. All of a sudden a frantic horse race was starting up in her chest and the thunder of galloping hooves threatened to drown out everything else.

But on the outside she remained calm. She turned and there he was, the man whose photograph she'd seen in last week's newspaper. The man whose genes she shared.

Without him, she wouldn't exist.

And now he was here, heading towards her, and she was feeling . . .

Nothing.

Nothing at all.

Good, that was good. She hadn't wanted to feel anything and her wish had evidently been granted.

Indifference was the order of the day.

'Oh Lily, my baby . . .' As he said it, Keir Bourne tentatively held out his arms and Lily took a small step back. Something about the delivery of the words felt off, as if they'd been someone else's idea. She became aware of a small man with a huge Nikon taking photos from the other side of the road. Shaz, meanwhile, was watching and listening with her phone in her left hand and an avid smile on her face.

To avoid a hug, Lily shook hands with Keir Bourne and said, 'I don't remember meeting you before.'

'It wasn't for very long, just a few minutes. And it was twelve years ago, so why would you remember? But it's wonderful to see you again now. It's been like torture, knowing I was missing out on so much of your life. Not a day's passed when I haven't thought about you, Lily. All these years I've dreamed of us getting to know each other. You're my flesh and blood, after all . . .'

Lily was struck by the irony that she'd felt more – so much more – when she'd first met Declan just a few short weeks ago. They might not share a bloodline, but the bond between them, the instinctive connection, had been there from the word go.

People were stopping to see what was going on, to watch and listen to the family reunion that was being so assiduously recorded by the photographer.

'Can we move somewhere more private?' Hearing the familiar rhythmic clunk of Dan's metal crutch on the pavement behind her, Lily realised that word of the meeting had spread and he'd come out to support her. Flashing him a look of gratitude over her shoulder, she turned back to Keir. 'Follow me.'

'Can I come along too?' Shaz had her cheery-but-sympathetic face on.

Lily shook her head. 'No.'

'Darling,' said Coral as Lily led Keir Bourne towards the gates of Goldstone House, 'if you want me with you, just say.' Her cool nod in Keir's direction indicated precisely what she thought of him.

Lily was grateful, but there were too many customers; they couldn't all be left to fend for themselves. 'It's OK, I'm taking Dan with me.'

Shaz said, 'Well if you're having Dan, surely Keir could have me in with him? I'd be as quiet as a mouse, I promise!'

The photographer was still clicking away alongside them, muttering *yes, yes* to himself each time he got a good shot. Shaz was giving Dan a hopeful smile.

'Oh dear, how can I put this?' said Lily. 'Still no.'

Chapter 35

'You're hurt,' Keir said, once the three of them were alone in the kitchen of Goldstone House. 'I understand that. You've heard your mother's version of events, but you've never heard mine.'

'Go on, then.' Lily sat down at the kitchen table to keep some distance between them. He was well dressed, wearing a dark blue crew-neck sweater over a white shirt and dark grey trousers that looked brand new. Had he made the effort just for her?

'Look, you have to understand how young we were. I was living at home, working for the family business. My parents went ballistic when they found out Jo was pregnant. And it was Jo's decision to take the money they gave her and disappear. I was the one who was abandoned,' said Keir. 'If she'd stayed with me in Exeter, we could have made a go of things, I know we could.'

'That's not what she told Coral,' Lily said evenly.

'But Coral wasn't there, was she? Listen, I'm sorry you lost your mum, but maybe it made life easier for her to tell people she'd been abandoned. Maybe it was her way of getting sympathy . . . oh dear, I don't mean it badly, but perhaps she thought it was the best way to deal with a difficult situation. But she was a fantastic girl and I did love her.' He gestured helplessly. 'I'm just trying to explain that I know you think I'm the bad guy here . . . but what if I'm not as bad as you think?'

Wasn't he? Lily didn't believe him. She wanted him to leave. But now that he was here, she also wanted to learn more details from him about her mum.

'Tell me about how the two of you met.' At least she could do this; hearing the stories from Declan about his adventures with Jo in Barcelona had been such a joyful experience, creating brand-new memories for her to treasure forever. Even if her mum's relationship with this other man had ended badly, their first months together must have been happy.

'Um . . . well, I suppose we were in a bar.'

'And?' said Lily.

Keir looked baffled. Finally he shrugged. 'We must have got chatting somehow. Then I'd have offered to buy her a drink . . . then we'd have talked some more.'

'Do you remember?' said Lily. 'Or are you just guessing?'

'I kind of remember. It was twenty-seven years ago,' Keir protested. 'But when you first meet a girl, that's what you do, isn't it?'

'What was she wearing?'

He frowned. 'Jeans? And . . . some kind of top?'

'Well let's hope so,' said Lily.

He began to smile, then saw that she wasn't smiling back. 'Sorry, I'm not great at noticing clothes. But I know we really liked each other. At the end of the evening we arranged to meet up again, and it went on from there.'

Lily said, 'What did you buy her for her birthday?'

'I didn't know this was going to be Twenty Questions.' He

261

half laughed and gestured vaguely. 'Um, a box of chocolates, I expect. And some flowers.'

'What kind of chocolates did she like?' Lily knew her mum had hated the dark kind.

'Er . . . Black Magic?'

It was like trying to drag memories out of a brick wall. Shaking her head in disbelief, Lily glanced across the kitchen at Dan, who murmured, 'Romantic.'

'Look, I'm sorry if I'm not saying the right things here, but I'm doing my best. And I'm still your father.' Keir took a deep breath. 'Can I just say, I'm glad you've had a good life. I'm sorry your mum died. And I'm so proud of you. Seeing you in the paper with Eddie Tessler was just . . . Is he here, by the way? I'd love to meet him. Shaz says if we could get a couple of photos of you, me and Eddie together, that would be—'

'Oh my God.' Anger flared in Lily. 'Is that why you're here? Is that all you care about – meeting Eddie?'

Hastily he shook his head. 'No, no . . . that was Shaz's idea, not mine. She was the one who wanted me to ask that.'

'Of course she was,' said Lily tightly.

'This isn't fair,' said Keir. 'You're my daughter. I've wanted to get to know you for years.'

'But you didn't,' Lily retaliated.

'Because your mother thought it was for the best. I stayed away for that reason, for *your* benefit. She'd arranged your life and decided it wasn't going to include me. But that wasn't my fault . . . I'd have done anything to get to know you.'

'I don't believe that for one minute.'

'Well it's true.'

Lily said coldly, 'Handy for you, too. If you'd been that keen, though, I'm sure you could have made some effort.' She didn't even care; God only knew why she was arguing the point. The sooner he was out of here, the better.

'I did make the effort.' Keir's jaw jutted. 'I came down here, remember? Twelve years ago.'

'Allegedly,' said Lily. Who was to say he hadn't been lying about that too?

'I did. It was in December. I met you for a few minutes.' He glanced over at Dan. 'I met you too.'

Dan raised an eyebrow.

'Right here? Was I working out in the yard?' said Lily.

'No. You'd just arrived home from school on the bus. You,' Keir pointed at Dan, 'were pretty sarcastic. Then you both headed off and I carried on hearing all about you from this girl I'd met in the café.'

'You asked a load of questions about me and she told you everything you wanted to know. Why would she even do that?'

'Honestly?' He broke into a smile at the memory. 'Because she liked me. A lot.'

'But this girl never told me you'd been here,' said Lily. 'That makes no sense. Why wouldn't she?'

'I don't know, maybe because she was embarrassed? Because she regretted what she'd done?'

'This is bullshit,' Dan broke in. 'None of it's true. He's bluffing, making the whole thing up.'

'I'm not,' said Keir. 'We spent the night together at the Valentine Hotel.' The veneer of charm was sliding away. 'Had a very nice time, if you know what I mean.'

What a lowlife. 'So what was her name?' asked Lily.

'I can't remember.'

'That's handy, isn't it?' said Dan. 'It's almost as if this mystery female never even existed.'

'Oh she existed all right.' The note of triumph was audible

263

in Keir Bourne's voice; he was almost smirking now. 'And I may have forgotten her name,' he went on, directly addressing Dan, 'but I definitely remember that she was your sister.'

A stunned silence reverberated through the kitchen. Lily heard her own heartbeat thundering in her ears. She waited for Keir Bourne to say, 'Ha, fooled you'; for it to have been his idea of a sick joke.

But he wasn't laughing. Instead he was looking decidedly pleased with himself.

Across the room, practically vibrating with fury, Dan said, 'You're a disgusting human being.'

'And a liar,' said Lily.

'Ah, you'd like it not to be true.' Keir Bourne shifted on his chair. 'But it is.'

'You don't even know her name,' said Dan.

'Oh come on. From the look of you, I don't imagine you remember the name of every girl you ever slept with.'

'Fuck off,' said Dan. 'How dare you? Patsy wouldn't touch you with a bargepole.'

'Patsy. That's it, that's her name. She was the one who introduced you to me at the bus stop. I was wearing dark-rimmed glasses,' said Keir. 'She was wearing a red coat. It was just starting to snow.'

Lily was barely breathing. The tiniest memory was beginning to unfurl, like a sprouting seed sending a tendril of green up through the earth. Patsy, greeting them at the bus stop with a stranger in tow . . . a man in glasses who had said something trivial to them . . . and Dan had given him a typically cheeky answer. It had been a cold afternoon and Patsy had protested that they should be wearing coats too. That was as far as Lily's memory went. She and Dan had run off down the road. Since that day she hadn't given the chance encounter another thought.

Dan had evidently been dredging up details of that same afternoon. He said suddenly, 'You were there because you were waiting to meet someone off the bus. But they weren't on it.'

Pleased, Keir Bourne said, 'Well done. See? I knew you could do it if you tried.'

'So you lied about that. And you lied to Patsy as well. She had no idea who you were.'

Lily felt sick. It was hideous enough to think of this man flirting with Patsy, let alone anything more intimate happening between them. But it was beginning to seem as if it might actually be true. God, poor Patsy when she found out; she'd be devastated. Maybe they wouldn't tell her. If she were to discover she'd once slept with this vile man, she'd just die.

'Putting it all together now? And yes, we spent the night at the Valentine,' said Keir Bourne. 'Pretty nice place; expensive, too. So you see, there's no need to look down your noses at me and accuse me of lying.' There was a definite edge to his voice. 'Because I haven't lied about anything at all.'

Dan had already said it; now it was Lily's turn. Icily she reminded him, 'Except Patsy didn't know who you were.'

'And that's where you're wrong again,' said Keir Bourne. 'You really shouldn't jump to conclusions. She knew.'

'How fucking dare you?' Dan's spine was rigid, his face closed with fury.

'Don't believe me? Again?' Keir was enjoying himself now. 'Go on then, ask her yourself.'

Chapter 36

It was called facing the music.

Except there wasn't any music.

Not that it would help if there were. This, Patsy knew, was the very worst time of her life and all she could do now was endure it and suffer the consequences.

She had known what was going on the moment her mobile had rung and Dan had said, 'He's here. We're in the kitchen. Will you come over and join us?'

And Dan, in turn, must have known at once that she knew when she simply said yes without asking why.

Now she was walking down the road in the direction of Goldstone House, about to explain why she had done something for which there was no excuse.

How many times had she gone through it in her mind, desperately attempting to justify her decision? The years slid backwards all over again as Patsy relived the initial outrage when she'd discovered his true identity. Her disgust and fury had been visceral. He'd lied to her, seduced her with his charms and persuaded her to have sex with him because she'd believed he genuinely liked her.

Yet again, needless to say, she'd been wrong.

And then what was she supposed to do? It was snowing heavily outside. Her security-conscious mother, having double-locked and bolted the front door of the cottage, would be fast asleep in bed. If she walked home, she wouldn't be able to get in. At three o'clock in the morning, she could hardly start banging on other people's front doors either.

Although now, of course, Patsy wished more than anything in the world that she had. Curling up on the bench next to the bus stop and spending the rest of the night getting covered in snow would have been so much better than staying in that room, in that huge velvet-canopied four-poster bed.

With an adulterer whose name happened to be Keir Bourne.

But finally, because there simply hadn't been a viable alternative, she had fallen into a miserable, guilt-racked, exhausted sleep.

At seven the next morning she'd slid silently out of bed, washed and dressed herself while Keir Bourne slept on, then finally prodded him into wakefulness.

When he turned and saw her standing there in her red coat, he said casually, 'You off, then?'

'You need to leave here and never come back. I mean it.' Her knuckles whitened as she gripped the straps of her handbag. 'Never, ever. Lily doesn't want to know you, she's happy as she is. Coral and Nick are her parents now.'

'Fine. Suits me.' As he said it, Keir smothered a yawn.

'Promise me you'll stay away.'

'Is this about Lily? Or about you?'

'Both.' Her armpits prickled with humiliation; it was shameful enough that she'd allowed herself to be picked up by a stranger and had ended up spending the night with him, let alone that he'd turned out to be Lily's father. 'You have to promise. Nobody's ever going to know you were here, and they must never find out about . . . this.'

He was smiling, unconcerned. 'Us sleeping together, you mean?'

Patsy wanted to cry but she couldn't allow it to happen. She wanted to peel off her own skin. She'd betrayed Lily and betrayed herself. She was a disgusting human being.

'I mean it,' she told Keir Bourne. 'Or I'll tell your wife.'

Not that she ever would have done, but he wasn't to know that. He'd hastily agreed with her and made the promise. The snow had stopped falling, a gritting lorry had already trundled past and the road was now passable. Keir would leave the hotel, leave Stanton Langley and she had his word he would never return.

Twelve years on, he'd broken that promise.

Oh God, she'd arrived at Goldstone House. Patsy braced herself. It was all about to go off.

Lily knew the moment the kitchen door opened and she saw Patsy's face, white with terror rather than illness.

Because of course Patsy hadn't been taken ill last night; she'd simply got the shock of her life.

Well she wasn't the only one.

First Keir Bourne turning up, having sold his story to the paper. And now this.

This.

'He says you spent the night together at the Valentine.' Dan wasted no time in getting to the point.

'We did.' Patsy was looking as if she wanted to be sick.

'And you knew who he was.'

'Not at first. Not for hours. Not until after . . .'

'Then you found out,' Dan continued, 'but you still stayed there with him.'

Patsy opened her mouth to protest, then closed it again. She nodded miserably.

268

'Even though you knew who he was,' Dan went on, the disgust evident in his voice.

'I'm sorry.' Patsy shook her head miserably. 'It was snowing and too late to come home. But I still shouldn't have stayed.'

'See?' said Keir Bourne. 'I told you I wasn't lying. And then she made me promise I'd never come back, never try to contact you again. Not for your benefit,' he added, addressing Lily with an air of vindication. 'She just wanted to make sure her guilty secret was safe.'

'Oh God,' said Lily. 'You knew he came here to see me. You knew he was *interested* enough to do that, to see how I was doing, but you never told me. You decided I didn't need to know.'

Still too ashamed to cry, Patsy said wretchedly, 'You must hate me.'

Lily stared at Patsy and it was like looking into the eyes of a stranger. Oh well, seeing as everyone else was being honest all of a sudden, and seeing as she was feeling about as hurt and betrayed as it was physically possible to feel . . .

'Do I hate you? Right now? Honestly?' All of a sudden, she had to say it. 'Yes, I do.'

There was a moment of charged silence, then Patsy said, 'You can't hate me more than I hate myself.'

Dan watched as Patsy left the kitchen, stifling a sob as she closed the door behind her.

Lily saw the faint smile on Keir Bourne's face. 'You're a pretty unpleasant human being, aren't you?' she said. 'Do you still cheat on your wife?' Her dark eyes blazed. 'Doesn't matter, I don't need to know. Anyway, I never want to see you again. You're nothing to me. Never have been, never will be.'

It was her turn to stand and walk out.

'And then there were two,' said Dan. 'In case you're wondering, however much Lily despises you, I despise you more.'

Keir Bourne shrugged and said nothing.

'Seriously, why the fuck did you do this? You don't care about Lily, so what's the point?'

'I needed the money.'

'Oh, great.'

'It's all right for people like you. You couldn't begin to understand. My marriage ended a few months ago, my wife kicked me out of the house, I'm living in a crappy bedsit. Not having enough money to enjoy yourself is depressing,' said Keir. 'When I saw the photos of Lily in the paper and realised who she was, I was pleased she'd done well for herself. Then I happened to mention it to one of my mates down the pub, and he said I should call the newspaper, ask them how much they'd pay for a story. But I didn't, because I told myself I wasn't that kind of person.' He stared down at the table for a couple of seconds.

'How did they find you, then? By hiring Derren Brown?'

'My mate called the paper and told them about me. Shaz turned up at the pub that same evening. She was very persuasive,' said Keir. 'Once she has her mind set on something, it's hard to say no.' He sighed. 'And she made me an offer I couldn't refuse.'

'How much?' said Dan.

'A grand.'

'What? Are you serious? That's the offer you couldn't refuse?'

'Again, when you don't have any spare cash, that's a lot.'

'So you've come here and caused all this mess . . .' Dan indicated the kitchen door, through which first Patsy then Lily had departed, 'for a thousand pounds. Lily's your biological daughter and you've done this to her. Wow, you really are a hero.'

'And I suppose you've never made any mistakes in your life,' Keir retaliated.

He was growing up, Dan realised. Maturing. A couple of years ago he wouldn't have thought twice about launching himself at Keir Bourne, even in his currently crippled condition. He still had one good leg to stand on and one good arm capable of landing a punch that would demonstrate his utter contempt for this man and what he'd done. One perfect punch and bugger the consequences.

But he wasn't going to give in to that urge, tempting though it was. The damage may already have been done here; however, there was something to be said for preventing possible future damage. Breaking Keir Bourne's jaw wouldn't be such a clever move.

God, though, just for that split second wouldn't it feel great?

'I'd better go and find Shaz, tell her what's going on,' Keir Bourne said wearily. 'I don't suppose there's going to be any more photos they can use.'

Oh, the temptation . . .

'Don't get up,' said Dan as the older man went to push back his chair. 'There's something else I need to say to you first.'

Patsy found Sean and Will sunbathing in their back garden, reading the Sunday papers and blissfully unaware of everything that had gone on.

Well they'd hear about it soon enough. Everyone would know by this time tomorrow. Stanton Langley might have plenty of good things going for it, but keeping secrets wasn't one of them.

'I did a bad thing and now I'm running away for a bit.

271

Sorry to mess you about.' She handed the keys to the salon over to Will. 'Can you apologise to my regulars and say I'll be back next week?' If they even wanted to let her do their hair after this. 'I've called Jenna and she's going to fill in while I'm away.'

'Whoa, hold on, what's happened?' Sean sat up and took off his sunglasses. 'What's this about?'

'I'm a terrible person and now everyone knows about it. I need to go, because I'm a coward and I just can't face anyone for a while. Ask Lily or Dan, they'll tell you what I did.'

'Oh Pats.' There was concern in Sean's eyes, those kind grey eyes she'd encountered for the first time just a few short months after her tryst at the Valentine Hotel. She'd been so thrilled to meet Sean, had thought her luck had changed at last . . . ha, had even imagined that in some cosmic way she'd been forgiven for the shameful incident with Keir Bourne.

Except of course the cosmos had been playing the long game and had had one last triumphant twist in store.

Patsy was still trying hard not to cry. Sean said, 'Is it a man?'

'Isn't it always?' She could barely squeeze the words out past the lump in her throat.

'Oh sweetheart.' He wrapped his arms around her and gave her a consoling hug. Patsy let it happen, because there would be no more hugs once he found out what she'd done.

Not from anyone.

Chapter 37

Arriving home on Friday afternoon, Declan found Gail already there, having let herself into the house in order to start preparing dinner.

'I finished work early.' She gave him a brief kiss on the lips before turning back to attend to the salmon fillets and broccoli. 'Thought I'd surprise you.'

Battered cod and chips would have been the real surprise. Declan said, 'I just need to go upstairs to the office and check through a couple of contracts.' He shrugged off his jacket and left his phone and car keys on the kitchen worktop.

'How long will you be?'

'No more than twenty minutes.' He put his hand to his heart. 'And that's a promise.'

Upstairs in his office, he kicked off his shoes, then waited a couple of minutes before making his way back down to the kitchen, where he found Gail going through his phone with the thoroughness of a KGB agent. So his instincts had been right after all. He stood in the doorway and watched as, head bent and fingers darting at the speed of light, she scrolled through his emails, instant messages and recently called phone numbers.

Utterly oblivious to his presence behind her, she jumped a mile when he said, 'What are you doing?'

The phone slid from her fingers and clattered on to the worktop. Ah, she'd moved on to photos. Reaching past her and scooping it up, Declan said, 'Looking for anything in particular? Maybe I can help you find it.'

Caught out, Gail went on the attack. 'You were on the phone to Lily this morning for twenty-three minutes.'

'I know.'

'You've spoken to her four times this week.'

'And? She's had a lot going on. You know that.' What with Keir Bourne's reappearance, followed by the Patsy bombshell, it had been a traumatic few days for Lily.

Gail lifted her chin. 'So you're still planning to drive down tomorrow and spend next week there.'

'You know that too. I told you I was.'

'You can't stay at Goldstone House with Lily. You just can't.' Shaking her head, Gail said, 'Absolutely not.'

Declan was incredulous. 'You can't seriously be thinking there's anything going on between Lily and me.'

'*I* don't think that, but other people might. And you can't tell me there isn't something suspicious going on. There was another number you rang this morning, with the local code for Stanton Langley. Who was that?'

'I don't know, maybe it was the plumber working at the cottage.'

'Except it was a landline number,' Gail retorted. 'You got off the phone to Lily and called it two minutes later.'

Declan nodded, remembering. 'Yes, that was me calling Coral.'

'Ah, now we're getting to it. What about?'

Only the fact that he'd already made his decision meant that Declan didn't mind answering the question. He said evenly,

'Coral was wanting to cancel her trip to the South of France because she didn't want to leave Lily, what with everything that's happened. Lily asked me to speak to her, to persuade her to go.'

'And did you?'

'I did.' It had actually been a confusing scenario, seeing that given the choice, he would have far preferred Coral to postpone the holiday so she'd still be at home while he was staying there. But he'd done as Lily wanted and assured Coral that he'd be around to keep an eye on things. Because he knew from Lily how much the break in Grimaud would mean to Coral. And he'd eventually managed to make her see sense and agree to fly to Nice.

Even though it wasn't what he wanted.

Oh well.

'Interested in Coral, are you?' Gail said it lightly, but there was a faint edge to her voice.

'No,' said Declan.

'Sure about that?'

Jealousy had always been the ultimate turn-off for him. Luckily, years of bidding at auction had honed his poker face; he was skilled at not giving anything away. 'Quite sure, thanks,' he said calmly. 'How long has the phone-checking been going on?'

'Not long.'

How had she even known the code to unlock it? By covertly watching him, Declan supposed, since it wasn't a number he'd ever written down. He thought back to the couple of occasions recently when he'd opened his office drawers upstairs and sensed that the contents weren't exactly as he'd left them. He gazed steadily at Gail. 'Have you been going through the papers in my office too?'

She hesitated just long enough – presumably wondering if he'd had CCTV installed – to confirm what he'd begun to suspect. He shook his head. 'OK, well I think we've reached the end of the line here.'

Gail flushed. 'What line?'

'This.' He indicated the two of them. 'Us. I'm sorry, I can't cope with being spied on.'

'But I just had to—'

'No, you didn't. And I never imagined you'd do it. I didn't think you were the type.'

'Oh for heaven's sake.' Gail's voice rose. 'That's just it, I'm *not* the type! I've never been like it before, but you've forced me into it by being this way.'

'This way.' Declan shrugged. 'What way?'

'Oh come on, you know . . . that place. Everything to do with Stanton Langley . . . that cottage you've bought, the people there . . . and if you ask me, I bet—'

'Well I'm not asking you,' Declan cut in. 'I don't want to know.' He meant it too; Gail could be cutting when she wanted, and he couldn't bear to hear whatever dismissive comments she might be about to make. 'This isn't working out. I think you should leave now.'

She blinked. 'You mean it's over? *We're* over?'

'That's what I mean, yes.'

'For real?'

'For real.'

'What about this?' Gail pointed to the salmon fillets and broccoli sitting sadly in their white ceramic baking dish along with a shallow puddle of rice wine vinegar and a smear of wasabi.

Did anyone seriously like wasabi?

'You can take it with you if you want,' said Declan. Personally,

276

for the next few months he was planning on giving salmon and broccoli a miss.

Gail gathered herself. 'I'll go and get my things,' she said coolly.

She was only gone for a few minutes; it didn't take long to collect together her toothbrush, toiletries bag and expensive silk nightdress. When she returned to the kitchen, she was in complete control once more. 'I hope you're sure about this. You may live to regret it.'

'I may,' Declan agreed, because she still had her pride.

'And then you'll be sorry. Because if I leave now, that's it. No going back.'

Thank goodness for that. He shook his head. 'I know.'

'OK, well I'll be off then.' Gail placed his spare front-door key on the kitchen worktop. 'I daresay we can be civil about this. No need for any awkwardness.'

Relieved, Declan said, 'Definitely no need.'

'Seeing as we know so many of the same people,' said Gail, 'I hope we can let them think our decision to separate was mutual.'

Ah, back to keeping up appearances. Declan nodded gravely. 'Easier all round.'

'Can I just ask you one last time? Is there anything going on between you and any of the women in Stanton Langley?'

Declan shook his head, and this time he was being entirely honest. 'While you were searching my phone, did you find anything?'

'No,' Gail admitted.

'That's because there's nothing to find.' He spread his hands. 'And that's the honest truth.'

'Right. OK, I believe you.' Evidently relieved that she was leaving the relationship without having been cheated on, Gail nodded. 'I do.'

'Thanks.' Why was he even thanking her? He had no idea.

She kissed him politely on both cheeks, as if they were distant acquaintances who'd bumped into each other in the street. 'I'll be off then. Just put foil on top. Take it out after twenty minutes.'

'Sorry?' The mind boggled; what on earth was she talking about?

'The salmon and broccoli,' said Gail.

'Oh, right, of course.' Declan wondered how next door's cat would feel about wasabi. He showed Gail to the front door, extremely glad she hadn't sobbed.

'Just a word of warning, though, before I go.' She paused in the doorway. 'There may be a few awkward moments ahead for you with Coral.'

The hairs rose on the back of Declan's neck. 'What?'

'Just giving you the heads-up.' Gail regarded him with amusement.

'Why? I don't know what you mean.'

'Have you seriously not noticed? She has a crush on you.'

A whoosh of adrenalin had him in its grip. At least his look of disbelief was genuine. Stunned, he swallowed. 'What makes you think that?'

'Simple.' Gail shrugged. 'I asked her.'

What? *What?*

He raked his fingers through his hair. 'Are you serious? When?'

'Last weekend. You know what I'm like,' said Gail. 'If I want to know the answer to something, I'll ask the question.'

Or scroll through a phone.

But the phone thing was irrelevant now. 'Hang on, you're telling me you asked Coral if she had a crush on me and she said yes?'

More amusement. 'Oh no. She said no.'

He stared at her. 'I don't get it. So she doesn't, then.'

'Declan, do keep up. I'm a woman, aren't I? She definitely does. I can tell.' Declan continued to look stunned. 'See what I mean about awkward? But I thought you deserved to know so you can let her down gently. Forewarned is forearmed, after all.'

'Right,' Declan said slowly.

'Anyway, I'm off now. Bye.'

'Bye.' Still in something of a daze, he heard himself say, 'Sorry.'

Evidently pleased with herself for having shared Coral's secret with him, Gail said smugly, 'No need. Your loss.'

Chapter 38

Declan left his house on Saturday morning aiming to reach Stanton Langley by midday. He knew that Coral had booked a cab at one to take her to the airport. Obviously he had no intention of saying anything about what Gail had told him, but just the thought of seeing Coral again before she left for France was enough to make his heart race with anticipation.

He'd barely slept last night, going over and over in his head the words Gail had uttered. She'd been so completely sure of herself, too. And if her deduction was correct . . . well, that made all the difference in the world.

Roadworks on the motorway meant one lane was closed. Traffic was heavy; it seemed as if half of London had decided to escape the city this morning and were all doing it at the same time. This was fine, though: Declan had anticipated the holiday exodus and factored the delay into his time schedule.

Until a caravan got tangled with a lorry and ended up lying on its side across both remaining lanes, causing a six-mile tailback and a fair amount of colourful language amongst those caught up in it.

By the time Declan arrived in Stanton Langley and pulled up outside Goldstone House, it was 1.15.

'Hello!' Lily greeted him with a hug. 'How are you? You just missed Coral, she left less than a minute ago – poor thing, she was starting to panic because her taxi was late turning up. You must have passed her at the end of the street!'

So the silver taxi he'd seen at the traffic lights had contained Coral. For a moment Declan felt like a small child being told he'd just missed Father Christmas.

Oh well, she'd be back in a week. It wouldn't kill him to wait, would it?

Aloud he said, 'She'll have a great time over there.'

Lily beamed. 'I know, it's going to do her the world of good. She used to love painting so much. I bet she'll have a fantastic week.'

Deliberately dismissing thoughts of Coral having a fantastic week in the South of France, Declan said, 'And how are you doing?'

'Not too bad. Keeping myself busy. Look, you don't need to sleep at Weaver's Cottage—'

'It's fine, I promise.' He shook his head; they'd already discussed this on the phone. Gail had been right when she'd said other people might find the idea of him staying at Goldstone House inappropriate. 'I really don't mind at all.'

Lily's eyes were sparkling. 'Ah, but this is a whole new plan. Dan had a text from Patsy this morning saying she isn't going to be back for another week. So you can stay with Dan.'

'Patsy's away for another week? Is she OK?'

'I imagine so. I haven't rung her to ask, if that's what you're wondering.' Lily's shrug was deliberately offhand. 'We don't know where she is. But she's apparently spoken to Jenna, who's staying on to cover for her at the salon.' She paused, then changed the subject. 'So anyway, how about that for an idea? You and Dan at his place?'

It would certainly be more comfortable than sleeping on the floor at Weaver's Cottage. 'How does Dan feel about it?'

'Hey, he's the injured party who can't carry a cup of tea out of the kitchen without tipping it over himself like Mr Bean.' Good humour restored, Lily said, 'It was Dan's idea.'

'In that case, perfect,' said Declan.

'Hooray.' She hugged him again. 'Oh I'm so glad you're back!'

The piece in this Sunday's edition of the newspaper appeared online just before midnight. It was far smaller than last week's double-page spread. Dan swung his laptop round so they could view the screen, and Lily and Declan leaned across the table to read the article.

Lily, who had been bracing herself all evening – all week, if she were being honest – saw that it was essentially a non-story. Having scanned Keir Bourne's words, she felt the tension seep out of her body, all the pent-up anxiety magically recede.

'Oh, thank God. I thought he was going to say all sorts of horrible things.' She took a glug of Dan's wine, because her own glass was empty. 'But he hasn't badmouthed me at all.'

Now that he hadn't, she almost felt guilty for having thought he might.

'Well, what would that have made him look like? Anyway,' Declan raised his own glass to her, 'good news. Here's to you.'

'Cheers.' Lily clinked and took another glug.

'I'd say cheers too,' Dan said mournfully, 'but someone stole my drink.'

Lily studied the photos accompanying the article more carefully. The first, of the reunion itself, looked every bit as uncomfortable as it had felt: two strangers awkwardly encountering each other in the street. The second, presumably taken afterwards, showed Keir Bourne looking sad, and the accompanying text quoted him as saying, 'It wasn't the outcome I was hoping for, but I respect Lily's decision not to want any further contact with me. There's nothing more to be done. I just wish her and Eddie Tessler all the very best for the future.'

The third and final photograph was of Keir Bourne's ex-wife and teenage daughter, neither of whom spoke to him any longer. The ex-wife, Tanya, had told Shaz, 'You want my honest opinion? Sure about that? OK, Keir Bourne was a lousy husband and father who was capable of turning on the charm when it suited him. He had several affairs that I knew of, and I'm sure there were plenty more I never got to hear about. Our lives are far happier now without him around to mess us about, and I don't blame Lily one bit for not wanting anything to do with him. That kind of hassle has to be the last thing she'd need.'

The daughter, Sasha, was equally blunt. She said, 'Lily's well off out of it. Trust me, she hasn't missed out on anything, not having our father in her life. I'm fifteen years old and last Christmas he gave me a teddy bear he'd bought in a petrol station on Christmas Eve. I know this because he left the receipt in the plastic bag it was wrapped up in.' Finally, asked if she was curious to meet her older half-sister, the girl had replied, 'To be truthful, I'm not bothered. I mean, Lily's pretty and everything, but the two of us don't look anything alike. Seeing photos of her doesn't make me long to meet her just because we happen to have the same biological father. Especially when we both wish we didn't. Still, she seems like a nice person, so good luck to her. And if she happens to read this, here's a message from me: Hi, Lily, you had a lucky escape!'

Lily finished reading. 'That poor girl. She sounds great, though.'

Dan smiled. 'She sounds exactly like you.'

Ha, she hadn't even realised it, but of course he was right. Studying the photograph more closely, Lily saw the clean angles of Sasha's face, the bright, defiant gleam in her blue eyes and the determined tilt of her chin. She was small and pale, with poker-straight dark hair. There might not be any physical similarity between them, but Sasha's comments were undoubtedly the kind she herself would have made at that age.

'Good for her,' she said with affectionate empathy. 'She'll be fine.'

'You could contact her if you want to,' said Declan. 'Write a letter, tell her you'd like to meet up.'

But Lily was already shaking her head. 'It's OK, she's not interested. You can't force these things. She knows where I am if she changes her mind. And there's no hurry. Maybe she'll be in touch a year from now, or ten years. She's only fifteen. Let her do it in her own time.'

Declan walked Lily back to Goldstone House, then returned to the cottage and helped Dan clear away the dishes on the living-room table.

'Thanks for offering to put me up,' he said as Dan poured them both a nightcap.

'No problem. It's good to have you here.' Dan raised his tumbler of Scotch. 'You haven't mentioned Gail all evening. Is she going to be coming down any time this week?'

Declan paused; he hadn't told Lily his relationship with Gail was over. But that was at least partly because he hadn't wanted to detract from Lily's own current issues. He shook his head. 'She's not coming down. We've called it a day.'

'You have?' Dan was interested. 'Why?'

Well he wasn't going to tell him that. Declan shrugged. 'Just wasn't working out. You know when it's right . . .'

'And it wasn't right,' Dan concluded with a nod. 'Same with me and Anna.'

'I haven't told Lily. She's got enough to think about at the moment.' The other, somewhat less altruistic reason was to do with him wanting to be the one who told Coral so he could see her reaction face to face.

'Fine, it's just between us.' As Declan began filling the bowl with hot water and Fairy, Dan said, 'I'm not great at washing up, but I can put stuff away.'

'No problem. I'll do this bit. Can you pass me those plates?'

Limping across the kitchen, Dan carried the plates over with his good hand and Declan plunged them into the bowl.

'We're like Jack Lemmon and Walter Matthau in *The Odd Couple*.' Dan grinned. 'Two single men living together. Can I be Walter Matthau?'

'Definitely.' Unable to resist asking, Declan rinsed a plate and said, 'What caused the split between you and Anna, then?' Not that he'd ever met her himself, but Lily had told him all about Dan's revolving-door attitude towards dating the opposite sex.

Dan glanced at him, then shrugged and looked away. 'Like I said, pretty much the same as you. When I was younger, I'd just go out with whoever I liked because they were easy enough to spend a bit of time with. But I'm getting older now and it needs to be more than that. It needs to mean more. If they aren't someone you know you definitely want to spend the rest of your life with . . . well, it just seems kind of pointless.'

From the look on his face, Declan guessed that Dan had surprised himself with this confession; at a guess, it wasn't the kind of thing he'd find easy to admit to work colleagues and friends his own age.

'I think you're probably right. Good for you.' Declan nodded easily. 'It'll happen one day. How about Lily?' he continued, changing the subject to what had been uppermost in his own mind tonight. 'What do you think's going to happen when Patsy comes back? Do you suppose they'll be able to sort themselves out?'

When there was no reply, he turned to look at Dan and saw how very much it evidently mattered to him. There was heightened colour in his tanned cheeks and tension visible in his jaw. Finally he exhaled and said, 'Bloody hell, I hope so. But I really don't know.'

Chapter 39

'Hey, how are you?'

Lily experienced a fresh pang of guilt at the sound of Eddie's voice. 'Um, I'm fine, but a bit, you know . . .'

'Let me guess. Busy.' His response was good-natured but resigned. Which was hardly surprising, seeing as this was the third time today he'd called her and she'd been unable to speak to him.

'I'm sorry, it's just been chaos here, I've been rushed off my feet. And there are people queueing up now . . . Can I call you back later?'

'You said that three hours ago.'

'I know, we haven't stopped for a minute. Look, I'll definitely call you at six o'clock.'

'Fine,' said Eddie. 'Let's hope I'll be free then.'

'Sorry.' Lily lifted her hair away from where it was stuck to the back of her neck.

'It's OK, I know what it's like.'

'Excuse me,' snapped a tall woman clutching two cast-iron door knockers and a handful of doorknobs. 'Could I possibly buy these, or shall I just put them in my handbag and leave?'

'I have to go,' Lily told Eddie.

'Don't work too hard,' he said in the moment before she hung up.

Cheek.

At 5.30, Lily closed the yard for the day. Once she'd locked up the office and said goodbye to Marty, she headed over to the house, where she found Dan waiting for her on the doorstep.

He grinned at her. 'Hi. Looking hot.'

'In a fabulous way or a sweaty way?' Since her hair was once again plastered against her neck and her T-shirt was dusty and damp, Lily suspected she knew which.

'Stop fishing for compliments, you.'

'What's that?' She pointed to the cool box at his feet.

'It's an ambulance.'

'Ha-di-ha. I mean what's in it?'

'Change of plan.' Having earlier volunteered to cook dinner at the cottage for the three of them, Dan picked up the cool box and followed her into the house. 'Declan's staying on at Weaver's Cottage to get the kitchen finished before the work-tops arrive tomorrow. He won't be back before midnight. So I thought I'd take you somewhere special instead.' He gestured with pride at the cool box. 'I've done us a picnic.'

'Nice. And how are you planning on taking me there exactly? By giving me a piggyback?'

'You'll have to drive us,' said Dan.

As if she hadn't guessed. 'Where are we going, then?'

'Back in time.' His dark eyes glittered with mischief. 'Don't ask. You'll like it, though, I promise.'

'Give me half an hour.' She kicked off her flip-flops and headed for the staircase. 'I need to shower and change first.'

Under the stream of lukewarm water, Lily massaged her aching temples and let the shampoo suds cascade over her face. It had been a long week. She'd been working hard, keeping herself busy in order not to have to think about Patsy. The weather had grown steadily warmer and today the sun had blazed down, turning the yard into a complete heat-trap.

Dressed once more, this time in a purple cotton sundress, she threw herself on to the bed and called Eddie in New Zealand.

'Hi,' he said when he answered. 'Sorry, it's my turn to be busy now.'

Lily's heart sank. 'Oh no, that's a—'

'Joking.' This time she heard the smile in his voice. 'I'm fine to talk. How are you doing?'

'Shattered. Did I wake you up?'

'It's OK, I couldn't sleep anyway. The joys of jet lag. How's Declan getting along with the cottage?'

'Oh, he's been working on it non-stop. They're going to finish installing the kitchen tonight. How about you? What d'you have planned for today?'

'Interviews . . . we're recording a chat show first, then there's a four-hour press junket this afternoon.'

Lily said teasingly, 'And are there any gorgeous females out there?'

'I wouldn't notice. How about you, any irresistible male customers?'

'God, loads.'

He laughed. 'I miss you.'

'Miss you too.' He was currently on a tour of New Zealand, Australia and Singapore, and from there he had to fly back to New York; they wouldn't see each other again until the week after next. 'Sorry about today.'

'Don't worry, can't be helped. Goes with the territory.' His voice softened. 'We'll make up for it when I get back.'

Lily wiggled her toes and smiled up at the ceiling. 'Yes, we will.'

'You said thirty minutes. You're late,' said Dan when Lily re-appeared. He made himself look disapproving, but the sight of her caused his heart to leap. She was wearing a short purple dress, silver flip-flops and his favourite scent.

Lily said, 'I was talking to Eddie,' which didn't make his heart leap, but he was used to putting on a brave front.

Reaching for the cool box – cleverly, he'd worked out how to loop the handle over the grippy part of the aluminium crutch – he said, 'Come along then, let's go.'

'Bossy.' Lily gave him a nudge.

'Hungry,' said Dan as they made their way over to the car.

Twenty minutes later, she realised where they were headed. 'Are we going to The Leap?'

'It's possible.' Dan grinned at her. 'Go on then, you know the way.'

They'd almost reached Hestacombe, a village to the west of Stanton Langley. Lily duly turned left and drove along the narrow farm track.

'Oh my God, I can't believe we're back here,' she marvelled. 'I haven't thought about this place for so long. Remember that summer? What if there's still a bull in the field? If there is, I'm not risking it.' She raised her eyebrows at Dan's still-plastered foot. 'And you definitely can't.'

'There's no bull. I checked.' Two days ago, in a taxi on his way to a physiotherapy appointment in Cheltenham, he'd spotted the turn-off and asked the driver to make a quick detour down the track. The bull was long gone, the field currently empty.

Thank God.

At the end of the overgrown track, Lily parked on the verge. Hauling the cool box out of the boot of the car, she opened the gate to allow Dan through, then closed it behind them.

'This is exciting.' She grinned at him as he limped beside her along the perimeter of the field.

'I thought you'd like it.' Dan was pleased with his idea to bring her here. 'You deserve a break after the week you've had.'

He was still slow, though getting better at moving along as the broken bone in his foot had begun to heal. It took them ten minutes to make their way in single file along the stony path that led down through the woods to the water's edge.

The trees thinned out, dried grass stalks whipped their legs as they approached their destination, and they finally reached the sun-dappled grassy clearing, with Hestacombe Lake stretching out directly in front of them.

'Wow,' said Lily.

'I know.' Dan stood beside her and together they surveyed the magical view. The sky was pale cobalt, the water reflecting it a pewter-tinted shade of blue. On the other side of the lake stood the picturesque village of Hestacombe. There were holiday homes visible amongst the trees, and a small artificial beach that had been constructed by the owner of Hestacombe House. They could see several people on the beach; a couple more were swimming and splashing around, and birds were darting and swooping through the still summer air. That was the popular side of the lake, close to a road and easily accessible to all.

This side was the better one, though; it was the secret side most people would have no idea how to reach. A group of them from school had discovered it one chilly day during the Easter holidays, and made it their own. As summer had approached and the days had grown longer and warmer, they'd taken to cycling over here most weekends, hanging out together, playing music, drinking illicit bottles of cider and inventing games to entertain themselves. Once the summer holidays had arrived, it had practically become a home from home.

'Nothing's changed. It's exactly the same,' Lily marvelled. She put the cool box down on the grassy bank, opened it and shook out the thin blanket. Once the food had been arranged to her liking, they sat down and Dan unscrewed the cap on the bottle of wine he'd packed, along with two acrylic tumblers.

'Here you go, you can have one glass.' He poured and handed the first one to Lily.

'Cheers,' she said when his tumbler was filled too. 'This is a luxury we didn't have back then. Posh wine in glasses.'

Dan grinned. 'We used to take turns swigging Blackthorn cider out of a plastic bottle.'

'I always was a classy bird.' Lily tossed a cherry tomato high into the air, caught it in her mouth and crunched it in half with her teeth.

'See? You still are.'

'I know. Sophisticated, me.' She clapped a hand to her chest. 'Through and through.'

God, he loved her so much. For a moment Dan found himself winded, unable to speak. He really did love everything about her, from her dancing brown eyes to the way those spirals of tawny-blond hair bounced over her smooth, tanned shoulders, to her unfailing ability to laugh at herself.

He leaned back with his legs stretched out in front of him and watched the surface of the water shimmer as iridescent dragonflies hovered and danced over it, inches above the surface. He could so clearly remember the time Lily had been floating on her back in the water with her eyes closed and he'd swum silently up behind her. Just as he'd been about to surprise her, a huge dragonfly had darted in front of his face so suddenly that he'd let out a yell and tried to bat it away in a panic, like a complete wuss. Lily, in hysterics of laughter, had never let him forget it. Ever since, during quiet moments, it had become something of a standing joke to blurt out, 'Dragonfly, waaaah!'

Now, idly nudging his leg with her bare foot, she pointed half a Scotch egg at the dancing dragonflies and said, 'Do you remember that time you—'

'Yes, I do.' He rolled his eyes. 'Thanks so much for reminding me.'

'Ha, that was hilarious.' Lily flailed her arms, miming his abject horror. 'You were such a big girl's blouse.'

'So you've told me, three or four hundred times.'

She laughed. 'Some things improve with repetition. Oh my God, look! I can't believe it's still there . . .'

Lily was lying on her back now, pointing up into the branches of the huge sycamore tree behind them. Following the direction of her index finger, Dan saw the remains of the old grey rope fastened around one of the thicker branches overhead. Once it had been five metres long; now only a short length with tattered ends remained.

'It seemed like such a good idea at the time.' Dan was rueful; it had been his idea, after all.

'Oh, come on, it was a brilliant idea.' Lily turned her head sideways to look at him. 'What happened to Kyle wasn't your fault, was it?'

Chapter 40

Wasn't it? Dan's mouth was dry. Apart from anything else, he'd been the one who had bought the rope from the hardware store, carried it all the way down here and climbed the tree in order to tie it securely around that branch. He'd done it so they could take a running jump from the top of the slope, swing out over the water like Tarzan, then launch themselves through the air and into the lake. He'd gone first to test it out, and everyone else had followed his lead. It had been the highlight of that long, hot summer, providing countless hours of fun and resulting in their meeting place being renamed The Leap.

They would have carried on doing it too, if Kyle hadn't had his accident, making a catastrophic error whilst attempting that double somersault.

Instead of releasing his grip on the outward swing, Kyle had held on too long and let go on the return one, but had gone for the double somersault anyway. Everyone had seen him cartwheel through the air then land on the very edge of the lake in less than three inches of water.

The sound of him landing – it had been a hideous combination of watery splash and bone-crunching thud – was something Dan knew he'd never forget.

'It was an accident,' said Lily. 'Poor Kyle. Scary at the time, though.'

It had been bloody scary. Kyle had lain there on his side, white-faced and clearly in tremendous pain. It had taken twenty-five minutes for the paramedics to locate and reach them, but it had seemed like hours. Dan had knelt in the water beside him the whole time, not daring to move Kyle's crumpled body. Instead, he'd kept the injured boy's head slightly elevated so the water didn't flow into his mouth.

Once the paramedics had arrived, they'd strapped Kyle on to a stretcher and with some difficulty managed to carry him back up the hill to the waiting ambulance. The next day the rest of them discovered he'd sustained multiple fractures to his pelvis.

Kyle had spent the next couple of weeks in Cheltenham General Hospital and the remainder of that summer recuperating. His parents had then relocated to somewhere in the north of England, so he never did return to their school and none of them ever heard from him again.

'I wonder what he's doing now,' Lily mused. She pulled a face. 'I wonder if he made a full recovery.'

'Of course he did.'

'You don't know that. He might be hobbling around on sticks. Or in a wheelchair.'

'Don't say that.' Dan felt sick.

'He could be, though,' said Lily. 'We just don't know. Poor Kyle, he was a funny little thing, wasn't he? Always so desperate to fit in with the rest of us, but he never really did. God, and his mother was scary.'

'When did you ever meet his mother?' Kyle had only arrived at the school six months earlier and had lived several miles from Stanton Langley, in a village called Compton Drew. As far as Dan was aware, none of them had encountered his parents.

Lily reached over for the punnet of raspberries, then lay back and rested them on her flat stomach. 'It's a secret.'

He turned his head to look at her. 'What?'

She popped a raspberry into her mouth. 'OK, it *was* a secret. I'm sure he won't mind me telling you now. He invited me over for tea at his house one day.'

'He did?' Dan paused. 'Is that the secret? Are you sure you want to work for MI5?'

'Sarcastic.' Lily gave his ankle a gentle kick. 'He asked me to pretend to be his girlfriend, if you must know.'

'Seriously? Why?'

'His mother had been giving him a hard time, wanting to know why he wasn't going out with anyone. Poor Kyle. When he told me, I couldn't believe she'd be like that. Then I met her, and she was worse. The first thing she said to me was "So you're Kyle's girlfriend? Thank goodness for that, we were beginning to think he was gay."'

'Ouch. What a witch. And she actually meant it?' Dan said in disbelief.

'Oh definitely. She was a horrible woman.'

Now he felt even worse. That poor kid. 'And presumably he *was* gay.'

'Nope. He said not. He told me he was straight but shy. And he was only sixteen, for crying out loud. Can you imagine how awful it must have been, having your mother coming out with stuff like that?'

'So you just went over to his house for tea and that was it? She was convinced?'

'I went over there four or five times. His mother ended up really liking me.'

296

'But there was never anything going on between you and Kyle?'

'Of course not. We just held hands a bit and pretended to be boyfriend and girlfriend for a few weeks. Then we broke up.'

'I can't believe you did all that,' said Dan.

Lily shrugged. 'No big deal. I felt sorry for him, so I helped him out.'

'You're actually quite a nice person, deep down.'

'And you're actually in danger of getting rolled into the water.' Lily nudged him playfully.

'I'm amazed you never mentioned it before. All these years and you kept it to yourself.'

'Maybe because it was no one else's business. And if you'd found out, you'd probably have made fun of him.'

Dan smiled; he loved that Lily had resisted the temptation to tell a story that would have been amusing *and* shown her in a good light. She was also right about the making-fun-of-Kyle bit. Well, prior to the accident, at least.

They both gazed out over the lake in companionable silence for a couple of minutes. Following that day, the farmer who owned the land above this side of the lake had put up a No Entry sign and, rather more persuasively, installed a bull in the field. He'd evidently also cut down the rope hanging from the tree. Since then, none of them had been back. Until today.

'Oh, Coral called earlier,' said Lily. 'It was lovely to hear her sounding so happy. She's having a fantastic time in Grimaud.'

'That's great.'

'I'm so glad we managed to persuade her to go. And she's painting again . . . What are you looking at?'

Dan smiled. 'You.' Whilst she'd been gazing up at the sky, he'd thought it was safe to study her profile in the early evening sunlight: the angle of her cheekbones, the dusting of freckles across her nose, the sweep of her gold-tipped lashes above the clear whites of her eyes.

'Why? Do I have something on my face?' She rubbed her hand vigorously around her mouth. 'Is it crumbs?'

'It's OK. You're fine.' It wasn't something he could say out loud, but Lily's mouth really was his favourite mouth in the world.

'Have you heard from Patsy?'

She was still watching the sun filtering through the branches. Her hair was spread out across the grass beneath her head and a ladybird had just landed on her pink bra strap. Was it a good sign that she had asked?

'I had a text this afternoon. She asked me if I thought you missed her.'

Silence. Dan realised she must miss Patsy but couldn't bring herself to admit it. After a few moments he said, 'She also asked me if I thought you'd ever speak to her again.'

Lily swallowed. 'And what did you say?'

'I told her I didn't know. I thought I might ask you this evening.'

'Hmm.'

'What does *hmm* mean?'

'Honestly?' She sighed. 'Oh Dan, you know me. I'm not the not-speaking-to-someone type. But I still can't believe she did it. All these years she didn't tell me he'd been here. She had no right to keep something like that to herself. If she hadn't slept with him, she'd have told me, I know she would. But she needed to cover her tracks so she kept quiet. Every time I think about it, I just feel . . .' Lily clenched her fist and pressed it against her chest. 'It makes me feel sick.'

'I know.'

'I can't help it. She did a bad thing.'

Dan nodded. 'Have you ever done a bad thing?'

'Of course I've done bad things. But not that bad,' said Lily. 'Nowhere near.'

'Go on, then. Tell me some of your not-so-bad things.'

'OK.' A glimmer of a smile. 'Well . . . I made you some cheese on toast once. I dropped it face down on the kitchen floor and there wasn't any more bread left. So I scooped it up, smoothed all the melted cheese back over the top with a knife and sprinkled it with black pepper so you couldn't tell anything had happened.'

'Did you also spit on it?'

'What? No!'

'In that case,' said Dan, 'I forgive you.'

He wouldn't have minded even if she had.

'Thanks, I feel so much better now.' Lily shot him a sideways look. 'Is this your attempt to make everything all right? Because I don't think it's going to work.'

'Come on, is that the worst thing you've ever done? I mean, seriously?'

'Right. I'm trying to remember.' She concentrated hard, then said, 'OK, I bought two cushions in a supermarket once and the cashier made a mistake and only charged me for one of them. I should have told her, but I didn't.'

'Oh my God, I bet you felt *really* terrible about that,' said Dan.

'I did! Oh . . .' She realised he was making fun of her. 'Shut up. I *did* feel bad about it.'

'Now tell me the very worst thing you've ever, *ever* done. And please don't say it was the time you put an empty crisp packet in the green recycling bin.'

Lily reached out and pinched his wrist, then gave the matter some thought. Finally she said, 'Just after I'd passed my driving test, I reversed the van into a postbox and smashed the brake light. I swore blind to Coral and Nick that I'd seen a red car reverse into the van then drive off.'

'And did they ever find out the truth?'

'No.'

'So I could tell Coral when she gets back from France.'

Lily gave him a look. 'You could. But it's hardly a life-changer, is it? Is that why you're doing this?'

Dan wasn't entirely sure what he was doing; he was kind of freestyling, making it up as he went along.

'Your bad things aren't bad enough.' He topped up his glass of wine. 'You've never even told a string of lies and broken some guy's heart.'

Apart from mine. Which doesn't count.

'Sorry,' said Lily. 'If only I had a secret double life as a serial killer. Go on then, what's the most awful thing you've done?'

Dan tilted his head to look at her. This was the bit he had decided to tell her.

'Oh dear.' Lily's eyes were bright with anticipation. 'Too many to choose from, I suppose. Hard to narrow them down.'

'It was my fault that Kyle smashed his pelvis.' Now it was Dan's turn to feel a bit sick; he'd actually said it out loud. At last.

Chapter 41

'What? No it wasn't. I was there,' said Lily. 'I saw it. He got his timing wrong, that's all.'

OK, time for some brutal honesty. Aware that his was a story that decidedly *didn't* paint him in a good light, Dan took a deep breath. 'Kyle got his timing wrong because he was terrified. I'd told him he had to go for the double somersault, and if he didn't do it, we didn't want him tagging along with us any more. I said if he wimped out, that was it, he'd be out of the group. And I saw the look on his face. I knew he was petrified, but I let him go ahead and try it anyway.' He paused. 'So that's why it happened, and it was all my fault.'

'Wow.' Lily was staring at him, incredulous. 'Why? Why did you say that to him?'

Oh, the crawling shame. Not just of having done it, but of revealing his own behaviour to Lily.

'I don't know. I guess I just didn't like him that much. He was quiet and awkward and I used to catch him looking at me. He used to watch you too, all the time. It creeped me out a bit.' It had actually creeped him out a *lot*. 'I suppose I thought it would either force him to go ahead and do it and make him more interesting, or get him to leave our group. Which most of us would have been happy about.'

Lily was frowning. 'But . . . I never heard you say anything mean to him.'

'I didn't. Apart from that day. I just came out with the challenge on the way down there and wondered what he'd do. I actually thought he'd chicken out.' Dan shook his head. 'Obviously I wasn't expecting it to end the way it did.'

'And Kyle never said anything. I visited him in hospital and he never told me.'

'He didn't say a word to anyone,' Dan agreed. 'I knew it was my fault. He knew it was my fault. And I've felt guilty about it ever since.'

'Poor Kyle. I wonder what happened to him.'

'I know, I've thought about that too.'

'As bad things go, that's a pretty good one, though,' said Lily.

'Thanks.'

'I haven't done anything like that.'

'Clearly not. If you had, it might make it easier for you to understand how it feels.'

'OK, see that little bit of rope dangling up there? Climb up and swing from it,' said Lily. 'Then let go and land on those rocks. I'm ordering you to do it.'

'You're joking,' Dan told her, 'but I'm serious. I think you should do something you'd feel guilty about.'

Lily bit into a ripe strawberry and thought for a moment. 'Don't make me go shoplifting. I won't do it. God, imagine getting arrested.'

'Hang on, you've got a—' Dan stopped himself as the thought struck him. He'd been about to tell her the ladybird was now tightwalking its way along her narrow pink bra strap. Stunned, he let this new thought rattle and swoop through his brain like a micro-rollercoaster. OK, this was something he genuinely hadn't planned in advance, but would Lily believe him? And should he do it?

More to the point, did he dare to do it? And if he did, what would it do to *him*?

'I've got a what?' Lily was still waiting for him to finish the original sentence. She peered down at her front, then wiped the corners of her mouth once more.

'Here, let me.' Sliding closer and half sitting up so the arm he'd been supporting himself on was now free, Dan carefully coaxed the ladybird off the satin strap with his thumb and nudged it into the palm of his hand.

'Oh no, you can't be serious.' Lily was shaking her head. 'I'm not killing a ladybird. Don't ask me to do that.'

Despite himself, Dan started to laugh. The way her mind worked never failed to entertain him. 'I'm not asking you to murder a ladybird.'

'Oh. Well, good.'

As if it had had quite enough of this kind of dangerous talk, the ladybird spread its wings and flew off.

And now Dan was no longer laughing. His heart was bumping crazily against his ribcage at the prospect of what he was about to do. He'd known Lily long enough and well enough to know for sure that she'd never been unfaithful to a boyfriend.

For a start, there hadn't been that many of them.

Secondly, it simply wasn't in her nature to be underhand. It would never occur to her to even be tempted.

'OK,' said Lily. 'What *are* you thinking?'

She was still lying on her back with her hair spread across the grass beneath her head. Dan sat at her side, gazing down and breathing in the faint fresh scent of her shampoo. 'How about if I ask you to do something that wouldn't get you arrested?'

'Like what?'

'How are things going with you and Eddie?'

'Great,' said Lily.

'Where is he now?'

'That's a stupid question. You know where he is. New Zealand.'

'And you'd never cheat on him. You just wouldn't, I know that too.'

Lily pulled a what-are-you-on-about face. 'No, of course I wouldn't.'

'OK, so . . . how about if you kissed someone else?' Dan looked at her. 'Would that make you feel guilty?'

'Yes.'

'It wouldn't have to wreck your relationship, though. And he'd never know about it. You wouldn't tell him, and nor would the other person, who you know you can absolutely trust. It would just be between the two of you. Completely private.'

He could see the pulse flickering at the base of her throat, the sheen of her skin there, the movement of her neck as she swallowed. Then her gaze locked back on him and she said, 'So you're saying it's something I could do that would make me feel ashamed of myself and then I'd understand what it felt like to have done a bad thing.'

'That's pretty much it. Seems like a logical plan to me.' He smiled fractionally.

The silence stretched between them. High above their heads, birds were singing to each other in the trees, and from across the lake came the sound of a car driving up through the village. Closer to hand, a bee buzzed amongst the clumps of wild celandines and dog roses.

Finally, her voice husky and barely above a whisper, Lily said, 'It's not just Eddie who mustn't know. You have to promise not to tell anyone else.' She swallowed again. 'Anyone at all.'

Oh God, it was going to happen, it was actually going to happen.

'I promise.' Dan nodded slowly. 'And you know you can trust me.'

'Go on then.' Her dark eyes huge, her breathing uneven, Lily reached up and lightly touched the side of his face. 'Let's do it.'

He lowered his mouth to hers, hesitated for a second a millimetre above it, then closed his eyes and made the first contact. His lips brushed against hers and he felt her tremble . . . which was quite a feat considering the amount of turmoil engulfing his own body right now.

Oh, but this was something he'd longed to do – had dreamt of doing – for *so* many years. Was it any wonder his hormones had gone into overdrive? He was kissing Lily, properly kissing her at last, and the reality of it was every bit as dizzying as he'd hoped. Her lips were soft, she tasted of summer and strawberries, and her fingers were sliding around the back of his neck . . .

It was a mind-blowing experience, and one Dan knew he'd never forget as long as he lived. Two weeks ago, in the kitchen of Goldstone House, he'd held and reassured her and it had felt fantastic, but this was up to a whole stratospheric new level. It wasn't perfect, what with one arm still being strapped into a sling, but imagine what it would be like if he had both hands free . . .

OK, it hadn't been nearly enough, but it was going to have to do, seeing as this so-called exercise was meant to be for Lily's benefit, not his own. It almost killed Dan to kiss her for one last second then ease away, but he somehow managed it.

For a long moment it seemed as if the air was vibrating between them. He looked at Lily, from her beautiful mouth to her even more beautiful eyes, and waited for her to break the silence. What he wanted her to say, of course, was, 'That's it, I'm going to tell Eddie it's all over . . . *you're* the one I want to be with . . . it's you, it's always been you . . .'

He held his breath, silently willing her to say it.

Oh God, and she was still gazing up at him. What was going through her mind?

'Well, it worked,' Lily said at last, and there was a faint tremor in her voice.

'It did? How are you feeling?'

'Terrible.' She exhaled, then broke into a rueful smile. 'Just awful.'

'Why?' What he wanted was for her to shake her head in disbelief and say: 'Because now I know how much I love you.'

She briefly closed her eyes, then opened them again. 'Just like you said. Because now I've done something I shouldn't have done. And it's not fair on Eddie. I've betrayed him. He doesn't deserve that.'

Not the reply he'd been hoping for, to be honest, but probably the one he'd expected. Oh well, the fantasy had been nice while it lasted.

'Well that's good. So it's mission accomplished. We set out to make you feel guilty, and now you do.' He could still feel the imprint of her warm mouth on his, but the moment had passed; it was time to revert to friendship mode. He shrugged and said flippantly, 'That's what I call a result.'

'Well, thanks.'

'Don't mention it.' He smiled briefly, as if she were some just-met girl who meant nothing to him. 'All part of the service.'

306

Lily nodded. She sat up and reached into the punnet of raspberries. 'You won't tell anyone, though? You do promise?'

It lacerated him to think she still needed to be reassured. 'I've already promised. You know you can trust me.'

'I thought I could trust other people.' Her expression was rueful. 'Turns out I couldn't. I suppose I'm— *Ow!*'

Dan's gaze had been fixed on her eyes. If he'd been paying more attention, he would have seen the wasp perched on the raspberry she was putting into her mouth. By the time he batted it away, it was too late. Lily had been stung on her bottom lip.

'Bastard wasp!' She clapped her hand over her mouth and let out a squeak of pain. 'That *hurts.*'

'Here, let me look.' Dan knew she wasn't allergic to wasp stings; he suspected he just wanted an excuse to touch her again. Moving closer and nudging her hand away, he held the side of her face and studied the site of the sting.

Not a lot to see, to be honest.

Just a bit of redness and maybe a slight swelling.

'If it was a snake bite, I'd offer to suck out the poison,' he said.

'That's really helpful. Thank you. If my lip swells up like a balloon, I'm going to look ridiculous,' Lily fretted. At that moment, her phone began to ring and she let out a groan of despair. 'Oh no, it's Eddie.'

Dan moved back, Lily flapped her hand at him to stay silent and he spent the next few minutes listening to her telling Eddie that she'd just been stung on the lip by a wasp whilst neglecting to mention where she was and who she was with.

By the time she ended the call, her bottom lip was visibly bigger and she was visibly more upset.

'What is it?' said Dan.

'Oh come on, you know perfectly well what. We did that thing we did . . .' Lily gestured helplessly between them, 'and less than a minute later I'm stung by a wasp. On my *mouth*,' she emphasised.

'And?'

She stuck out her swollen bottom lip. 'If that isn't karma, I don't know what is.'

Chapter 42

Twenty-four hours had passed since That Kiss, and Lily was still so shaken by the experience she was beginning to wonder if she'd ever feel normal again.

Oh God, though, it had been *so* completely and utterly mind-blowing. She'd expected it to be a bit special, what with her having secretly wanted to kiss Dan for years, but no way had she expected it to take her over like this. It was like having your body infiltrated by a spirit and being incapable of controlling any aspect of it. Her brain was flatly refusing to concentrate on anything else. Her heart quickened every time she thought about Dan – which was *all* the time, pretty much – and production of adrenalin was in overdrive.

Plus, there was the guilt issue. Because there was undoubtedly guilt there. But try as she might, Lily knew she definitely wasn't feeling anywhere near guilty enough.

She heaved a sigh and looked at her reflection in the dressing-table mirror. What a mess, what an unholy mess. And what had she done? Only ended up making her own life that much more difficult.

Because it clearly hadn't meant anything to Dan. He'd come up with the idea on the spur of the moment and done the deed without stopping to think twice about it. Boom, kiss administered, job done. She was the one who should have guessed just how much turmoil it would set off. She should have said no when he'd first made the offer, laughed it off and not allowed it to happen.

Except she hadn't done that, had she? Instead, like a complete numpty, she'd let him go ahead and do it, unleashing all kinds of bodily havoc.

Twinnnnnngggggg went her phone, and Lily jumped, because pretty much everything was making her jumpy right now. Then she did it again when she saw the text that had flashed up on the screen from Eddie.

Skype??

Oh God, she couldn't, just couldn't do it. Not yet, not while she was in this much of a state. It was hard enough speaking to him on the phone. Actually looking him in the eyes and pretending everything was fine was definitely more than she could handle right now.

Hastily she texted back: *You'd get a fright if you did – my lip's swollen up like a football. I look awful.*

You see? Even that wasn't true, her lip was fine. She was lying to conceal her guilt, but the real guilt wasn't what Dan thought it was.

As far as he was concerned, the plan had been that she would feel bad because she'd physically kissed another man.

What he was blissfully unaware of – thank *goodness* – was the fact that she felt bad because it had been the best kiss, the best thirty seconds and the most heavenly *experience* of her life.

Another text from Eddie lit up the phone's screen.

I don't mind how scary you look. Xxx

Lily texted back: *Maybe not, but I do! Can't talk now, I'll call later. Hope your TV thing goes well. Xxx*

310

He replied: *OK. Love you. X*

Excuse me? Lily looked at the message again. He'd definitely written *Love you* at the end.

OK, that was weird. He'd never said those words to her before, so why would he be texting them now?

Did he actually mean it?

Was he texting the fact that he loved her because it was less terrifying than saying it to her face?

Did she even want him to be saying it, given the situation she currently found herself in?

Lily closed her eyes, then opened them again and gave her reflection in the mirror a get-real look.

Because it wasn't as if she had two lovely men after her and all she had to do was choose which one she liked best. Eddie Tessler was really nice, but he was from a show-businessy parallel universe and she suspected she was a bit of a novelty, more of a passing whim for him than anything serious and lasting. And she was fine with that, because deep down she knew theirs was a relationship that had never been destined to last. It was a dalliance and it was fun, but it would never be long-term. There were too many differences between them for that.

Whilst Dan was simply Dan, her oldest friend and the last person you'd ever want to get properly involved with, because Dan just didn't *do* proper involvement. If she were to give him her heart, he would break it.

And life in Stanton Langley would be awkward for ever more.

Which was why she had – *had* – to get over the kiss.

Her phone burst into life and she saw that Eddie was now calling her.

'Hi,' she said. 'I'm still not Skyping.'

'I know. It's OK. This is a bit embarrassing actually. I pressed send on that last text before realising what I'd done.'

During the ensuing awkward pause, Lily started to laugh. 'Thank goodness for that. You didn't mean it!'

'Exactly.' Eddie sounded relieved. 'It's how I used to end texts to my last girlfriend. I just did it this time without thinking. I didn't want you to wonder what it meant . . .'

'I *was* wondering,' said Lily, still smiling. 'It seemed a bit weird. Anyway, mystery solved. I'm glad you called to explain.'

'And I'm glad you're OK about it. I mean, I do like you a lot, you know I do . . .'

'But it's too soon for any of that love stuff. God, yes.'

'Thanks. Bye,' said Eddie.

'Bye. Love you,' teased Lily.

'Haha, very funny.'

Less than five seconds after ending the call, another text arrived. This time it was from Dan.

Where are you? Have you fallen asleep? Dinner's ready and we're waiting for you to get your lazy backside over here, or I'll eat all your roast potatoes myself. X

Lily dusted a bit of powder over her freckled nose, slicked on some lip gloss and jumped to her feet. She could put on a carefree face and carry on acting as if they were just friends.

She had to, because they *were*.

Rapidly she texted back: *Touch any of my roast potatoes and you're a dead man. On my way.*

Then she paused and added a single kiss, to match the one Dan had used to end his text to her.

One tiny electronic kiss. Who'd have imagined the amount of upheaval a real-life one could cause?

★ ★ ★

312

Declan had never before worked so hard or such long hours. OK, maybe he had, but never before with such intent and purpose. The last week had been a blur of activity, coordinating other workers and getting as much done as humanly possible. In his mind, he'd wanted everything finished by the time Coral returned home from the South of France. Superstitiously – and he'd *never* been superstitious in his life – he'd decided that if the renovation could be completed, all would be well.

He bloody hoped so, anyway.

The other idea that had been unfurling in his brain was one that ran along the lines of how about if he were to completely change his mind about the cottage? Because if everything did work out as he very much hoped it would, maybe he needn't sell or rent it out after all. He could afford to keep it for his own use, make it *his* escape from the pressures of city life, *his* idyllic weekend retreat . . .

And now it was Saturday afternoon. Weaver's Cottage had been transformed and Coral was at this very moment on her way back from the airport.

Declan stood in the centre of the knocked-through kitchen-diner with its stunning room-length view over the valley and the rolling hills beyond. The kitchen units were white and the worktops dark green, the surfaces illuminated by pools of light from the spotlights strategically installed beneath the wall units. With its white floor, sleek silver accessories and accents of crimson, it was unrecognisable as the cluttered, unsanitary nicotine-stained kitchen that had belonged to Old Malcolm for almost seventy years.

He'd taken the call from Lily an hour ago. 'Coral's on her way home. Are you going to be at the cottage this afternoon? Because I told her how much work you'd done and she can't wait to see how it's looking now. She said if your car's outside, she'll stop off and you can give her the grand tour.'

Whereupon Declan, who had actually planned to drive into Chipping Norton to get his chainsaw fixed, had casually replied, 'Oh, I'll be here.'

Twenty minutes later, he heard the sound of a taxi pulling up outside the front gate. Unable to play it cool and wait for the doorbell to ring, Declan pulled open the door, waved to Coral and called out, 'Hi!'

She was looking fantastic, bright-eyed and happy. Oh God, it was *so* good to see her again.

'Hooray, hello! I'm *longing* to see everything you've done.' She jumped out of the taxi and greeted him with a hug before breaking away as the driver hauled her turquoise suitcase out of the back. 'Oh thank you so much.' Extending the handle and taking charge of the case, Coral paid him before turning back to Declan. 'Is this OK? Will you be able to give me a lift home after we've finished here?'

'Of course. No problem. I could have picked you up from the airport,' said Declan. 'It wouldn't have been any trouble.' Ha, talk about understatement; it would have been the very opposite of trouble.

'Oh no no no.' Coral waved her free hand. 'I won't let anyone do that. It's so mortifying when the flight's delayed and whoever it is ends up having to wait for hours to pick you up.'

'So you get a taxi instead and the flight's never delayed.'

'Exactly that.' She grinned at him. 'Sod's law. Works like a charm every time.'

Declan took the case from her. 'Come along then. Let's get inside.'

'Can't wait,' said Coral. 'I've been looking forward to this.'

314

Not as much as he had. Declan led the way into the cottage, his heart thudding with anticipation. He would show her everything that had been done first, get it out of the way, then tell her that his relationship with Gail was over. He'd pictured her reaction so many times . . . of course she would be surprised, then sympathetic . . . but there would also, with a bit of luck, be a glimmer of relief and hope in her eyes. And then he would confide in her the reason for his having ended it, and he'd witness the expression on her face, of disbelief mingling with growing joy and delight as she finally understood what he was—

'Oh my goodness, look at this place, what a *difference*,' Coral exclaimed as she stepped into the kitchen-diner. 'It's fantastic!'

While she was gazing around in wonder, Declan secretly gazed in wonder at her. She was wearing a pink and white striped shirt and her favourite jeans. Her tan had deepened, accentuating the clear blueness of her eyes, and her blond hair was fastened up at the sides with white clips, which revealed her slender neck. The idea of kissing that neck was—

'So you listened to me, then.' Smiling, she swung round to him.

'Sorry?' It was hard to stop thinking about her neck.

'The splashes of red.' Coral pointed to the velvet cushions on the window seat, the blinds and the glossy wall tiles behind the sink. 'I can't believe you remembered.'

Declan remembered every single word she'd ever uttered. On the day of the property auction, he'd been explaining to her that he normally redecorated in neutral colours and she'd said, 'Oh, but don't you love a pop of colour? Something bright to liven things up? I just think it makes all the difference!'

'I gave it a go,' he replied good-naturedly. 'And you were right.'

'You've done a great job. Seriously, I love it.' Coral was investigating the cupboards now, opening and closing drawers, admiring the spectacular view from the window. 'I could live here myself.'

There were so many possible replies to that, but before he could even formulate one, she was off, disappearing into the living room to admire the light ivory decor (with accents of mulberry and plum). Then she ran upstairs and he showed her the bathroom, followed by the smaller spare room, and finally the main bedroom. In here the walls were sunny yellow, the carpet was thick and pale gold, and the fitted units were white. This time the accent of colour was supplied by the view from the windows, of the valley spread out below them.

'You've done it,' Coral said simply. 'It's just perfect.'

What Declan wanted to say was: *So are you*.

But it was too soon. Instead he nodded. 'Thanks. It's turned out well. I'm happy.'

Coral was smiling up at him. 'So you should be.'

Hopefully he was about to become happier. 'Shall we go downstairs and have a coffee? I want to hear all about your holiday. Did you have a great time?'

'Oh, the best. I'm so glad I went.' She moved past him, wafting unfamiliar perfume in her wake.

'You smell different.' Declan couldn't help saying it as he followed her down the staircase.

'I know, I bought it in a little shop in Saint-Tropez. Fancied a change. What do you think?'

'Nice.' Was it nice? He wasn't so sure; it was heavier and spicier than the scent she'd always worn before. To change the subject, Declan said, 'You're looking well.'

Because that was definitely true.

'Thanks.' Back in the kitchen-diner, Coral occupied one of the crimson-cushioned stools around the central island while he switched on the coffee-maker. 'I feel fantastic. Everyone there was so friendly. And I've got back into painting, can you believe it? It's like a miracle!'

'Lily told me you had.' Declan smiled, because she was glowing with happiness and her joy was contagious. 'I can't wait to see what you've done. And, you know . . .' he indicated the walls around them, 'if you did feel like donating one to a deserving cause, that'd be great.'

'Well maybe. Then again, you haven't seen them yet.' Coral's eyes were sparkling. 'Anyway, how's Gail?'

Talk about the perfect opener. Aware that the moment had arrived, Declan wiped his suddenly prickling palms on the sides of his trousers and opened his mouth to say, 'Actually—'

'Ooh, made me jump!' Coral pulled her phone out of her jeans pocket as it broke into what sounded like a load of inebriated jazz musicians at the end of a long night. This was new too. When she saw who was calling, she said, 'Sorry, can I just answer this?'

'Of course.' Declan opened the glass-fronted cupboard on the wall above the coffee machine and took down two stainless-steel cups and saucers. You knew you liked someone when you gave them a cup *and* a saucer.

'Hi. Yes! Oh gosh, that was quick!' Coral swung her legs as she spoke to whoever was on the other end of the line. Was it Lily? Or one of the staff at the yard? Her eyes bright, she listened for a few more seconds, then said, 'OK, well this is perfect. Just before you reach Stanton Langley, you'll pass the Valentine Hotel on the left-hand side of the road, then about five hundred metres further on there's a cottage with a dark green Audi parked outside. Declan's just been showing me everything he's done to the place . . . honestly, it's amazing. But yes, I'll look out for you. See you in a minute! Bye!'

Chapter 43

There was a slow, lurching sensation in Declan's stomach, like descending fifty storeys in a lift. The tone of her voice and the light in her eyes belatedly told him that he really didn't want to hear what was coming next.

Except he was going to have to hear it.

'Don't worry about coffee.' Coral was already sliding down from her stool, reaching for her shoulder bag. 'And no need to give me a lift into the village either. That was a friend of mine on the phone.'

Her cheeks were flushed as she fiddled with the fastening on her bag. Declan murmured politely, 'Oh yes?'

Don't say it, please don't say it.

'His name's Trent and we met on the painting holiday. It was just the most amazing coincidence: there were seven of us staying there and it turned out he lives only fifteen miles away from here, in Cirencester!' Coral shook her head in disbelief. 'Isn't that crazy? And we hit it off from the moment I arrived. I just . . . oh gosh, it sounds silly to say it, but it felt like fate,' she rattled on. 'As if it were meant to happen. The years since Nick died have been so difficult and so lonely, I honestly never imagined I'd feel this way again. I thought I'd had my happy life, as much as I deserved, and now it was over. But then the feelings came back and . . . well, it happened. Like everyone always tells you, just when you least expect it. I went to the South of France to get back into painting and there he was. Trent. He lost his wife five years ago and felt just the same as me. But all it took was a couple of hours on that first evening and we just knew something special was happening. It was like . . . magic!'

Declan nodded. He was lost for words, but Coral was gazing at him, waiting for him to speak.

'That's . . . great news.' He forced himself to smile and sound delighted for her. 'Fantastic. I'm so pleased.'

I'm also lying.

'Thanks. I can't tell you how brilliant it feels.' She laughed. 'It's like being a teenager again. I'm all . . . fluttery!'

OK, this wasn't helping matters at all. It simply wasn't what he needed to hear. And now, in addition, they could both hear the car slowing to a halt outside. Ten minutes ago it had been a taxi bringing Coral back to him, the most wonderful sound in the world. Now it was the complete opposite.

'Here he is.' Coral jumped up and reached for her suitcase. 'Come on, you have to meet him!'

Oh joy. But what other choice did he have? Declan followed her out of the cottage.

'You found us,' Coral exclaimed happily.

'Oh my God, look at you. Even more beautiful than I remembered.' Trent was tall, fair-haired and as tanned as she was. He was wearing a green checked shirt, blue linen shorts and deck shoes. 'Come here,' he ordered, holding out his arms to her. 'I've missed you so much!'

They hugged. Trent kissed her on the mouth. Declan averted

his gaze until Coral pulled away and explained laughingly, 'He's joking. His flight was only two hours earlier than mine.'

'I still missed you, though.' Trent gave her waist a squeeze, then turned to Declan. 'Hi there, Dec, I've been hearing all about you. And your lady friend, of course. Grace, is it?'

'Gail,' said Coral. 'She's lovely!'

Trent was enthusiastically shaking his hand. Now wasn't the time to make the announcement. Declan said, 'She isn't here, I'm afraid.'

'Well I can't wait to meet her too. I'm looking forward to getting to know all Coral's friends. Has she been telling you about our time in Grimaud?'

'Um, kind of.'

'Ha! Not *all* about it, obviously. No, but it was great. Best week of my life. Mind-blowing.' He winked cheerily. 'Lucky me, eh? OK, let's get this case into the back of the car . . .'

The suitcase was stowed in the boot of his very clean bottle-green Vauxhall Vectra. Trent then held open the passenger door and ushered Coral inside. Coral, fastening her seat belt, said to Declan, 'We're all having dinner at the Star tonight. You'll join us, won't you? I'll book a table for seven thirty.'

'Great.' Could he bear to? Maybe, maybe not.

'We'll see you later,' she said.

Revving the engine, Trent raised his hand in farewell. 'Bye for now!'

They drove off in a cloud of dust, and Declan realised there was no way he could share dinner with them; it would be just too hard to handle after the hopes and plans he'd had for her return.

It looked like Gail had been wrong about Coral's feelings for him after all. Or maybe it had been a fleeting mini-crush

321

that had now been well and truly eclipsed by the all-consuming, all-singing-and-dancing love affair that had swept her off her feet.

Declan sighed. Either way, he'd messed up and missed out.

As they drove away from Weaver's Cottage, Coral silently congratulated herself on having handled the situation without doing anything embarrassing. It was fine, she'd managed it, she hadn't made a fool of herself and there'd definitely been none of those giveaway looks of longing that Gail had previously observed. She'd learned from her earlier mistakes and retained her dignity. Thank God.

Mind you, it was a lot easier when you had a distraction in the form of Trent.

'You OK?' As they stopped at the traffic lights, he briefly rested his left hand on her knee. 'What are you thinking about?'

Coral admired his profile. 'I'm thinking we had a perfect holiday.'

'We definitely did. And now we're back home. On to the next phase. I just hope Lily likes me.'

'Of course she will.' Coral's tone was reassuring.

Seriously, though, what a difference a week could make. It wasn't something she'd expected to happen, but it had. Trent had been a revelation. He had, by his own admission, fallen for her the moment they'd met. And yes, it had caught her by surprise, but as he said, that was just the way he was. What you saw, with him, was what you got. If you knew what you wanted, why bother shilly-shallying about? Just seize the moment and go for it.

Coral had been won over by his enthusiasm, his openness, his honesty. As a widower, too, he knew what she'd been through. He was empathetic. Most of all, though, he liked her and wasn't afraid to show it, and he was available. Which meant she was allowed to like him back. After the agony of having to hide her feelings for Declan, who was so lovely but so completely *un*available, it had come as a relief. Here was someone she *could* allow herself to fall in love with.

OK, it was too soon to call it love, but so far it had been a wonderful experience. She'd found herself relaxing and feeling normal again . . . and just loving the *sensation* of feeling normal. The last week had been a joyous whirl of sunshine and laughter, conversation and wine, and the gloriously pleasurable zing of growing attraction for this new man whom fate had brought into her life.

Ironically, too, she owed it all to Declan and Gail. If she hadn't been panicked by Gail's terrifyingly astute observations, she would never have landed up in Grimaud and met Trent.

Funny how fate worked, sometimes. You never could tell, could you? Trent wasn't Declan – if she were being honest, he wasn't even close – but he was single and he was offering her a future. Coral's heart skittered at the thought of it; she'd taken an unexpected new direction and maybe it was the right one.

This could be the start of a whole new life.

Patsy arrived back in Stanton Langley at ten o'clock on Saturday evening. The cottage was unexpectedly tidy. Empty, too. She sent a quick text, and two minutes later received the reply.

Right. Not ideal, obviously, but it had to be done.

Sick with fear, she walked down to the high street and crossed the road to the Star. The sky was pitch black, with only a sliver of moon visible above the trees behind it. The white fairy lights strung up outside the pub glittered in the darkness and made it look so much more welcoming than it could well turn out to be.

She knew they were in there. From here, she could hear the sound of music, voices and laughter. When she walked in, would the place suddenly fall deathly silent, like in *High Noon*?

Her mouth was dry and she could no longer feel her knees. The last time she'd faced Lily, the encounter had ended just about as badly as it was possible to end.

Patsy braced herself. It was time to find out if this one was due to be worse.

'Well?' Coral said eagerly while Trent was up at the bar ordering a fresh round of drinks. 'Do you like him?'

Which was one of those questions to which it would be impossible to reply no.

Luckily Lily didn't need to. She nodded and said, 'He's really nice,' because it was so clearly what Coral wanted to hear. And Trent did seem nice; there was nothing to actively dislike about him. It was all just a bit sudden and unexpected, that was all. Like Coral, he was in his late forties and had been widowed. He worked as the manager of an electrical store in Cirencester, loved to listen to jazz music and was a keen amateur water-colourist in his free time. He had an open face, good table manners and was cheerful and friendly. He was also quite clearly besotted with Coral.

If Lily was completely honest, it did feel the tiniest bit odd seeing him holding Coral's hand, stroking her fingers and slowly rubbing the small of her back, but this was only because she wasn't used to witnessing such public displays of affection from someone who still felt to her like a stranger.

Then again, he wasn't a stranger to Coral. She'd finally found someone she liked, and that was all that counted. It was definitely a good thing to have happened to her.

'Suspicious Minds' was playing on the music system as Trent

brought their drinks back to the table, and a few of the regulars were joining in with the chorus.

'Ah, Elvis Presley. Can't beat a bit of Elvis. Elvis the Pelvis,' said Trent, sitting down and taking a gulp of lager. He winked at Coral. 'Love me tender. Can't help falling in love.' He reached for her hand once more and gave it a squeeze. 'The wonder of you.'

Yikes, and now he was gazing dreamily into Coral's eyes. Was he about to burst into song and start serenading her? Lily exchanged a glance of alarm with Dan, who promptly leapt into the breach with 'Speaking of pelvises . . .'

Oh God, now what was *he* about to say?

'Sorry, what?' Coral was looking baffled too.

'Remember Kyle, the boy we were at school with? The one who had that accident at Hestacombe Lake and broke his pelvis?'

'Of course I do,' Coral exclaimed. 'That poor boy, wasn't he in hospital for weeks? And the farmer put a bull in the field after that so the rest of you couldn't get down to the lake.'

Dan nodded. 'Lily and I were wondering what happened to him after his family left the area. We wanted to look him up, but neither of us can remember his surname.'

'McSomething. Or MacSomething,' said Lily. 'I'm not sure I ever even knew his name, not properly. It was MacLanan or McLanahan, or McClannon . . . or MacAllen . . .' She shrugged. 'We tried googling, but it was hopeless.'

'And I can't help you,' said Coral. 'I never even met him. No clue, sorry. Oh—'

Her eyes had widened. For a split second, Lily thought Kyle's name had somehow come to her. The next moment, she realised it hadn't; Coral was staring straight past her across the pub.

Lily met Dan's dark eyes once more and saw the concern

in them, coupled with a lack of surprise. That was when she knew who had just walked in and, in all probability, who had texted him ten minutes ago.

Well it had to happen at some stage. Patsy couldn't stay away forever and never come back.

Chapter 44

It was by the sheerest coincidence that the previous Elvis track had just faded away and been replaced by the opening chords of 'Devil in Disguise'. Whooping with recognition, and oblivious to the awkwardness of the situation, the regulars cheerily greeted Patsy's arrival, then returned their attention to the impromptu singalong.

Lily looked at Patsy and Patsy looked back, her expression carefully masked as she slowly threaded her way between the tables.

'How are you feeling?' Dan kept his voice low.

Lily shook her head. 'I don't know.'

Across the table, Coral was explaining to Trent what was going on. Leaning sideways, Dan murmured, 'Do you want me to kiss you again? Because I will. Right here in front of everyone.'

Lily couldn't move; his mouth was millimetres from her ear and her ear was fizzing like a firework, hyper-aware of his proximity. She whispered, 'Shush, stop it.'

'OK. But you never know, it might help.'

Of course it wouldn't help. But the awful thing was, she wanted it to happen. Not here, though, and not now. In private.

Oh God, stop thinking about it.

But she knew what Dan was doing and why he was doing it. Patsy was his big sister, his only living relative, and he wanted all this to be over. He hadn't asked her to forgive Patsy, but of course that was what he wanted.

And now Patsy was standing directly in front of her, swallowing with difficulty, her hands clasped and her fingers twisted together. You could see her knuckles whitening with the tension in her grip.

'Lily, I'm sorry. I know, I know, I can keep on saying it and it's never going to be enough, but I don't know what else I can do.' Patsy's face was pale, and the violet shadows beneath her eyes betrayed how little sleep she'd been getting. 'I just wish there was something—'

'Don't.' Lily shook her head as she pushed back her chair and rose clumsily to her feet. She wrapped her arms around Patsy and hugged her hard. 'It's all right, you don't have to do anything. You made a mistake, that's all. But I still love you.'

'Oh God.' Choking up, Patsy let out a sob like a honking goose. 'Really? *Really?*'

'Of course really.' And now Lily's eyes were brimming too. 'You've been gone for two weeks. I've missed you so much.' It was true, it was so true. She'd wanted to punish Patsy, but in doing so she had only succeeded in punishing herself. The two of them had both been feeling terrible. Forgiving Patsy meant all the anger could melt away, the hurt and the resentment evaporate into thin air. Tightening her hold, she whispered, 'I'm sorry too.'

'Oh Lily, you haven't done anything to apologise for.'

Well she had, but it was nothing to do with Patsy.

Lily exhaled with relief. She looked across at Dan and saw him smile. Forgiving Patsy for having done wrong meant she could forgive herself for kissing Dan. Or, more to the point, kissing him and enjoying it so much she hadn't been able to stop thinking about it ever since.

Forgiving herself, it turned out, was easy. Now all she had to do was figure out how to erase the memory of That Kiss from her brain . . .

Then it was Coral's turn to embrace Patsy and say, 'We've all missed you. Where have you *been*?'

An extra chair was pulled up at the table. Sean, working behind the bar, brought over a drink for Patsy and gave her shoulder a squeeze. 'Welcome back.'

Patsy rested her hand on his for a moment and looked up at him with gratitude. 'Thanks.'

At the other end of the pub, Elvis had given way to Queen and everyone was now belting out 'Bohemian Rhapsody'. Patsy shook her head. 'No one's taking any notice of me being here. I thought the place would fall silent and I'd be glared at. I expected to be public enemy number one.'

'They don't know,' said Lily.

'Really?' Patsy clutched her chest in relief. 'You didn't tell them?'

'No one else needed to know,' said Coral.

'Oh God, thank you. Thank you so much. I was so scared. Where does everyone think I've been?'

'We just said you'd gone up to London to help out in Rosa's salon because two of her senior stylists were off sick.'

Patsy nodded, because this was entirely feasible. 'OK, right.'

'And where were you really?' said Lily.

'Dredging a canal in Norfolk.'

Double-take time. 'You *what*?'

'It's one of those voluntary projects to clear up the water-ways. You spend all day every day scooping gloop and weeds

329

and rusty bikes out of a stretch of canal, and in return they put you up in a caravan and give you three cooked meals a day.'

It was like hearing Patsy announce that she'd been working in a sewer or down a mine. Lily said, 'You? Dredging a canal? But that's everything you hate in the world.'

'I know. I think that's why I did it. Couldn't afford to go anywhere nice, so I decided to do something awful instead. It seemed like the right thing to do. I suppose I wanted to punish myself.'

'Oh *Patsy*. And was it better than you thought? Did it turn out to be fun after all?'

'No, it was revolting. Mud and rats and millions of mosquitoes. And the smell of it was just . . . *eurgh*.'

Grasping at straws, Lily said, 'Were the other volunteers nice, though?'

'God, no, they were awful too. I was sharing a mouldy two-berth caravan with an old hippy called Rain. You know how people always say nits prefer clean hair? Well that turns out to be a big lie, because Rain has a headful of nits and she hasn't washed her hair for the last twenty-three years.'

Lily tried not to shrink away. Patsy saw her flinch and they both burst out laughing. Oh, the joy of knowing all the bad stuff was behind them; everything was completely back to normal. The connection between them was as strong as it had ever been.

'Where's Declan?' Patsy looked at Dan. 'You said in your text he was staying at our place with you. I thought he'd be here tonight.'

'He was going to be,' Lily explained. 'But something came up this afternoon, some emergency with one of his properties, and he had to drive back to London to sort it out.' It had been so lovely having him down here all week; she'd been disappointed when he had called her earlier to tell her he was leaving and wouldn't be able to join them this evening. She hoped the problem wasn't too desperate; he'd sounded a bit subdued on the phone.

'He's finished Weaver's Cottage,' said Coral. 'It's amazing.' She shook her head. 'He said he'd be quick, but we didn't think he'd be this quick.'

'I can't believe so much has happened while I've been away.' Patsy looked at Coral, then at Trent sitting beside her with his arm around her waist. 'Looks like you've been pretty speedy yourself.'

'Hi. Trent Barrett.' With his free hand, Trent reached across the table and enthusiastically pumped Patsy's hand. 'Guilty as charged. A week ago I went away on a painting holiday and met the most amazing woman in the world.'

'Oh don't!' Coral was laughing and blushing.

'Don't be modest. I'm saying it because it's true.' Trent pulled her closer to him. 'When you know, you know.' He gazed deep into Coral's eyes. 'And believe me, I know. Which makes me the luckiest man in the world.'

'You definitely are,' said Patsy with a warm smile.

Lily wanted Coral to be happy, but she couldn't help wishing the lovey-doveyness could be dialled down a notch. She glanced sideways at Dan, who came to the rescue once more.

'Hang on, did Kyle's family move to Liverpool after they left here? I've been trying to remember, and for some reason I'm thinking Merseyside.'

He wasn't; they'd already been through this and concluded they had no idea where the family had headed. But Lily said, 'Ooh, maybe you're right.'

'Who's this?' said Patsy, joining in.

331

'We were just talking about him before you came in,' Dan explained. 'Kyle, the one from school who ended up in hospital after that accident at The Leap.'

'Oh I remember.' Patsy nodded. 'Kyle McLinehan. Poor lad, how is he now, do you know?' She paused. 'What? Why are you all looking at me like that?'

Lily said, 'Did you *know* him?'

'No.'

'But you know his name was McLenehan,' said Dan.

'Not McLenehan. Mc*Line*han,' Patsy corrected him. 'His mother came to the salon one time, not long after the accident had happened. She had a trim.'

'You remember that from ten years ago?' Dan was incredulous. 'And you actually remember how to spell her surname?'

'She was a bit terrifying,' Patsy confessed. 'She saw that I'd written it down wrong in the appointment book and told me off. It was like being back at school, to be honest – she made me rewrite it properly and say it out loud. But it meant I didn't forget it. Mc*Linehan*.'

Dan already had his phone out. He tapped in the name and said, 'Bloody hell.'

'What? Show me, show me.' Lily leaned across, ready to peer at whatever he'd found. Hopefully it wasn't a news story about a poor put-upon boy going berserk and doing away with his scary mother.

She heard Dan start to laugh with relief. 'Thank God for that,' he murmured, then turned his phone so she could see the screen too.

And there was a photo of Kyle McLinehan, older now of course but still instantly recognisable, wearing a racing helmet and mud-splattered jockey's silks and with his arms held joyously aloft as he celebrated victory in the winners' enclosure at Ascot.

'He's a jump jockey,' Lily marvelled as Dan scrolled on down. 'He's not in a wheelchair!'

'Not at the moment,' Dan said drily. 'Listen to this . . .' He expanded the text and began to read aloud: '"In the last decade, spectacular wins have been interspersed with equally dramatic injuries; in addition to fractured femurs, arms and collarbones, a horse landed on McLinehan last year, leaving him with serious internal injuries and a fractured skull. He recovered well, however, and was back racing within months. More happily, earlier this year he and his wife welcomed the arrival of their fifth child."'

'All those injuries,' Lily marvelled.

'And five kids. Basically, Kyle doesn't hang around.'

'If we'd known anything about horse racing, we'd have heard of him,' said Lily. Then she jumped as beneath the table and out of sight of the others, Dan gave her hand a squeeze.

He was only doing it to signal his relief that Kyle was OK, but it gave her a jolt all the same. Worse, it made her want to kiss him. *Oh help . . .*

'Looks like he's done all right for himself,' said Patsy. 'Five children too. When his mother was telling me about him, she was absolutely convinced he was gay.'

'He's won loads of races.' Lily was still reading the information on Dan's phone screen. 'Ha, remember how Gail was boasting at the barbecue about how she was friends with Frankie Dettori? Next time she's down, we can boast back about knowing Kyle McLinehan.'

'Except she's not going to be back down here.' Dan stopped abruptly. 'OK, I wasn't supposed to say that.'

'What?' Lily was puzzled. 'Why not? What's happened?'

Dan hesitated, then shrugged and said, 'Oh well, it's not like it was a *proper* secret.'

It wasn't exactly reassuring to discover he wasn't that great at keeping any kind of secret, proper or otherwise. As if the memory of their supposedly secret kiss wasn't already preying on her mind enough. Anyway, never mind about that now. 'Dan, what's going on?'

'Declan only didn't mention it because he thought you had enough on your plate, what with the stuff with Keir happening and Patsy disappearing. But he told me last week,' said Dan. 'It's all over between him and Gail. We won't be seeing her again.'

'Wow.' Lily boggled. 'Do we know why?' Although she had to say, they'd spent the last week with Declan and if he was heartbroken he'd been disguising it like a champion. Until today when he'd had to rush back to London, if anything she'd have said he seemed even more cheerful than usual.

Dan said, 'It was his decision. There's no one else involved. He just realised things weren't right.'

'Well I bet Gail got the shock of her life.' Lily could just picture her reaction. 'She doesn't seem like the kind of person who'd expect to be finished with.'

'No one goes through life expecting to be finished with,' said Dan.

Patsy said, 'I do.' She pulled a face. 'And I'm always right.'

'We're going to find you someone nice.' Lily had already decided, while they'd been hugging each other, that this was going to be her new resolution. Turning to Coral to back her up, she said, 'Aren't we? Between us we'll make it happen.' Because Patsy might have made mistakes in the past, but she did deserve to be happy.

Coral blinked. 'Sorry. What was that? I missed it.'

'She's miles away.' Trent laughed and, with his arm wrapped around her shoulders, gave Coral another of his overenthusiastic hugs. 'Wakey wakey, pay attention, honeybun – you were daydreaming about our last night in Grimaud, weren't you!'

Eww again; but Coral was looking embarrassed, smiling apologetically and shifting in her seat. Plus Trent was looking smug.

So maybe he'd been right.

'OK, can I just say I wasn't being nosy.' Patsy blurted the words out as Dan made his way back into the living room much later that night.

'About what?' Dan frowned as he put down the plate of cheese on toast he'd just made in the kitchen; why on earth was Patsy looking at him like that?

Then he saw that she was pointing to his laptop, lying open on the coffee table between them.

'All I did was glance at the screen as I was reaching for the TV remote. By the time I realised it was your bank statement, it was too late. I'd already seen his name.'

'Whose name?' But Dan had already figured it out. And Patsy knew that he knew.

She gave him a big-sister head tilt. 'Come on, you're many things, but you're not stupid.'

Apart from his unbelievably stupid love for Lily. Except Patsy still didn't know about that, thank God.

She was now pointing to a transaction on the screen. 'There. On Sunday the twenty-ninth of June, you made an online payment of three thousand pounds.' She paused, then said evenly, 'To Keir Bourne.'

Fuck.

And the way she'd emphasised the amount made it sound like a lot.

OK, it *was* a lot. But it had seemed like a good idea at the time.

Dan exhaled. 'I thought Lily had been through enough.'

Patsy was looking at him as if she knew better. 'Just Lily?'

'OK, and you too,' he admitted. 'Both of you.'

'That's why there was no story the following Sunday. No more awful embarrassing details.'

Dan nodded.

'You paid him off.'

This was true, and he knew it had been a bad thing to do, like paying a ransom to kidnappers. But he'd wanted it to be over, had wanted Keir Bourne to go away, leave them alone and not inflict yet more pain on those whose lives he'd messed up. Bourne had been due another thousand pounds from the newspaper for the follow-up piece. When Dan had offered him two thousand to keep quiet, he had hesitated, torn but visibly tempted.

Three thousand had sealed the deal. Right there and then, in the kitchen at Goldstone House, Dan had keyed the necessary bank details into his phone and transferred the money into Keir Bourne's account.

His parting shot had been: 'And if you're ever tempted to ask for more or renege on this agreement, think again. Because I know people who'd be only too happy to bring you to your senses. If you know what I mean.'

Needless to say, he didn't know anyone, but had uttered the words with a hopefully convincing note of threatening menace.

Keir Bourne had nodded and appeared to believe him anyway. He hadn't been able to scuttle away fast enough, like the cockroach he was.

'Well, it was a crazy thing to do.' Patsy was looking emotional. 'But thank you. So much.'

'Don't worry about it. Let's not mention this to Lily, OK?'

'OK.' Patsy broke into a wobbly smile, then jumped up and hugged him. 'You're not a bad brother, you know.'

'I know.'

'It's good to be home.'

'I'm glad you're back too.'

Patsy wiped her eyes and said hopefully, 'Can I have some of your cheese on toast?'

'OK, now you're really pushing your luck,' said Dan.

Chapter 45

It was Patsy's birthday.

Happy birthday to meeee, Patsy sang quietly in her head.

Not out loud, that would be embarrassing. And people would stare.

This morning she'd gone into work and there'd been cava and cake. People had popped in and out to wish her many happy returns and bring her flowers. Sean and Will had given her the most beautiful Vivienne Westwood red leather purse, Lily and Coral had bought her a stunning Venetian mirror and Dan's present had been two tickets to see Beyoncé at London's O2 Arena and spend the night in a glitzy four-star hotel in Canary Wharf.

She loved her friends and family so much. She also knew that it was more than she deserved.

Then at lunchtime Kath from Derring's Farm had come into the salon and told them about her grandson, ill in hospital in Baltimore and desperately in need of funds to pay for life-saving surgery. Poor Kath had been in a state; she hated to ask, but they were raising money via an eBay charity auction and if anyone had anything at all they could donate to the cause, her family would be so grateful.

Patsy had slipped home, explained the situation to Dan and returned to the salon with the tickets for the Beyoncé-and-hotel-stay package. Kath had been overwhelmed, but Patsy had insisted. Much as she'd always longed to see Beyoncé performing live, giving her birthday present to a worthy cause made her feel better and went some way towards assuaging her continuing guilt.

The excellent news was that since Kath's son had put the tickets up on the fund-raising page this afternoon, bidding had already reached £550.

And Patsy knew she'd done a good thing.

The time was now five to eight and her date was due to arrive at any minute. She tried hard not to wonder if doing a good thing might mean things would go well this evening in a karmic kind of way. But that wasn't why she'd done it.

She hadn't even meant to come out on any more internet dates. Having done a *lot* of serious thinking in the past few weeks, Patsy had made up her mind to alter her life and stop being so desperate. From now on she was going to sort herself out, live life on her own terms and knock the neediness on the head. She'd also thanked Sean and Will for their kind suggestion but explained to them that she wouldn't be taking them up on the offer. She wanted a baby, but also important was being able to share it with someone she was truly in love with. And if she were destined to never meet the right man and remain childless . . . well, so what? It was what happened to thousands of women, and if they could cope with it, then so could she. It wasn't the end of the world.

Sean and Will had been brilliant, thank goodness. They'd agreed that this was the right decision for her. And when she'd finished apologising for having dashed their hopes, they'd told her it didn't matter a bit, and that now they knew for sure that a family was what they wanted, there were plenty of other avenues to explore.

For now, though, as far as she herself was concerned, Patsy had taken the decision to just stop thinking about it. What would be would be.

The door to the wine bar swung open and Patsy's stomach did its habitual anxious lurch. But it wasn't him; it was two blond girls in skin-tight dresses and strappy heels.

His name was Rick, he was thirty-seven and an architect, and he lived right here in Cheltenham. During her fortnight away from home, she hadn't accessed the dating site once. Having made the decision to give it up, it wasn't until after her return to Stanton Langley that she'd seen Rick's messages. Several of them, but not in a stalky or scary way; he'd simply wondered why she hadn't replied to his emails.

Patsy had emailed him back to explain, and he'd said well wasn't that a shame, he'd missed his chance. Then he'd asked if she wouldn't consider making an exception, just this once . . . and they'd fallen into a routine of exchanging jokey messages pretty much every day. Finally she'd succumbed because he'd sounded funny and genuine. And when he had set the date for this evening, she hadn't told him it was her birthday. It wasn't important; he didn't need to know.

Maybe if tonight went well and they saw each other again and again, she would tell him the truth about the day of the first date and together they'd laugh about it.

OK, getting way ahead of herself, as usual. Let's face it, the chances were that Rick would turn up, turn out to have all sorts of annoying traits, and she'd be back home by ten o'clock all ready to start the rest of her new and improved man-free life.

The door swung open at eight o'clock on the dot and a middle-aged couple came into the wine bar.

At three minutes past, a man arrived to collect his wife, who'd been having a drink with friends from work.

At ten past, the door opened once more to admit another couple, and this time every muscle in Patsy's body stiffened in horror. The woman was tall and elegant with sleek dark hair and a prominent Roman nose that suited her high-cheekboned face.

The man was Derek.

Derek, he of the turquoise Lycra leggings and tandem obsession, whom she had last seen disappearing down the road alone on his bicycle built for two.

Except this evening he was wearing normal clothes.

Oh God, oh God, please don't let him spot me . . .

But fate – or God – wasn't that magnanimous. As Patsy attempted to study the wine menu at such close range that it was making her eyes cross, Derek stopped dead in his tracks. 'Well, well, look who it is! Hello, Patsy, what are you doing here? Waiting for another blind date?' He glanced at the watch on his bony wrist and feigned concern. 'Oh dear, was he meant to be here by eight? Not looking good, is it? I do hope he isn't going to embarrass you by not turning up!'

Such a loud, carrying voice. Other people in the bar were nudging each other and whispering. Some were giving her sympathetic smiles but others were clearly finding it hilarious. And the worst thing was, Patsy knew she absolutely deserved it.

'I hope so too.' She forced herself to remain outwardly composed. 'Hello, Derek, you're looking well. Sorry about our date.'

'No problem. Your loss.' He slid his arm possessively around his companion's waist. 'I'm glad you jumped off my tandem. If that hadn't happened, I wouldn't have met Andrea, would I? She loves cycling. We're a perfect match.'

'That's great. I'm happy for you,' said Patsy. It was true, but she was also mortified for herself.

'Thank you. We reap what we sow. Maybe I deserved to meet someone nice . . . and you didn't.'

'Definitely.' Patsy nodded. 'I think you could be right.'

'Come on.' Andrea gave Derek a nudge. 'Let's go through to the other bar, shall we?' She turned back to Patsy. 'Can I just say? You really missed a trick there, but I'm glad you did. He's one in a million, and he's all mine.'

'Let's leave her to her date.' Derek was smug as he cast another ostentatious glance at his watch and pulled a face. 'Ooh dear. That is, *if* he turns up.'

They made their way through to the conservatory bar at the back of the building, leaving Patsy wreathed in awkwardness. It was like wearing the opposite of an invisibility cloak. Derek and Andrea might have disappeared, but the thirty or forty other customers were still here, casting sly glances in her direction and thinking she deserved to be stood up.

Because Derek was actually looking perfectly normal this evening, what with his trendy choppy haircut, nice shirt and well-fitting jeans.

It was hugely tempting to get to her feet and announce, 'Look, he turned up for our first date wearing turquoise Lycra leggings, OK? And a cycling helmet.'

But she couldn't; she just had to sit there and sweat it out. And it was almost 8.15 now. Why wasn't Rick here yet?

Time crawled by in that special slow-motion way it had a habit of slipping into when you were most desperate for it to move faster. The doors swung open to admit several more customers, none of them Rick. Quarter past became twenty past, and Patsy experienced the sinking feeling of rejection. Five more minutes, then she'd leave. Maybe three more. She was surrounded by people murmuring to each other, smirking at the non-arrival of her date. If she were to walk out now, they'd all burst out laughing and start discussing her utter humiliation and comeuppance. That would be fun for them, wouldn't it?

OK, one more minute, then she was off. There'd been no text messages from Rick and no response to the one she'd sent him eight minutes ago. Enough was enough; even the bar staff were covertly watching her now, waiting to see what she'd do next. In fact, it was definitely time to—

'Excuse me. Are you Patsy?'

Patsy swivelled round so fast she almost cricked her neck. But it wasn't him. She'd seen several photos of Rick, and he was tall and thin with short dark hair and a scar through his left eyebrow.

'I'm Patsy.' This one was medium height and broad-shouldered, with tousled fair hair and blond stubble on his cleft chin. He was wearing a checked shirt and unfortunate burgundy trousers. 'Is this about Rick?'

Every eye in the wine bar was upon them; no one was even bothering to pretend not to be eavesdropping.

'Um . . . yes.' The late arrival looked awkward.

OK, having him hover in front of her table like this was just drawing even more attention. Patsy pointed and said, 'Sit down. Is he not coming?'

Although she already knew the answer.

He cautiously sat opposite her as if suspecting the chair seat were scattered with upturned drawing pins. 'I'm sorry. No, he isn't.'

Chapter 46

'Is it because he's dead?'

A shake of the head. 'No.'

Right. 'Is he trapped at the foot of a deep ravine with severe injuries and no way of climbing out?'

'No.'

'That's a real shame,' said Patsy. 'You might like to warn him that he'd do well to avoid going near the edges of any deep ravines for the next few weeks.' Just to give Rick the benefit of the doubt, she said, 'OK, is he ill?'

Another weary head-shake. 'He isn't ill. He's just a prize dick.'

Surprise surprise.

'And you're . . . what? His best friend, his brother?' *Another prize dick?*

'Neither. I hardly know him. But he's spent the whole afternoon drinking at the cricket club. His friends kept reminding him he had a date this evening but he said he couldn't be bothered going. And nobody else seemed to care; they were just laughing and making jokes about it. To be honest, that's what they're like. But I thought it couldn't be much fun for you sitting here on your own wondering what was going on, so I asked him where the two of you were meant to be meeting up.'

'Well that was decent of you.' Unlike bloody Rick. 'Sorry, I don't know your name. But thanks anyway. Bastard. I mean him, not you . . .'

'I'm Oliver.'

'Right. Patsy. Oh, you already knew that. Sorry again.' Patsy exhaled and shook her head, looking down at her hands in order to avoid glancing around the room. 'Is everyone staring at me?'

'No, of course not.' Pause. 'OK, a bit. Oh God, are you going to cry?'

'Definitely not.'

'Well that's good.' He sounded relieved. 'So . . . um . . . I just came to let you know.'

Poor Oliver; he couldn't wait to get out of here. Patsy nodded. 'Of course. Thanks again, I appreciate it. Very kind of—' Oh shit, here came Derek and Andrea, making their way back out. Just as Oliver began to get to his feet, Patsy grabbed his hand and hissed, '*Sit*.'

Like he was a *really* naughty dog.

Startled into obedience, Oliver sat back on his chair a split second before Derek looked over and said, 'Well how about that then? Her date finally turned up. Better late than never, eh?'

Thinking fast, Patsy said, 'There was an accident on Lansdown Road.'

'Between a minibus and a Vauxhall Corsa. I was lucky she was still here waiting for me.' Oliver smiled across at Patsy. 'Sorry again. I hate being late.'

'Well keep an eye on her,' said Derek. 'And if you give her a lift home later, mind she doesn't jump out of the car window when you're not looking.'

Patsy said, 'Don't worry, I won't be doing that.'

When the door had closed behind Derek and Andrea, Oliver said, 'How was that? Did I do OK?'

'More than OK. You were *very* good.'

He broke into a grin. 'What was that about the car window?'

Patsy hesitated, then realised she might as well tell him; she had no more dignity left to lose. 'He was another internet date. I wasn't expecting him to turn up on a tandem. He wouldn't stop talking about bikes so I jumped off the back and let him cycle off without noticing I'd gone.'

Oliver burst out laughing. 'Ha, brilliant. Good for you.'

'Maybe tonight was my payback.' Patsy was rueful, although Rick had evidently been no great loss. Then she noticed the way Oliver was looking at her. 'What?'

'I kept getting this feeling I'd seen you somewhere before, but I couldn't place you. Except now you've mentioned the internet dates, I think I've got it.' He stopped, thought for a moment, then wagged an index finger in the air. 'OK, did you go on a date a few weeks ago with a guy who interrupted every single thing you tried to say?'

Patsy sat back, stunned. 'You mean James? Are you *serious*? Do you know him too?'

'I don't know him at all. I was there. You were having dinner at The Greengage in Nailsworth, right? We were at the next table.'

Patsy covered her mouth. She'd been aware of the couple seated a few feet away but hadn't paid them any attention. She shook her head. 'It's my mission in life to provide entertainment for eavesdroppers.'

'Sorry, we couldn't help it. Each time you opened your mouth to say something, he just talked right over you. About his ex-wife, mostly.'

'He was a nightmare.' Patsy sighed. 'I can't believe you were there.'

'Thank goodness your brother had that accident so you had to rush off.' Oliver's mouth twitched.

Patsy nodded. 'It was good timing.'

He indicated her phone on the table. 'Have you arranged for someone to call you again this evening?'

'Well I have, but I'll be back home before it happens. Look, thanks again for coming to tell me about Rick.' She picked up her handbag and rummaged for her car keys. 'OK, time to make a move. Did you drive here or can I offer you a lift?'

Oliver glanced at her almost empty glass of orange juice. 'Or . . . I don't *have* to leave. We could stay here and have a drink. If you wanted to, that is. I mean, I'm in no hurry. Although maybe you are. God, sorry, as if you haven't had a bad enough start to the evening . . .'

'Where's your wife?' Patsy's tone was cool. 'Or your girl-friend? The one you were with at the restaurant the other week.'

He slowly nodded. 'Oh, her. Were we holding hands, snuggling up together? Kissing?'

'I didn't really notice. I don't think so.'

'Well thank goodness for that.' Oliver pulled a face. 'Because I don't have a wife or a girlfriend. That was Nadine,' he said. 'She's my sister.'

For the next hour, the conversation zigzagged in all directions. When he asked about her family, Patsy found herself telling him about Dan's career as a pilot and his lifelong love of flying.

'You see? That's a cool thing to do. Guess what form of transport my younger brother's obsessed with? OK, you won't

347

guess, so I'll tell you.' Oliver shook his head in despair. 'Steam trains. He can't get enough of them. Seriously, he's even dragged me along with him to a couple of shows.'

Ding went Patsy's brain, sparked by the memory of Tess in the salon offering to have a word with her husband about getting her fixed up with one of his fellow steam train enthusiasts. She smiled inwardly at her mental image of the men with their flat caps and untrimmed beards.

OK, probably best not to relate that tale to Oliver.

But twenty minutes later, when he happened to mention that one of his friends from work lived in Chipping Norton, Patsy said, 'Oh I love that place. The little theatre just off the high street is so brilliant. My friend Finola lives there too and we always go along to their Christmas pantos.'

'Finola?' Oliver sat up. 'Married to Will? Will is the friend I work with! They had this amazing barbecue the other week . . . it was the best night ever, I've never laughed so much in my life.'

The little hairs had risen on the back of Patsy's neck. That had been the evening she'd had her disastrous date in the Star with penny-pinching Marcus. And she'd dithered about whether or not to bother driving over to Chipping Norton afterwards but had ended up deciding against it.

Whereas if she *had* gone along, she would have met Oliver . . .

'I was invited to Finola and Will's barbecue too,' she said.

'You weren't there, though.' Oliver shook his head. 'If you had been, I'd have definitely noticed you.'

She'd even wondered if it could have turned out to be one of those potentially life-changing *Sliding Doors* moments. How spooky was that? She smiled and shrugged. 'You're right, I didn't go.'

At eleven o'clock, the manager of the bar called last orders, just as Oliver was telling Patsy the story of how he'd lost his keys last year, on Christmas Eve.

'. . . And it had just gone midnight, so of course it cost a *fortune* to call out a locksmith.' He laughed at the memory. 'Not the best start to Christmas, or to my birthday.'

'Your birthday's on Christmas Day? Oh wow,' Patsy marvelled. 'That must be weird. *Is* it weird?'

Oliver shrugged easily. 'I'm kind of used to it by now. When's yours?'

'Um . . . July.'

'Ah, you were a summer baby. When in July?'

Whoops, bit embarrassing. 'Second half.'

Oliver beamed. 'Same as my sister. What date?'

'The twenty-fourth. So when you and your sister were young, did she lord it over you because—'

'Hang on,' Oliver interrupted. 'The twenty-fourth?'

Patsy nodded and felt herself reddening.

'Of July?'

She nodded again.

'But . . . that's today,' said Oliver.

'I know.' She felt inexplicably ashamed.

'Oh Patsy.' He gazed into her eyes. 'I'm sorry. You should have said.'

'Doesn't matter.' She broke into a smile. 'There might have been a bit of a dodgy dip in the middle, but the rest of it's been great.'

At that moment the manager clanged the bell and called out, 'Time! Time now at the bar.'

'Wait!' Oliver jumped to his feet and rushed over. Evidently having sweet-talked the manager, he returned triumphantly bearing two glasses and one mini-bottle of Prosecco.

349

'Here we go. Better late than never.' He divided the sparkling wine between them. 'Cheers. Happy birthday.'

Their glasses clinked together. Patsy said, 'Thank you.'

'Rick missed a trick.' Oliver's eyes glinted with mischief. 'The dick.'

'I'm glad he did,' said Patsy. *Ooh, daring*.

Oliver looked pleased. 'I'm glad too.'

By 11.30, the staff were busy tidying up and it was time to leave the almost empty bar. When Oliver excused himself to visit the men's loo, Patsy found herself approached by the female half of the only other remaining customers. In her fifties and well dressed, she teetered over on high heels.

'Hello, hello! Sorry, I'm a wee bit tipsy, but can I just say we've been here all evening and we heard what happened. This one seems really nice, though. I know looks-wise he's no Ryan Reynolds, but you can't have everything, can you? I mean, not saying he's ugly, he's just a bit ordinary, but that's OK! And you can always smarten him up, can't you? The important thing is that he sounds like a really nice guy and the two of you are getting on together so well.'

'Erm . . . he's behind you,' said Patsy.

'I am.' Oliver, back from the loo, nodded in sympathy.

The woman's husband reached for his wife's hand. 'Sorry, is she burbling again? Once she starts, she can't stop. Just ignore her. She doesn't mean any harm.'

'It's fine,' said Oliver. 'I agree with everything she says.'

Had there ever been such an amazing, unexpected evening? Patsy caught his eye and felt something inside her click into place, like the very last piece of a jigsaw puzzle. She smiled and said, 'So do I.'

Chapter 47

Lily had delivered a Victorian marble fireplace and a stone birdbath to a customer in Stow-on-the-Wold. Arriving back in Stanton Langley at six o'clock, she saw Eddie and Dan sitting together at one of the tables outside the Star.

Her heart leapt at the sight of them as their heads turned in her direction. She parked the van and jumped out, and Dan said, 'I'll leave you two to your reunion. Bye.'

It was still a novelty to see him walking normally, without a limp or using the aluminium crutch for support. For a couple of seconds Lily watched him heading for the car he was now able to drive again. Next week he had his appointment with the aviation medical examiner and an hours-long session booked on the simulator to establish his proficiency and physical fitness before he could return to work.

Then Eddie said, 'Hey, come here, you've no idea how much I've missed you,' and drew her towards him for a kiss.

Typically, it was at this precise moment that three teenage boys on bicycles pedalled past, emitting ear-piercing wolf whistles along with a cry of 'Go on, give 'er one!'

It was hard to kiss romantically when you were snorting with laughter.

'Sorry,' said Lily. 'Bloody hecklers.'

'I don't believe it.' Staring after them, Eddie said, 'The kid on the left? That's the one I gave all those signed photos to. Little shit.'

It was Tim, or Tom, younger brother of Jess, the waitress at the Valentine. Luckily Eddie was amused rather than outraged. Lily said, 'That was my fault. He did sell them on eBay.'

'I didn't doubt it for a minute.' Eddie smiled down at her, his hands resting on her bare shoulders. 'Anyway, I really have missed you.'

'I've missed you too. How's it going with the screenplay?' She knew the struggle he'd been having with it for the last couple of weeks.

'Don't ask. The harder I try, the more the words refuse to come out and the worse it gets. Come on, let's go.' He was leading her towards his car now, parked just down the street.

'Where are you taking me?' said Lily as he accelerated away from the kerb.

'Sshh, it's a surprise.'

She assumed he'd booked a room at the Valentine, but before they reached the hotel, he pulled up outside Weaver's Cottage.

He pointed to the To Let sign planted in the front garden. 'You know, I really thought Declan might decide to keep it for himself.'

'I wondered that too,' said Lily. 'He put so much effort into it. Still, I suppose that's his job. Anyway, he came down for a flying visit yesterday to let me know he's decided to rent it out. He couldn't stay, though; he's snowed under with work at the moment.'

'How is he? Well?'

Lily hesitated. 'I think so.'

Eddie said, 'Do you think he misses Gail?'

'He hasn't seemed very happy recently.' Lily paused, then nodded. 'I think maybe he does miss her. A lot.'

'Well you never know, maybe they'll get back together. But in the meantime, there's a cottage sitting empty.' Eddie swung open the driver's door of the car. 'Want to show me round?'

'It's locked. I don't have a key.'

Next to her, Eddie delved into his jeans pocket and held up a key with a label attached. 'That's OK. I do.'

There was a playful look in his eye that for the life of her Lily couldn't figure out. What on earth was he suggesting? Because if this was his idea of a fun game – that they could sneak into an empty cottage and have wild reunion sex in there – well, there was absolutely no *way* she would go along with such a—

'Oh God, are you thinking what I think you're thinking?' She must have been looking as horrified as she felt, because Eddie said, 'Please don't think it! That would be *so* weird. Listen, I saw the To Let sign up outside when I arrived back this afternoon and asked Dan about it. He told me what was going on. And I called into the estate agent's just before they closed. They trusted me with the key, what with me being a movie star and all.' He smiled, reaching across for Lily's hand. 'How would you feel if I took a year's lease out on this place, hmm? Does that sound like a pretty good plan to you?'

Lily swallowed and wondered if her heart was *visibly* hammering against her ribcage. It sounded as if it should be a brilliant plan.

In theory.

Oh help, this was awkward. She was doing her best to look surprised and delighted, but the muscles in her face felt as if they'd forgotten how to do it, and meanwhile the uncomfortable silence was lengthening and Eddie was watching her, reading her face like a book.

He might be many things, but he wasn't stupid.

'Well there we have it, looks like I've got my answer.' He carefully slid the key back into the pocket of his jeans.

'Sorry,' said Lily. Oh God, was it worse being rejected when you were a famous film star? And what if she were making the most terrible mistake? Because he *was* famous, he *was* a film star, and millions of females would think she'd completely lost her mind. How many ordinary girls turned down an opportunity like this?

'It's OK. I had my suspicions. I kind of did it to see if I was right.' Eddie paused, then added wryly, 'And I was.'

'You're fantastic,' said Lily. 'It's not you, it's definitely me. I must be mad.'

He half smiled. 'Goes without saying.'

'What made you have your suspicions?'

'The other week when I signed off that text with *Love you*, it was a genuine mistake and I had to call you and let you know that. I thought you'd be disappointed but trying your best to hide it. You weren't, though.' He was watching her intently. 'Quite the opposite, in fact. You were relieved.'

This was true. Lily recalled the moment of alarm when she'd first seen the words. Followed by the exquisite feeling of let-off-the-hookness when he'd called to apologise and explain.

She said, 'I could have been pretending to be relieved.'

'You weren't, though.'

'No.'

'Oh well, at least now we know.'

'But I do really like you.'

Eddie dipped his head. 'Thanks. I like you too. Slightly more than you like me, but that's OK.' His tone was rueful. 'My ego can probably handle it.'

'What with all the other millions of girls out there, jumping up and down and screaming, *Pick me, pick me.*'

'Well, quite. I daresay I'll recover. But it's going to be a struggle to find someone else like you. I know you don't think you're special,' Eddie went on, 'but you actually are. You're funny and brave and principled and honest. And I really hope we can stay friends.'

Now he was making her feel terrible. In order to hide her guilty face, Lily leaned across and gave him a hug. Against the soft cotton of his expensive pale blue shirt, she breathed in the scent of him and knew it would stay with her for the rest of her life. Her voice muffled, she said, 'I hope so too.'

They stayed like that for a few seconds more. Finally, realising there was another confession she had to make, Lily pulled back and shook her hair out of her eyes. 'OK, there's something I need to tell you. And this is your fault, because I wasn't going to, but you just called me principled and honest, so now I have to say it.'

'Sounds intriguing.' Eddie looked amused. 'What is it, have you been unfaithful to me?'

He was saying it as a joke, because it was the least likely option he could think of. Feeling sick but knowing she had to go ahead, Lily nodded. 'Yes.'

'*What?*' That made him sit up. 'Are you serious?'

Hastily she added, 'Not sex.'

'Oh, right.' His shoulders relaxed. 'So . . . what kind of unfaithful, then?'

'It was a kiss. A proper kiss. That was all, but it definitely felt like being unfaithful.' She knew she had to explain. 'I was talking to a friend about the situation with Patsy. They asked me if I'd ever done anything really bad that had made me feel terrible and ashamed of myself. And I couldn't think of anything

355

bad enough. So they thought I should do something . . . and, well, that's what it was.'

'Right. So, did it work?'

Lily nodded, her mouth dry. 'Oh yes, it did.'

'You really felt terrible,' Eddie prompted.

'Yes.' Oh God, and now her brain was remembering it all over again . . .

'But it made you realise how Patsy had been feeling, and that's how you were able to forgive her.'

Lily nodded again.

Eddie said thoughtfully, 'I did wonder.'

'Well anyway, that's it, that was what happened. So now you know. And I'm sorry.'

Another look, followed by a crooked smile. Then Eddie drew her towards him and gave her a kiss on the forehead.

'No problem. Very honest of you. Look, I'm going to drop you home now and head back to London. But I meant it about us staying friends.' As he started the car again, he gave her arm a squeeze.

'Good.' Glad he didn't hate her, Lily added, 'And thanks.'

Back at Goldstone House, she gave him one last hug. 'Fifty years from now, when you're up on stage collecting your Oscar for lifetime achievement, I'll be the annoying old woman in the nursing home boasting to everyone that one magical summer we had an affair. And nobody will believe me, which will be *so* annoying.'

'If that happens, I'll come and visit you,' said Eddie. 'Then they'll believe it.'

'I'll hold you to that. Can you bring your Oscar with you?'

'Of course. And it could have lasted longer than one summer. Your decision, remember. Not mine.'

Lily shrugged and smiled. 'Oh well.' She'd expected him to

ask more questions, but he hadn't. Which was probably a good thing.

'I'll tell you something, though,' Eddie said as she climbed out of the car. 'It must have been one hell of a kiss.'

Chapter 48

It wasn't right. Coral had tried so hard to make it work, but it just wasn't happening. Tiny niggling problems, building up over the last few weeks, had become impossible to ignore. In fact you could almost say they'd been multiplying like bacteria.

She stifled a burst of laughter and turned away so Trent wouldn't see. Finding the situation funny really wasn't appropriate under the circumstances. Maybe she was hysterical with relief at having realised that it was OK, she could end this relationship, it was *allowed*.

Oh, but how many couples could lay the blame for their break-up on a single speck of mould on a sandwich?

'What are you doing?' Trent's voice was laced with suspicion. 'Turn round and look at me. Are you *laughing*?'

Oh dear, he'd seen her shoulders shaking. The game was up.

'You *are* laughing,' he announced.

'Because I can't believe you're making this much fuss about a sandwich.' They'd constructed them earlier this morning, because he'd announced that they were going for an eight-mile walk along the Cotswold Way and would need to take supplies with them. When Coral had suggested stopping at a lovely pub

358

for something to eat and drink, Trent had replied, 'No, let's not do that, they just rip people off. We'll take our own.'

But the loaf of bread in his kitchen evidently hadn't been the freshest. By the time they'd stopped for lunch, the heat of the day had got to it, and Trent had stared in horror at the blue dot on the outside of his cheese and pickle sandwich. 'Oh God, I don't believe it! What am I going to do now?'

It had taken Coral a few seconds to realise he wasn't joking. Calmly she had reached across, pinched together her thumb and forefinger, and removed the blue dot. 'There you go, sorted.'

Which had caused Trent to look at her as if she'd just murdered a kitten. 'You can't do that!'

'I just did. What's wrong?'

'You seriously expect me to eat that sandwich now?'

Was he three years old? Was this one of those hidden-camera TV shows? To humour him, Coral said, 'You don't have to. Here, I'll have that one and you can have mine.'

'You'd eat a mouldy sandwich?'

'It isn't a mouldy sandwich. I've taken the mould off. But even if I hadn't, it wouldn't hurt me. It isn't a decomposing rat.'

She gave him her own sandwich and Trent turned it over, his brow furrowed with suspicion. If he'd had a magnifying glass, he would have used it. Finally he pointed, said, 'This one's got it too,' and threw it to the ground in disgust. That was when the giggles had begun to rise up and Coral had had to turn away. If ever Trent was invited to be a contestant on *I'm a Celebrity . . . Get Me Out of Here!*, he should probably say no.

'Antonia would never have laughed at me.' His tone was accusing. 'She wouldn't have eaten a mouldy sandwich, either.'

This was another less-than-endearing habit that had begun

to grate. He'd taken to bringing his late wife more and more often into conversation. Which was fine, of course it was, apart from the fact that he invariably held Antonia up as the pinnacle of perfection to whom all others needed to aspire. Antonia had never been given a parking fine. She'd loved listening to his favourite jazz albums. She'd always polished her shoes before leaving the house. She'd never forgotten to put the oven timer on and burnt the casserole. And she'd never, *ever* folded over the corner of a page to keep her place in a book – only complete heathens did that.

And now it was as if a ticker-tape was running through Coral's brain, emblazoned with all the other things she found frustrating about Trent. The baby voice he put on when he wanted her to make him a cup of tea. The way he tried to imitate the accents of people on TV, all the way through whichever programme they happened to be watching. His predilection for using unfunny catchphrases over and over again and thinking they were hilarious every time.

Not to mention his habit of calling her Pumpkin.

Since she was hungry, Coral valiantly controlled her mirth and ate the sandwich. Trent said, 'That is repulsive. You're making me feel sick watching you.'

'You don't have to watch me.' She swallowed the last mouthful. The sandwich hadn't been that great anyway; instead of butter, Trent only kept cheap margarine in his fridge. 'Look, I don't think we're right for each other, do you? Not really.'

His expression changed to one of alarm. 'But Pumpkin—'

'We had a holiday romance and it was fun,' said Coral. 'And I'm grateful to you for making me realise I could feel normal again, but I think we've gone as far as we can go.'

'Pumpkin—'

'Please don't call me Pumpkin.' Coral shook her head. 'I don't like it.'

Trent looked confused. 'But Antonia always liked it when I called her that.'

Oh God. 'I'm not Antonia, though. We're different people.'

'You certainly are. She loved being called Pumpkin. And I loved it when she called me Mr Snuggles. I *asked* you to call me that,' said Trent, aggrieved, 'but you haven't done it once.'

Eurgh, just the thought of saying it made her shudder. Coral said, 'I'm not really a nickname-y sort of person.'

Trent looked at her, a picture of disappointment. 'Antonia was.'

Let's face it, they were both disappointed. He'd thought he'd found someone capable of getting him over the loss of his beloved wife. And it had been like that for her too. Poor Nick, she hadn't forgotten him, but she'd definitely been clinging to the hope that a relationship with Trent would help her over her embarrassing crush on Declan.

Except that hadn't happened; the embarrassing crush hadn't gone away. Anyway, that was all completely irrelevant. Coral gave herself a mental shake. The lettings agent was still looking for long-term tenants for Weaver's Cottage, and Declan was back in London. He hadn't been down to Stanton Langley for weeks. Not only was he out of the picture, he'd never been *in* the picture in the first place. All she had to deal with at the moment was *this* failed relationship.

Still, no relationship was better than being stuck in one that wasn't right. And she definitely wouldn't miss having to endure that awful jazz music Trent loved to listen to. See? There was always a bright side.

'So that's it, then,' he said. 'Over.'

'I think so,' said Coral. 'Don't you?' She *knew* so, but it seemed only fair to be polite.

He grimaced. 'Fine. I just hope eating that sandwich doesn't make you ill.'

Coral smiled. 'If you're honest, you're probably hoping it will. So you can say you told me so.'

He gave her another of those long, unamused looks of his. 'You're not perfect, you know. In case you think you are.'

Oh goodness, retaliation for having been laughed at. So much for being polite. Coral said, 'I don't think I'm perfect.'

'My Antonia used to go to a salon for a full professional manicure every week. Her nails were always immaculate.' Trent's lip curled with derision as he pointed to her hands. 'Yours are a disgrace.'

Chapter 49

For Declan, the last seven days had been like dog years. Time had never passed so slowly; every hour had felt like a week.

It had begun as a normal phone conversation with Lily as he was making his way on foot to an appointment on Pall Mall. They'd been discussing a TV espionage series they were both currently enthralled by, chatting about what he'd been up to in London and catching up with everything that had been going on in Stanton Langley. Then Lily had added, 'Oh, and it's all over between Coral and Trent. Turns out he wasn't the one for her after all.'

Just two casual sentences, but they'd had the power to stop Declan dead in his tracks as he crossed Trafalgar Square, causing two tourists to cannon into the back of him and a flock of startled pigeons to rise into the air.

Somehow he had got through the rest of the telephone conversation without Lily thinking he'd lost his mind. Hopefully he'd sounded more or less normal. In the real world, for the next couple of days, he'd managed to carry on working, attending meetings, making appointments and arranging for all necessary tasks to be carried out.

But inside his head he felt like a teenage boy, fizzing with excitement and anticipation and willing time to pass because there obviously needed to be a break between Coral finishing with one man and finding herself on the receiving end of a declaration of love from another.

Furthermore, the break needed to be long enough not to rush and possibly overwhelm her, but not so long that she had time to meet someone else. No way was he going to risk letting *that* happen again.

The original plan had been to leave it for a fortnight, but Declan had soon discovered he couldn't wait that long. Yesterday he'd cancelled his meetings for today and called Lily to let her know he was on his way down.

'Oh, brilliant.' Lily had been delighted. 'We haven't seen you for weeks. I've missed you!'

'I've missed you too.' *All of you*, he'd added in his head.

And now yesterday was today, and he was almost there. The last time had gone horribly wrong; Declan knew he had to be prepared for it to happen again. But he also knew he had to try. Give it his best shot. Find out once and for all if Gail's instincts had been right.

And if it turned out she'd been wrong all along . . . well then at least he would know. He'd have his final answer.

'Yay, you're here! Excellent timing!' Lily greeted him with enthusiasm. 'Give me five minutes to finish closing up, then we'll have a drink. I sold that church pulpit this afternoon, by the way . . . Oh, and this fantastic old lady turned up and bought the red velvet coffin . . . she said she'd love to be buried in it because it looked so cosy!'

'That's great. Is Coral in the house?' Like a master spy, Declan had already noticed there was no sign of her out here in the yard or in the office. 'I'll go on over and say hello.'

'Oh, she isn't here.' Lily's words caused his stomach to tighten

364

and the words *not again* to reverberate through his brain. 'She said we'd run out of balsamic vinegar and chocolate biscuits, so she's gone off to do a supermarket shop.'

He breathed again. The big out-of-town supermarket was six or seven miles away on the Cheltenham road. All of a sudden Declan couldn't bear to wait a minute longer; he had to see Coral as soon as possible.

'Damn, I meant to stop off there and grab some champagne . . . completely forgot. I'll go and pick some up now.'

'Hello? No need.' Lily pulled her phone out of her pocket. 'I can just give Coral a call and she can get it for you while she's there!'

No, no no no. Declan's mind was made up, and he was going to do it if it killed him.

'There's something else I need to buy.' He saw the confusion in Lily's eyes. 'It's something for you . . . a surprise. I won't be long . . . back soon . . . oh, and don't phone Coral to say I'm on my way. I'll surprise her too!'

'OK.' Bemused, Lily shrugged and watched him back away. As he turned and headed for the car, she called out, 'But if my surprise happens to be chocolate truffles, I like milk, not plain.'

You might think there were only a couple of items you needed to buy, but start pushing a trolley up and down the aisles of a huge supermarket and it soon began to fill up.

Then again, wasn't this why she was here? Having lost her nerve when Lily had cheerfully informed her that Declan was on his way down from London, Coral felt again the rush of adrenalin she'd experienced at the realisation that she was about to come face to face with him once more.

And like a perfectly mature and sensible forty-eight-year-old woman, she'd run away.

Well, driven away. In an outright panic.

Which was completely pathetic and ridiculous, because he'd still be there when she arrived home with her bags of shopping, but at least this way she had an extra hour to mentally prepare herself for his arrival.

Pausing in the loo roll aisle, Coral reached for the sixteen-roll multipack of their usual brand and added it to the trolley. Oh God, look at her hands; she stopped to examine them, conscious of Trent's parting comment last week. Spending so much time in the reclamation yard had always been hard on her nails; she kept them short, unpolished and workmanlike.

Had people been raising their eyebrows at her hands for years, inwardly appalled by the sight of her plain, unglamorous nails? Should she maybe head over to where they sold the make-up and buy a bottle of nail polish?

Since procrastination was the order of the day, she wheeled her trolley over to the aisle that segued from shampoos and shower gels to shaving equipment, pharmaceuticals and cosmetics. She was usually in a rush, so it made a nice change to be able to loiter and browse. And goodness, there were so many kinds of polish to choose from.

Two women a bit further along were looking at lipsticks, comparing shades on the backs of their hands. Idly listening in, Coral wondered whether she should treat herself to a lipstick too.

'Beigey-pink, that's your colour,' the dark-haired woman told her blond friend with an air of authority. 'Don't go for that purply one, whatever you do.'

Coral paid attention; the woman sounded as if she knew what she was on about. When they'd moved away from the lipsticks, she would choose a beigey-pink one for herself.

'Oh my God, what are you buying *that* stuff for?' The blond one let out a muffled shriek and jabbed her finger at the slim cardboard package she'd just spotted in her friend's hand. 'Eurgh, gross!'

'It's OK, calm down.' The brunette laughed. 'I don't *have* piles. You use the cream under your eyes to shrink your eyebags and tighten the skin. It's like a miracle, I promise you. A facelift in a tube! All the top beauty experts swear by it.'

The blond woman stared at her in disbelief, then turned and clip-clopped back down the aisle. Returning with an identical tube, she brandished it at her friend. 'OK, but only because I trust you. You'd better not be having me on.'

Once they'd headed off to the checkouts, Coral moved along to the make-up section and chose the beigey-pinkiest of all the lipsticks. Then she selected a nail polish to go with it. Who knew, maybe in future people would stop shuddering with revulsion at the sight of her naked mouth and fingernails and life would change out of all recognition.

Finally she sidled down to the bottom-cream section and picked up a tube of the stuff the two women had bought. Well, if it was as miraculous as it sounded, may as well give it a whirl. She dropped the tube into the trolley and covered it with some of the much-nicer-to-look-at bags of fruit and veg. OK, now it was probably time to pay; this supermarket might stay open until ten o'clock in the evening, but she really couldn't put off seeing Declan for that—

'Hi,' said Declan's achingly familiar voice in her head.

No, not in her head. *Behind* her head.

'Hwaargh!' Coral spun round to find him standing right behind her. Oh God, and she'd actually emitted a ridiculous-sounding squawk, like a rugby player doing a haka.

'Whoops, didn't mean to make you jump. You were miles away.' He smiled. 'Sorry!'

She clapped her hand to her breastbone. 'It's OK, you just caught me by surprise. What are you doing here?'

Which, seeing as he was standing in front of her clutching a security-tagged bottle of Laurent Perrier in each hand, wasn't the brightest of questions.

'I've just completed on that Georgian property in Kensington. I thought we should celebrate.' He raised his arms, because she evidently wasn't clever enough to recognise two bottles of champagne when she saw them. 'Anyway, how are you? Looking well! It's good to see you again.' Belatedly he leaned across to greet her with a friendly kiss on the cheek, but the corner of the shopping trolley was trapped between them. It promptly ricocheted off Coral's hip, banged against the supermarket shelving and sent a piled-up display of cardboard packets careering into her trolley and on to the floor.

Not painkillers. Nor indigestion tablets. Or vitamin pills, oh no.

It had to be dozens of packets of condoms, didn't it?

'God, sorry again. My fault.' Declan began hastily scooping them out of the trolley.

'Doesn't matter! It's fine! Let me do that . . .' Desperate for him not to delve down and find the Other Packet, Coral took over. 'Why don't you go and pay for the champagne?'

'It's OK, we'll go together. I can help you with everything at the checkout. Are you all done?'

All done? She was overdone. The supermarket had air-conditioning, but she could feel her skin prickling with perspiration as they made their way over to the line of checkouts. While they queued, Declan said, 'Sorry to hear about you and Trent, by the way.'

'It's all right. Those things happen. Well, you know that; it happened to you too. You go first.' Coral gestured at the conveyor belt as the customer ahead of them finished paying.

'Ooh, I say!' The middle-aged cashier beamed up at Declan as she rang up the two bottles. 'Someone's got something nice to celebrate!'

Declan smiled back and said, 'I hope so,' at the exact moment Coral said, 'He definitely has!'

Which caused a bit of confusion. 'Oh, sorry,' said Coral. 'I thought you said the deal was done?'

'Ah yes. That one is.' Declan looked momentarily flustered. 'But there's another one I'm still keeping my fingers crossed for . . .'

'I was wrong, then.' As the cashier took his card, she confided, 'When customers buy champagne, I always try to guess why. At first when I saw you two together, I thought you were celebrating your wedding anniversary . . .'

'We're not married!' Coral blurted out.

'. . . and then I saw you weren't wearing wedding rings, so I decided it was your birthday and he was taking you out somewhere lovely for dinner.'

'It's not my birthday. We're just friends.'

The chatty cashier shrugged, unruffled. 'Ah, right. Isn't that a shame? Oh well, never mind.'

'Want me to unload your trolley for you?' offered Declan.

'No, I'll do it! You can help with the packing if you like.' Coral began busily piling things along the length of the conveyor belt. The friendly cashier started scanning the items through the till. Declan filled up carrier bags. While he wasn't looking, Coral found and deftly removed the tube of pile cream from the trolley and placed it on the non-moving side of the conveyor belt beneath a rack of sweets. *Phew, done.* She finished the rest of the unloading, then moved the trolley up to the other end and began transferring the filled carriers into it.

'Hello? Is this yours?'

The voice was clipped, authoritative and boomingly loud. Turning, Coral saw a tall woman in her late sixties brandishing the tube of pile cream. *Of course she's brandishing it, because this is my life.*

'No, not mine.' She shook her head. 'Thanks, though.'

'Well I believe it *is* yours,' the woman persisted. 'Because I saw you take it out of your trolley.'

'Is it yours, love? What is it?' The friendly cashier reached out an upturned hand for the item. 'Want me to put it through the till?'

'No, I don't,' Coral's voice went a bit high-pitched, 'because it isn't mine. And I don't know what it is because I've never seen it before.'

It felt as if everyone in the store was now listening to the exchange. Flustered, Coral lifted a bag into the trolley.

'Except you *have*,' retorted the woman, who clearly had no intention of backing down. 'And I'm a GP, so shall I tell you why the fact that you're denying it makes me so cross? Because you're ashamed of your own body, that's why! Too embarrassed to admit you have an intimate problem that some people might find amusing.'

Oh God, where was a hole in the ground when you needed one to swallow you up? Coral said, 'But—'

'You!' The loud woman pointed an accusing finger at Declan. 'Would you still love her *if* she had piles?' As she said it, she put sarcastic air-quotes around the word *if*.

'Yes,' said Declan. 'I would. Of course I would.'

Coral just wanted to die.

'Except they aren't a couple.' The cashier shook her head at the loud woman. 'They're just friends.'

'And I don't have piles,' Coral protested.

'Oh I give up. Some people just don't want to be helped.' The loud woman dropped her wire basket to the floor with a crash and stalked off.

'Ah, wasn't this one great?' The cashier beamed and jerked her thumb at Declan. 'Jumping to your defence like he did, saying he'd still love you even if you did have piles. What a star!'

'I don't have them, though,' Coral said faintly. 'I promise.'

But everyone was looking at her and smirking. Worse still, she knew none of them believed her for a second.

Having paid for their shopping, Declan removed his credit card from the card reader and said brusquely, 'Let's just get out of here, shall we? Right now.'

Mortified, Coral felt herself blushing all over again. Oh dear, he'd clearly had enough.

As they left the store, she blurted out, 'I'm so sorry about that . . . how embarrassing. Look, confession time. I overheard someone saying that stuff was a miracle cure for eye bags . . . that's all it was. I should have said so straight away . . . I thought I'd give it a try, but then you turned up and—'

'I meant it,' Declan interrupted her.

'Oh, sorry. Of course.' All of a fluster, Coral realised he didn't want to listen to her garbled explanation; he just wanted to be out of here, out of the car park, probably well away from her. 'Well look, you *can* go, I'm fine to unload the trolley on my own, my car's right there—'

'What are you talking about?' said Declan.

'You want to get out of here.' As she steered the trolley over to where her car was parked, Coral said with a slightly hysterical laugh, 'And who can blame you?'

'OK, stop.' Declan reached for the handle and brought the trolley to a halt. 'We're at cross purposes here. When that madwoman asked me if I'd still love you, I said yes. Just now, when I said I meant it . . . well that's what I meant.'

Coral stared at him. What? Oh. *Oh*.

Declan paused too, as if listening to the words that had just come out of his mouth. He raked his fingers through his hair. 'OK, I didn't plan for it to happen quite like this, but I'm saying it now. I'd still love you. I just would. Because . . . I already do.'

Coral was trembling. She wanted to ask if this was a joke, but knew it wasn't. All she could say, with a squeak in her voice, was 'Really?'

Declan nodded. 'Oh yes, really. You're amazing. The only reason I bought that cottage was so I'd have an excuse to keep coming down here.'

Oh God, imagine that.

'I had no idea. You didn't say anything.'

Declan shrugged. 'I didn't know how you felt about me. I thought maybe you weren't ready for another relationship.'

'And you had Gail . . .' she reminded him.

'I know. I felt bad about that. But she was the one who told me you liked me.'

'*Gail* said that? Oh my God! How did she know?' Feeling herself flush, Coral stammered, 'I m-mean, she asked me, but I said it wasn't true.'

Declan was searching her face for clues. 'Was it not true?'

'Are you kidding? Of course it was true. I was mortified!'

'So then I finished with Gail, but in the meantime you'd run off to Grimaud.'

'Hello? *Because* I was mortified.'

'And then you met Trent . . .'

'Because I was so completely desperate to get over you! Plus,' said Coral, 'still mortified.'

'Well I think you can stop being mortified now.' Declan's voice softened as he drew her towards him. 'I want to kiss you, but I don't know if I can do it here.'

'Really? Why not?'

'Well I don't know if you've noticed, but we're standing in the middle of a supermarket car park. It's hardly the most romantic setting.'

'Oh I don't know. Feels quite romantic to me,' murmured Coral.

He broke into a smile and lowered his voice. 'Also, people are watching us.'

She wrapped her arms around him and felt months of fear and anxiety melt away. This, *this* was what she'd been waiting for. Pausing with her mouth millimetres from his, Coral smiled back at him. 'Good.'

And it turned out that if you wanted it to be, and if you were with the right person, a supermarket car park could be a wonderfully romantic place after all.

Chapter 50

It was the last week of October, and autumn had well and truly arrived. But today was a sunny, cloudless day so Lily was able to see everything. From up here, the leaves on the trees glowed red and gold as if they were on fire.

'Look over there.' Dan was leaning across, pointing out of the window on her side. 'Waterskiers on the lake.'

Lily gave his arm a swipe. 'Will you stop looking out of the window? Watch where you're going!'

'Hey, calm down.' He waggled the wings for a second, just for fun. 'This isn't a car. I can't steer it off the road.'

'Well keep your eye on the instrument panel. I still can't believe you're allowed to drive one of these things. And I really can't believe I'm letting you drive *me*,' said Lily.

'You're being very brave.' He kept a straight face. 'Although when it's a plane, we do tend to call it flying, not driving. That's the technical term for this up-in-the-air business.'

It did all look incredibly technical, though. There were so many flight instruments: dials, switches, levers and different-coloured square buttons. Dan had already listed them, rattling off explanations of vertical speed indicators, airspeed indicators, the magnetic compass and the altimeter. He appeared to know what he was talking about, which was a relief. Lily, who had never seen him actually *being* a pilot before, kept sneaking sidelong glances at this new professional version of Dan, in his crisp white shirt and dark trousers, with his combed-back hair and aviator sunglasses. No wonder he was endlessly being propositioned by girls.

The next minute, she clutched the sides of her seat and yelped, 'What's happened? Are we crashing? *Oh God . . .*'

'Will you relax? We professionals prefer to call it beginning our descent. Look, there's the River Tamar.' Dan was pointing again. 'We're crossing into Cornwall. Not long now before you're reunited.' He sounded amused. 'Try not to make a fool of yourself, OK?'

'I'll do my very best.' Lily was used to his teasing now. The view of the press was, naturally, that Eddie Tessler had been the one to end the relationship, and since neither of them had commented on the situation, Dan had played along with it. Whether or not he believed it was another matter.

'Have some dignity,' he said now. 'No bursting into tears and begging him to take you back.'

'I'll try not to do that. And in return, can you try to land this plane?'

'Land it? Oh dear, that could be tricky,' said Dan. 'Hang on, let's see if anyone's left a manual in the glove compartment . . .'

It had been Eddie's idea to hire Dan for the day. He was currently making a film in north Cornwall and needed to fly over to Paris for a meeting with an Australian producer. As soon as the meeting was over, he'd be returning to Cornwall. Aware that Dan was now fully recovered and back working for the airline, Eddie had asked if he was free that day and able to lease a small plane to take him to France and back.

Which Dan, with his dreams of one day starting up his own charter company, had been only too happy to do.

And when Eddie had suggested that Lily might like to fly down with Dan and visit the film set, she'd jumped at the chance.

She smiled at the sight of Eddie walking towards her. The awkwardness was behind them now, and it was great to see him again after that last afternoon in Stanton Langley back in July. While Dan completed the necessary paperwork in the tiny airport office, Lily gave Eddie a hug. 'What have they done to you?'

'I know.' He ruffled his hair, cut spikily short and dyed white-blond for his role in the film. 'I keep catching sight of myself in mirrors and getting the shock of my life. Yet another reason why being a screenwriter beats acting.'

They'd kept in touch by text, but Eddie had been vague about that side of things. Lily said, 'Did you finish that screenplay, the one that was giving you so much trouble?'

Eddie grimaced and shook his head. 'It was a nightmare. I gave up on it in the end. How's everyone at home?'

'All good.' Lily had kept him updated with the goings-on in Stanton Langley. 'Oh, I know what I meant to tell you! In the last couple of weeks, I've heard three different people talking about things that have happened in the village and each of them used you as a time reference. It was all "When Eddie was here" or "Just after Eddie left". It's like you're a memorable date in the diary, like Christmas.'

He looked pleased. 'That's quite an accolade.'

'You're the only VIP we've ever had in the village. You never know,' said Lily, 'we might end up with a giant statue of you up on a plinth outside the pub.'

Dan emerged from the office. 'Everything's sorted. All ready to go?'

'Absolutely.' Eddie was already holding his passport, phone and wallet; there was nothing else he needed. Pointing to the car park, he said to Lily, 'My driver's waiting to take you over to the film set. Mira's going to look after you. We'll be back by five thirty.'

'I'll be fine.' Lily was looking forward to seeing Mira Knowles again. 'I can't wait to watch the filming.'

'Oh,' Eddie turned back as he and Dan headed across the tarmac to the little plane, 'and there's something I want you to take a look at, too. It's in the car.'

'What is it?'

His smile was enigmatic. 'Something.'

'Is it a photograph?' said Lily.

'No.'

'A boa constrictor?'

'Not a boa constrictor either, amazingly.'

'Will I like it?'

'No idea. I hope so.' As he followed Dan to the plane, Eddie called over his shoulder, 'You can tell me when I get back.'

The car was an elongated black Mercedes. The driver waiting to open the rear door for her wore a smart grey suit and tie. It was a long way from lanky Dave in his jeans and holey jumpers who ran Dave's Cabs in Stanton Langley and regarded a day without pickled onion Monster Munch as a day wasted.

But that was real life. This, today, was the fantasy one Lily found fun to visit but still undeniably weird to experience. She paused to watch as the plane containing Dan and Eddie left the ground and rose into the duck-egg-blue sky, bound for Paris.

Then she climbed into the back of the limo and saw the A4-sized envelope waiting on the seat with her name on it.

Inside was a handwritten note from Eddie:

That last screenplay you kept asking me about? It was awful and I gave up on it weeks ago. Wrote this instead. Have a read and let me know what you think. Be honest.

E xx

PS Yes, I know, you're always honest!

The note was attached to the title page of a printed-out screenplay. Lily did a metaphorical double-take when she saw what it was called, because it was how he'd always jokily referred to his initial stay in Stanton Langley:

Five Days Away.

They'd arrived at the film set. It had taken forty minutes to get there from the airfield, but Lily had barely noticed the journey, so engrossed had she been in the film script. Having struggled so badly with the last one, Eddie had evidently taken to heart the age-old advice to write what you know. She raced through it, half dreading what the ending might be. When she saw what he'd written, she closed her eyes and rested her head back against the cream leather upholstery. To her huge surprise, a tear spilled out of each eye and slid down either side of her neck.

It wasn't real life, obviously. Not *real* real life, because that would never allow such a neat storyline with all the loose ends tied up. But enough of it was real to make it instantly recognisable. In the opening scene, Eddie finds himself holed up inside a central London hotel, besieged by paparazzi and at the end of his tether. His manager and his publicist are giving him grief and he needs to escape.

Cut to: In the dead of the night, he's secretly bundled into a tiny Cotswold cottage belonging to someone he's never met. The woman promises on her life not to tell a soul he's hiding there.

Cut to: Eddie is alone in the cottage when someone starts trying to break in by picking the lock of the front door. He comes face to face with Lily, who lives in the village and is already having a pretty eventful day of her own. It's her twenty-fifth birthday, and she's just read a life-changing letter written to her by her mother, who died when she was eight—

Lily's eyes snapped open as the window slid down and she heard a familiar voice saying, 'What's she doing? Is she fast asleep? Lily, it's me! WAKE UP!'

To be fair, the voice would probably be familiar to a large percentage of people on this planet.

'I'm not asleep . . . Oh good grief.' Lily hastily brushed away the tears. 'He didn't warn me you were going to look like *that*.'

Mira grinned. She was wearing a nun's habit, a huge prosthetic nose and a fake whiskery wart on her cheek. Well, hopefully a fake whiskery wart.

'Sorry! Isn't it brilliant, though? I can go out like this and nobody gives me a second look.'

Lily raised her eyebrows. 'Really?'

'Oh well, not in the habit. But if I change into jeans and a sweater, I can walk around St Carys and no one even knows it's me. *So* cool. Anyhow, how are *you*?' Mira enveloped Lily in an enthusiastic embrace. 'Try not to knock my wart off!'

For the next hour, Lily was shown around the location where they were filming and introduced to the rest of the cast and crew. The action was taking place in and around a clifftop hotel overlooking a surfing bay on the north Cornwall coast. The film was an action comedy drama featuring a billion-dollar heist engineered by a seventy-five-year-old grandmother and her niece, played by Mira masquerading as a nun. Eddie's role was that of the detective aiming to foil their dastardly plot.

Lily watched from the clifftop as Mira was filmed scrambling down the steep path to the beach in her nun's habit and a pair of Union Jack wellingtons; she then had to race across the beach and throw herself down on the sand behind a faded blue rowing boat.

It all took ages. The director wanted endless retakes, and each one meant Mira having to be rigorously de-sanded and sent back up the path before setting off again.

'I'm exhausted just watching it,' Lily said to the girl next to her. The girl's name was Sophie and she was married to the owner-manager of the hotel in whose grounds they were standing.

Sophie, who'd been taking photos of the filming with an impressive-looking Nikon, said, 'And it's easy to slip, too. I once tried to stop a pushchair that was falling down that path.' She pulled a face. 'It's steeper than it looks from up here.'

'Did you manage to stop it?'

'Just about. Wasn't a soft landing, though. I was pretty battered and bruised.'

'Ouch.' Lily winced in sympathy and nodded at Sophie's front. 'Were you . . .?'

'Oh no, thank goodness.' Sophie's eyes danced as she briefly rested her free hand on the watermelon-sized bump beneath her sweatshirt. 'That was two years ago, way before this happened. I take a bit more care getting down that path now I'm pregnant.'

By three o'clock, the shooting moved on to involve other actors, and Mira's work was done for the day. Having changed out of her habit and peeled off her wart, she and Lily retired to a quiet corner of the hotel terrace for coffee and cake.

'So have you noticed how wonderfully patient I've been?' Mira finished a slender slice of lemon torte and licked her fingers with relish. 'All afternoon I've been dying to ask you and I haven't!'

Lily kept a straight face, because Mira was as transparent as a child. 'You want to play Squares?'

'Well obviously I want to play Squares. I *love* Squares. But right now I want to know what you think about Eddie's screenplay.'

'Have you read it?'

'Of course I've read it!'

'And?' said Lily. 'What's your verdict?'

'Well I think it's completely amazing. But I want to know what *you* think.'

Lily dropped another spoonful of sugar into her coffee cup and looked thoughtfully across the table at Mira. 'I think . . . you haven't read it.'

Mira looked confused. 'What? Why do you say that?'

'I'm very clever.'

'Well you're not, because you're wrong.'

'OK then,' said Lily. 'Because Eddie wrote a message for me on one of the pages. It said: "Don't talk to Mira about this, by the way, before I get back. She's bursting to know what it's about but I refused to let her read it. I wanted you to be the first." Sorry.' Lily grinned at the look of indignation on Mira's face.

'Honestly. What a sneaky bastard.'

'Quite funny, though.' Lily was consoling. 'He knows you so well.'

'That man drives me nuts. Seriously, he's the most annoying person in the world. OK, can you give me any clues? I just want to know what it's like!'

'Can't tell you. He wants to discuss it with me when he gets back.'

Mira gave her a piteous look. 'Oh please. Just the teeny-tiniest hint.'

'Still no.'

'Is it good, though?'

Lily paused, then nodded. 'Yes, it's good. And that's all you're getting. We're changing the subject now.'

'Fine, fine.' Reaching into her emerald–green leather shoulder bag, Mira whipped out a notepad and two ballpoint pens. 'In that case, please can we play Squares?'

Chapter 51

'Well?' said Eddie.

The driver had picked Lily up from St Carys at five o'clock and brought her back to the airfield just as he and Dan were coming in to land. During the forty-minute journey, she'd leafed through the screenplay again and thought about what he'd written.

Now they were sitting facing each other, drinking hideous cups of tea from the vending machine. The screenplay lay closed on the red Formica table between them.

'You sound like Mira,' said Lily.

'Ha. Did she try to trick you?'

'Of course she tried to trick me.'

'And did you tell her anything?'

'I did not. But you'll have to when you get back to that hotel or she really will burst. Like an egg in a microwave.'

'And now you're doing exactly the same thing to me,' said Eddie.

'What would you do if I said I hated it?'

'I'd destroy it,' he replied without hesitation. 'Delete everything from the computer. No one else has seen a single word of it. If you aren't completely happy with what I've written, no one else ever will.'

Luckily she didn't need to make him do that.

'I think it's amazing,' she said, and saw the relief on his face, the relaxation of tension in his jaw.

'Really?'

'God, yes. I mean, I'm no expert, but the way you've done it . . . everything about it . . . well, do *you* think it's good?'

A faint smile lifted the corners of Eddie's mouth. 'Modesty aside, I'm pretty sure it's the best thing I've ever written.'

'Wow. And how does that feel?'

'A damn sight better now I know I don't have to delete it.' He sat back on his grey moulded plastic chair and exhaled with relief. 'So you're fine for me to show it to a few people, then?'

Lily nodded. 'I think you should.'

'There's still no guarantee it'll get made, of course.' Having forgotten how awful it was, Eddie took a sip of the vending machine tea and grimaced. 'Other people have to like it too.'

'I know. But I bet they will.'

'God, this is disgusting.' He gave up and pushed the plastic cup to one side. 'Anyway. Are you OK with the way it ends?'

Lily's stomach contracted, because she'd been waiting for him to get to this bit. 'Yes, why not? It's fictionalised, isn't it? You've based the story on what happened to us, but you have to give it a proper conclusion. That's what people want when they go to see a film. You can't just leave them wondering what happens to everyone.'

Eddie said, 'I used poetic licence.'

'Exactly.' Lily nodded vigorously in agreement. 'You couldn't have a boring old real-life ending, could you? That'd be a complete let-down. And Dan won't mind either, he'll think it's hilarious.'

Silence. Eddie was watching her. 'How about if it isn't poetic licence?' he said finally.

Lily's heart began to race. 'But it isn't real, is it? Because it hasn't happened. You just wrote it that way.' In the screenplay, Eddie's character made his peace with the idea of fame and returned to work with fond memories of the girl who had helped him during his five days away. And Lily's character ended up getting a romantic happy ending with the long-term friend whose bad-boy lady-killing ways had only ever been a cover, a way of concealing his true feelings for her.

Eddie's gaze was unwavering. 'What if I wrote it that way because it could be true?'

'It couldn't, though. In a film, maybe. But not in real life.' Her palms were prickling with embarrassment now, because she was practically coming out and admitting it. Oh God.

'Then again, you never know, do you? Not until you give it a try.' He shrugged. 'Just putting it out there.'

He knew. She didn't know how he knew, but he did. Abandoning all pretence, she said, 'When I told you I'd kissed someone else, you never did ask me who it was.'

This time Eddie gave her one of those famous movie-star smiles of his, the kind that had turned a million girls' knees to mush and helped to propel him to stardom. 'Oh Lily, there wasn't any need to ask. I already knew.'

The drone of the aircraft's engine was comfortingly steady as they flew through the night sky back to Oxfordshire. Cocooned in inky darkness, Lily peered at the silver stars above them, the almost-full moon over to their right and the snaking lines of golden dots from the car headlights, street lamps and illuminated buildings on the ground far below.

At least Dan, piloting the little plane, didn't know what was going on inside her head. Eddie had promised her that much.

'By the way,' Dan broke the silence between them, 'when Eddie told you he hadn't said anything to me, he was lying.'

Lily's stomach abruptly plummeted as if they'd hit an air pocket. Unable to look at him, she stared directly ahead. 'Said anything to you about what?'

'Everything. All of it.' His voice was steady. 'The whole lot.'

And he'd chosen this moment to announce it. Terrific. Lily cleared her throat and adjusted her headset. 'Why are you telling me this now?'

'Because I have to. And I thought it might be easier up here. Can you do something for me?'

'Like what?' *Jump out of this plane right now, with no parachute? Easily.*

'Close your eyes,' Dan instructed, 'and listen to me while I tell you a story.'

Was this the voice of doom? Was he about to let her down gently; explain to her that of course he hoped they'd always be friends, *good* friends, but there couldn't possibly ever be anything more than that?

It was, after all, exactly what she had done to Eddie.

Talk about tit for tat.

'What kind of story?' said Lily.

'A true one. Go on, keep your eyes closed. And I know this won't be easy, but if you could also manage to keep quiet and not interrupt, that would be great.'

Lily's nails were digging into her palms. Her mouth was dry and she felt sick.

'Right. Are you sitting comfortably?' Dan paused. When she'd nodded, he said, 'Then I'll begin. There was once a boy who liked to torment a girl. When they were young, he did

386

it all the time and it was practically the highlight of his life. Then as the years went by and they got older, he realised he liked her in a whole different way. But the girl didn't feel the same about him, so nothing ever changed. To make himself feel better, the boy did everything he could to find someone else he liked more, but that turned out to be pretty much impossible, because that person simply didn't exist. So he carried on being just good friends with the girl he wished he could be more than just good friends with. And although he always hoped that one day she'd change her mind about him, he'd pretty much given up on it ever actually happening.'

Lily's eyes were still closed. Dan's voice was low and intimate, seeping through her headset and into her brain.

'So anyway, that's the story part over,' he continued. 'Now we'll move on to the screenplay thing. Eddie talked to me about it on our way over to Paris. I didn't know you'd told him about that kiss . . . at the lake. He said when he heard about it, that was when he knew for sure. Then he asked me if he was right. And I said yes. Then he said didn't I think it was about time I did something about it and told you the truth? And he was right, of course. But it turns out I'm a coward when it comes to saying stuff like that, which is why I'm doing it now, up here where you can't run away. I love you, Lily. I always have loved you and I always will. But if you don't want to hear this, all you have to do is ignore me and we'll pretend it never happened. OK, we can't pretend it didn't happen,' Dan amended, 'but we can never mention it again. If that's what you'd prefer, all you have to do is open your eyes and change the subject . . . point out of the window and say something like, "Ooh, is that a UFO over there?" And then I'll know.'

Lily opened her eyes, her throat so choked with emotion she couldn't speak. The next moment she spotted a small but intensely bright ball of red light rising up through the night sky, heading towards them. Letting out a muffled shriek, she pointed and yelped, 'Oh my God, it's a—'

Then the red ball transformed into a giant crimson chrysanthemum that was instantly joined by sapphire, bright white and orange bursts of light exploding beneath their flight path like gigantic flowers blooming on fast-forward.

'It's a firework display!' Belatedly realising that Dan might think she was choosing a creative way to change the subject, Lily exclaimed, 'It was a firework I saw, not a UFO! I love you too!'

He turned to look at her as they flew over the multicoloured carpet of fireworks exploding far below them. 'Really?'

'Really!'

'In a just-good-friends way, do you mean?' He'd sounded so calm before, but he wasn't feeling calm at all, Lily realised. He was double-checking, being cautious, needing confirmation, and it just made her love him more.

'Not in a just-good-friends way at all. Quite the opposite kind of way, actually.' She felt her stomach unknot and broke into a smile, finally unafraid to reveal her true feelings; at last she could be honest. 'There's never been anyone else for me either. It's always been you.'

'I can't believe this.' Dan reached across for her hand. 'I just can't believe it's happening. I want to kiss you, but . . .'

'You have a plane to fly,' said Lily. Every single cell in her body was zinging with anticipation at the thought of what lay ahead. 'Are we nearly home yet?'

He gave her fingers a squeeze. 'I suppose we've waited fifteen years, so another fifteen minutes won't kill us. Unless . . . have you ever had sex in a cockpit before?'

'Waiting might not kill us,' said Lily, 'but sex in a cockpit definitely would. Let's get our priorities right and land safely, shall we?'

Dan was grinning at her. 'You're the boss.'

Chapter 52

One year later

It wasn't every day you got to see yourself plastered across a huge poster advertising a hotly anticipated, about-to-be-released movie. Lily couldn't stop gazing up at it.

OK, it wasn't actually *her* face on the poster, but it was the face of the actress bringing her to life on the screen. And having your character played by Mira Knowles was still pretty amazing, not to mention surreal.

'Well?' said Dan, at her side. 'How does it feel?'

'Weird.' Lily leaned against him. They'd viewed the poster online, but this was the first time they'd experienced it in the flesh, so to speak; full-sized and on display for everyone to see.

'Wait till millions of people have seen the film. That'll be weirder.' Dan brushed his warm mouth against her cheek. 'We should check in to the hotel. You haven't heard from Patsy, have you? She didn't reply to my text.'

Right on cue, Lily's phone began to ring. She glanced at the screen. 'This is Patsy now. Hi, where are you? Have you left yet?'

'We're not going to be able to make it.' The line was crackly and Patsy was sounding distant and out of breath. 'I'm having contractions. Oh Lily, it's happening, I'm in labour!'

Lily's mouth dropped open. '*What?* Oh my God, really? Right this minute? Are you in hospital?'

'We're heading there now . . . ooh *ow ow owww* . . . hang on a sec . . .'

'She's having the baby,' Lily told Dan. 'They're on the way to the hospital. Right now!'

Dan regarded her with amusement. 'You sound so astonished. She has been pregnant for the last thirty-nine weeks, you know. It had to come out sooner or later.'

Lily gave him a thump on the arm. 'I know, but it's exciting! Pats, can you hear me? Do you want us to come back?'

'OK, contraction's passed, I'm here again. No way,' Patsy exclaimed. 'You've got a premiere to go to. No no, you do your thing and I'll do mine. We'll see you tomorrow . . . Ooh, this weather! Is it raining in London?'

'Still sunny here.' Lily glanced up at the clear blue sky. 'Hasn't rained at all. How's Oliver doing?'

'Trying to be brave on the surface, but underneath he's panicking like a— *Ooooh!*'

'Well tell him to drive carefully,' said Lily. She loved Oliver, they all did. The night Patsy had been stood up had turned out to be the best night of her life.

'*Aaaarrgh,*' Patsy gasped. 'I will!'

Patsy's last *aaaarrgh* hadn't been another contraction. Rather, it had been due to the fact that she'd discovered the flooded lane they were travelling down was more flooded than they'd first thought.

To be fair to Oliver, you couldn't say he hadn't been driving carefully. He'd driven very carefully indeed through the water when it was only a few inches deep, and there had been no indication whatsoever that the lane would suddenly dip and the water become much deeper. Poor Oliver, it wasn't his fault; he wasn't familiar with this nifty short cut she'd told him to take.

Patsy, who was familiar with both the short cut *and* the sudden dip, had been too busy talking to Lily to pay attention. The rain was lashing down around them, on the radio there were reports of flash-flooding throughout Gloucestershire and Oxfordshire, and there were warnings that the emergency services were at full stretch. Patsy looked at Oliver, the man who had made the last year the happiest of her life, and saw his hand tremble slightly as he turned the key in the ignition.

Rurr-rurr-rurr-rurr-rurr . . .

Nothing happened. The engine was flatly refusing to start. It was like trying to turf a sleeping teenager out of bed with a plastic spoon.

Patsy witnessed the growing panic in Oliver's eyes as the realisation sank in that they could be in real trouble here. And as if in sympathy with the tension in his jaw, the ominous tightening sensation started up again inside her stomach. As before, the first few seconds were fine, then it carried on beyond an acceptable level and became a wave of pain so intense it took her breath away. Ow. *Ow.*

Rurr . . . rurr . . . rur . . . rur . . . rur.

'OK, here goes.' Abandoning his attempt to start the engine, Oliver opened the driver's door and jumped into a foot of murky brown water. 'Maybe if I can push us out, it'll do the trick.'

He was strong, but not that strong. Under the circumstances, Rambo himself might have struggled. As Patsy clutched her enormous stomach and panted her way through the contraction,

Oliver tried and failed to move the car either backwards or forwards. Climbing back inside like a sodden drowned rat – actually, more like a drowned bear – he said in a strained voice, 'We'd better call an ambulance.'

If there was one available.

Patsy's phone, which had slid to the floor during the last agonising contraction, began to ring.

In their central London hotel, Dan was stretched out on the huge bed in their room, watching as Lily began getting herself ready for the evening ahead. Her hair, still wet from the shower, was rippling down the back of her white towelling bathrobe. Her dress was hanging up in the steamy bathroom to get the last few wrinkles out of the peacock-blue silk. It was early, still only four o'clock, but they were meeting Eddie and Mira for a catch-up before the main event.

'What are you looking at?' Lily was eyeing him through the mirror as she smoothed foundation into her cheeks.

'Some girl I fancy,' said Dan.

'And why are you watching her?'

'Just wondering if I've got a chance of persuading her back into bed.'

'You already had your chance, and you took it.' Lily's eyes sparkled as she finished blending in the foundation and reached for her pot of blusher.

Dan loved to watch her doing her make-up. She was fast, but the result was always impressive. He loved the way she widened her eyes as she applied mascara to her long lashes, then leaned forward and raised her eyebrows in order to brush darker shadow into the sockets of her eyes. He adored the way she put on lipstick, pouting, then pressing her lips together. And he knew he'd never tire of watching her tilt her head this

393

way and that as she sprayed scent behind each ear, along her collarbones and – always the final squish – down her cleavage.

Basically, he just loved every single thing about her, more than he could have imagined possible. His friends and work colleagues might tease him for having become a one-woman man, but they didn't know the half of it. If they could only be aware of the thoughts that went through his brain, they wouldn't believe he was the same person. But he was, and he was finally the person he'd always wanted to be. Being with Lily had made his life complete, and he knew without a shadow of a doubt that he never wanted them to be apart.

Hence the plans he'd made for tonight . . .

The call on Patsy's phone had come from Sean, just to let her know that he and Will were about to leave Stanton Langley and head up to London for the premiere. When she told him where she was, Sean had said at once, 'Don't bother calling an ambulance. Stay where you are. We're on our way.'

They arrived twenty minutes later, appearing through the torrential rain like two knights on a shining white charger.

OK, in a muddy grey Range Rover, but Patsy wasn't complaining. Her contractions were now less than five minutes apart and she was in a world of pain.

'Has she had it yet?' Sean leapt down from the passenger seat and was instantly up to his knees in water. Within two seconds his hair was plastered to his head, his sweatshirt and jeans soaked through. 'No? Jolly good. Let's get her out of there, shall we?'

'Huuuurrrgh.' Patsy clenched her teeth as the next contraction seized her in its remorseless grip. 'HUUURRGHHH.'

Will backed up the Range Rover, sending waves of water whooshing into the footwell of the car. Oliver and Sean linked arms and between them managed to carry Patsy across to the 4x4 and lift her on to the back seat. Oliver waded back, collected her case and locked the car. Then the four of them headed off through the biblical downpour to the hospital where Patsy was due to give birth.

Thirty minutes later, they sloshed into the car park. Will pulled the Range Rover up outside the entrance to the maternity unit and Sean raced inside, located a wheelchair and brought it out for Patsy to be loaded into.

'I feel like a sack of potatoes,' Patsy panted as they pushed her into the reception area.

'That's exactly what you feel like,' said Sean. 'Only heavier.'

Despite the pain, Patsy laughed and tried to hit him. The receptionist said cheerfully to Sean, 'So you're baby's father, I take it?'

'Not me.' Sean shook his head. 'I'm the ex-husband.'

'Oh, right. Sorry! Is it you, then?' Taking in the impressively broad shoulders and huge biceps, the receptionist beamed at Will.

'Ow, ow, wrong again.' Patsy puffed her way through the next contraction. 'He's my ex-husband's boyfriend.'

'But you never know,' Will said cheerily, because they were currently interviewing potential surrogate mothers, 'you might see us back here in a year or two when we have one of our own.'

'Right! I see!' The receptionist, who had clearly encountered every possible variation in her time, turned to Oliver and said brightly, 'So how about you, dear? Third time lucky, or are you a taxi driver just here to pick someone up?'

'Ow ow *ow*,' said Oliver, because Patsy was squeezing his hand so tightly his fingers had gone blue. Then he broke into a huge smile suffused with pride. 'I picked her up fifteen months ago. Yes, I'm the father.'

'Well that's great,' said the receptionist. 'And how many of you are staying for the birth?'

'Not me!' Will looked horrified.

'Nor me.' Sean took the keys to the Range Rover from Will. 'We're off to the cinema to see a film.'

Oliver rubbed his crushed fingers. 'Looks like it's just me, then.' Then he rested his hand on Patsy's shoulder and shook his head in wonderment. 'I'm going to be a dad. I can't believe it.'

'I'm going to be a mum.' Patsy smiled up at him.

'We're going to have a baby,' Oliver marvelled.

'And it's not going to be born on the back seat of a broken-down car, thanks to us.' Sean struck a manly pose. 'We're like gay superheroes.'

'OK, the midwife will be along to see you any minute now,' the receptionist told Patsy before turning her attention back to Sean and Will. 'So! What film is it you're off to see?'

'It's called *Five Days Away*,' said Will.

'Oh *that* one – gosh, I had no idea it was even out yet! It was filmed not far from here, did you know that? Starring Eddie Tessler and Mira Knowles . . . ooh, I love those two,' the receptionist exclaimed. 'I've heard it's supposed to be really good . . .'

Prior to the premiere, everyone had gathered in a private room at the hotel where they were staying. Champagne was served, members of the cast and crew met up once more with the characters Eddie had based his screenplay on, and the producer and director both gave brief speeches to say how incredibly proud they were of the end result.

'Any news about Patsy?' Once the speeches were over, Eddie joined Lily, who took out her phone and checked that no new texts had come through while it was switched off.

'Not yet. Oliver said they'll be back in touch once it's over. We're not allowed to call them because apparently she's busy being in labour and it's distracting. So who knows when we'll hear? Could be any minute now,' said Lily. 'Or tomorrow morning.'

'That's the trouble with babies,' said Eddie. 'They're such divas. So self-centred and unpredictable.'

Lily said, 'And now it's my turn to ask. Do you have any news?'

'About what?'

'Whatever you like. But I'm kind of wondering if there's anything you'd like to tell me about you and Mira.'

Silence. Eddie was looking at her. Finally he said, 'Are you a witch?'

Lily grinned. 'Considering you're actually a pretty good actor, you haven't been able to hide it very well. Even Dan noticed something was going on with you two. And he's a man.'

He gave in with good grace. 'Oh well, we're just trying to keep the press off our backs for a bit longer. It'll come out sooner or later. Two years we've known each other, three films we've made together, and all that time we were just friends. Then a couple of weeks ago we met up in New York and everything changed.'

'That's brilliant.' Lily truly meant it. 'I'm so happy for you.'

'It might not last. It's great at the moment.' As he spoke, Eddie's gaze settled on Mira across the room, talking to Will and Sean. 'But you never know how things will work out, do you? Especially in our business.' He pulled a face. 'I'm still pretty new to it, remember. Mira was a child star – she's been famous her whole life. She's incredible and I love being with her, but she hasn't exactly had a normal upbringing.'

Turning to look at them from thirty feet away, Mira winked

at Lily. 'On the other hand, I have amazing hearing. Ears like a bat!'

The waiters were collecting up glasses; it was time for everyone to leave the hotel and make their way across to Leicester Square.

'Heard anything?' Coral joined Lily and Eddie while Dan and Declan went to check the cars were waiting for them outside.

'Still no news. You look fantastic,' said Lily.

'Do I? Are you sure?' Coral smoothed down her coffee silk dress. 'These heels are killing me. I can't believe I'm about to walk down an actual red carpet!'

Declan was at the doorway, beckoning to them. Lily said, 'You can take your shoes off as soon as we're inside the cinema.'

'But I don't want to rush in,' Coral protested. 'It's going to be my one and only real-life red carpet experience. I want to make it last as long as I can.'

Chapter 53

'RRRRRAAARRRGGGGGHHHHH.'

Patsy was roaring now. Oh God, the unearthly *noise* she was making; she sounded like a wild animal, and she felt like one too. Panting hard and aware of the perspiration trickling down her forehead, she opened her eyes and gasped, 'Sorry . . . I'm sorry, is this completely putting you off me?'

Oliver mopped her forehead with a wrung-out cold flannel and smiled down at her. 'It's not putting me off you.'

'Are you sure? Because what if you're thinking this is the most hideous experience of your life and you can't stand the sound of me howling like a . . . ow, like a wolf . . . owwww . . . oh make it stop . . . waaahhhhh!'

'OK, listen to me,' Oliver said when the contraction had eased off. 'You look beautiful. You're having my baby and I'm not going anywhere. I already love both of you and one of you hasn't even been born yet.'

The warmth of his reassuring words flooded through her. Patsy felt her heart swell and her anxiety recede. This wonderful man was the best thing that had ever happened to her; with Oliver at her side she could do anything, including giving birth to something the size of a prize-winning pumpkin.

'Right then, Patsy,' the midwife announced from her position at the foot of the bed. 'You're ten centimetres dilated, my darling. It's all systems go now. Time to start pushing this baby out!'

Lily and Declan were standing back, watching the stars of *Five Days Away* do their thing on the red carpet for the barrage of cameras as photographers jostled for the best shots.

'Enjoying yourself?' said Declan.

'Well I haven't spotted any runaway mice this time, which is a bonus. It's a lot easier not being the centre of attention. Although some people seem to be having fun.' Lily twisted the crystal-studded bangle on her wrist and smiled at the sight of Coral being photographed with the actresses who'd played her and Patsy in the film. Coral was loving every glamour-packed second, every camera flash and scream of delight, not to mention the buzzy air of excitement that was—

Whoa.

Lily's gaze, which had been skating idly over the massed crowds lined up on the other side of the barriers, suddenly screeched to a halt. She zoned in on the face of someone she'd never met but whom she was nevertheless pretty sure she recognised.

Oh goodness, was it really her?

The girl was small and thin with a pale, heart-shaped face, straight dark hair falling to her shoulders, and unflinching bright blue eyes. She was wearing a stripy grey sweater under a pink puffa jacket and was clutching a phone in her hand.

From here she blended in perfectly, looking like every other film fan.

It was the way she was completely ignoring the stars on the red carpet in order to look at Lily that was the real giveaway.

Declan touched her arm. 'Everything OK?'

'Yes.' Lily nodded. 'I've just seen my half-sister.'

'*What?* Where?'

'At the front of the barriers. Pink puffa jacket.' As Lily was murmuring the words, the girl raised her free hand slightly, did a little wave and broke into a crooked smile.

'I see her now. What are you going to do?'

'Ignore her.' Lily waited, then gave Declan a nudge. 'Hey, she's my half-sister. I'm going to go over there and say hello.'

'Push, Patsy! Take a deep breath and push down as hard as you can!'

'HMMMPPPLEURGHHHHH!'

'And again! Come on, Patsy, you can do it,' cried the midwife.

'GUUUURRHHHHFFF!'

'That's it!' Oliver was urging her on too, letting her grip his hands and heroically not complaining about the pain she was inflicting on him.

'One more push. I can see the head,' the midwife said. 'Let's get this done, shall we? OK, brace yourself, here we go . . .'

'Hi.' Sasha's eyes were bright. 'Do you know who I am?'

'Of course I do. I recognised you straight away from your photo in the paper.'

'And are you OK with this? I mean, me turning up today?'

Lily nodded. 'Oh yes, definitely!'

It wasn't something she'd mentioned to anyone else, but deep down, a tiny part of her had wondered if it might happen like this one day.

'I didn't even know for sure if you'd be here,' said Sasha. Up close, she had a scattering of freckles across her nose and the faintest sign of a dimple in her cheek. 'And I know I said last year I wasn't bothered about meeting you, but . . . well, that was then. I'm older now. More mature. I thought maybe I'd like to see you after all.'

She was sixteen and full of spirit. Charmed, Lily said, 'I'm glad.'

'In case you're wondering, I'm a lot nicer than my father. Our father,' Sasha amended.

Lily said, 'Well that's good. Hopefully I am too.'

The younger girl's thin face lit up when she smiled. 'I suppose we could hardly be worse. Honestly, you didn't miss out on anything growing up. You were better off without him.' She hesitated. 'Could I take a photo of us together? Would that be all right with you?'

'I'd love it,' said Lily.

When it was done, she said, 'They're going to want us to head inside in a minute. Can I see you later?'

Sasha pulled a regretful face. 'The thing is, I've got to catch the train home. School tomorrow. It's GCSEs this year,' she explained. 'I want to get as many A stars as I can.' After a pause she added frankly, 'Maybe next summer when exams are over we can meet up again. You could give me your number if you like, so I can text you. I wouldn't be a nuisance, I promise.'

Lily took the girl's phone and keyed in her number. 'You wouldn't be a nuisance anyway.' She handed the phone back. 'I've never been a big sister before. Text me whenever you want. I'd like that very much.'

The red carpet had been cleared and the press pen had emptied. Lily, along with the rest of their party, was making her way through the cinema foyer when Dan's phone rang.

'Whoa!' He stopped in his tracks and held up his hand. 'It's Patsy.'

Everyone in the foyer fell silent. Cast and crew alike had

got to know Patsy during their weeks of filming in Stanton Langley. There'd also been some lively betting on the weight of the baby when it arrived.

'Hey,' said Dan, 'how's everything?'

Lily loved the way Dan's voice softened as he spoke on the phone to his sister.

He listened for several seconds before breaking into an unstoppable grin. 'Yes? That's brilliant. Fantastic. Well done, you! Listen, are you decent? OK then, let me call you back on FaceTime. You can tell everyone yourself.'

And seconds later, with the volume turned up to maximum, Lily and Coral and the others surrounding Dan saw Patsy's flushed, happy face appearing on the screen of his phone.

'Hello, hellooo!' She waved from her hospital bed. 'Sorry to interrupt your premiere, but I've got someone here for you to meet. He weighs eight pounds and two ounces and we love him to bits!'

Everyone cheered as Patsy lifted up her newborn son, wrapped in a white blanket, and presented him to the camera.

'For those at the back who can't see,' Dan announced, 'it looks like a baby.'

'He's beautiful,' Lily exclaimed. 'You clever thing!'

'I know! Thank you.' Patsy was beaming. 'I'm so happy.'

'I don't believe it. Eight pounds two ounces.' Dan shook his head in resignation. 'And I had twenty quid on eight five. This is bad news. Hey, Pats, I don't suppose you could pop him back in for a few more days so he can—'

'No, Dan,' Lily chimed in. 'She probably doesn't want to do that.'

'Dan?' Patsy was firm. 'Lily's right.'

'You see, this is what I have to put up with,' Dan said mournfully. 'A sister who's just plain selfish.'

'Don't worry,' Lily shook her head at Patsy, 'I'll deal with him later. You get some rest now, you deserve it. Have you chosen a name yet?'

'Not yet.' Patsy glanced down with pride at her son. 'We thought we'd wait until he arrived, then see what he looked like.'

'Risky,' said Dan. 'What if he looked like ET?'

'If he had,' said Patsy, 'we'd have named him after you.'

In the darkened cinema, Lily was completely wrapped up in the film playing on the screen. She'd read the script, watched some of the scenes being shot on location, and Eddie had even shown them the initial rough-cut version, but actually seeing the polished end result was just the most extraordinary experience. Somehow, from the real-life bones of a story, Eddie had written something amazing, and the director had brought it to the screen in a way that was both funny and sad, quirky and emotional. Eddie was playing himself, her own character was played by Mira, and a gorgeously charismatic up-and-coming actor called Ronan Morrell had captured Dan's character to a T.

It was fictionalised reality, but so recognisable that Lily felt as if she were living and breathing the film, even those scenes created by Eddie that had never actually happened.

And now the film was nearing the end. Next to her, Lily felt Dan reach for her hand, and as always, the intimacy of the gesture gave her a thrill. Up on the screen, Eddie was being presented with an award for his work, receiving a standing ovation and listening to the applause as it rang out around the theatre. Then it cut to the next scene, with him being driven back along a winding road to his multimillion-dollar home in the Hollywood hills. There, barefoot and still clutching his award, he wandered alone through the vast empty rooms, then stood on the terrace gazing out at the glittering view spread out below . . .

And then it cut to the cottage in the Cotswolds where he'd first met Lily. But that had been then, and this was now. Outside, visible through the window, snow was falling. Inside, in the living room, a fire was burning in the grate and the squashy, faded blue sofa was occupied by Mira and Ronan playing the characters of Lily and Dan. They were lying contentedly together, laughing and playing with a boisterous mongrel puppy with a waggy tail and soft oversized paws.

This bit, Lily knew, had needed several takes, because the puppy had kept doing little wees of excitement over Mira's jeans.

In the cinema, Dan leaned closer and whispered, 'We could get a puppy if you like.'

On the screen, the camera panned in and you could see that the Lily character was wearing a ring on her left hand. The Dan character was saying something that was making her laugh harder.

In the cinema, real Dan said in a low voice, 'Fancy getting married?'

Lily's heart gave an adrenalin-filled jolt. She whispered back, 'I wouldn't mind. Who to?'

She felt Dan shifting in his seat, altering his grip on her left hand. The next moment something smooth was being slid on to the third finger, and he was murmuring in her ear, 'Sorry, I'd get down on one knee, but there just isn't room.'

In the almost total darkness of the cinema, Lily held up her left hand and blinked in disbelief at the rectangular diamond glinting back at her.

'Oh my God. Is this *real*?'

Dan was smiling. 'Well believe it or not, I didn't buy you a ring from a market stall.'

She loved him so much. *So much.* 'You know what?' Her voice quavering with emotion, she shifted towards him and reached over to stroke the side of his beautiful face. 'I think I might quite like to marry you.'

'Good,' Dan whispered. 'I think I'd like it too.'

They'd managed to miss the closing moments of the film but it really didn't matter. Up on the big screen, the credits had begun to roll and everyone else in the audience was breaking into a tumultuous wave of applause that reverberated around the huge theatre. But it was all just background noise now. Lost in the moment, Lily gazed at Dan as he took her in his arms. 'You and me . . .'

And when he'd finished kissing her, she saw the look of genuine love in Dan's eyes as he said, 'Oh yes, definitely. *Always.*'